# KILLJOY

## ADRIENNE LOTHY

**BOOK TWO OF THE STARHAWK TRILOGY**

AN MM ENEMIES TO LOVERS SCI-FI ROMANCE

ISBN 979-8-9904977-2-6 (e-book)

ISBN 979-8-9904977-3-3 (print)

Book Cover by Seaj Art.

First edition 2025.

*For JP, lover of minions*
*& June on the moon*

# The Starhawk Series Reading Order

Kestrel

Killjoy

Starhawk

# CONTENT ADVISORY

Dear reader,

Inside this book are: detailed depictions of hallucinations and mental illness due to isolation, depression and self-loathing talk by a main character, on page violence and murder, deaths of characters' family members, under-negotiated kink, drug use and references, smoking, drinking, consensual-non-consent roleplay, knife play, toxic masculinity, shame regarding bottoming and being sexually submissive, references to trafficking, slavery, sexual assault, and mentions of past domestic child abuse. Sexual assault is occasionally directly referred to by a four lettered word, beginning with R. Some of these scenes are depicted with mild and limited description.

This book is intended for adult readers only. The author does not condone murder or violence outside of fiction.

With respect and gratitude,
Adrienne

# Chapter One

# INSURANCE

Niko drew in a steadying breath, then patched the call through. Lady Death's holographic contact photo stared back at him, her expression grim. Accusing. His mouth grew dry as he waited for it to ring. After several seconds of silence, an automated beeping picked up, the universal symbol for a dead line.

*Shit.*

He sighed, thinking of his options. Back in the bedroom, Elliott was still asleep. Niko sat alone in the vast and empty cafeteria. He'd needed space for this call, needed to work himself up to it. Now that he finally had, the ex-hunter's contact was dead.

*So, what now?* He drummed his fingertips along the arm of his wheelchair, thinking. The industrial white lights of the facility buzzed quietly overhead. One had a slight flicker that Niko had noticed once and could never unsee. It only added to his sour and anxious mood as he glanced at it now.

There was someone else he could call, an old contact that had collected dust for years. Niko grimaced at the very thought.

Aleksander "Aleksi" Mikhaylov. Illicit goods runner, general twatwaffle, and Niko's ex-boyfriend. It hadn't ended well.

Aleksi knew Lady Death, though. He'd worked to secure her exclusive and first-serve stock on rare black market goods—including plentiful RapiGel and the corrosive bog-theun toxin—and Death paid him handsomely. Niko hadn't spoken to either in over three years now, but he knew they'd still be working together. Aleksi never turned down good money, and Death had the credits to spare.

Reluctantly, he scrolled down—way, way down—through his list of contacts until he reached Aleksi's. He'd long since replaced his contact photo with an image of a yauntha'guur, often considered one of the most gruesome looking animals the galaxy had unfortunately ever evolved.

"Okay," he murmured. "Let's do this."

He patched the call through and was almost disappointed when it began to ring. It rang on and on—so long that Niko was about to give up—before he heard muffled sounds on the other end of the line.

"Uh, hello?" Aleksi said, voice grossly familiar. Niko hated him so much. "*Niko?*"

"Hey, Aleksi. Yep." He wanted to make this brief. "I need Lady D's new number."

Aleksi gave the same consideration to Niko's obvious attempt at keeping their interaction short that a ship's engine did to a pigeon it encountered. "Oh my god, Niko. Wow. It's really been a while. You know, imagine my surprise when I saw your pretty face on the news. We all thought you were dead." He laughed. "You've been up to a lot lately."

Niko wanted to throttle him. "Yep. Hey, can you get me Lady—"

"How did you even end up mixed up in that? And where have you been these last three years? It feels like it's been forever."

"Aleksi."

Aleksi's tone flattened. "Come on, Niko. At least humor me."

Niko ran a hand over his face, praying to the spirit of his kind and benevolent mother for patience he didn't have. "It's complicated. And none of it is what Galapol is presenting to the media."

*As for the last three years,* Niko thought, *I've been touring Mt. Gofuckyourself. It has a great view.*

"So, he's not actually killing people?"

"Uh, no, he is, but—"

"Huh. I never imagined you'd throw in your lot with some-body like that. Truth really is stranger than fiction. Hey, speaking of which, you know that real mean old bastard? The Xermotl that everyone was scared of, with the rumors about collecting eyeballs from his bounties and keeping them in jars?"

Niko sighed. "Yep."

"Well, he got too old to keep it up and works as a pastry chef now. They say he likes to add extra icing to everything." When Niko said nothing, he continued, "You know, like, *eye*-sing—"

"Wow."

"Yeah. So, what's he like? Kestrel."

"Um, Aleksi—"

"Did you fuck him?"

"Wh-what?"

"You totally did, didn't you? I saw he was gay. They mentioned he had some boyfriend who was interviewed. The moment I heard you ran off with him, I thought, oh, they're totally fucking. They can't not be."

"Alek—"

"I can't believe you're fucking the galaxy's most wanted sniper. Does he have good aim when—"

"*ALEKSANDER!*" Niko shouted. Aleksi fell quiet. "For fuck's sake."

The other man sighed. "Still upholding the name 'Killjoy,' I see."

"I just want to talk to Lady D. I need her number. It's important."

Aleksi's tone shifted to something more serious—dark, even. "Are you sure you want to do that? I don't think she's very happy with you."

Niko's skin crawled. *Great. That's great.* "I wouldn't be asking if it wasn't that important."

"So, here's the thing," Aleksi started. "The Lady has changed things up in the past few years. New phone, new policies. A group of mercs actually almost got her. She doesn't talk to people outside of a restricted list when it comes to calls now, and got a lot more paranoid."

"So, tell her it's me. She knows me."

"Funny how you come knocking out of the blue, after years of silence, when you're *totally fucking* the galaxy's worst killer. Would *you* trust you in this situation?"

"I— No," Niko relented. "Not really."

"I always liked you, Niko." Niko couldn't really say the same. "So, I'll help you. Why don't you meet with me, and I'll take you to her? We can have a meeting together and I'll plead your case."

Niko's stomach twisted in a sharp pang of unease. "You can't just talk to her and have her call me? If she's that paranoid—"

"Niko. I could sing your praises until my face turns Heenvan blue. But you know how she is. It's been *years* and you left her high and dry. Didn't hold up your end of the bargain. And now Kestrel. She doesn't know who you are anymore. You have to be there to show her and defend your honor."

"Fuck," Niko murmured. He buried his face in his hands.

"I'll vouch for you, Niko," Aleksi said. "Consider this my apology."

Niko sighed. He didn't want Aleksi's apology. Even if it had been given sooner, it still wouldn't have mattered. The man had all but killed anything they'd once had as quickly and efficiently as Elliott took down his targets. Niko had really liked him, once upon a time. But that was a lifetime ago, and he'd felt nothing but bitter contempt since. And now he'd long since moved on.

He had no other choice, though. Aleksi clearly wasn't going to give him her number, and from the sound of it, she wouldn't answer if he did. *Unless he's lying*, Niko thought. He'd become quite experienced with the man's dishonesty.

Niko hated cheaters.

This was probably a trap. He felt it, deep in the marrow of his bones. This was Baouban all over again. If he even got to see Lady Death and this wasn't just a ruse to try and isolate and kill him, maybe she would do the deed instead.

Over three billion credits was an insurmountable sum of money. Even Niko's *comparatively meager* hundred and twenty million since he'd last spoken to Baouban was a game changer for almost anyone. And Niko was about to dive into the shady underworld of the black market again—a society spread across the stars, governed only by a single emperor: capital gain.

"*Fuck*," he said again. It was stupid. It was suicidal, even. But if he wanted to help expose the sickening truth about what and who Honeybliss was to the public, he had to do it. He had to try. This might be their only chance.

For every victim of Honeybliss. For Elliott.

"Okay, Aleksi."

The other man gave him coordinates to a parking garage in Dainna, a gargantuan asteroid-turned-black-market-hive. Niko had been there before, worked there before, played and partied, in another lifetime. Dainna's surface was perpetually ablaze in a crowd of kaleidoscopic holograms advertising everything that lay within, just beneath the thick layer of rock—bars, casinos, brothels, vendors of every exotic item anyone could dream of. Arena matches, seedy hotels that lifted any personal item not secured in the night, and strongholds of influential underworld denizens, Lady Death included.

He felt like a sardine leaping headfirst into an ocean of circling sharks.

When he hung up the call, Niko caught a glimpse of pale gold in the corner of his eye. Elliott was leaning in the doorway, one arm wrapped around himself, the other rubbing sleep from his eyes.

"Hey, babe," Niko said.

"I heard you yelling."

*Oops.* The cafeteria was a good way out from the room they slept in, but with the eerie and oppressive silence that always permeated the facility, Niko wasn't surprised he'd managed to overhear. Especially with ears that had been conditioned to listen for shouting after years spent in an abusive household.

"Yeah, uh, somebody on the phone was giving me the runaround. I'm sorry for waking you."

"Somebody? The illustrious, so-called 'Lady Death?'"

"No, I couldn't get through to her. She changed her number. Come here." Niko held his hand out, and Elliott pushed off the doorframe and crossed the all-too-large, all-too-empty cafeteria. He sank down into a chair across from Niko and took his hand.

"So, what's going on, then?"

Niko had spent long enough around him to start picking up little tells. The question was innocuous enough, but something about the way Elliott didn't look him in the face when asking and held his shoulders slightly rigid betrayed his underlying anxiety.

Niko sighed, leaning back in his wheelchair. "Ugh. There's somebody I used to know who still works with her. So, I called him to try and get her new number."

"Okay."

"He says she's turned paranoid over the last couple of years due to a near-miss on her life, though, so she doesn't take calls outside of a vetted list and won't talk to me because I'm all over the news for pairing up, of course, with an infamous assassin."

"Right."

"So, uh." Niko waffled around. "So. Uh. I'm going to go there and meet with them both."

"Absolutely not."

"Elliott. We can't give up this opportunity. It may be our only chance. And there's nobody in the galaxy like Lady Death. If anyone can make sure every planet gets made aware of the shit Honeybliss has done, it's her. It's well worth the risk."

"No. Niko, no." Elliott stood up, releasing his hand. He looked upset.

"I have to. This is bigger than me. It's probably a trap, but—"

"It *is* a trap. It's obviously a trap."

"I know. *I know*, Elliott. You're right. But I have to try anyway. If I gave up now, what would I be?"

Elliott shook his head tightly. "We'll find another way." His voice was clipped, tone final.

Niko drew in a slow breath, willing himself not to entertain the anger rising in him. Elliott was the last person he wanted to snap on. He knew the man was only trying to look out for him in the same way he himself looked out for Elliott. It was the Starlight Awards all over again, with Elliott wanting to retreat and survive, and Niko pushing deeper beyond the point of return.

They'd only just barely survived that.

"This *is* the way, Elliott," he said at last. "This is it. We have to talk to her. I can't get through to her anymore and I don't know anyone else who can help."

"They're going to eat you alive if you go in there."

"I'll be careful."

"Like you were with Baouban?" Elliott snapped.

They stared at each other for a moment in silence, Elliott's gaze assertive and cold, before finally yielding back to a wounded sorrow. He wrapped his arms around his waist tightly. "I'm sorry. That was unfair."

"Elliott. Let's not do this right now. We're not— I'm on your side. If there were any better way to do this, I would. But I have a plan. I'm already thinking of what I can hide on the suit if things go south. I—"

"I'm going with you."

Niko gaped at him, his brain briefly going offline. "No. That's— No. That's the worst possible idea." Elliott had to be goading him at this point.

"Of course, I'm not going to just stand there and hang off your arm," Elliott said instead. "I'm not an idiot. I'll keep in stealth and use the shield generator. They won't even know I'm there. You can consider me insurance."

"I don't know about this, Elliott," Niko said, his stomach turning sour now.

"It's this way or not at all."

Niko opened his mouth to protest, a hearty '*Since when do* you *get to make the rules?*' readied. He let it die on the back of his tongue. It had, after all, been Niko who had only just gotten them surrounded by Galapol agents, with no way out. And it had been Niko who'd afterwards asked Elliott to help rein him in when his own stubbornness wouldn't relent.

So, they had each other at a disadvantage.

"Fine," he conceded. "But stay in stealth and don't say a *fucking* thing. I mean it, Elliott."

"I know."

They fell into charged silence, Niko slumping in his chair and Elliott standing with his arms folded.

"There's, uh, one other thing," Niko said.

"What's that?"

"The guy I'll be meeting... His name's Aleksi Mikhaylov. He's. Um. My ex."

"Oh. Okay."

Silence lurked between them again, before Elliott finally added, "Is there something more to that?"

Niko sighed. "No, I— It's— I don't know. I just wanted to mention it, in case he says something or references something from the past. I don't know."

"You mean in case he tries to get you to make up for lost time and screw his brains out?"

Niko could taste the bile on his tongue. "No. No. Those days are long gone. I'd rather fuck a yauntha'guur."

Elliott smirked. "If I think too hard about that, I might find it insulting."

Niko couldn't help but smile, a gentle wave of much needed amusement and relief washing away some of the tension.

"Really, though, Niko. You're a living, breathing person with life experience, and I'm not going to get jealous of the time before we ever crossed paths. I won't hold it against you. You had a boyfriend. You had sex. It happens."

Affection blossomed through Niko as he looked at him. Affection, and appreciation. "Yeah. You're right. I'm just being weird."

"As long as you don't want to go shack up with him again, what do I care?"

Niko shook his head. "No. I—I really had a thing for him a long time ago. But one night, I'd gotten my bounty quicker than I'd anticipated and the job ended early. I decided to surprise him. Went back to our place and found him balls deep in a Heenva woman." He winced. The experience was years ago now, far separated from where and who he was in life at this point. And he'd found something far better since, someone Niko was willing to defy a galaxy for. But the memory still, and would always, hurt.

Elliott grimaced. "That's rough."

"Yep."

He moved around the table and pushed Niko's chair back, then sank sideways into his lap. He looped his arms around the back of Niko's neck, so that their faces were inches apart. His beauty, airy and ethereal, always left Niko breathless—seeing his contours and details up close was always a delightful reminder of that.

"I can make him have a happy little accident," Elliott purred. "'Here lies Aleksi, who tripped on a bullet.'"

Niko laughed and shook his head. It was one thing to joke about vengeful killings of abhorrent ex-lovers with a sympathetic party. It was a whole different thing to do it with Elliott Kestrel, notorious assassin. "Yeah, a bullet that was aimed right between the eyes and moving six hundred miles an hour."

"Which he tripped into."

Niko shook his head again. "Seriously, though. He's a shit-tier person, but he doesn't deserve to die. I just... want to finish this as quick as possible and talk to Lady Death."

"It's a trap," Elliott said. "He's so obvious it hurts."

"Yeah." Niko sighed, the weight of his future pressing down on him hard. "It is. You're right. We both know it is. So, we'll just have to keep our wits about us. It's not just him, either. We're going to Dainna, which is one of the biggest black market outposts in the galaxy, so it's... everyone. Everyone will probably try to kill us.

"Actually." Niko sat up straighter, looking at Elliott. "You were able to find my phone number before. Do you think you could find whatever her new number is? We wouldn't even necessarily need to go there, then."

"It doesn't work that way," Elliott said. "You were on a regular service and registered. In these sorts of shady pockets, people tend to be more paranoid and make their phones untraceable. Like you and I do now. I found that out when I was researching Honeybliss."

"Damn. Right, yeah."

"So, you're still absolutely committed to this path?" Elliott asked.

"Unfortunately."

"Then I'll be sure to bring my lucky knife."

"You have a lucky knife?"

"So far they've all been lucky, but I especially like the one I killed Matteo Ricci with."

"Hey. Speaking of killing, though," Niko started, "unless it's absolutely necessary, let's try to avoid it there. Even if it all goes south, I mean. Which it probably will. We're not there to kill just because people want a chance at a bounty so high it would leave them set for ten lifetimes."

"I know that, Niko."

"I know you do. I just want to make sure we're on the same page, just in case. I know how tense things can get when adrenaline and fighting for your life gets involved." He'd only just barely stopped Elliott from killing Fourier—though, in the end, the Galapol agent had ended up dead, regardless. "These guys aren't Honeybliss. Some of them do pretty shitty things. Some are thieves and pirates. Some run predatory casinos, deal drugs. Most of them have killed before, but it's almost always inside crime. Defending your supply, taking out a rival, punishing betrayal. That sort of thing."

Elliott tilted his head. "You've had a lot of experience with that kind of life, haven't you?"

"Yeah. Spent a lot of time in and out of black markets."

"So, one day you shoot the shit with some nefarious underworld drug lord and the next, you're chumming it up back in Station Twelve with Galapol?"

"Uh. Yeah, it was kind of like that, actually," Niko mumbled, scratching at the wiry stubble on his cheek. It only now occurred to him that his life might be a little bit weird.

"How is that possible?"

"So, I'm kind of like a daywalker, right?"

"A... daywalker?"

"Yeah, like in the movies. Half-vampire, half-human. They're of both worlds, darkness and light, and can walk in the sun, but usually hunt—"

"Please tell me you really didn't just compare yourself to a vampire."

Niko grinned. "Really, though, like I said before, I had a reputation and a niche. So long as I brought Galapol the *real* trash, they were willing to overlook... well, a lot."

"Huh. Okay. I can see how they'd work out a deal like that with you. But what about your black market connections? They had to know you were working with Galapol, right? Why didn't they just shoot you in the back of the head and call it a day?"

"There are some people there who would in a heartbeat, believe me. But it's like any other society, right?" He found himself stroking his fingertips up and down the gentle ridges of Elliott's spine, and hadn't realized when he'd started. "You can't make a blanket assumption about the people of the market. Everyone's different, and everyone has their own set of morals and standards. There are a lot of people there who, believe it or not, are actually pretty damn decent. People who keep their honor and dignity. They might do some shady things, sure. But they keep to their own and would never tolerate anything like what Honeybliss does.

"The pockets I kept to were like that—unless I was hired to do clean up. Then I'd venture in further to some of the really dicey territory. There was always the opportunity for good pay in the market itself to keep it regulated. Some guys were truly reprehensible. You have to be pretty fucked up when you're so legitimately awful that other criminals think you need to be put down. They were just insane, or went too far, or started getting a reputation for being utter monsters. Usually, it took some time but eventually someone would step up and hire somebody like me to go out and, uh, 'take care' of them.

"I guess it's like you and Honeybliss. What you're doing isn't by any means legal. But you're doing it for a greater cause. Instead of the black market, you're cleaning up the whole galaxy. When Lady Death learns what's really going on, she'll respect you."

"Respect," Elliott said quietly, as though tasting a foreign word. "I wonder, though, if she's going to respect me more than she respects three billion credits."

Niko swallowed. It was the question he couldn't answer, and yet the one this all came down to.

"I—I want to tell you she will. The person I once knew would, for sure. Out of anyone in the market, she had the most honor. Her and—" Niko deflated a bit. "And Baouban. I guess in the end, I can't promise anything. I just know we have to try. It's not enough to kill these bastards. I want the galaxy to know what they did and never celebrate or protect them again."

"You're starting to sound like me," Elliott said.

"You might be rubbing off on me."

Elliott leaned in and kissed him—long, gentle, warm. It felt so good to be joined with him like that, even so briefly. When he pulled away, Niko reached up to pet his untamed blond hair.

"We're going tomorrow night, so make sure you're ready by then," Niko murmured.

"Why not just get it over with tonight?"

"Mmh," Niko grunted. He had to tell him eventually. "So, you're not going to like this, either."

"Splendid. Let's hear it, then."

"I'm supposed to meet with Zann tonight. I actually have to leave soon."

Elliott went stiff in his arms. This time, he didn't argue, remaining, instead, silent.

"Elliott..."

"Why?"

"Because he—" Niko scrambled for the words. "He deserves to know why I turned against him."

"I don't feel good about this. You're meeting in a likely isolated location, by yourself, with a Galapol agent—"

"Former Galapol agent," Niko corrected. "Who's my brother."

"It's a conversation you can have over the phone, Niko."

"No. I can't. Not with him. I owe him this in person."

"I thought you already told him about Honeybliss and sent him the files."

"I did. He promised me we'd open an investigation when this was over. But I never got the chance to actually speak to him about it. Especially not after he watched them. I just want one chance to talk to him about it all. To explain, and to ask what he knew, too. And I don't want to do it over the phone. He's my best friend. He and my dad are the only family I have left."

Those last words seemed to impact Elliott. He closed his eyes and turned his head away. Niko felt himself winning this argument. He knew that family was important to Elliott, that he couldn't bring himself to get in the way of that.

"I'm sorry. I have to do this," said Niko.

"I'm going with—"

"No. Not for this one. This one's just me and Zann. I *need* this. I promise it'll be okay."

Elliott was quiet for a long while. Niko wondered what he was thinking, and considered begging it out of him. In the end, he kept quiet too.

Finally, Elliott said, gentle but firm, "We're not going to survive this for long if you're always out meeting with people. It's only a matter of time before someone tries to be another Baouban."

Niko rubbed at the back of his neck. He knew this all must be jarring to Elliott, after living in absolute isolation for, at the very least, several months. "I know, Elliott. I know that. After these two things, I'm done. One's for our cause—and you. The other is for me."

"I know, Niko. You're right. I'm sorry."

"It'll be alright. It's going to be okay." Niko had to say it, though he didn't know whose benefit it was more for—Elliott, or himself. He tried to push away the memory of how close they'd just come to losing it all. "We'll make it through this. We always do."

CHAPTER TWO

# BOYFRIEND

THE LAST TIME NIKO was on Celelast had been the darkest days of his life. A quick look at the familiar architecture—empty, derelict apartment buildings with broken windows, this section of city long since abandoned for more modern projects—left his heart in his throat. His breath came quickly now, in short, panting gasps, as visions of falling through a window just like those, surrounded by glimmering glass shards just before the impact that had changed his life forever overtook his sight.

Niko exited the ship and ran a hand over his face, trying to banish the visions, trying to steady himself. The air was cool here, but he was sweating.

The fact that Zann chose this spot to meet haunted him. He tried not to look into it too much, tried not to think of what message his brother might be sending. In the end, Celelast was a private place to meet, the entire dwarf-planet being half run down and abandoned, an old outpost inhabited only by a dwindling but stubborn population of outlaws, ruffians, and laborers.

*Should have asked him to meet on Sunorrna.* But that place seemed sacred, somehow, something intimate, a breath softly exhaled and suspended in time. A quiet memory that existed only between Elliott and himself.

Maybe Niko could make a new memory of this old dump. Maybe it could be the reunion he longed for with his brother. Something to replace the trauma and looping re-experience of falling whenever he even heard the name.

*In the end, you did it to yourself anyway, asshole,* a cruel thought reminded him. *Nobody pushed you out that window.*

Niko started toward the memorial park. It was overcast and windy today, a sort of biting, temperamental wind that picked up in random gusts before calming again. Trash was strewn about the old memorial grounds. A defaced and vandalized statue of the human business mogul, Edorren Duna, who had founded the now-dead sector of city had a damp napkin stuck to his face. Bird shit painted a crusty river down his left arm.

Beyond the statue was the old park, where long-neglected playground equipment stood, chains jangling and groaning when the wind pushed around the old swings and rusty merry-go-round. Whatever laughter and children's joy once filled this park was long since gone. The idea of kids being here, let alone ever being happy, was something Niko couldn't picture.

Or maybe they had never been happy. This place had been abandoned and moved on from for a reason.

Zann was there, sitting alone on an old bench. He held a cigarette between his lips, the purple smoke carried away on the biting wind. He'd quit years ago—they both had. Niko knew things were bad for him if he'd gone back to it again.

He watched his half-brother from afar for a moment, heart aching at the sight of him. He didn't know where they stood now, nor if they'd ever be alright again. He didn't know how much Zann had known about Honeybliss, either—only that he'd, when pressed, admitted he was aware they were real. That they'd done horrible things.

They had both betrayed each other; it was a double-sided blade that wounded.

Zann glanced up and saw him. He must have felt eyes on him. He had always had the same kind of uncanny instinct Niko did. For a moment, they simply stayed like that, gaze meeting gaze, Zann's face half shrouded behind a dancing haze of smoke. Then he waved Niko over and patted the bench. "Don't just stand there, Niko," he called.

Niko hesitated, casting one last glance around. The old park and silent buildings surrounding it revealed nothing. He tried to shake his unease, but it wouldn't budge. There was something else that lurked within it, something deeper, and more sinister. Paranoia. His skin crawled beneath the suit; the uncanny feeling of hidden eyes on him tugged at the edges of Niko's attention.

*We're not alone.*

Maybe Elliott was right. Maybe this was all a trap, and countless Galapol agents were staged, just waiting for the order to take him down for good. He shook his head, trying to push the thought away. He had to trust Zann. After all, he'd come this far.

His paranoia could just be a product of the anxiety that being back on Celelast induced in him.

Niko was grateful that Elliott was still back at the facility. If anything happened now, at least the other man would be alright.

He had to take some solace in that.

Niko made his way across the park, through the old and long-abandoned playground equipment. Up close, he was surprised it still stood at all. None of it had seen use in obvious years, maybe decades. He sank down onto the bench beside his brother, looking over at him. Zann smelled of tobacco, and a faint whiff of the aftershave he'd always favored. It made Niko nostalgic for when life had been less complicated.

"Want one?" Zann asked, holding out a pack of cigarettes.

Niko hesitated, considering it. The stress he'd been under lately was incredible, and it would be nice to have another outlet for it. He shook his head. "No, thanks. I've picked up enough old bad habits lately. Probably don't need another."

"You look like shit," Zann said, tucking the pack away.

"Yeah, you've been saying that lately," Niko said.

"Because you do."

"Zann..." Niko started, shaking his head. "I want to say I'm sorry. I'm sorry that I hurt you back on Neema. I'm sorry for knocking you out. I'm sorry for... getting you kicked out of Galapol."

"Replaced by fucking Fourier, of all things. Probably for the best, or I'd be in a body bag right now, instead."

Niko winced at the memory. It still made his stomach churn to recall the horrible sight—and *scent*—of two dozen Galapol special ops agents dismembered, dead and dying from Bubblegum's explosives.

"You know," Zann continued, taking a drag. "Kulna interrogated me. Fucking Kulna. Had to go into the room and be recorded and sworn in and everything to tell them I didn't know jack shit about you and your new boyfriend."

"I never wanted you to get caught up in anything like this," Niko said. Guilt sat heavy in his chest, greater than any pull of gravity.

"I just want to know *why*, Niko? Why throw your lot in with this guy, of anyone? Why him?"

Niko shifted uneasily. "I learned about Honeybliss. It just hit too close to home, Zann. Everything that's going on that just gets turned a blind eye to. They killed his sister—"

"That's not what I'm talking about. I saw those cute little sexy texts and that photo. Made me want to pour bog-theun corrosive into my eyeballs. That's more of Elliott Kestrel than I *ever* wanted to see."

Niko felt himself flushing.

"You were getting in with him long before you downloaded those files. 'You kissed me back?' On Uula? Seriusly, Niko?"

"I, uh—" Niko squirmed again, at a loss for words. "I— Yeah. Yeah. I guess so."

"So, what the hell?" Zann tossed the cigarette butt on the ground, crushing it beneath his shoe, where it was destined to fester with the scattering of other forgotten trash blown across the old park grounds.

"I don't—" Niko felt suddenly like a small child caught sneaking sweets red-handed. "I-It was just tactics. Part of the game. He— I—"

Zann sighed, clearly done with this line of questioning upon seeing that it was going nowhere. "Niko, brother, you need to stay away from this."

"Stay away?"

"Yeah. I'm saying you need to leave whatever the fuck you have going on right now. I can get you a safehouse, a new temp ID. I'll figure something out. Come on, man. You're not thinking about any of this."

Irritation flared through Niko and he shot Zann a scowl. "I'm not *thinking*? I've done nothing *but* think since this whole thing started."

"Yeah, with your dick, maybe."

"It's not like that."

"No. No, no. You are. How the hell do you know this guy isn't just *using* you, Niko?"

"Using? What?" The idea was incredulous. "No one's using anyone in this situation. I agreed to help him because I actually saw what he's getting at."

"Yeah. I know you must really, really like him. Especially if you were willing to fuck off the way that you have to help him start knocking off galactic celebrities."

"I—"

"But," Zann continued, steamrolling right over him, "my question is, Niko, does he like you?"

"Yeah, Zann. Somehow, he does."

"How sure are you of that?" Zann's voice had a dangerous sort of tone, the same kind Niko had heard him use during interrogations when he'd found a weakness to exploit and circle like a vulture. The one he got as he walked a suspect into their own logic trap.

"What?"

Zann eyed him, leaning back and draping an arm across the back of the bench. "I'm asking if this guy is using you as just another survival tactic."

Niko's head swam. The suggestion was egregious. "No, Zann. We're equals. We work together in this. There's no using or being used here."

"Are you *sure*, Niko?"

"Yeah. I am."

"All I'm saying here is that you're someone I would describe as 'pure of heart, but dumb of ass.' I know you like this guy. Clearly you do. But who was the biggest pain in his ass before this? You. Who was the one getting in his way and fucking up his plans, over and over again? *You.* You were the only one able to keep up with him and get close and he knew that.

"What happens when he realizes you're too good at your job to be neutralized through conventional means? He goes a different route. This guy's got a long history of being a smart bastard. You've seen how he strategizes and how he works. His texts were taunting you, too. Like he knew you wanted it bad and that it messed your head up. If you were someone willing to do anything to keep going with your mission, and the one person who kept threatening to ruin it all and take you down was someone you could trip up with a little seduction, would you?

"...You know what, no. Don't answer that. You have too good of a heart. But my point is, someone else might be willing."

"Zann, no—"

"But even further than that, he didn't just throw you off, did he? He outright converted you to his cause. You're his personal fucking champion now. You go out, take the hits, help him accomplish whatever he wants to get done, and all he has to do is give you some nice pats on the head, tell you he really likes you, and suck your dick a few times. Win, win, right?"

Anger boiled over inside Niko, a white-hot torrent felt in every taut muscle. Before he realized he'd done it, he found himself standing, glaring down at Zann. "No, you don't get it. Don't try to twist this into something manipulative. It's never been like that. He's not like that. All he ever wanted was for someone to just fucking *listen*. And I chose to listen."

"I'm just saying," Zann said, not moving an inch, still leaning back languorously against the bench. He raised his eyebrows. "I love you, Niko, but I'm not so sure you'd know how to recognize if that's what was going on."

"Of course I would, Zann." Niko wanted to spit the words at him. "Why don't you try giving me a little respect? How long have I been hunting bounties successfully before this?"

"Those bounties weren't Kestrel. They didn't have his brains. Or looks. How well do you actually know this guy, Niko?" Zann asked.

"Back at the Starlight Awards, when things went south, I'd told him to leave. To take the *Soñadora* and get out alive. I wanted him to. He had every chance to. But he didn't. He refused. He came back for me. He fucking *sacrificed* himself for it. He had no reason to. If this was only ever just tactics and convenience, he would have left me to it while he got away. If that other hunter hadn't... stepped in, he would have ended up caught and dead. That's not manipulation, Zann."

"It could be," Zann said, "if he thought you both still had a chance of getting out at the time. What was it you said when I asked you to come back to hunting? 'Sunk cost fallacy' and all that? Could have been trying to protect his investment."

"Don't. Don't make this into that. It's not that."

"Look. I'm not saying I don't empathize with the guy. I do. Of course I do. But there is a non-zero chance he might also be trying to survive this in his own way too. And that might just be through you. In a way you don't see."

"No," Niko said. Memories of Elliott unraveling after their failed hit tore through his mind. Elliott had been beside himself, all rage and despair. He'd tried to push Niko away, tried to drive him out of the mission—so he wouldn't be hurt again. He'd been almost hysterical about it. He'd started tearing into himself, saying he deserved to die.

Niko shook his head. "I know that's not what it is, Zann. And I know you're looking out for me here. I appreciate that you are. But you have to trust me with this. There's more to him than that. He was tearing himself apart when we got back. He blamed himself for the whole thing, for almost letting me die. When it was *my* fault. I was about to apologize to him for fucking the whole thing up, but he only blamed himself. That wasn't manipulation. It was genuine despair."

Zann sighed. He leaned forward, fishing out the pack of cigarettes from his coat pocket, but then seemed to think about it some, and simply held it instead. He looked up at Niko again. "Just— I'm not trying to piss you off, Niko. But I want you to keep a real careful eye on this, okay? You don't have anyone else there in your corner right now, and if he *was* just pulling your strings, would you even see it?"

Niko opened his mouth to argue, but stopped short. As much as he wanted to reject what Zann was saying, his brother had a point. He had never been great with being able to see betrayal coming, nor lying, even when it was right in front of him. Aleksi had been a perfect example of that—the man had been cheating for months before Niko caught him. He'd never even suspected a thing. And now Baouban, too.

He could at least admit to that personal shortcoming.

But, just as he had with Zann before, Niko wanted to choose faith. He wanted to believe in Elliott. Right now, they were all that each other had. And Elliott had been through so, so much, driven to the point of desperation.

Niko nodded at him. He would relent that much, if nothing more. "I'll be careful, Zann. I promise." After a long silence, he spoke again. "There's something I need to know, too."

"What's that?"

"You said you'd heard of Honeybliss. That there were rumors. You said you knew they'd done fucked up shit. Just how much did you know, Zann?"

Zann ran a hand across his face. He chewed at his bottom lip, looking up at the overcast sky. "Look, can you sit your ass down and stop looming over me?" Niko sank back onto the bench beside him, and he continued. "Yeah, so. I've heard of it. I know it's a thing. I know what they do. They kidnap and disappear people." He looked at Niko, holding his hands up. "But I don't know who's in it. I couldn't give you a list to save my life, except for what's in the files you gave me. I don't even know how long they've been around, just that they've been here a while."

"Elliott says he sent those files to Galapol almost three years back. He says he sent them to Station Twelve. Did you know? Did you get them?"

"I didn't. I didn't hear a thing about that. Whoever got them was real quiet about it, if that's the case. I've just heard people talk about it over the years. Sometimes cases come up. People come to us to try and investigate some of the missing. But it doesn't usually get far."

"Why not?" Niko asked.

"Because, Niko, and this is what you need to understand, here. Honeybliss really is untouchable. When I say untouchable, I mean you do not fucking *think* about looking at them. You don't think about thinking about it. They're so big and so powerful it's beyond what we can even do. This is an entire network of the most influential assholes in the entire galaxy. Some of them *are* their governments. They're more powerful than Galapol. They've fucked up cops before, gotten them fired, killed, even disappeared themselves. You want proof? Look at what you sent me."

Niko winced, remembering some of the files that had included the torture and violations of former Galapol agents. Niko hadn't connected the dots, hadn't realized they'd been singled out for actually trying to go against the grain and make some noise.

Zann wasn't fucking around.

"You have to believe me, Niko," Zann continued. "I hate shit like that. I despise it as much as you do. It's vile, it's awful. We went into this whole thing together to help people, and I still want to do that. But this? This was beyond even our reach. If we so much as sneezed in their direction, entire governments were going to turn their gazes our way."

It all made Niko ache. "That's why it's so important. What Elliott and I are doing. I want to make the difference that nobody else can or will. We're stopping them from hurting anyone else."

"Yeah, but at what cost, Niko? You already have the entire fucking galaxy out for your head. And every time you go out there, you risk getting yourself killed."

"How is it any different from bounty hunting? Every time I went out on a job, I had that risk."

"You know this isn't the same. You never had every other bounty hunter, Galapol agent, and planetary government out after your ass."

"That's—" Niko sighed. "That's fair. I won't stop, though, Zann. Not until every one of them is gone. It's an ugly business, and what you said before is right. It *is* scaring people. They don't understand. But I have a plan to change that. We need to stop the copycat murders from happening. We need to show people why we're doing what we're doing."

"Yeah? And how are you going to do that, Niko?"

"Lady Death."

Zann eyed him up and down. "You told me things didn't end so well with her."

"No," Niko admitted. "But I'm going to try and amend it. I'm going to meet with her tomorrow."

"You're going to go into the fucking black market, where your ass is worth a quadrillion credits, and hope you're greeted with open arms and a smile? Here I thought you just said you were going to be careful. Even you can't be that naive."

"No. I know. We're walking into a trap. I know what it is. But I don't have a choice. We need to get a message out, or more innocent people are going to die for this bounty. And she's capable of doing that."

"We? *We're* walking into a trap? You're seriously bringing your boyfriend?"

Niko tripped over the word. It wasn't the first time Zann had called Elliott that. He opened his mouth to speak, to object to the term. But... was it wrong? What was Elliott? What were they? They had grown so close as to be inseparable lately, living together, working together, sleeping with one another. Niko felt something deep, intangible, and raw for Elliott. Even thinking about him made Niko's heart skip a beat.

He decided to ignore it for now. It wasn't what mattered in Zann's question, anyway. "Yeah. I don't really love it either, but he insisted on coming. He's going to stay stealthed. Hopefully I can get what I need and get out quick without any trouble."

"You realize on the scale of one to fuck-awful that this idea is about a one hundred. Right?"

"I know, Zann. But I have to do it. Everyone Honeybliss hurt deserves it. We can prevent more from being taken and killed. And we can prevent any more copycat murders. We're going to end Honeybliss for good."

"Well, you always used to be a crazy son of a Toliai. And ambitious. I'll give you that." He eyed Niko for a moment. "Despite everything, I missed this. I missed *you*. It's good to see you not acting like a zombie anymore. Even if it means you're out fist-fighting the universe with Elliott Kestrel."

"Not the entire universe. Just the galaxy."

"Right," Zann said. "Well, that makes it way more manageable."

"I feel awake again for the first time in years, Zann," Niko admitted. "It feels good to be fighting again."

The two of them fell into a long silence before Zann finally spoke again.

"Shit. You know," he said slowly. He ran a hand over his short-cropped coils. "Maybe it's time I do something about it too."

"What?" Niko looked at him.

"Honeybliss. I knew they were out there, but didn't do anything about it. They were beyond what I could do. They were too big. I let them be too big; we all did. Maybe you have the right idea. Even if you did it in the most asshole, chaotic way possible."

A multitude of feelings ran through Niko. Elation, hope, joy. Fear and sorrow. He wanted to ask Zann to join him, to work with him. Niko knew his brother would excel at researching, at strategizing, at bringing down those who wrecked and ruined. It was what the man lived for. The three of them working together as a united team would be unstoppable.

The question was on the tip of his tongue.

But he couldn't dare ask that of him—doing so would only lead down a dangerous, deeply lonely path. He couldn't strip Zann's very life from him. He'd already cost him his career.

"Zann, I don't know. I don't want you to be at that kind of risk—"

"Niko. Wasn't it you who said before that we don't back down from the hard stuff?"

"I— Yeah. I did."

"So don't coddle me. Maybe I can help you out from the outside, somehow. I'll think of something."

"Just be careful, okay?" Niko said.

"Real rich, coming from you, Niko."

Another quiet lulled over them.

"How's, um," Niko mumbled. "How's Dad?"

"He's pretty broken up over you, still," Zann said. "He's under Galapol's protection, though. They're keeping a close eye on him. I harassed them until they agreed to post constant surveillance. They might be bastards for firing me, but I made sure they're going to take good care of him. It's the least they can do."

Niko wished that information comforted him more than it did. "Do you think it's going to be enough? If—"

Zann cut him off. "It's going to have to be. What else am I supposed to do?"

Niko nodded. *Unless I brought him to the facility.* The idea of depressed and anxious Oliver, stuck and isolated in the too-quiet, too-empty halls of the facility while he and Elliott were out on a hit made Niko nauseous with constricting grief. A safehouse wasn't guaranteed to be safe at all, anymore. Somewhere like Celelast or Sunorrna were just as lonely as RM-9832642G, maybe worse. And both had their own inherent dangers. Maybe if Lady Death didn't want the credits on his head...

The black market hive inside Dainna wasn't a place for Niko's father, either, though.

He'd really fucked up. Niko hadn't been thinking at all.

But the alternative had been to let Elliott get killed by Zann, or be given a harrowing public execution at the hands of Galapol—or any other number of planetary governments out for his head.

Before Niko could spiral further into the despair of that thought, Zann stood up. He followed suit.

"Listen, no more disappearing acts this time. I'll stay in touch with you through that burner phone. So keep an eye out," Zann said.

"Come here." Niko opened his arms wide. He pulled Zann into a tight hug that he realized probably wasn't quite pleasant for his brother, given the suit.

When they separated again, Zann eyed him warily up and down. He jabbed an accusing finger at him. "And one more thing. Don't ever body slam me in that armor. I didn't appreciate that shit."

Niko smirked. "Then don't shoot my boyfriend. I didn't appreciate that shit, either."

"Yeah, well, you just make sure that boyfriend's worth it, huh?"

"He is."

They parted ways, Niko glancing back over his shoulder as he wandered back through the desolate old playground and memorial park, stealing one last glimpse of his brother. Zann was watching him, too. He struggled to light up another smoke as the fickle wind picked up.

"Keep in touch, asshole," Zann shouted.

Niko flipped him the bird.

He made his way out through the old park and toward where the *Soñadora* waited. The warmth of his reconnection with Zann faded as he cast another look around. His surroundings were just as they'd been before he spoke with Zann. Darkened, shattered windows peered out at him from distant abandoned buildings, their rooms steeped in murky shadows. The park itself remained empty, scraps of old napkins and a paper cup caught up in flight by the wind, only to snag on clusters of scraggly plants, temporarily bound again in a sojourn to nowhere.

Everything was quiet, and he was alone.

But Niko found the hair on the back of his neck rising. Someone had seen. Someone had noticed him here, had watched. Had lingered, quietly. He didn't know how or why, but he couldn't shake the feeling. Had Zann been tapped, somehow? Had Galapol been watching him in secret and decided to follow?

It wasn't out of the question that Galapol might have eyes on Zann.

He reached the *Soñadora* and paused before entering, giving one final sweep of the ruinous landscape. Overgrowth and long neglected weeds sprouted through cracks in the old concrete. The decrepit playground equipment creaked and moaned, metal against unoiled metal as it was pushed about by the wind. The apartments in the background sat quiet, empty, dark. Still. Nothing had changed. Niko glanced up at the roof of the tallest one. He half expected to see Elliott there, perched, sniper rifle in hand. But he was greeted only by miles of emptiness.

Yet hunters' instinct told him that someone had been watching.

And was watching still.

Niko climbed into the ship, hastily locking the door behind him, paranoia rapidly spiking again. He did a quick sweep of the cabin, the bathroom, even under the bunk. He checked the interior and exterior security cameras. Nothing had been disturbed. Nothing was bugged.

He didn't want to linger here any longer. Niko sank into the pilot seat and began take off procedures to return to the only place he could even somewhat call home now—the quiet facility on Elliott's eternally frozen, forgotten moon.

CHAPTER THREE

# BACK IN TOWN

*"I MADE YOU A PRESENT!"* Elliott shouted as he entered the Murder Room. The heavy bass and rhymes of Royce RG vibrated the ceiling intercom speaker above them, nearly drowning out his voice. Niko glanced up at him from a pistol he had disassembled and was cleaning. Elliott's lips were curved up in a mild, sly crescent. Niko could tell he was trying to hide how pleased he was with himself.

He turned the music down. "Yeah? What's that?"

"I'm not going to tell you. You'll have to come see." Elliott disappeared around the doorframe.

Niko had to suppress his own grin as he wheeled out of the room after him. He tried to predict what 'gift' might refer to—maybe a new gadget, explosive, or something utterly and completely wild. Whatever it was, he hoped it wasn't another cake—Elliott had attempted to bake one for him once with the limited supplies they'd had, and it had wrought an apocalypse on his taste buds. Niko was still recovering.

Elliott led him out of the facility proper and down the ramp to the immense hangar. *Good. Not a cake this time.* The relief Niko felt was palpable.

Rap music still carried quietly over the hangar's speakers, though it felt far away and like an echo of civilization rather than any kind of enjoyable experience. The rubber of Elliott's combat boots squeaked lightly against the floor, painting a rhythm to the constant, quiet hum of Niko's wheelchair. They were clearly heading towards the *Soñadora Despierta*.

"Uh?" Niko grunted out, curiosity—and a little bit of concern—taking over. That ship was his baby. Perhaps, even, his true soulmate. Though Elliott might be a close second. "There's something on the ship?"

"You could say that," was all Elliott seemed willing to clarify. "Come on."

He made his way up the ramp, which had been left deployed. Niko followed shortly after, glancing around once he was in the ship's cabin. Nothing seemed different. Not an item was out of place.

Elliott stepped aside and gave a sweeping, dramatic gesture towards the door to the cockpit. Niko's heart leapt into his throat. *Tell me he didn't fuck with the controls.* He made his way over, then saw it: a rather crude looking electronics panel welded to the side of the console.

"Um, Elliott?"

"Go on. Try it." It had a simple switch on it, from which a dozen different wires and delicate silvery threads protruded. Niko reached out and flipped it. A familiar deep, brief hum reverberated through the entire ship and Niko stared up at Elliott wide-eyed.

"No fucking way."

"Way."

"I have to see this." Nothing seemed to have changed from the inside. Niko made his way back out of the ship, down the ramp, before turning the chair. He let out an involuntary whoop of sheer excitement, giddiness bubbling up in him, replacing any of his previous trepidation as he peered out at the faintly perceptible distorted outline of where the *Soñadora* stood. He could see right through it. Elliott had somehow installed what he'd named the Ophthalmic Refraction Apparatus—or ORA—powerful enough to hide an entire ship.

"Oh, hell yeah. I can get into *so* many wrecks with this."

Elliott was beside him now, arms folded over his chest. "Asshole. But you *will* have to be cautious with how you utilize it, of course. It also has to pull from and drain the battery so you'll only want to use it during strategic opportunities. This hangar does have a charger, but if we get stranded because of it, we're fucked."

"Damn. This is great." Niko looked up at him. He could feel the grin all over his own face, something that went deeper than the skin. Happiness. It was almost as though the muscles that formed his smile themselves delighted in the pleasure of being, emotion and physicality inseparable from one another. "You're incredible. Really. Thanks, babe."

"I don't know why I hadn't considered it before. I've only ever used it for myself—and eventually you. I didn't know if I could make it work for something as big as this ship, but I was thinking last night and figured out how to make an amplifier. I worked on it all morning."

"Hey," Niko said. Elliott looked down at him as Niko held his hand upward in anticipation of a high five. His green eyes narrowed piteously for a moment, but eventually he acquiesced and slapped Niko's hand with his own, their high five emitting a satisfying and singular, crisp *clap* that left Niko's palm tingling. Elliott's mouth betrayed his own burgeoning joy now, twitching upwards at the corners despite his best efforts to appear serious. He coolly looked away.

"I'm going to go shut it off before it does start draining the battery," he murmured, and wandered off into the ship, seeming almost to ascend straight up into the air and vanish into nothing. Niko watched in fascination as the *Soñadora* seemed to materialize before him again, opaque as it had ever been, with another deep sound. Elliott re-emerged and joined him once more.

"So, uh," Niko said, "you ready for today?"

The air around them almost seemed to cool as Elliott's eyes grew somber and distant. "I don't know that we'll ever be fully ready for a foray into somewhere like that, Niko. But we're as ready as we can be."

Niko nodded, swallowing back a lump of nervousness catching in his throat. "Hey, you regularly go crawling into massive charity galas, award ceremonies, political debates, and concerts," he said, aiming for a bit of levity. "How bad could a criminal market be, compared to that?"

"I suppose we'll find out soon enough," Elliott said, but something in his expression softened a little, his eyebrows raising. "But whatever happens, I'm glad to be there with you."

Niko guided the *Soñadora* into the wide gates of Dainna's Tenntha District docking station. Every visible surface was buried under a ghostly wash of holograms, all advertising different goods and experiences one might find within the giant, crowded asteroid. Unlike most docks, no one stopped or checked them in. They weren't scanned by a flurry of security bots, nor contacted over radio. This was a place of general lawlessness; if you even knew about the existence of Dainna and were willing to venture there, chances were, you were someone who fit right in.

Niko had thought briefly to try out his new stealth toy, but after a lengthy debate with Elliott on the way there, he'd relented to the other man's conclusion that parking while invisible in a typically crowded, high-traffic area probably wasn't going to work out in his favor. Not to mention the issue with the battery drainage. The ship had no outer markings to set it apart from any other model KZ-114. The only risk he carried was someone potentially recognizing it by its particular mods and additions.

Elliott peered out the windshield as Niko navigated around a trio of small Dvaab ships making their way out. Niko couldn't help but smile at the other man's obvious fascination—since they'd gotten near, his eyes had grown wide and watchful. His face and hair were awash in a spectrum of shifting colors as they passed by various clusters of neon holograms.

"So," Niko said as he drifted toward the parking level Aleksi had agreed to meet at. The entire dock was a labyrinth of small platforms to anchor a ship to, layer stacked upon layer. A violently neon blue hologram reading TEN-8-5A indicated he'd reached the right sector. "Welcome to Dainna. Biggest black market bastion in the galaxy."

A whole spectrum of holograms reflected in Elliott's eyes. When he spoke, it was with a quiet, breathless awe. "I've never been anywhere like this."

"Wish I could give you the grand tour, but yeah. Speaking of which. Elliott, we need to discuss a few things. I need you to keep in stealth and not make a peep the entire time we're here. No wandering off, nothing weird. Just stay quiet and let me do the talking."

"Talking. Right. I'm sure that's what Mikhaylov's here to do."

Niko sighed. He hated the idea of this going south, but Elliott was right. It was an inevitability at this point. He didn't really want to fight Aleksi. In fact, he didn't want to see his shitty face at all, but beggars couldn't be choosers. And Niko had one route now to meeting Lady Death.

"I won't kill him though, since you asked so nicely," Elliott said.

"That's reassuring." Niko guided the ship in to rest at the TEN-8-5A docking platform, where it connected with a magnetic tether. He let out a long breath, hoping to drain some of the tension from his body. It didn't help. "Alright. Do your thing, Elliott."

"In a moment," Elliott murmured. He stood.

"The sooner the bet—"

Elliott swooped in and planted a long, warm kiss on Niko's lips. Niko yielded to him, letting him in. It made him melt, all heat and electricity. Elliott always made him feel this way.

When Elliott pulled away, Niko grabbed his wrist. "Hey."

"Yes?"

He hesitated. "What are we?"

Elliott frowned. "That's a vague question."

"I mean," Niko shifted, suddenly feeling squirrely and regretting the question. "What—do you think—you and me—are we—"

"Oh," Elliott said, eyeing him. "We're partners in crime. Gay space crime."

"No, um. Do you think, uh, it would be, you know—" Niko found himself staring up at the ceiling instead of Elliott as he talked. It was easier to look anywhere but at him. "Like, would the label 'boyfriends' be weird?"

Elliott laughed. "I don't think it's weird at all, Niko. Do you want to call me your boyfriend?" His voice dropped to a low and sultry, teasing tone.

Elliott's words wormed their way straight into some molten, hot part of him. Niko pulled the suit's glove off and reached out again to take his hand. Then he ran his thumb along the map of the tendons there, his mood turning briefly luminous—giddy, even—despite all that lay ahead of them. "I do. I do want that."

"I do too, Niko. I want you to be my boyfriend."

*All he has to do is give you some nice pats on the head, tell you he really likes you, and suck your dick a few times. Win, win, right?*

The thought crept unbidden into his head and Niko nearly grunted with annoyance.

Fucking Zann.

He pushed it all away. He wanted to enjoy this small victory. Their mission—and lives—had become so difficult lately. It was nice to have something Niko could take true solace in. Or, rather, *someone*.

Elliott left him with a smile, gaze meeting gaze. He vanished right before Niko as he activated his stealth. Niko could still feel the warmth and touch of his hand against his own before it finally pulled away. He missed him already.

*Well*, Niko thought as he peered out the windshield at the crowded, vibrant parking deck. He latched his glove back into place. *It's now or never.*

He stood, weapons already latched to his back, belt, and side, then wrapped an old scarf that had belonged to Elliott around his face until only his eyes remained visible. It was a shitty cover at best, but it would keep him from being immediately recognizable to anyone passing by.

Niko had no doubt Galapol had made sure to plaster his face everywhere for the galaxy to see, with his lucrative bounty attached. This place may have been outside of Galapol's influence, but it was home to a multitude of hunters. Very *hungry* bounty hunters.

He stepped out of the *Soñadora* and walked down the ramp. It was both a comfort and source of quickly growing anxiety not to be able to clearly see Elliott. He had to trust that the other man kept close like he'd instructed him to.

And that no one else happened to bump into or notice him there.

All around them, the scents of various fried foods and street meats floated by from stalls, pop up shops, and carts. People of every species wandered around them, going about their own business. Some sort of Gheroun cultural music played from a nearby speaker. Niko was just glad that for once it wasn't Hayura or Kuliedi Taan, the galaxy's current popstar obsessions. Neon holograms and advertisements continued to assault his retinas at every turn; there was simply no escaping them. A maze of doorways led to shops selling anything imaginable, legal or not, bars for weary travelers, and other dens of pleasure.

The crowds around them were certainly different from what he'd grown used to lately—the people here had all sorts of modifications, body art, and clothing that could only be described as loud. The species that possessed hair often had it dyed in shades so vibrant they rivaled the adverts and signs around them for attention.

Niko shouldered his way through them all. No one was polite here; you either pushed your way through crowds, or you got shoved around instead.

He paused, glancing around, before spotting Aleksi, who was leaning languidly against a stack of crates stamped with a symbol Niko didn't recognize. A new gang or trade faction who had arisen since his last foray here, maybe.

His blood turned to ice at the sight of his ex's familiar face as the man turned to look in Niko's direction. He was still as handsome as he'd ever been, with straight, black, glossy hair, hazel eyes, olive skin, and a five o'clock shadow. Niko felt no attraction though—in fact, the sight of his well-formed features only made him feel even more resentful than he already did. Whatever had once been between them was now well and truly dead, rotting in the ground for years.

Aleksi's eyes met Niko's and he grinned in recognition, all perfect white teeth. He raised a hand in greeting and made his way over. Niko tensed instinctively, shoulders rising as the other man approached. His skin crawled. He fought the urge to turn and walk right back into the *Soñadora*.

Or punch Aleksi. He definitely wanted to punch that smug grin off his face.

"Hey, bud. Wow," Aleksi said once he stood before Niko. "Nice scarf."

"'Bud?'"

His smile widened, eyes squinting into little crescents now. Niko saw he was getting crow's feet around them. Aleksi's voice dropped to a low murmur. "Or I could say your name, you know, loudly. Here, in the middle of Dainna."

Niko grunted. "Fair point." He was ready to be done with this already.

"So, you ready to meet the Lady?"

"Yep."

Aleksi turned and started walking deeper into the mingling alien crowds, weaving through food and weapons stands. He gestured with a jerk of his head for Niko to follow.

Niko kept up with him. He wanted so badly to mumble to Elliott over their private frequency—*Get a load of this chucklefuck.* But he kept his mouth shut, slipping between clusters of armed people who would sell his soul to Galapol, Honeybliss, or any higher bidder if they so much as caught a whiff of who he really was. His pulse spiked as he thought of Elliott having to subtly navigate the tight crowds without betraying that there was, somehow, an invisible but physical presence wandering around.

"I talked with her and she was pretty adamant about telling you to fuck right off," Aleksi said as they walked. He ducked under a beaded curtain and Niko did the same. The thing tinkled softly as they passed through into another long corridor full of shops and fast, pulsing, muffled music. "But I finally got her to agree to at least talk with both of us here. She said if I'm willing to vouch for you after all these years that she'll at least listen. She's always had a lot of honor, despite everything."

"Yep."

"She's moved her compound since, too. It's in the Vaiyya district now."

"Okay."

"*He actually thinks he's clever,*" Elliott quietly marveled over their frequency. His voice, delivered as a soft whisper, eased Niko a little. It was a comforting reminder that he was near. As problematic as that very fact equally was.

"You used to be a lot more talkative, you know?" Aleksi said, casting a glance over his shoulder at Niko.

"Uh huh."

Niko heard a soft snicker in his earpiece again. It made him smile beneath the scarf.

"*This guy's really dense, isn't he?*" Elliott whispered.

His smile widened.

Aleksi walked briskly, leading Niko through side corridors and greasy alleyways. Some were lined with destitute people, likely outcasts who'd been booted from casinos, brothels, or bars from lack of funds or poor behavior. Aleksi nearly tripped over a Gheroun woman who was mostly a pile of dirty rags, dirtier tentacles, and only one eye remaining of three. She growled at him like a feral animal.

"Ma'am. Sincerest apologies," Aleksi said, putting a hand on his chest. "Beautiful tentacles, by the way. Very plump."

Niko wanted to punch him again.

"*What do you think would happen if I dropped him on his ass while stealthed, and how angry would you be on a scale of one to ten?*" Elliott murmured.

Niko barked out a laugh at their unexpected alignment. Aleksi glanced at him again, flashing another grin as he mistook Niko as being amused by him. He shot Niko a wink that made him nearly shudder.

*"It smells so good here, Niko. We should lift some of that street food before we go,"* Elliott whispered. *"I'm salivating."*

"I don't know if you want this shit," Niko finally mumbled back, unable to help himself. He tried to keep his voice to a low murmur so Aleksi didn't hear. "Tends to be laced with hard stuff."

*"Would make things more interesting than Mikhaylov is."*

"The last thing anybody needs right now is you suddenly showing up armed, in the middle of Dainna, tripping balls off hallucinogens."

*"You don't think that sounds like fun, Niko?"* Elliott teased.

The reckless, less-than-sane part of Niko *did* think that sounded fun. But he wasn't about to let Elliott know that. Especially right now.

Elliott wasn't wrong, though—everywhere they went, they were submerged in tantalizing scents, oily fried fats that hung thick in the air, mingled with salt, zest, and uniquely alien spices.

And a little bit of drugs.

Aleksi led him to the Vaiyya district, a crowded industrial zone where rare ores were bought and processed, and stolen, hot vehicle and ship parts were made quick work of.

"She's rebuilt here now. Entrance is through here."

*"This is legitimately insulting,"* Elliott whispered over the comm. Niko grunted a quiet agreement.

"Alright, Aleksi. Show me where she is," he said flatly. He resisted the urge to roll his eyes.

They approached a huge, windowless building made with patchy, corrugated steel. "One sec," Aleksi muttered as he paused before a rusty side entrance. He keyed in the entry code, then pressed his thumb to the biometric scanner. The lock clicked and Aleksi pulled the door open.

Niko muttered so quietly that he wasn't even sure Elliott was able to hear. "If she were really here, she'd have guards posted at this door. Death is a people person and runs on connections. He should have known that."

"*He's not even trying*," Elliott quipped with an admonishing click of his tongue.

Niko stepped through the door and into a vast garage full of various disassembled ships, overhead lamps hanging high above and washing the place in dim yellow light.

"*Ask if he can just spare you and get on with the backstabbing now*," Elliott whispered. "*I'm bored. And hungry.*"

Niko couldn't help himself. "Soooo. Lady Death works in ship parts now, huh?"

"Eh, sometimes," Aleksi said, walking between two towering, half-stripped ships whose models Niko didn't recognize. They looked vintage though, likely favored by collectors. "But these actually aren't hers. Her place is further back inside the building."

"Uh huh."

They reached the far end of the garage, where stairs led up to a mezzanine which connected to two sets of doors. Aleksi paused at the foot of the stairs and tilted his head.

"She should be here any—" He pulled a pistol out from inside his jacket and shoved the business end towards Niko's face. "Second."

Several mercenaries appeared, stepping out from behind derelict ships, their own guns at the ready, all trained on Niko.

Niko sighed. He looked at Aleksi with disappointment.

"Sorry, Niko. Your bounty's just too good to pass up. But I'll buy a bottle of aged Uulan red in your honor."

"*Finally,*" Elliott muttered. "*Maybe now we'll actually get somewhere.*"

Niko raised his hands in mock surrender and shook his head. The mercenaries fired on him, all their bullets uselessly pinging off his shield as the shockwaves of their impact rippled through the air. He unlatched his own rifle and took a quick shot aimed for Aleksi's foot, but the other man was too fast, leaping behind half a beautiful XR-193 racer that looked to have its windshield missing and cockpit gutted.

He heard Elliott drop two of the mercenaries—if the grunts and moans of pain were any indication—and spun to take down another, shooting her in the arm.

"Shit!" She lurched and dropped the gun, cradling her wound before shrinking away from him.

Niko turned back to where Aleksi was hiding.

"You really think I didn't see this coming, Aleksi?"

"I don't know," Aleksi called out from his hiding spot. "You missed a lot of things going on right in front of you for a long time, dude."

Niko really wanted to give him a bad day. "You always were an asshole. Here I was hoping people could change."

Aleksi appeared briefly around the side of the XR-193 and fired quickly on Niko, but like the others, the bullet didn't even come close. Elliott caught him with a shot through the shoulder and Aleksi staggered back before disappearing again, leaving a trail of blood droplets in his wake.

"*Ooohh,*" he ground out, his voice gravelly from pain now. "You brought your new fucktoy too. Perfect. He's the one I really wanted."

"Fucktoy?" Elliott purred. He wasn't whispering anymore. "The only one getting penetrated here today is you. By a bullet."

"Yeah? I heard these do a pretty good job at wrecking your ass." Aleksi appeared again, quick, EMP grenade in hand. Niko didn't give him the chance. He was on Aleksi in an instant, barreling into the other man. He grabbed him by the neck and threw him to the ground. Aleksi slammed down into it hard, the breath knocked out of him. The grenade tumbled away uselessly, bouncing across the floor, the pin still in.

"Aleksi. Knock it off," Niko said, staring down at him. "You're not going to win this. Just take us to where she actually is."

Aleksi wasn't ready to quit just yet, it seemed. He leapt up, jackknife in hand now, that he drove toward Niko's neck. "Hey, remember this?"

A pang of shock and annoyance jolted through Niko as he recognized its design—a twin of his own knife, and a gift he'd given the other man years ago. Aleksi was infuriatingly quick, almost as much as Elliott had been. Niko deflected the hits with his arm, though, the blade all but useless against his armor. Then he punched Aleksi hard enough to send the other man reeling.

*Fuck. That was way more cathartic than it should have been.*

He heard Elliott take down two more of the mercenaries in the background, the shots coming from different angles as he quickly maneuvered about. Only one remained active now, and Niko turned and shot at him, missing. The merc returned fire back on Niko which the shield stopped again, then panicked and tried Niko's own tactic, rushing him instead.

Niko overpowered the man, wrestling him back and throwing him to the ground like he'd done with Aleksi. Elliott swept in quick, knocking the mercenary's gun out of his hands.

"Okay, okay, okay," Aleksi said, raising his hands in surrender now that his hired help had been dismantled. A trail of dark blood ran down from his left nostril where he'd been decked and his nose sat at an angle now. The shoulder Elliott had shot sagged limply. He looked utterly depressed. "Fine, I get it. I'll take you to her for real."

Niko trained his rifle on him. He didn't trust Aleksi not to pull something tricky again in a last-ditch effort. "Do it. And don't fuck around this time. We're not going to be so merciful a second time. Am I clear?"

"Clear as crystal," Aleksi said flatly.

"I heard you were back in town," a deep, feminine voice boomed out across the garage from behind them. It was terrifyingly familiar.

Everyone involved in the failed ambush froze in place. Niko's heart dropped as he slowly turned and stared at the Heenva whom everyone called Lady Death. This wasn't how he'd wanted to make her acquaintance again.

"Oh. *Oh shit,*" Niko heard Aleksi mutter under his breath. Clearly, the asshole hadn't been actually expecting her here, either.

Death was a robust, tall woman with generous curves. Her blue, scarred skin showed in patches, purple hair tied back in a severe bun. An eyepatch covered her missing right eye. She was exactly as Niko remembered.

Flanking her were several of her own guards. He vaguely recognized a few of them.

"So, uh, Niko showed up and tried to use me to—" Aleksi started, his voice suddenly gone shaky.

"Shut up. Just shut up," Niko snapped at him.

Aleksi ignored him. "He's got his serial killer fuckbuddy here with him. The one with the sniper rifle, who's, you know, *murdering* everyone—"

"Do you know what 'shut up' means?" Elliott asked. He knocked Aleksi to his knees, the act looking odd and seeming to come from nowhere with Elliott's stealth still in place. "You're a liar and an idiot, and now you're in time out."

"Show yourself," Death demanded. Her people trained their guns in Elliott's direction.

"Shit," Niko muttered. This was falling apart fast.

Elliott deactivated his stealth, appearing before Death and her guards.

To her credit, the Heenva merely eyed him up and down, sizing him up. He kept *Repartee* lowered at his side, not showing any hostility towards her either. She could easily take him out before he'd ever have a chance to defend himself. Niko tried not to dwell on that fact—but it was all he could think about.

"In the very flesh," she marveled.

Niko swallowed nervously. "I—I need to talk to you. It's why I'm here. Why we're here."

Death's gaze swiveled toward Niko again, cold and displeased. She pursed her lips and her branching antennae flickered with a faint and dangerous glow. "Why would I have any interest what-soever in talking to you, Killjoy?"

"So, they actually do call you that," Elliott said.

"You have some real balls," Death continued. "The audacity you have to set foot on my turf after you disappeared without ever honoring your debt would impress me if it weren't so pathetic. And now you want to *talk*."

"You didn't mention that part," Elliott murmured.

Niko may have forgotten to bring up their bad blood and his unpaid debts when regaling him with stories about the Great

Revolutionary of Sala. The plan was a little more convincing that way.

"You're right," Niko said, looking at her. He latched his rifle onto the back of his suit and raised his hands in a gesture of goodwill. "It *was* pathetic of me. And it was wrong. So, I've come to finally repay that debt. Whatever you ask, I'll do it."

"Don't trust these guys. Are we really just going to ignore that he brought *Elliott Kestrel* with him?" Aleksi had gotten to his feet again.

"I'm not ignoring anything," Death said patiently. She eyed Aleksi and his bloodied nose, then looked back at Niko. "Why are you and *Elliott Kestrel* roughing up my people in an old parts garage?"

"Alek—" Niko started.

Elliott cut him off. "Mikhaylov got too big for his britches and decided he wanted to use the fact that Niko needed to see you to instead stab him in the back for his bounty."

Niko glanced sharply at Elliott, his pulse spiking as he realized the man whose reputation made people do dangerous, uncharacteristic things was negotiating the situation now.

*You had one rule. One. To let me do the talking.*

Death looked at Elliott now, her expression turning sour with disgust. Her antennae flashed sharply in a brief, intense glow. "Is that so?"

"It is," Niko said. "He led us here for an ambush."

"A pathetically obvious one," Elliott added in. Then he muttered, "You have really poor taste in men, Niko."

Niko scowled at him. "You're kind of insulting yourself with that one too, you know?"

"Anyway." Elliott looked back at Lady Death far more boldly than Niko liked. "You should tell your minions to try a little harder next time." He tipped his chin up with a hint of regal pride and challenge.

Niko winced. They were both going to finish this exchange as corpses.

Death turned her gaze on Aleksi instead, though, eyeing him up and down. She didn't look pleased. "My *minions* don't back-stab people."

"Look, I can explain," Aleksi said, suddenly sounding nervous. He held up his hands placatingly. Death stared at him in vicious silence. "Let's be reasonable here. You've seen his bounty. It would leave you set for a lifetime and more. It would leave all your people set too. They'll all be taken care of. This guy fucked off on you anyway, right? We can split it. Fifty-fifty solid. I brought him here and—"

Death shot Aleksi between the eyes, the sound thundering through the warehouse. He dropped to his knees with a solid *thud*, then fell forward onto his face. A puddle of dark blood spread out from beneath his head, reflecting the dim lights above.

Niko gaped in utter horror, momentarily breathless. "*Why?*"

"Clean this up," Death barked at her guards, ignoring him. They fanned out and shot any of Aleksi's mercenaries who had been left behind and stranded due to their injuries. Niko flinched with each fatal gunshot. He glanced at Elliott, who looked quietly upset, his brow drawn into a subtle frown, skin pale with his own barely expressed shock. He didn't seem interested in clever quips and comments anymore.

When it was done, Death turned her unimpressed gaze on Niko again. "The two of you, come with me."

Niko nodded to Elliott. The other man vanished as he reactivated the ORA, but Death shook her head.

"No. You stay in sight." It wasn't a request.

Elliott reappeared, watching her warily.

"Come on," she said, then turned and walked away. Niko cast one last glance at Aleksi, feeling ill. He lay unmoving, the puddle of his blood still growing beneath him. He'd never get up again.

Niko had despised the man, but hadn't wanted him to die.

He waited for Elliott to make his way over, then walked side by side with him. Death's guards formed a ring around them as they exited the parts garage.

"You okay?" Niko murmured. He knew how well Elliott took getting others caught up and killed—even if they were greedy assholes in the end. He was probably blaming himself, too, especially given it was his comments that had helped seal Aleksi's fate.

"I'm fine," Elliott replied, his voice clipped and tense.

Niko eyed him. Elliott pressed his lips together into a tight and severe line that made Niko ache. He knew him well enough now to know he was anything but fine. Niko reached out to touch the back of his hand, when one of the guards snapped at Elliott, jolting both men.

"Put your weapon away."

He did, slinging *Repartee* over his back. Niko was surprised they hadn't tried to outright take it from him. It was a stunning—and completely unexpected—show of trust from Lady Death for the galaxy's most notorious killer. Niko hoped it was a good sign, that perhaps she might still trust him, too, after everything.

They made their way back through the winding, neon-shrouded corridors of Dainna in a direction Niko was familiar with this time. She'd never moved her compound—but that wasn't really surprising. Death's guards kept to their tight formation around Niko and Elliott as they walked, guns out.

The news of their presence would sweep across all of Dainna within the hour, he knew—and somehow already had begun to, given that Death had even shown up—but nobody dared to try their luck, even as Niko watched the eyes they passed by widen with shock and recognition, all fixated on Elliott. Some even glanced at Death and moved away, nervously keeping a distance.

Even Dainna gave her respect. That was the power Lady Death wielded.

Power that Niko might just be able to use to hit Honeybliss where it hurt. They just had to survive this, first.

*Nothing to it, right?* Niko thought. *It'll be all downhill from here.*

# CHAPTER FOUR

# NO ONE IS YOUR FRIEND

THE NEARER THEY DREW to Lady Death's compound, the more antsy Niko grew. None of this had gone how he'd hoped, but the two of them were still alive and about to finally have an audience with her. That was what mattered now.

But there were some things Elliott still needed to know.

"Elliott," Niko murmured. The guards could probably overhear everything he was about to say, regardless. Especially the Dvaab ones, whose hearing was exceptional. "I need you to keep your mouth closed once we're in here. I mean it, this time. Let me do the talking."

"Fine."

"There's another thing, too. Just— Be respectful when you're in there. To Lady Death. To her wives. She has two, and you need to know about them both. One's a Quwa-quay woman named Yalsa—"

"Quwa—"

"I *know* that Quwa-quay are typically bi-gendered," Niko hissed, glancing around at the guards and Death nervously. "But Yalsa is a woman. And if you want to suggest otherwise, you're going to eat a bullet of your own, courtesy of Lady D. Do not fuck around with any of this."

"I wasn't going to suggest otherwise."

"Good."

"You have a lot of homicidal friends, don't you?" Elliott, the galaxy's most wanted assassin, whispered.

"Yeah, I do." Niko reached over and pinched the other man's ear the way his own mother used to do when he, Zann, or Ryen had been being assholes. He couldn't help himself, despite the gravity of everything they'd just endured and all that lay ahead of them still. Elliott shrunk away, as far as the tight ring of their armed escort would allow, though Niko caught the faint ghost of a grin on his face.

"There's also Sweetheart," Niko continued.

"Everyone has a weird name here, don't they? I'm reconsidering 'the Dickfister.'"

"You'd fit in more than you know. Anyway, she's a Xermotl and has been here as long as I can remember. You need to treat her with the *utmost* respect or—"

"Let me guess. I get my own special bullet for dessert."

"You're catching on. Call her ma'am or miss, defer to her. Treat her like she's a goddess. It's—it's a whole thing. Lady Death does not tolerate rudeness to Sweetheart. Probably above anything else in the galaxy."

"I can't wait."

They were nearing the compound now, a big, multi-tiered concrete structure that featured hardy, bulletproof windows with steel bars welded to them and thick blackout curtains blocking the view in or out. It was just like Niko remembered. That he'd ever even briefly believed Aleksi when he'd said she'd moved left Niko ashamed. Death would never hide away in fear. But time did weird things to people, he knew. It had made the underworld's most trusted provider of safe shelter and secret keeping betray him for credits.

"Nice place," Elliott whispered. "The iron bars are a delicate touch."

"*Elliott,*" Niko muttered.

Their group entered through thick, guarded double doors. The entryway guards nodded to Death and eyed Niko and Elliott closely, but professionally tamped down on any surprise they may have felt, maintaining stoic poker faces.

High ceilings with simple and sturdy but mildly artful chandeliers hung above them all, casting a warm, dim glow. Each chandelier differed from the next, giving a quirky and eclectic vibe. A few tall, exotic potted plants from alien worlds were scattered about, shoved into various corners. Patterned rugs laid out a path before them, with framed artworks and paintings from some of the most renowned artists the galaxy had ever known—alive and dead—adorning the walls. Each painting was probably worth as much as Niko had ever earned in his lifetime.

Velvety curtains were drawn closed over the windows, giving a sense of enclosure and privacy. This place was every bit the den he remembered it being. Niko just hoped he could come to feel as welcome in its walls as he had always been before. He unwound the scarf from his face, feeling like he could finally breathe again.

The compound interior was bustling with people who worked for and were loyal to Death.

As Aleksi had unfortunately shown, she didn't tolerate disloyalty.

They paused in their various activities and conversations to blankly stare at Elliott. Niko glanced around uneasily from one person to the next, suddenly wondering all over again if he'd made the right choice by ever coming here. And especially by bringing Elliott with him.

A spindly, lavender Xermotl began making her way toward their group. Anyone in her direct path immediately moved themselves out of her way without hesitation. Her movements were elegant, dainty, careful even. Sweetheart had always reminded Niko of a ballet dancer. Her translator chip was affixed around her neck to a pink leather collar which had a heart and bow on it. The voice that emerged from the chip was soft, feminine, high in pitch. It fit her perfectly.

"Welcome back, Mistress." She extended a spade-shaped, delicate hand to Lady Death, who paused to kiss it.

"Mistress? *Kinky*," Elliott whispered.

"Do. Not," Niko warned him.

Even the guards surrounding them nodded their respects to Sweetheart. They murmured polite greetings.

Sweetheart turned to peer at Niko, her patterns glowing brightly in a golden sunset orange of excitement the moment she recognized him. Her four large, glossy eyes blinked as though doubting what stood before her. "Killjoy? Is that really you?"

"Sweetheart, ma'am," Niko said, bowing his head demurely. He felt Elliott's fascinated gaze on him. "It's good to see you again. You're as lovely as ever. Maybe even more so. It's... been a while, huh?"

Sweetheart's patterns shifted to a gentle pink which signaled the Xermotl form of a smile. "You're too kind, Niko. May I call you Niko, still? I'm sorry if it's awkward now—"

"It's not awkward, ma'am. We're friends, right?"

She clasped her hands together. "It's delightful to see you again after so many years, dear friend. You look very well, Niko. Everyone is going to be so excited to talk to you again." She said it in the way only rare, truly benevolent souls did—with sincerity and care, rather than empty platitudes. Being near her, despite everything, put Niko a little more at ease. "I do hope that life has been kind to you during your absence."

*Not really*, Niko thought, his mood souring again slightly. Between his fall and injury, the years of pitch-dark depression that followed, and the galaxy wanting him dead now, life had mostly been particularly unkind.

*With a few exceptions.*

He glanced at Elliott, then smiled. "I can't complain. Things are pretty good lately. I hope you've been doing well, too." Elliott's green gaze held its own quiet smile before Niko looked back to Sweetheart again.

She squinted two pairs of eyes happily at him. Then she turned her quizzical gaze to Elliott and Niko felt himself tense.

*Don't say something weird to her*, he begged. *Please.*

He was definitely going to say something weird to her.

"How astonishing," Sweetheart marveled, touching absent-mindedly at her collar. "I recognize your face from the news. Everyone talks about you, all the time. Elliott Kestrel, if I'm correct?"

"You're correct, ma'am," said Elliott, putting on the smoothest smile Niko had ever seen from him. He was so handsome, even Niko found himself getting distracted from his thoughts. Or any thought at all. "I'm flattered that you recognize me. Niko's told me a lot about you and it's all been heaps of praise. He certainly wasn't lying, it seems. It's truly my pleasure to finally get to meet you."

Niko appreciated the merciful lie thrown his way. He'd neglected to say a thing about Sweetheart before today.

Sweetheart's patterns turned a deep chartreuse—which had taken Niko years to learn was Xermotl code for blushing—at Elliott's compliments in a way she never had with Niko. It was all he could do to keep himself from rolling his eyes. It seemed even the married alien woman wasn't immune to Elliott's handsome face as he put on the charm.

Elliott looked every bit right then a golden-haired playboy and not a habitual murderer of planetary leaders.

"I don't wish to offend, Mr. Kestrel—"

"Please, ma'am. Elliott's fine, I insist."

Sweetheart blushed again before continuing. "But if I may, I'm quite curious what business you have here visiting our home? Especially someone with such... *renown* as yourself." She said it like she was meeting a favored celebrity.

In the end, Niko figured it was better to have someone fawning over him like this than the quiet, keen-eyed murmurings coming from everyone else around them.

Lady Death cut in and answered before Elliott could. "We'll talk about that later, Sweetheart. For now, I want you all in the conference room."

Death walked on ahead and Niko's armed party followed. The guards had their guns lowered now, but still kept them out. Sweetheart gave Elliott an elegant wave, squinting happily, and Elliott waved back at her.

"It's a pleasure to make your acquaintance, Elliott," she said. "Be well."

"Likewise, miss."

They entered the conference room, another large, thickly-walled chamber with the curtains drawn closed and dim, warm lighting hanging from above. Niko remembered this room. It was, more or less, the same, with a few small changes. Some of the more beat up chairs had been replaced, and the plain table from years before was now upgraded to one with a delicately artful cherry blossom branch design hand-carved across its surface, carefully engraved with gold inlay. The center of each flower had a sizable diamond, all trapped under layers of smooth, transparent resin.

"I really hope you can trust this woman," Elliott whispered. His voice was tense again, any charismatic pretty-boy act all but vanished. "Or we're about to be fucked." He cast a nervous glance over his shoulder at the one—and only—exit to the room which now had two guards standing shoulder to shoulder, blocking passage. The room was filled with a dozen people, both old faces Niko recognized and new ones he didn't. Some were people he'd once called good friends. Others were business acquaintances he'd seen come and go in passing. All of them may as well be strangers now.

Niko swallowed. He hoped the same thing as Elliott. He'd thought he could rely on Baouban, though, and it hadn't led him anywhere good. He'd known he probably couldn't rely on Aleksi, but even then, some deeply buried glimmer of hope remained, stubborn and resilient, up until the man had predictably pulled a gun on him. If Lady Death turned on him too, he truly had nowhere else to go and no one left to turn to anymore.

"Have a seat," Death said as she stood beside the largest and most comfortable-looking chair at the head of the table. The guards moved to line the walls of the room, silently standing alert. Everyone else present stayed standing as well, keeping as much distance as possible from the conference table. Some bowed their heads together and murmured, while most stayed quiet. Every eye was on Elliott and Niko now. They both glanced at each other warily, neither seeming too keen on the idea of sitting.

"It's not a request," Death said.

Niko acquiesced, pulling out a chair that faced the door midway down the table. He sank slowly into it. It creaked beneath his weight, the sound scratching against the quiet tension of the room. Something caught his eye through the doorway behind the guards—a glimpse of pale, pearlescent white, ethereal as a specter. Yalsa.

She peered at Elliott with sharp, lustrous eyes half-hidden behind a softly glimmering, sheer veil. Niko had always been a little wary of her; the Quwa-quay woman seemed far too clever for her own good and had a particularly ruthless nature to her. She'd never spoken with Niko much, either, having kept a distance—even when he'd been around often and on great terms with Lady Death.

A moment later, Yalsa slipped from view, but Niko could feel her still. He knew she was still there, lurking just out of sight, listening just on the other side of the wall, a silken shadow.

It wasn't just Lady Death they had to place their trust in. It was every other person who lived with and worked under her in this compound.

That realization made this all the more intimidating.

Elliott followed suit and settled into a chair beside him to his left, placing himself between Niko and Lady Death, despite clearly being terrified she was going to try something. A brief flash of memory—Elliott putting himself between Niko and a line of Galapol agents when everything had gone wrong at the

Starlight Awards—made something mournful and raw stick in Niko's throat.

Elliott sat tall and rigid, unmoving in his seat. The discomfort emanating from him was almost palpable to Niko, but he knew it would be imperceptible to almost anyone else in the room—Elliott did a respectful job of keeping his own expression stoic. Niko fought the urge to reach out and take his hand beneath the table.

Death sat last, satisfied that they were cooperative, it seemed, and leaned back in her chair, regarding Niko with a sour expression. She folded her hands over her waist.

"I heard about Baouban," she said.

"Mmh," Niko grunted.

"It's unfortunate. But not surprising. No one is your friend anymore, Niko." She'd switched away from his black market name, and back to his given one. "You're worth more than anyone's goodwill now."

Sweat trickled down the back of his neck. "Even you?"

She eyed him for a long moment, tilting her head in thought. Chandelier light glinted off the polished onyx of her rings. Niko didn't remember her being fond of jewelry before. "You shouldn't have come here. And you shouldn't have trusted anyone, given your... uniquely lucrative situation now. Not anyone. Not even me."

Niko tensed. They needed to find a way out. Fast. He'd been wrong, had made a mistake—

"You're taking stupid, blind risks. Those are rookie mistakes," she continued, "that you should have grown out of a long time ago. You made yourself vulnerable by coming to Dainna. But I don't care a lick about your bounty. I care that you said you wanted to repay the favor that you owed me."

He nodded, trying to will his wild and anxious heart to calm as it hammered against his ribcage. He put an armored hand on the table. "I do. I'm here to do that now. Anything you need."

Death leaned forward across the table, staring right into him. Her chair creaked as she did. "It's been years. What took you so long?"

Niko swallowed and cast a flickering glance around. The sweat that he'd felt on his neck before now covered his entire body. Adrenaline clawed through his veins. He was about to share a fatal vulnerability with a room full of underworld crime syndicate members. A vulnerability that could cost him dearly. He'd cut off contact with them all a long time ago, simply dropping off the map.

Not to mention, money had begun rewriting almost every relationship he'd once had, it seemed.

He'd been extending his hand to a lot of people lately. He knew it was a matter of time before it got bitten again, and hard. Death had warned him that he shouldn't trust her. But Niko decided to, anyway.

"I—I got injured badly on that final hunt. It wasn't good. I shattered my spine in several places and broke my legs. It was so bad, I didn't think I'd ever be able to hunt again." He tried to keep it vague, to walk the tightrope of honesty while also protecting the fact that without the aid of the suit, he still couldn't walk. Nor would he ever. "I was down for the count. And it left me ashamed, because I did it all to myself. I threw myself away to get him. Just to make sure *he* didn't make it out either.

"I was in a pretty dark place. So, I hid away. I was a mess. I should have contacted you. I should have contacted a lot of people. It was wrong to vanish like I did. I never meant to leave your favor unpaid. It's not how I ever wanted to end things with you."

Death looked at him for a long while in silence, gauging what he'd told her, before finally giving a slow nod. Niko sagged in relief at realizing she'd accepted the truth of his revelation.

"And now you're finally back to hunting?" she asked.

"I—uh—well, kind of—"

"Kind of?"

"He was hunting me," Elliott cut in. Niko looked at him, nervous all over again. Elliott and rules didn't seem to get along well. He could feel all eyes in the room turning toward the blond man now.

"Interesting. Yet you don't seem to be in handcuffs," Death said.

"Actually, *he's* the one *I* got handcuffs on—"

"*Elliott,*" Niko said, nearly choking. He flushed as he glanced around, then cleared his throat. To his surprise, some of the oppressive, harsh mood broke, though. A few people chuckled and a smile cracked across even Death's severe face.

"Elliott Kestrel isn't who the media has made him out to be," Niko continued. "That's why we came to you, actually. Other than repaying this favor and finally making things even between us. I... I have to ask you for help again. I know the audacity behind that. I wouldn't bother you with this if it wasn't this important. It's bigger than me. It involves the entire galaxy."

"Go on," Death said.

"What Elliott is doing isn't just senseless violence, like the news has been portraying. There's a—" He searched for the right word. "A cabal out there called Honeybliss. A network."

"I've heard that name uttered before in the worst parts of town," Lady Death said. "But never enough to know much more than that."

"Right. A lot of the galaxy's elites are a part of it. Kings, politicians, celebrities. He showed me all of it. The same people who by daylight contribute to peace talks and charity funds are engaging in trafficking in the dark. They *buy* people and torture and rape and kill them. Just... because they can get away with doing it. They're beyond legal consequence at this point. Galapol won't touch it, because even they're scared shitless of them."

Death eyed Niko, then turned her gaze on Elliott, sweeping him up and down. "I want to hear the rest of this from you."

Elliott cleared his throat. "...Honeybliss has existed in some form for decades. At least. Maybe more, but it gets hard to tell after a certain point. Since the earliest data I could find on them and connect together, they've been responsible for thousands disappearing across the galaxy every year. They have so much collective money and influence that it all just gets swept under the rug, like Niko said. They pay people to keep it invisible to the public eye.

Hackers, assassins. Smear campaigns. People who will rewrite and ruin public records. Any method, so long as it keeps the silence.

"You won't find it anywhere now, no matter how hard you look. They used to share videos and photographs between each other on the dark web, but it's not even there anymore. They've scrubbed it all clean. But I researched them a few years back and compiled a collection of all their dirty little grotesque deeds before they had the chance to delete it all."

"So, it's a massive problem. But why come to me about this?"

"I tried distributing it on the internet, but they have AI-driven algorithms that catch and erase it within minutes. I've tried bringing it to the media multiple times in the past, but Honeybliss has all the reputable outlets bought. Their fingers are *everywhere*, in every pie. We're talking about the most influential figures in the entire galaxy, some with multiple planets at their beck and call. Every time I tried something new, it got worse. They sent hitmen after me eventually and I had to flee my home. They rewrote my medical history and public records and made me look broken. Unstable and unreliable. News outlets wouldn't touch it and Galapol gave me the cold shoulder. Eventually, I decided to just... take care of them myself, instead.

"But you were the Revolutionary of Sala. I know who you are. You won victory for your people in their civil war when there was no hope left through seizing control of and hacking all your planet's communications towers and satellites. You got your message out across the galaxy at large and requested aid. You got out the truth that your oppressive government tried to silence. I—I actually wrote part of my Master's thesis on your method."

Niko was in awe of him. Elliott had presented himself so well, had spoken with such clarity and dignity that it left him feeling a little breathless and dazed. He felt a rush of affection blossom warm in his chest and fought to tamp down the smile that wanted to grow across his lips.

He wasn't the only one.

Death smiled too. It seemed even she was charmed by Elliott. She looked pleased to have her work recognized, her remaining eye carrying a fond shine that made Niko ache with nostalgia. She used to look at him like that, a long time ago.

"So, you want me to take these files and get them past the wall of silence," she said.

"Precisely. Niko says you have the unique connections to do something this big. Combined with your experience..."

"There's more to it than getting the data transmitted," Niko interjected. "There've also been copycat kills picking up since we started hitting back at Honeybliss. People intentionally trying to fuck things up and pin it on us. All with the single purpose of driving the bounty higher. They're killing innocent people. We need to also get a live broadcast message out to show we don't condone any of it and aren't associated with those murders. More are happening every day at this point."

"I see," Death said. Her gaze was alight with fascination now, her branching antennae pulsing with a faint blue. "How did you even learn about any of this in the first place? Honeybliss?" She looked at Elliott again.

Niko's heart dropped.

All the quietly building brightness in Elliott dulled instantly. "I— They— I—" He was fumbling now.

"They took his sister," Niko said quietly, trying to help say what he couldn't.

Elliott glanced at him, gaze dull with pain. Then he simply nodded.

"What happened to her?" Death pressed.

Niko winced. Lady Death was an honorable woman through and through, but she was tough, and she was blunt, and she didn't shy away from what was painful.

In the end, these were all the same questions he himself had once pelted Elliott with in the past. It made Niko ache with discomfort and shame, knowing he'd taunted him about Cleo's fate.

Elliott struggled again, before finally saying, "She suffered. She's gone now." The clipped simplicity of his statements felt somehow particularly brutal, like the sharp blade of a knife. Somehow, it felt to Niko like Elliott was only driving that knife back into himself. "You'll see it on the videos if you want to watch them."

Niko reached across the gap between them under the table and found his hand. He wrapped his own around it and squeezed tightly. Elliott glanced at him again. Niko knew him well enough now to know he was clamping down hard on what must be an incredible, world-shattering pain. They locked eyes for a moment, and Niko gave him a heartbroken, reassuring smile.

*I'm here*, he mouthed silently to Elliott.

"Send me these files." Death then read him her new number and Niko recorded it onto his phone too. Elliott busied himself with his phone.

With a quick dismissive wave from Death, the room began to disperse. It seemed their meeting was formally over. A few people ambled about or hung around still, but the guards exited with a nod, the doorway left unblocked now.

"Aleksi had a whole spiel about you not taking outside calls anymore after a near miss on your life," Niko said.

"And you actually believed him," Death marveled. He heard the chime of Elliott's files delivered to her phone. Before acknowledging them, she turned her gaze to Niko again. It softened a little, becoming something more familiar to the woman Niko remembered as his mentor. When she spoke, her voice was a fraction gentler. "I know you're upset about what happened to him and his friends."

Niko glanced away, but nodded.

"But you have to know why I did it. I had to send a message. If anyone else decides they can get away with going behind my back and trying what he did for easy money, they'll quickly realize that's not how it's going to work. I needed to shut that down, Niko. Or it was only going to happen again and again."

Niko nodded again. He hated what happened to Aleksi, but the man had done it to himself, in the end. Everyone knew not to fuck with Lady Death. Betraying her was as good as signing your own death warrant. Niko was almost surprised she hadn't tried to send someone after him too when he'd vanished on her.

Maybe she had just cared for him that much, even then. They'd had a bond once. She had taken Niko under her wing when he was young and dumber than he was now, full of sloppy ambition and unrefined technique. She'd taken the time to train him up in efficient bounty hunting. Lady Death had taught him how to survive.

And she had, maybe, become a little like the mother-figure Niko had desperately needed after losing his own.

A crime syndicate boss, ruthless badass of a mother.

"I'm going to take a look at these," she said. "And I'll make you a deal. You help me with that favor and I'll help you with yours."

Niko and Elliott glanced at each other.

"Alright," Niko said.

"Tonight, you're going to stay here. It's late, and I want to look through these before we talk again."

He felt Elliott's discomfort as the other man tensed beside him. He may have had a moment of connection with the woman who'd inspired part of his thesis, but now it seemed he had fallen back to his usual paranoia. "I—I don't know if—"

"Stay." Her tone was clipped and final. There was no room for negotiation. "You'll be safer in these walls than anywhere in the galaxy. No one gets through here who I don't want to."

Niko dropped his voice to a low murmur, trying to assure Elliott. "It's a sign of trust to her."

"Which is exactly why I don't love this," Elliott muttered back.

"Either we do this, Elliott, or we don't," Niko said. "We've come this far. And she's willing to help us."

Elliott relented, nodding. He fell quiet.

Death stood, and they followed suit.

"I'll get dinner sent to you shortly," she said. Then she came over and pulled Niko into a tight hug, something that both surprised and delighted him. He wrapped his arms around her in return.

It was like a dam breaking; the relief that washed through him with that embrace was palpable. Niko felt like he was finally back again, back in the past life he'd discarded for so many years. It was like slipping a dusty old glove back on. It still fit the same, like a second skin.

"Welcome back, Niko," she said, switching over to her native Sala Heenvan, where she'd always been most comfortable.

"Deleera," he murmured back in her language, using her given name. "I'm sorry, for everything."

"You're here now. Help me out and we'll be even. That's how we've always worked."

"Anything you need," Niko said. "I want to do that much."

"Niko, you could have really gotten yourself hurt coming back to this place. What if I'd decided on the same inclination as Baouban? As the Legend? As Aleksi?"

A heartbroken grimace pulled at the corners of Niko's mouth. "I knew the risks, Deleera, but I wanted to believe in you, if nobody else out there anymore. The day Lady Death starts putting money above people is the day I'll hang up my armor and retire."

"The armor looks good on you," she said, picking at his chest-piece. "A nice addition. But, Niko." She fixed him with a somber stare. "Don't ever stop fighting for what you believe in or what's right, based on the moral deficiencies of others. In the end, you have to carry your own banner high, even if it means being the one to lead the way alone."

"Yeah. I know," Niko said, glancing over at Elliott. The man had fought alone for so long, trying to put an end to the misery of Honeybliss. He had been abandoned and let down again and again, yet here he was now. He was so beautiful to Niko. "I think you'll really like him, D. He's such a good person."

Death looked over at Elliott now, who stood close by Niko's side. She switched back to Galactic Standard when she spoke. "What did you study for your Master's?"

"I majored in mechanical engineering and minored in computer engineering," he replied in flawless Sala Heenvan. Death looked taken aback, seeming impressed by him all over again.

"*You*," she responded in Sala Heenvan, "are someone very, very interesting who I'd like to get to know more. For now, though, you should both get rest."

Elliott looked thrown for a loop at someone wanting to actually be his friend. He said nothing, merely blinking at her. Niko couldn't help but be reminded of a computer that had crashed and was rebooting.

Then he frowned, remembering something. "Hey. How did you hear we were in Dainna in the first place?" He thought they'd done a decent enough job at appearing inconspicuous.

"Aleksi was stupid, as usual. He started texting his network that you were coming and promised them a lot of money if they wanted to help in his little scheme. Most of them joined in as the mercenary team you'd encountered. Fortunately, one of those friends was more loyal to me than to him. She knew you and I were close once and let me know what was up. She kept an eye on where he was leading you and reported it back to me. The idiot ran right into her and didn't even recognize her."

Niko frowned. *Wait—*

*Beautiful tentacles, by the way. Very plump.*

"The Gheroun woman?!"

Death only gave an enigmatic smile. "I don't give my spies away."

"So, you knew what he was up to all along," Elliott said.

"Yes. But I wanted to hear that weasel admit it himself."

Sweetheart peeked her head through the door. "Is your meeting over? I hope I'm not interrupting. I just wanted to say hi to Niko again."

"No, not at all, beloved. Would you do me the honor of taking these two... gentlemen to Niko's room?"

Sweetheart's patterns fluttered a delighted gold. "Anything you ask, Mistress."

It was Niko's turn to crash and reboot. Something buried deep inside him ached. He blinked at Death. "...My old room? You kept it this whole time?"

"I didn't want to give up on you, Niko," Death said. "I always hoped you'd turn up again one day. You were one of the good ones."

"She's downplaying that," Sweetheart said with a soft laugh that sounded like tinkling bells. Her four eyes squinted into mischievous crescents as though she were letting on a precious secret. "You're our family."

*No one is your friend anymore*, Death had told Niko.

But maybe he'd regained something better now, instead.

# CHAPTER FIVE

# IT DOESN'T HURT ANYMORE

NIKO WATCHED WITH BARELY held restraint as Elliott picked up a small XR-193 model ship off the dresser. It was the third time he'd done it now. He turned it over in his hands, picked at it a little, then set it back down. Then he wandered back to the door and checked the deadbolt lock again. He had stalked along the perimeter of Niko's former room twice already, inspecting every wall panel, cabinet, drawer, chair, and light fixture for bugs or hidden cameras.

The room was much the same as the rest of the compound—with heavy curtains over the window, a few colorful rugs on the floor, and a queen-sized bed. Even some of Niko's old trappings had remained undisturbed—the model XR-193, and some posters advertising ships, rap artists, and a couple of male nudes. The only thing that had been significantly changed now was that a stack of boxes had been shoved in the corner; they'd taken to using this space as storage. Elliott had given particular attention to the boxes, but they only contained spools of rare, handspun Yeuranian althaaema wool. Each box was easily a hundred-thousand credits. Maybe two.

Niko tried not to think that there was a good chance Aleksi had been the one to bring them here.

He couldn't entirely blame Elliott for his paranoia—not after everything they'd both been through. But as he watched him make his way to check the stack of boxes again, signaling the start of yet another round of investigation, he couldn't take it anymore. Niko stood and grabbed him by the wrist.

"Sit. Down. Please." He reminded himself of patient fathers at the supermarket trying to reason with their preschoolers.

"We should have gone back to the facility, Niko."

He repeated what had become a mantra in the past few hours. "It's going to be okay. This won't be like the safehouse. Lady D is different."

Elliott relented with a sigh. "I really hope that you're right." He looked around, seeming a bit lost now. Two empty bowls sat stacked on the dresser, the long handles of silver spoons protruding from them—the only thing left of the hearty mutton korma Death had sent along for their dinner. Niko's duffel bag sat in the opposite corner as the boxes. They'd been permitted to—both under cloak of stealth—go and grab their supplies and clothing from the ship for their stay. They'd agreed between each other to leave the chair back on the *Soñadora*. It wasn't something anyone in the compound needed to know about yet.

Niko needed to sit back down. Hours of trying to ignore a familiar old electric burning that had begun to claw at his legs was wearing him down. And making him testy, impatient.

He moved to the foot of the bed and sank down slowly onto it, wincing as he sat. A betraying hiss of pain escaped him. Elliott looked quickly at him with a sharp gaze of alarm.

"Niko? What's wrong?"

"Ugh. Nothing, babe."

Elliott's eyes narrowed. "Are you wounded? Did something happen during the fight?"

He clearly wasn't going to let it go. Niko sighed. "No, I didn't get wounded. It's just— Today's action fucked with my legs a little. It happens, sometimes. It's nothing."

Elliott only stared at him. After a moment, he said quietly, "It doesn't sound like 'nothing.'"

"It's just a thing that happens. Ever since I fell. Sometimes these missions trigger it. Sometimes it happens out of nowhere, when I've been doing nothing at all. It's just nerve pain. Shit misfiring from the old damaged connections. It'll pass."

He was starting to sweat, but resisted the urge to wipe it away—doing so would only highlight how much the mounting pain was actually getting to him, how severely it really burned. He didn't want to worry Elliott any more, especially now. The other man was already upset enough, bogged down under the heavy weight of restless paranoia. Niko didn't want to add to it all by making himself look weak or compromised.

Elliott drifted over to stand before him, though. When he spoke, his tone was softer. "What helps? What can I do to help you, Niko?"

A slurry of hurt and affection alike coursed through him. Niko ultimately shook his head. "It's not really that bad, honestly," he lied. "If it gets to be too much, I can just massage the leg muscles a little."

"Can I?" Elliott asked. "Will you let me?"

Niko hesitated. "You don't h—"

"I want to."

They looked at each other a moment before Niko finally glanced away and nodded. Elliott reached out and, with great care and no haste, stripped the armor from him, piece by piece, until Niko was in nothing but a gray tank top and black sweatpants. Elliott knelt on the floor and took his right leg. He trailed his hands along it, over the thick fabric, then began kneading at the muscles, starting with the ankle. Niko watched him and neither of them spoke. Elliott was so worshipful with his movements, careful with Niko like he were clay in the hands of an artist to be sculpted. It was almost too much to look at, too much to bear.

"Can you feel that, Niko?" Elliott asked.

"Mmh." He wanted so badly to say yes. "No. But it helps."

"It's alright if you can't. Lie back and just let me do this for you."

"Elliott—"

"Please, Niko. I want to help you. Just let me."

Why was it so hard? Why was it so difficult to let Elliott help him? Let him massage his abused, exhausted legs and damaged nerves? To let him simply take care of him for a while?

Why was it so hard to accept help?

Niko swallowed, pushing it all away, the urge to fight, to pull away, to snap that he was fine. The pain was probably just getting to him. He let himself lay back on the bed, staring up at the ceiling he remembered so well. He couldn't feel what Elliott was doing, outside of occasional electric, tingling jolts where his hands worked and kneaded, similar to muscles which had fallen asleep. But the pain was already lessening a fraction, too. It was far from gone, but it had diminished.

He let himself relax, the rest of his body finally untensing as he sank down deeper into the bed and closed his eyes. Niko stayed like that, letting himself drift for a while. He'd almost fallen asleep when Elliott's voice jolted him back into awareness.

"We're so vulnerable."

Niko sat up slightly, looking at him. Elliott was on to the left leg now, already up above his knee. He'd obviously been at it a while.

"I can put the suit back on," Niko started, feeling self-conscious and uncomfortable suddenly. "Just let me—"

"Niko," Elliott said, glancing up at him. "That's not what I meant. Just being here. We could be armored and armed to the teeth, and they could still just lob a grenade in here or something and we'd be dead before we could blink. And not even just these people. What if this place gets overrun? Everyone knows we're here, now. So much for keeping it quiet."

"I know," Niko said, letting himself lay back on the bed again. A yawn overtook him before he could continue. "I know that. But it's not going to happen, Elliott. They won't do that. And even if they did, I'm here. I'll take care of you. I'm not going to let anything happen to you. I promise. I'd do anything to keep you safe."

He meant it, every word, trying to push away feeling exposed, feeling somehow useless. In truth, he'd struggle to be able to make it to the small bathroom attached to their room by himself without the suit on or chair available, let alone defend Elliott from a coordinated ambush.

Regardless, the words found their mark, and Elliott's shoulders seemed to sag. Niko heard him let out a long, quiet breath. "I might not trust anyone here," he said. "But I trust you. And if you think we'll be alright, then we will be."

"Come here," Niko said. Elliott hesitated, then climbed up onto the bed, lying against Niko's side. Niko turned over to face him and wrapped his arms around him. Then he closed his eyes again, fatigue settling back in. The screaming in his legs had quieted to a burning whisper. "I've got you, Elliott."

"I know you do," Elliott said, and he sounded like he meant it. Despite everything, Niko couldn't help the smile that pulled at his lips.

He woke sometime in the night, groggy and out of it. For a moment, Niko couldn't remember where he was—had he fallen asleep on the ship? This wasn't the facility. Then it all came back to him, like a punch to the gut. They were in the heart of Dainna.

Niko glanced over at Elliott, who was staring quietly off into space. The other man seemed to snap suddenly out of his reverie, turning his gaze to meet Niko's.

"Mgh," Niko grunted. "What time is it?"

Elliott summoned his phone hologram. The light of it made them both recoil, squinting against the harsh blue. He quickly gestured it away. "Just past two in the morning."

Niko ran his hands up and down Elliott's back. The muscles of it were taut and tense. "Can't sleep, babe?"

"No," he admitted after a brief silence. "I can't stop thinking."

"You need to, Elliott."

"I can't."

Niko took his face in his hands, making him look at him. "You need to. What's happened, happened. We're here now. We're going to be alright. This is the opportunity we needed. The right path isn't often easy, is it? Think of how good it's going to feel to finally get everything Honeybliss has done out into the light."

Elliott seemed to struggle. "I—I can't, Niko. I've tried and failed for so many years to do that very thing, that I can't imagine it anymore. I can't even hope for it. To hope for it and be let down again is going to make me sick."

"We will, Elliott," Niko said. He ran his thumb along Elliott's regal cheekbone. "This time, we will. You're not alone anymore, right?"

"...Right. You're right. I'm sorry."

Niko stroked his hair for a while. He was beginning to wake back up now, and with clearer consciousness came awareness of his body. He didn't hurt anymore. Elliott's hands and a multi-hour nap, it seemed, had worked miracles.

"Hey," Niko murmured at him. He leaned in and kissed him on the corner of the mouth, testing how receptive Elliott was to the gesture. Elliott closed his eyes, seeming to bask in it, tilting his chin up toward him subtly. Then Niko kissed him fully on the lips this time, Elliott's own parting for him easily, and they met, tongue against tongue. Elliott clung tightly to a fistful of Niko's tank top. Reluctantly, Niko separated from him. "I can help you sleep, if you want."

Elliott's dusty green eyes searched him for a moment, before he spoke. "How are you feeling? Your legs."

"Better," Niko said. "It doesn't hurt anymore."

"Are you lying this time?"

Niko smirked, in spite of himself. "No, babe. Not this time. I'm doing alright."

"Then *please*. I don't want to think anymore."

Niko kissed him again and again, greedily now, letting each one be slow and sensual. He went for his long neck, unable to help himself. It was probably his second favorite part of Elliott. The other man emitted a soft sound, then sat up and climbed on top of him, one knee planted on either side of Niko's hips now, hands flat on the bed near his shoulders.

He bent down and took Niko's mouth with his own, penetrating him with his tongue. Then he murmured into his ear, breath warm against his skin, "Do you want me to fuck you, Niko? Would you like that?"

Niko did want that. Very, very much. More than he cared to admit. He swallowed, trying to catch his breath. He wanted to be filled with Elliott—the very idea was delicious. Even seeing the man positioned above him, looking down at him with a hungry glint to his gaze, hair hanging disheveled in his face, made Niko lightheaded. He felt himself straining against the fabric of his sweatpants now, just as voracious as the look in Elliott's eyes.

"Do you want to take my cock? You're so good at it," Elliott purred at him. He bent and nipped at Niko's earlobe. Then he slid his hand downward and cupped Niko's crotch through his pants and began to massage and squeeze him. It was like lightning struck through Niko—vibrant, pure pleasure and need. He drew in an involuntary breath at the touch. Then Elliott took Niko's hand and guided it to rest on his own needy bulge. "Last time, you took the whole thing like such a good boy."

*Whoa. Shit.*

Niko nearly choked at hearing those words. They did something terrible to him, and he felt his whole body flush with a surge of heat, his pulse pounding in his chest and throat now. It was all he could do not to tear Elliott's pants off right there. Not to beg him for it, beg to be filled with his hard heat until he ached from it.

Something feverish and wild overtook him. Urgent, starving fantasies wormed their way uninvited—but unrestricted nonetheless—through his mind. They came and pressed in on him before he could stop them.

Niko wanted Elliott to use him. Like a *thing*.

He wanted to exist only for Elliott's pleasure—to experience a surrender that was given wholly, completely.

He craved utter destruction, until only the breathless ruins of himself remained.

Niko had never had thoughts like that before. Or maybe he'd stopped himself before ever truly going there. But something about Elliott drove him to this strange state of existence, like the other man knew exactly what Niko wanted in some quieted part of himself and how to pluck its strings to harmony.

It made him absolutely wild. He felt outside of his body, floating, yet fully, intensely aware of its sensations all the same.

Niko wanted to be Elliott's very, *very* good boy.

But another thought came, unbidden, on the tail end of that: someone might see them.

It was absurd.

No one was going to enter this room at two in the morning. And if they did, it wasn't going to be for any particularly pleasant or amicable reason. He'd have far more to worry about than if an assailant might catch him in a compromising role.

Regardless, the idea of anyone knowing, of finding him on his back, penetrated and dominated hard by another person made Niko's face heat with embarrassment.

And shame.

What if Elliott was right? What if the room had been bugged? The possibility suddenly didn't seem so ludicrous.

He wasn't ashamed of Elliott. He knew he shouldn't be embarrassed to be with him—*however* they wanted to consummate their pairing. There was nothing inherently shameful nor demeaning in the least about receiving in a gay relationship. Nor about wanting to submit yourself to your partner.

How you liked it in the bedroom didn't dictate your masculinity.

He knew that.

But he couldn't shake it.

Niko had some shit to work through. Tonight had told him that, if nothing else.

"Actually," he mumbled, reaching up to trail his fingertips down along Elliott's side. "I want to be inside you."

"Mmh." Elliott gave a soft sound of acknowledgement. Niko searched his face for disappointment in the dim, barred neon light that trickled through their heavy curtains, but found nothing. Either Elliott truly didn't mind or was good at hiding it. "Alright, lover. However you like it, Niko." He bent down again, giving Niko a long and sensuous kiss he felt he didn't deserve. Niko tried to swallow the guilt down.

"Think you could grab the lube, babe? From my bag." He hated that he had to ask. That he couldn't do it himself.

Elliott climbed off him and rifled through Niko's duffel bag. It still had two bullet holes through it from Baouban's failed attempt on their lives. He came back, bottle in hand, and proceeded to peel his clothing off. Niko sat up and pulled his own shirt off, then his pants and underwear. He moved to the foot of the bed again, similar to how he'd been when Elliott had massaged his legs.

"Come here," Niko murmured, holding a hand out toward him. "Come sit in my lap."

Elliott handed him the bottle. He sank down into Niko's lap, facing away from him, then leaned against him so his back rested against Niko's chest. Niko's erection pressed against his ass. For a moment, they merely stayed like that. Niko wrapped his arms around the other man and held him tight against himself. He started planting slow and sensual kisses along his shoulder, working up along the curve of his neck. Elliott's wild, cowlicked hair had gotten longer; he had to push the ends out of the way now.

Niko left a greedy mark on him there, Elliott tipping his head to the side to give him full access and letting out a soft, low moan of pleasure. Then he simply buried his face in Elliott's hair, inhaling the scent that had become so synonymous to him with *home*.

There was something he wanted to say then, but stopped himself.

Instead, he murmured, "Let me get you ready."

Elliott leaned forward and Niko applied the lube to them both. Then he trailed his fingertips along Elliott's back, tracing the valleys that lie between each tendon, muscle, and gentle ridge of spine, until finally they brushed against the old hook-shaped scar on his shoulder blade. He thought to ask about it, was so curious, but this wasn't the right time. The realization that it had probably come from Elliott's shitbag excuse of a father hurt Niko's heart.

He would have to ask him later.

"Okay, babe," he murmured once they were both prepped. Elliott was ready for him and after another moment of readjusting, he sank down onto Niko, slowly, emitting a soft, choked sigh as he met him at the hilt. It felt incredible to be joined to him, inside him.

Niko stroked his unruly blond half-curls again, kissing his neck. He rested his hands on the other man's chest and stomach, palms flat against him, arms around him in an embrace. Elliott's heart beat wildly beneath his touch.

"Is it good?" Niko murmured.

"It's good. It's always good," Elliott said.

They simply stayed like that for a moment in stillness. Niko could hold him forever. Then Elliott began rocking his hips, moving himself against Niko. Niko wished he could aid him, could fuck into him. He slid one hand downward to grip Elliott's cock and began stroking it in time to Elliott's own movements.

He couldn't stop touching him, couldn't stop wanting to connect everywhere they could. Niko kissed him again and again, on the back, the shoulder, the neck, even the mouth when Elliott craned his neck so they could meet one another. Slowly, they built a rhythm, until Elliott was moving fast and hard against him.

A low, breathy, quiet moan slipped from Elliott that picked up in intensity the more they went and the harder they worked each other. It was Niko's favorite sound. He'd once tried to guess if the carefully-composed man kept silent, or gave in to vocalizing his pleasure in bed. That curiosity had long since been satisfied—Elliott was a moaner. No matter how it was they fucked.

But they were far from alone in the compound. And the last thing Niko wanted to do was draw attention to what they were doing—even if he was the one giving it to Elliott now. Some small part of him delighted at the thought, an inversion of his earlier fears. The idea of someone seeing Elliott riding him was darkly delicious in the same vein as the thought of someone noticing the blushing marks Niko had left along his neck and shoulders so often.

But actually drawing attention right now probably wasn't for the best and it certainly wasn't going to help Elliott get to sleep after this.

"*Elliott*," he murmured in chastisement. The other man only continued to moan though, his handsome, breathless voice coming with each exhale in a rhythm. "You're going to wake the whole damn building up."

"I can't help it," Elliott managed to get out. "Fuck, Niko."

It made Niko lightheaded to know Elliott was enjoying himself so much with him, that Niko could bring him to that kind of pleasure. To know he was losing himself so deeply he couldn't stop from crying out, even despite the situational paranoia he had from being in the compound.

*Fuck, that's hot,* Niko thought. *But it won't do.*

He slid his free hand up along Elliott's neck and jaw, then clamped it tight over his mouth. The other man gave a muffled cry as he did, seeming even all the more into their lovemaking suddenly. He arched his spine and tilted his head back until it rested against Niko's shoulder. Niko kept a firm grip over his mouth as Elliott bounced up and down against him, impaled, his muted moans still coming more than ever now.

He glanced down and saw in surprise that Elliott was gripping both of Niko's thighs hard, using them as the base to steady himself as he moved. He was beginning to sweat from the effort, his skin hot to the touch against Niko.

"You like that, babe?" Niko murmured.

A particularly prominent, strangled moan gave him his answer, the vibration of Elliott's resilient voice rippling gently across the palm of Niko's hand.

Niko pushed his thumb against the head of Elliott's cock, massaging it. Then Elliott seized up, back arching further. Niko could see he was gripping his thighs so tightly the skin had turned white where his fingers dug in. Elliott was close now.

He released his grip over Elliott's mouth and replaced it quickly with a forceful kiss, his own mouth taking up and claiming Elliott's. The other man gave a long, agonized, stifled moan against Niko's lips as he came, and the passionate, enthusiastic intensity of Elliott's ecstasy drove Niko to meet him there too, spilling himself within him. It was rare that he shared a climax with his lovers, but simply experiencing Elliott falling apart made Niko unable to hold it in either.

Elliott slowly parted from Niko's lips and gave a shaky, shuddering breath.

They stayed like that a moment, quiet, as Niko simply held him. As he slowly came back down from the high of Elliott, something else began to worm its way back in, unwelcome, unwanted.

Guilt.

*Was it okay? Was it really alright?* he wanted to ask. Clearly Elliott had enjoyed himself. Yet he couldn't shake the thought. This wasn't how the other man had wanted to do it. It was becoming clear he favored being the one to top, with something extra present too, subtle in the way Elliott had spoken to him when he'd started getting hot and heavy.

Elliott wanted to dominate him. And Niko had rejected that.

For not the first time that night, another cocktail of uneasy emotions churned through him. Guilt, and a new shame at turning down what his boyfriend had wanted from him. Guilt at having been embarrassed at the idea at all. Sorrow that something inside him wasn't ready to let himself go there yet. And shame all over again at the idea of ever actually letting it happen, along with the fact that Niko had quietly wanted it so, so badly. Even more than he'd actually wanted what they'd just done.

Niko didn't know where that came from—neither the want, nor the shame of it.

Elliott let out a long exhale, finally gathering himself. "Okay," he said, breathless sounding still. "I think I can try to get some sleep now. That wore me out."

"Good," Niko said, planting another light kiss on his shoulder. He felt all wrong now, though, tangled up and remorseful and like something that didn't belong here with Elliott.

Elliott got up and slipped off to the bathroom, then came back with a damp, warm wash cloth which he used to clean them both up. Niko felt a little bad for whomever they had on laundry duty these days—usually one of the newer recruits to join the compound, at least if this place still worked like it used to. That had been him, once.

When they were done, Niko scooted back up the bed and laid down. Elliott joined him. He rested his head against Niko and draped a hand over his waist, but didn't urge him to turn around nor hold him the way he usually did. The detail of it tore something inside Niko to absolute shreds. He'd grown used to usually falling asleep as the little spoon to Elliott. Niko wrapped around him tightly now instead.

There were so many things he wanted to say—and probably should.

*I'm sorry,* or *We should talk about this,* or *I wanted it too, but I'm ashamed and I don't know why.*

Elliott looked tired though, his eyelids already beginning to droop. It had been a long, demanding day—one full of tension, adrenaline, and combat. And it was nearly three in the morning now.

Niko added it to the list of things they needed to talk about later, when they were in a better place. He planted a long, warm kiss on Elliott's forehead.

"Get some rest, babe. I'm here. I won't let anything happen to you."

The other man closed his eyes and buried his face in Niko's shoulder. Niko could already hear—and feel—his breathing shift to something shallower, gentler.

Elliott was finally granted the peace of sleep, emptied of all thought.

Niko wished that he could join him. But now he found himself wide awake, instead.

# CHAPTER SIX
# SKEEVY LARRY

ELLIOTT SHOWERED IN THE morning and Niko stuck to a can of dry shampoo. There seemed to be a mutually shared aura of feeling like shit due to insufficient sleep. Once they were dressed and Niko was back in the suit, a knock came early to their door. They paused, eyeing one another, before Niko made his way over.

"Yeah?" he called warily, keeping it closed.

"Oh, please pardon me, Niko. I hope I'm not disturbing you. Mistress has requested you meet with her in the conference room again," came the soft voice of Sweetheart.

*Kinky*, Elliott mouthed silently at Niko. Niko scowled at him and mumbled back, "Don't. Don't even think about it." Then he unlocked and opened the door for her with a smile.

"Good morning, ma'am," Niko said. "Thanks for letting us know. We appreciate it."

Sweetheart squinted happily at him, her patterns rippling to a peachy warm tint. "I hope you slept comfortably and that our accommodations have been satisfying. Did you enjoy being back in your room?"

"Yeah, of course. I missed being back in this place. We appreciate your hospitality."

"You know that you're always welcome here, Niko. Your dearheart as well." She paused, holding her hands over her face in sudden horror, and cast a nervous glance towards Elliott. "I—I shouldn't have made assumptions. Perhaps I'm overstepping."

"You're not overstepping," Niko quickly corrected. He glanced over his shoulder at Elliott and gave him a small smile as their gazes met. "He's my dearheart."

Elliott smiled back, a warm and private thing. Something honey gold and liquid poured through Niko at seeing it.

"Oh! I'm relieved. Your dearheart is always welcome, as well. Please do come speak with Mistress, though. I think she's been waiting a very long time for you to uphold your bargain."

Niko winced at the reminder, but offered her a kind smile nonetheless. It was never an act with Sweetheart—despite living in a compound that could probably endure a nuclear strike, in the heart of a criminal society, she was single-handedly the sweetest, most genuinely benevolent person he'd ever met. Sweetheart had earned her name. Being kind to her was an unspoken, *harshly* enforced rule on Dainna—but it wasn't something Niko had ever found himself having to force.

He'd always liked her.

She had a certain sweet naivety that was both bizarre and refreshing in a place like this. He had no doubt that if Lady Death had viewed the rancid videos and pictures they'd sent her, she'd probably shielded Sweetheart from them all.

"Then we shouldn't keep her waiting," he said.

Sweetheart stepped aside, all four spindly, boneless legs moving with the inherent grace and elegance of a dancer. Niko noticed she had delicate pink ribbons crisscrossing up them. The ribbons terminated in bows that matched her collar. She waved happily to Elliott as they passed, and he flashed her his best show pony smile, all charm and charisma again.

He and Niko stepped out and made their way to the conference room, where Death was already waiting, swiping through some of the holographic photos displaying the galaxy's cruelest atrocities. Yalsa was there this time, hovering over Death's shoulder and observing the holograms, her long serpentine tail coiled around itself. She turned her gaze on Niko, eyeing him keenly from behind her transparent, jeweled veil.

Sweetheart had followed them. Niko froze in the doorway the moment he realized, blocking her view. "Uh," he started. "Ma'am, I don't think you want to see any of this."

"Why not? What's—"

Death stood when she saw them, gesturing the hologram away, and walked briskly over. She shouldered past Niko, then rested her hands gently on the Xermotl's shoulders.

"Beloved, you shouldn't be in here. Not this morning."

"Why not?" Sweetheart asked again. Her patterns faded to a distraught indigo. "I want to be near you and Yalsa. I want to see Niko again—"

"I know. We're going to spend time together this afternoon, remember? But what we're looking at now is terrible. Some of the cruelest, sickest things even *I've* ever seen. You don't need to have that in your pretty head, okay? It'll get stuck there."

Sweetheart hesitated. She glanced at Niko and Elliott.

"I'm not weak," she said quietly. Her patterns flared to a deep chartreuse, giving Niko pause. In all the years of knowing her, he had never seen the Xermotl woman actually angry before.

*Trouble in paradise?* Maybe not everything had stayed quite the same as he'd initially thought.

"No, you're not weak," Yalsa said from inside the conference room. "But you *are* soft. That footage is rancid bile. Watching it will only hurt you."

Elliott looked like he wanted to argue, but Niko subtly shook his head at him. Whatever was going on between the three of them, he didn't want to contribute to elevating an argument into an outright fight—nor did he want to piss Death off after only just getting back into her good graces.

Instead, Elliott only murmured, voice sullen, "It stays with you. I wish I'd never had to see."

Sweetheart finally relented, her patterns shifting to a morose, deep blue. "Okay."

"We'll talk about this later, alright?" Death said, casting Sweetheart a private and intense glance.

"Yes, let's," Sweetheart said, her eyes squinting and her patterns turning a faint teal in what Niko could only describe as a forced smile. "Bye, Niko. Elliott. Be well today." She made her way out and down the long hall that led to an elevator. Niko watched her go.

He glanced back at Death, puzzled by whatever that interaction had been, but she was staring at Elliott now instead, quite intensely.

"You," she said. "Come here."

Elliott hesitated, but before he could act, she stepped toward him. She reached forward and pulled the slender, blond man into a tight hug. Elliott went stiff, seeming utterly taken aback. His expression was outright panicked.

Niko was shocked as well, gaping at them in silence. Only after a moment did he realize his mouth was hanging open. A quick glance around the room revealed it had stunned everyone else present in the background too; the other compound denizens had stopped what they'd been doing, blinking at Lady Death.

Then she pulled away and clasped Elliott's face in her hands. He stared back at her with bewildered, wide eyes, a shade paler than usual.

"I saw the footage," she said so quietly that Niko could barely even hear, standing right beside them. This was a private conversation, it seemed, meant only for Elliott. She spoke in Sala Heenvan to him. "You know the one I'm talking about."

Elliott swallowed, his look of bewilderment quietly changing to something deeply pained. Pleading, even.

"You're strong," she said. "I am *humbled* by you, Elliott Kestrel. I am impressed by you. You have a resilience as rare as diamond."

Elliott was trembling now, seeming uncertain how to even respond to such words. He looked utterly devastated, broken.

Niko watched him reach up and tightly grip Death's wrists and hold them, her hands still cupping his cheeks.

"How did you—" she'd begun asking, but Niko couldn't hear the rest. Another voice came slithering in, louder and clearer, addressing him directly from several feet away.

"*Killjoy.*"

"Hey, Yalsa," he said a little uneasily. He glanced back at Death and Elliott, who were still talking to one another in near-inaudible tones. Elliott was telling her something now and she nodded at him. Niko wanted so badly to hear, but Yalsa spoke again.

"It's been a very long time."

*Not long enough. Fuck off, Yalsa.* Of course she'd had to start talking to him right now of all times.

He cast her a distracted glance again. "Yeah. Feels good to be back, though."

"I'm surprised you decided to show your face here after hiding away for so long. Quite brazen. But Deleera has always been soft on you." She had his attention now. He reluctantly peeled his gaze away from Elliott, focusing fully on the ethereal snake before him instead. Hesitantly, he stepped over toward her. "Though I wonder if you would have bothered *ever* coming back if you hadn't needed something from her now."

Niko swallowed.

*Fair point.*

"I—I always wanted to. I thought about you guys all the time. I missed this place, this life. But I wasn't really... doing so well, either."

Yalsa trailed her gaze slowly toward Elliott in the background. "Many Quwa-quay back home haven't been doing so well either after your lover murdered the Grand Sovereign before the eyes of millions."

Niko shifted uneasily, unsure of what to say to her. He didn't like where this was going.

"Though I see now why he did it," she continued. "Good riddance. They were a false, corrupted vessel. Soon, others will understand too. I respect your lover. That he was able to compile all this data and take their justice into his own hands after what happened with his sibling is fiercely admirable. That he has survived this long is perhaps even more so."

"Yeah," Niko said quietly. The graduation photograph of both siblings from his old Galapol files flashed through his mind—the shared joy between them, the obvious and unconditional love. He tried not to think about the glimpse he'd gotten of Cleo's video—Uru Taal looming over her like a nightmare, ignoring her pleas. The reminder that Elliott had at some point found footage of his beloved sister's torment and murder online—which Niko himself still couldn't even bear to fully witness—hurt him more deeply than he had words for. His heart ached for Elliott.

Niko cast a quick glance back at him again. The man looked shaken to his core, brows knit into a wounded frown as he nodded at Death, his eyes searching her face as she murmured something to him.

He wished he could have fucking heard it.

Whatever it was, Niko hoped it brought Elliott comfort. The man deserved it. He deserved far more support and love than his life had ever provided him.

"Though his methods are ham-fisted, to put it in your human terms," Yalsa said. Niko looked back at her. "The public vanity of his kills confounds his mission. If it were me, I would be taking them down in the dark. No one would ever know who I was. Nor who would be next."

"Yeah. I mean, that sounds like you," Niko said dumbly, not really knowing what else to say. It was always hard to talk to her; he had little connection. He'd always had the distinct feeling she disliked him, and had overheard her once describing him as a 'simple, puerile creature' years ago. "But that's the thing. He *could* kill them quietly and privately, but he wanted to send a message. In the end, shock and fear grabs people's attention in a way shouting or pleading doesn't. And I guess there's only so much screaming into a void that you can do."

"He certainly has the entire galaxy's attention now," Yalsa said, pulling her translucent shawl tighter around her shoulders. "*Everyone* wants a piece of your lover for themselves. And now they want you, too."

He opened his mouth to respond when Death cut him off. It seemed her conversation with Elliott was over. "Alright. Let's get down to business, shall we?" She made her way back into the conference room, sinking into her usual chair at the head of the table. Yalsa slithered after her, casting Niko one last, enigmatic glimpse over her shoulder, before she found her own seat beside her wife.

Elliott drifted past him. He seemed out of it, skin still drained of color, lips pressed tightly together. His eyes looked haunted, exhausted. Niko grabbed him lightly by the wrist and Elliott almost seemed startled to see him there.

"Niko."

"Hey. You doing okay, babe?" Niko murmured.

"I'm—"

"Don't say you're fine." They looked at each other for a moment. "Don't."

"I'm... not sure," Elliott said slowly instead.

Niko nodded. He could appreciate the honesty, at least. "We'll talk about it, okay?"

"I—" Elliott's eyes glazed over, turning dull. He was retreating somewhere inside himself. "I don't really want to talk about it anymore," he admitted.

Niko swallowed back a lump growing in his throat. "Okay. That's alright. I'm here if you need anything, though, okay?"

"Thanks, Niko."

They made their way to the table and sat. Niko glanced over at him; Elliott appeared calm and perfectly, stoically composed now, but Niko knew by the near translucency of his complexion that he was still barely holding himself together.

Two small canisters of LightningLace sat unsealed on the table near Death—stimulant street drugs widely used for keeping awake for long hours and maintaining focus. She must have stayed up all night combing through Elliott's files.

"I see now why you want people to know that this is happening. I've seen some shit in my life, but this collection of files takes the piss out of anything else. And I believe I can pull together the resources to help you. It's going to take time to prepare it and get every moving part in place. So, I want you to make good on your favor to me, first. I assume that's agreeable to you?"

Niko swallowed, but nodded. Whatever she was about to ask, he was ready. It had been so long and he was tired of hiding away.

Death opened her phone hologram to his contact—which still had a decade old photo, youthful, bright-eyed, and grinning—and sent him a file, which chimed on Niko's phone seconds later. He opened it, revealing a plethora of information on a haggard and skinny, pasty human man with empty eyes and a cagey expression.

"They call him 'Skeevy Larry,'" Death said. Niko half expected a sarcastic *'Charming'* from Elliott, but the other man stayed quiet beside him. "He's a drug lord who's risen in power over the last two years to the point where nobody wants to take him on. He has very much outstayed his welcome. He has a cute little reputation for spiking women's drinks at the local bars and doing things to them not too unlike these videos you've sent me. He's an all-around oxygen thief. Waste him for me."

Niko blinked. He'd expected, somehow, something much, much *more*. The unpaid favor had haunted him for years, had slowly grown in his mind in size and complexity. This was nothing more than the simple type of clean-up job he'd been given time and again when he'd been a regular here. Niko nodded. "Okay. Yeah. Fuck this guy."

Death looked at Elliott, raising her eyebrows. "This is your specialty too, isn't it? Go with him if you want or stay here. Either is fine."

"I'm going with him," Elliott said, not missing a beat.

Death nodded. "I expected as much." She shifted her gaze to Niko. "Do what you do best, then. Get rid of him for me, and access to the galactic public is yours."

Niko didn't have to be told twice.

They were served breakfast first—tom yum with shrimp and a side of delicately sliced, candied meat from a ten-legged Heenvan livestock Niko recalled as maybe kauloai or kaauluuo. They ate with everyone else this time in the dining hall—a space not so different from the conference room, with a long table at its center. The dining hall held a far less inherently oppressive aura, though, and everyone spoke more freely here. Niko tentatively joined in with them, finally daring to make small talk with a few people he'd once called friends. Elliott engaged with no one, drawn deeply inward as he ate. Whatever had been exchanged between Death and himself continued to leave him quieted and sullen.

Then it came time to get down to business, so they set out together, trying to navigate the multi-level labyrinth that formed Dainna's many districts, aimed toward the coordinates Death had given them of Skeevy Larry's own compound, both men moving about under the cover of Elliott's ORA stealth devices.

Back on Dainna again now, Niko found himself wishing he could take Elliott out on the town, touring some of the old bars and eateries he'd used to haunt in his previous life.

A date. That was the proper label for it. He wished he could pause everything and take his boyfriend on a date. To have a moment where they could both just forget about the crushing gravity of everything for a while and instead drift into the neon haze.

But that wasn't what their lives allowed for, anymore.

Larry lived in the Saauva district, deep in what would have been hostile territory even on a good day for Niko, and full of a migraine-tangle of neon lights and crowded holograms advertising a menagerie of illicit entertainments. Brothels, bars, casinos, drug dens and more all lined the crowded streets as fast music with a deep, shuddering bass sounded from inside one of the businesses. They moved carefully to avoid drawing close to any crowds, keeping to back alleys.

"How's your suit battery?" Elliott murmured. They'd wandered a good twenty minutes before he finally spoke.

"It's fine," Niko said. "I should be good for another day and a half, two days maybe. This way." They turned down a long, decrepit back alleyway that even the scavengers and addicts had left abandoned. The corridor smelled vaguely of what Niko could only describe as rotted corn, which left him a little confused—and disturbed.

A single, dim streetlight illuminated the far end. They were otherwise cast in darkness. Elliott had a pair of night vision goggles he slipped on, but without the helmet to his suit, Niko was at a disadvantage, left to make his way along through the dark. Elliott tried to point out where littered refuse and obstacles were, but Niko cursed as he still nearly tripped over a discarded mannequin leg. Where the fuck that thing had even come from, he didn't want to know.

*"Quiet,"* Elliott hissed. After another long pause, he spoke again. "So, I'm curious. What exactly is this favor meant to repay, anyway? Lady Death seems pretty hung up on it. Did she loan you credits?"

Niko was almost insulted. "No. Nothing like that. She gave me information. For my, ah, personal hunt. She's the one who pulled strings and found out where my family's killers were, then pointed me their way. She did it with the agreement that I'd return a favor for her, too. We traded a lot like that. Death works with an honor system and takes it pretty seriously. If someone helps you, you help them in return when they ask. And she'd helped me with the clear understanding this meant I owed her too.

"It's how she has so much influence and connection. She helps a lot of people out. By never repaying her for locating the people even Zann and I hadn't been able to find for years, and then disappearing without so much as a word, I dishonored her pretty badly. So, I'm grateful to get this chance to make it up."

"Couldn't she have done this herself? It's a simple hit job, right?"

"Maybe. I don't know all the politics going on these days. I've been out of it for too long. There's usually some sort of power balance that doesn't get crossed without repercussions. Even if not, she's got a lot going on. Death's power comes from influence and connections. She regularly has people taking care of back-end business, so she doesn't have to busy herself with it."

"So why 'Skeevy Larry,' then? Do you have some particular connection to this guy?"

"Nope," Niko murmured, careful to navigate around a car that had been left parked haphazardly across the alleyway. Nearer now to the single streetlight, he could make out that its tires had been long since stolen and it had several bullet holes in the driver's side door. "It's more of the principle of it. It wasn't a particular favor. It's just *a* favor. Trade for trade. I do this and our years of unsettled debt will be even."

"I assume she's going to want something in return for helping us with all this," Elliott said.

Niko frowned. "Probably, yeah. She spoke like Larry *is* the exchange, but that doesn't make any sense. It's not anything you'll need to worry about, though. I'll take care of whatever she wants done."

"And I'll help you," Elliott said. "Like you've helped me."

Niko smiled, the expression lost under the stealth cloaking and veil of dark. Maybe Zann would call it all sunk cost fallacy—that Elliott was investing in keeping Niko happy and alive so that Niko kept helping him. But just as he'd done with Zann, Niko chose to believe in Elliott, pushing all the doubts and fear away. The man before him was sincere and empathetic underneath the controlled exterior.

And Niko felt more deeply for him every day they spent together on this great and crazy adventure.

"Alright," he said, slowing a little. The alleyway branched into several more now, all becoming more labyrinthine, with towering structures surrounding them. He pulled up his phone hologram to check, squinting hard and bringing it to the tip of his nose to try and read it under stealth. "We're coming up on it soon. He should be about two streets ahead to the left." He turned down the leftmost fork, into an extremely narrow alleyway full of low hanging wires and uneven, broken-up ground.

At least this one was somewhat illuminated by flat lights adorning an old fence.

"You know. She'll probably betray us in the end too, like everyone else does. But for the record, I very much like your friend," Elliott said.

"I've always looked up to her," Niko admitted. He ducked under a sagging, live powerline. It hummed ominously above him. "She took me under her wing when I was just a kid, new to hunting and stupid. Now I'm older, experienced, and still stupid."

Elliott laughed softly. It was a relief to hear that sound again. "You're not stupid, Niko. You're far from it." After a moment, he added, "You never told me why she picked *you* as her protégé."

"Honestly? I don't even know. I showed up in a bar here all banged up to hell and looking more dead than alive. She was there and saw me. For some reason she took pity on me. Came over and just... started asking how I ended up that way. And then gave me pointers. Eventually, it turned into her directly training me. Soon, I was living in her compound, running jobs for her."

"Incredible."

"The Legend gave me pointers too, but not to the extent she did. Some of my style is his, though, and some hers." They reached the end of the narrow alleyway and Niko paused. "Okay. We need to be careful up here. It should be on this street."

The narrow path gave way completely to a street that was barely maintained, the ground full of potholes and cracks, the sidewalks all but unwalkable. Trash and litter lay where they had been dropped in months and years past, no wind to blow it somewhere else and no one who gave a shit enough to pick it up. The whole place smelled like sour garbage and the ghost of expired, greasy food. A suspiciously still, chartreuse-tinted Gheroun lay on the far sidewalk. It was impossible to tell if they were dead or just sleeping off a bender.

Niko guessed the former.

"Delightful place," Elliott murmured. There was the quip Niko had so missed. "It speaks well of Larry's stand-up character."

"The sooner we're out of here, the better," Niko mumbled.

"Oh, you don't like it?" Elliott cooed in faux disappointment. "Here I was thinking we should look into buying a vacation house here, too. With a little picket fence. Or we could take up Skeevy Larry's abode, once we send him off."

"Hey. Speaking of which, there it is."

"Where?"

"Over there."

"I can't see where you're pointing, Niko."

"Oh, uh. To the left. The big-assed building." At the far end of the street was a four-story compound, not too different from Death's own. Niko could see two bulky guards leaning boredly against the wall, flanking the entry door. One was smoking something that definitely wasn't a cigarette. "This is going to be tricky. He's going to have people in there loyal to him. Probably a lot of them. We need to do it quick and quiet this time, I'm thinking. I know that's not your particular style."

"No, that's not *your* style," Elliott argued. "I'm adept at it."

"You're the one who usually kills people in big public spectacles—"

"But my *method* is quiet. *You're* the one who stomps around with your big metal armor and guns and explosives—" He paused. "Hey. Do you see that?"

Niko blinked. "Uh, where?"

"Top floor. There's a window to the right. If I were a crime lord with my own compound, I'd keep my quarters at the topmost floor. It's the hardest to get to and in the case of a raid, all three lower floors of your minions get sacrificed before hostiles ever make it to you. Plenty of strategic time to flee. Especially if you have any hidden escape routes installed."

"I—" Niko frowned. "Okay."

"I think we can get up there from the side of the building. You still have your grappling hook, right?"

"Yeah. But what about the sheet metal?" Much like Death's place, Larry's had thick steel bolted over parts of the windows.

"Simple. I can sear right through that via laser."

"Okay. Sounds like we have a plan, then. Let's go."

They made their way with particular caution toward the compound, careful to avoid tipping off the guards to their presence. As they circled around the compound grounds, Niko could hear their conversation.

"Weirdest part is that this guy was a bounty hunter before this, too."

Were they—?

"I know. Imagine turning down that money. Blondie must give the best head in the fuckin' galaxy."

"*He's not wrong*," Elliott whispered. Niko felt himself smirking.

"He's got to," the other guard agreed. "Estrella went and bought himself a six billion credit whore."

*Six billion credits now.* So, their bounty was continuing to climb. The number was surreal, almost unimaginable. Greedy people would be getting more and more desperate by the hour. They had to get the broadcast out. They had to make sure the bounty got canceled. Or even more innocent lives would be lost.

With that kind of money on the line, it was a wonder Lady Death or anyone else in her compound hadn't tried what most of Niko's old friends had by this point. Maybe, sometimes, honor really couldn't be bought. At any cost.

He found himself pausing to scowl at the guards, reconsidering just how 'quick and quiet' he really wanted to make this after all. He didn't love what they'd called Elliott, and found himself increasingly pissed off the more he thought about it. It would be therapeutic to crack their skulls together. They'd never see him coming with the ORA tech—

"*Niko*," Elliott hissed. "What are you doing? Come on. The window."

"...Yeah, sorry." He followed Elliott until they were straight below the fourth story window. "We'll need to ascend fast. I think the grappling hook and cable are going to be visible past a certain point."

"That makes sense. I'll be ready."

"Hey, come here," Niko said.

"Where?"

"Follow my voice—"

An invisible hundred and sixty pounds knocked clean into Niko, sending him stumbling back. He heard Elliott emit a strangled *unh* sound. Niko couldn't recover his balance in time, but the compound wall stopped him from going down entirely. He righted himself slowly, trying to catch his breath as adrenaline spiked through him.

"...I think I cracked my nose," Elliott said.

Niko couldn't help it. He started laughing softly.

After a moment, Elliott followed suit, the gorgeous sound of his laughter breathy and quiet.

"Look at us," Niko muttered.

"I *can't*," Elliott said. "That's the whole problem."

Niko laughed harder. He willed himself to quiet down. "Galaxy's number one most wanted right here."

"This is sad, Niko."

"Come on, babe," Niko said. He held out his hand. "Give me your hand. Just hold it out."

It took a moment of fumbling, but they found one another's hands. Niko pulled him tightly against himself and used the grappling hook. Once it caught on the roof overhang and he gave it a quick tug for stability, he hit the trigger and rappelled them both up the wall. They climbed onto the overhang and he retrieved the hook, tucking it back into his belt. Loud but muffled music came from inside the room, the bass intense enough to rattle the window glass.

"Nothing to it," Niko mumbled.

"Yes. We'll just say that," Elliott muttered. Niko heard him paw through a pouch on his utility belt and procure the laser. "Can you hold onto the welded metal here?"

Niko moved to the window and held the metal in place. "Uh, you're not going to end up running that through my arm, right? I mean, you can't exactly see me well right now."

"I'm starting at the top, so hold the bottom."

They worked quickly, Niko switching to grasping the top on Elliott's mark. When the metal was severed, he laid it down gently on the roof overhang. Freed of its barricade, the window beneath was unlocked and slid open easily. Heavy, bass-driven techno music pounded, flowing freely out from the open window now.

Elliott peeked in, pushing the curtains back just a smidgeon. "*Come on,*" he whispered, then slipped inside. Niko followed quickly as he could, nervousness briefly spiking through him at the fear of getting his unfeeling feet or legs caught on the window ledge.

He cleared it easily, to his relief, stepping down as quietly as possible into what indeed appeared to be Skeevy Larry's bedroom. Elliott was a little too good at being able to think like an asshole crime lord. He closed the window behind himself, hoping the guards didn't think anything of the brief increase in sound.

The room was shitty chaos—almost every visible piece of wall was covered in posters and graffiti, clothing, emptied vodka bottles and used syringes lying scattered around the floor and bed. The room smelled of stale smoke and despair. Two separate ashtrays were overflowing with ancient cigarette butts until Larry had at some point given up and started, apparently, leaving them lying around the top of a vanity dresser which sported a broken mirror. An old stained up couch sat by the bed, weeping its springs out through gouges and worn holes.

At the far end of the bedroom, beside a huge and expensive looking stereo system was the most horrific feature of the entire room—Skeevy Larry himself.

He was in nothing but his underwear, eyes closed, dancing enthusiastically to the music, bottle of half-drank vodka in hand. The guy actually had a tramp stamp that featured a credit sign flanked by two pistols.

For a moment, Niko and Elliott froze, simply watching.

"I finally understand what the term 'poetry in motion' means," Elliott marveled in disgust.

"...Yeah."

"Well, anyway, let's kill him," Elliott said, his tone lofty, all business.

"Right. So how are we gonna do this?"

"This is your favor, so you should do the honors this time."

Niko sighed. "Right. Okay."

"Here." Niko heard movement by the windowsill. Elliott then stepped away from it and Niko saw he'd left his knife lying there for him.

He was grateful Elliott hadn't tried to hand it to him in stealth, blade out.

"Thanks, babe." Niko grasped it and turned toward Larry. He wasn't used to this sort of killing style, of sneaking around and taking someone out from the shadows. But Elliott did it just fine, so he could make do too. How hard could it be?

He advanced through the room, moving slowly now, careful not to knock or crush any of the scattered trash with his feet, the knife clutched tightly in hand.

How to do this? Sticking it in his throat guaranteed a quick death, but it was so... messy. Niko hated the idea. In the head seemed grisly. Anywhere else and he wasn't guaranteed results. Neck it was, then.

He was almost to Larry when the man suddenly flung out his arm in a dramatic dance move, his bottle of vodka knocking straight into Niko and crashing to the floor. Both froze, Larry looking stunned and freaked out. "Oh—Oh shit. What?"

Niko panicked. He lunged for Larry with the knife, but the other man had caught on that something calamitous was going on and stumbled back out of the way. He started screaming for help.

*Fuck. Of course. Asshole.*

Niko did the only thing he could think of and grabbed Larry. He struggled with him, the knife dropping somewhere in the grime and mess below. For someone so scrawny, Larry put up a hell of a fight, powered by unholy strength from who knew what or where. Niko figured it was drugs. Any enigma that occurred on Dainna could almost always be attributed to drugs.

Niko finally got him turned around and held tightly against himself. He grabbed him by the head, then wrenched it to the side in one quick, strong jerk. The muted crunch of Larry's neck snapping was swallowed up in the pulsing beat of his techno music. Just like—Niko hoped—his earlier scream had been.

Niko was trembling. He let out a shuddering breath and slowly let Larry's carcass down, lying it in the broken bottle shards and piles of his own trash. He'd wanted to let it drop, to not touch it anymore, but was paranoid of the sound it might make.

"Shit," he muttered. He squatted down and fished around for Elliott's knife, finally finding it buried in what might have been an old sweatshirt.

Elliott deactivated his stealth and appeared beside him.

Niko opened his mouth to chastise him for it, but, well, fuck it. Just fuck it.

He deactivated his too, grateful to finally give a physical, visual presence to the two of them. Elliott stared down at Larry, a look of quiet disdain on his features.

"Wannabe. Honeybliss Lite," he muttered. Niko almost couldn't hear him over the music. He wanted to reach out and turn it down. It was adding to a slowly building tension headache likely caused by stress, but ultimately it remained their only cover against anything being wrong and alerting the rest of the compound just beyond the bedroom door. A glance at the door revealed—much to Niko's relief—a thick deadbolt that locked from their side. He held the knife out to Elliott and the other man took it.

"I thought this was supposed to be lucky," Niko grumbled.

"And I thought you were supposed to be good at this. It must be amateur hour."

Niko grunted. "Hey, he's dead, isn't he?" He summoned his phone hologram and snapped a quick photograph of Larry. "Come on, Elliott. We're done here."

"No," Elliott murmured. "Not yet. Hold on." He crouched on the balls of his feet, gripping his lucky knife. Niko saw a crescent of bare skin where his shirt and pants separated, the edge of his underwear peeking out.

"What're you doing?"

"Getting you proof," Elliott said simply.

"Wait, what? Proof?"

Without further explanation, Elliott took hold of Skeevy Larry's tattooed wrist and began sawing into the flesh with the serrated edge.

"Whoa! Elliott, what the *hell?*"

Elliott paused, still gripping Larry's wrist tightly. He peered over his shoulder at Niko, a single pale curl hanging in his eyes. "If *I* were your employer, I'd want definitive proof that you got the job done."

"That's—" Niko was more and more disturbed by what an apparently conniving and utterly ruthless crime lord Elliott seemed to be proving. Theoretically. "That's what the photograph was for."

"Well, we're bringing her hard, *solid* proof." Niko winced as he heard his knife grind up against the bone. The whole thing was grisly.

"Elliott, that's— No." He didn't have words.

The other man finished his task, holding the disembodied hand up victoriously above his head. Niko grimaced. Elliott stood and grinned at him, eyes squinted like a weird little cat proud of itself for bringing home a dead mouse.

He waved it at Niko.

"Don't," Niko said.

"Niko. Need a ha—"

"*Don't.*"

"You were so eager for a high five before. Want another?"

"Put it away, for fuck's sake."

Elliott tossed the thing at Niko. It was instinct to catch it, and Niko hated himself for it. Goosebumps crept along his skin in repulsion. Even attached to its body and warm with life, touching Larry's hand would have been nauseating to Niko. For once, he found himself grateful for being trapped inside thick, armored gloves.

"This was your job," Elliott said matter-of-factly, sliding his knife back into its sheath. "So, you carry the proof."

"I can't fucking believe this," Niko grumbled under his breath, trying to think of *somewhere* to stick it. He finally shoved it in a small utility pouch at his belt, then tried not to think too hard about it being in there. "Let's just go."

"Well?" Death asked once they were gathered in the conference room again. Several others had come as well, curious to overhear if the two of them had been successful.

"It's been taken care of," Niko said."Show her," Elliott said, eyeing him. "The proof."

Niko grimaced, rifling through the bag at his hip. He tossed the hand onto the conference table. It rolled once, then came to a stop with the pinky and ring finger stuck out, the distinct tattoos on them visible.

The room fell into a heavy silence, everyone staring at the hand, then at them. Niko swallowed. Beside him, Elliott looked proud of his trophy.

"What the fuck is that?" Death asked.

Niko glanced at Elliott. "Uh, a hand."

"I see that," Death said.

"It's Larry's—"

"I don't want this thing. Get rid of it."

Niko glanced at Elliott again, but Elliott only shrugged. They definitely needed to have a talk about bounty etiquette.

The rest of the room remained silent. The only one who seemed legitimately impressed was Yalsa, who focused on Elliott now with a keen, narrow-eyed approval, her head barely nodding. Niko remembered her *very* well now. Opposite to Sweetheart, Yalsa had always shared Elliott's more brutal view of getting things done.

Death stared at them expectantly, until Niko reached out and awkwardly retrieved the hand. He shoved it back into his pack and cleared his throat.

"Anyway," she said, after a lingering silence, "you've satisfied my conditions. I consider your favor repaid. You're in good standing with me, Killjoy." Niko felt the weight of three years as it sloughed off his shoulders. He heaved out a sigh. "While you were taking out the trash, I got to look at the remainder of these files. I'll help you make this big. I have connections who also owe me favors. We can interrupt and hijack public television transmissions and I think I can get past their algorithms with AI countermeasures. How big do you want to go?"

Elliott and Niko looked at each other, exchanging grins. Niko felt a little giddy. He was weightless, even sealed in the heavy suit.

Elliott turned his gaze back to her. He stood taller, straighter. When he spoke, he sounded a little breathless. "I want the whole galaxy to know."

"I appreciate your ambition," Death said, and nodded. "Your willingness to do to Honeybliss what no one else will has been admirable. Sometimes society needs the shit scraped off its shoes. You'll always be welcome here, Elliott."

Once more, Niko saw Elliott seem to fumble with knowing what to do, how to react. His cheeks colored and he briefly looked at the floor, before glancing around the room and at all the eyes that watched him back in silence. A few of Death's people nodded to him in approval and respect. In the back of the room, Yalsa pressed the palms of her pearlescent hands together in a gesture similar to prayer, showing her appreciation of him.

Elliott clearly wasn't used to having fans.

Nor, probably, respect.

He opened his mouth to speak, then closed it again, at a total loss.

"You too, Niko. You'll always have a home here. Anyway, this is going to take a few days to pull together. So, if you have business to take care of, do that now. And think of what you want to say. You'll get *one* chance, so make it count. I'll contact you."

"Thank you, Deleera," Niko said, his heart feeling full.

"You're welcome to stay here, or you can return to wherever you've been staying."

"We should—" Elliott looked at Niko. "We should get back. We have work to do, still."

"You know, I'm honestly kind of surprised nobody tried to make a move all night while we were here," Niko said.

"They did," Death said. Niko's blood turned to ice water. "All of Dainna was a hotbed of activity last night. I had patrols out everywhere in anticipation, though. We kept them back."

"I—" Niko blinked. "Why would you offer for us to keep staying here, then? It's such a burden on you."

"Because Sweetheart was right, Niko. And I defend what's mine. At any cost."

Niko was overwhelmed, gripped by so many emotions at once. Gratitude, guilt, awe. He was humbled.

"Before you go," Death continued, seeming to brush it off, "make me a comprehensive list of supplies you need. I'll get them from the market, quick."

Niko shifted uncomfortably. "I, um, don't have a lot of credits right now to—"

Death waved him off. "It doesn't matter. It's on me."

"Wait, really?" Niko asked, uncertainty creeping through him. He'd only just repaid Death's favor. He had no idea if she wanted this one repaid too. On top of helping them with Honeybliss.

"It's on me this time. Really. Don't worry about it, Niko. Just get what you need."

"Okay."

"What happened to your helmet? That suit has connection points on its collar." She walked over and stared up at him. The other attendees of their meeting dispersed, going back to their business around the compound.

"Uh, I lost it," he said, remembering how Elliott had pried it off and tossed it into the infinite sea of clouds that formed Uula.

They hadn't been on such good terms, back then.

He glanced over at Elliott, expecting to find the other man glued to his side, but did a double take when he saw him instead talking to Yalsa in the background. Something she said made him burst out into laughter.

*Okay then.* The two of them seemed to be hitting it off just fine.

"Talk to Noori next time you see her. She still deals in that sort of tech. Get it replaced and put it on my tab."

"Sure." Niko pulled her into a tight hug. "Thanks, Deleera. Really. For... everything."

"Don't disappear on me again," she said. "You were my favorite."

"I won't." He pulled away and grinned down at her. "Not this time."

"I mean it when I say you get one chance at this," Death warned him. "I'm going to have to pull all my strings and make the stars align for this to work. This is going to be the biggest favor I'll have ever called in. So make it count."

"We won't let you down."

# CHAPTER SEVEN

# VENGEANCE IS A KNIFE

BACK AT THE FACILITY, once they'd hauled the crates of supplies from Lady Death off the *Soñadora*, Elliott made his way to the Murder Room and Niko transferred back to his chair to get the suit charged before going to join him. Elliott had seemed deeply, quietly relieved to have new supplies. He hadn't mentioned it to Niko before, but it was an unspoken acknowledgement between them both that Elliott had only possessed finite supplies intended for one person, and the addition of Niko meant they'd been burning through them rapidly. Especially when Niko had the appetite of a Ghaelacuan geela-horse.

Niko was just grateful to get access to more flavors in the kitchen than salt and artificially flavored electrolyte powder.

After the constant neon lights, relentless thumping music and rich, spiced scents of Dainna, it was almost a comfort being back in the quietude and stillness of the facility. Elliott stood now, one hip out, arms folded across his chest as he regarded the wall of portraits gravely. Niko watched as his gaze trailed to the knife that still protruded from the center of Imperator Khaathra's face—the Gheroun leader whom Niko had once fought hard to keep Elliott from taking down on Uula.

"Her," Elliott said, simply.

"Yeah?" Niko asked, unease beginning to creep in.

"I want to take care of her and Iincha'cul now."

"Oh," Niko commented neutrally. He swallowed back a quickly rising nervousness, picking absentmindedly now at the arm of his wheelchair. "So, um, Elliott, I was thinking—"

"I'm not going to like this, am I?"

Niko sighed. "No. But hear me out, please."

"I'm listening."

"Why don't we lay low until we can get those files distributed? Deleera's going to help us finally get the information out about them that nobody—"

Elliott cut him off sharply. "And why would I do that?" His eyes held something dark and unmovable in them.

Niko blinked at him. "I mean, it can't really be swept under the rug or denied anymore if it all finally becomes public knowledge. Do we need to keep kill—"

"I will never stop killing them. Until there's no one left."

The room felt colder somehow; Niko could have sworn it dropped a few degrees. Elliott stood still and rigid, staring Niko down, all sheer, icy will and assertion. When Niko stayed quiet, he continued, "Even if the public knows, I still don't trust Galapol or the justice system to do anything about it. Most of these people *are* their own justice systems. Kings and emperors, prime ministers and presidents. Nothing is going to happen to them. They'll worm their way out like they always do.

"No, I want them gone. I'm not done killing them. I set out on a mission and I'm going to see it through, Niko. No matter what. I'll never rest until Uru Taal is dead."

Niko nodded. "So, why don't we go for Taal next and—"

"Because I want him to *suffer*, Niko. I want him to know fear. And misery. Just like he made Cleo feel. I want him to watch as all his little friends drop like flies, one by one, until he has nowhere else to run. I want him to realize there's no way out for him. Ever again. I want him to know, intimately, that he is going to die."

He was worked up now, breathing hard. Niko stayed silent, giving him a moment. An old intimate sorrow and dread wormed their way through him. It was obvious Elliott wasn't willing to relent, no matter how their situation changed for the better. He wasn't willing to accept any extended hand ready to pull him out of the deep dark of revenge. It was all too eerily familiar to Niko. It had consumed him once as well, and left him forever damaged. Vengeance was a knife that often cut its wielder, too.

When Elliott's breathing had quieted again, Niko finally reached out and laid his hand over the other man's, which had come to rest against the edge of the island now.

"Okay," Niko said slowly. "We're still in this, no matter what. But—"

"I'm not going to like this either."

"No. Probably not. But I think we need to at least rethink how we do this from now on."

Yalsa may have had a point. And he couldn't stop thinking about that now, her words echoing ominously through him.

Glimpses of the Starlight Awards flashed through Niko's mind—Galapol closing in, his options running out. Elliott beside him, about to be arrested or killed over Niko's failure. Both outcomes led to the same fate, in the end.

Niko couldn't let it all go wrong again. He wasn't ready to face that down.

"Khaathra and Iincha'cul are both going to have tight security right now, after the previous attempts on them. Their residences are probably going to be crawling with Galapol agents too. Especially knowing you were willing to show up at Jande Seiiren's place and not just at big events now. They're going to be expecting you.

"We should shake it up. We need to get smarter about all of this. If we keep doing the same things we've been doing, we're just going to end up cornered and dead. And once this information about Honeybliss is out to the public, *everyone* is going to be aware of who you're going after.

"You should reconsider doing any big events from now on. I know you wanted people to see exactly who your targets were, but once they have the info from your files, they'll already know who they are and exactly what they did. I can't imagine any Honeybliss member with half a brain is going to be willing to be in the public spotlight for the foreseeable future. They're going to get smarter about it, they're going to go into hiding. You were sending a message, but we'll have that message out to everyone now, and can just focus on taking them down instead.

"Let's start going in a new and random order, too. We'll still have hunters and mercs to contend with, especially if they don't cancel the bounty. But it'll throw off Galapol, at the very least, and make us harder to predict. They have your list of Honeybliss members, but will have no idea which we'll hit next. They'll struggle to choose where to allocate their resources. I know them. They can't be everywhere at once."

It would only hold up for a little while. The remnants of Honeybliss were already beginning to dwindle in number. The real challenge would come when they were down to the last individuals and it would no longer be hard to guess who came next. But for now, it was their best option.

Elliott didn't look thrilled, his brow drawn into a heavy scowl. Niko could tell he was turning it over in his mind. But the logic was undeniable. "Fine," he finally said. "We choose someone at random. It doesn't matter. They're all going to die eventually, anyway."

Niko let out a long breath, relieved. "Okay. So who—"

"You pick," Elliott said.

"*Me?*"

"Yes. Choose who gets it next. And we'll go for them. No more big events. We're hunting them now."

Niko hated himself for the small thrill that coursed through him at that last sentence.

"Okay, um." He wheeled to the grid of portraits, eyeing each one. Scribbled on them was various information, mostly incomprehensible in Elliott's handwriting. One stood out in particular, though—a single, semi-legible word that caught Niko's eye.

On the portrait of the Xermotl stage magician, Cnrys, among the chicken-scratch, read: *Eanan*.

The tranquil, oceanic moon.

"Him."

Cnrys was renowned for two things: his unparalleled stage magic tricks, and his bizarre obsession with humans and their cultures. The Xermotl had even gone so far as to undergo several cosmetic surgeries which had altered his original blue, patterned skin into something disturbingly resembling Niko's own dark bronze.

He was less known for being a violator and asshole, as shown in the cursed footage of Elliott's files. It didn't even surprise Niko that every one of the magician's victims had been humans.

Nor did it surprise him to see, now, that Cnrys's private beachside mansion looked tailor-built for human taste and standards, rather than anything resembling Xermotl culture—two stories, with a shingled roof, white plaster walls, and big windows from which to view the splendor of the sea.

The guy still hadn't managed to shake off the intrinsic love of and call to the ocean inherent in every Xermotl, though. And so Niko found himself on the shores of Eanan, standing side by side with Elliott.

They stood atop a large seawall which overlooked Cnrys's mansion and private strip of beach, hidden away under Elliott's stealth tech. Rich, golden sands glimmered below them, bordered by an endless expanse of brilliantly teal waters. Eanan's sun hung low in its sky, peeking from between scant, wispy clouds. If they worked quickly, they could make it out before dark.

"Finally got to take you to Eanan," Niko muttered, half-joking. Something about the statement wore him down a little, though. He wanted this in its full experience. He wanted to take Elliott here and spend a day or a week with him, to build the stupid sandcastles they'd joked about in the past. To sink into the warm sands and watch the tide come in. To just lose themselves in the ecstasy of simply being alive in each other's company.

He wished he could spend time with his boyfriend outside of the facility, and outside of hit jobs, just being people, lost somewhere together in the galaxy.

What would they be like, if they hadn't had to constantly hide away? How would Elliott be? There were so many things Niko could do with him. Places, experiences to show him, indulge him with. A fancy eatery or a loud pub with greasy fries and sports holograms in the background. Two tickets to a pop concert—he'd endure the plasticine music just to witness the other man's enjoyment. A beach, or a park, or a quiet night together just watching the traffic drift by the windows of Niko's old apartment. Movies—did Elliott like horror? Action? Romance? Did he like movies at all, or was he more of a reader? What books caught his passion, if so? There were so many things Niko wanted to ask.

It was strangely hard to focus on Cnrys and the mission they were on.

"It's nice here. I've never been," Elliott murmured back. He sounded detached. "Look. Easternmost window. That's him."

"Are we sure?" Niko forced himself to ask. He knew Elliott was probably peering through the pair of specialized binoculars he'd seen on his person before, but it was far more difficult to see without his own helmet visor to enhance and magnify the view. He'd taken the time to text the black market suit technician, Noori—the deaf woman hated trying to discuss business through phone calls and generally ignored them—and she'd promised to get a replacement helmet for him, the bill sent Lady Death's way. But for now, he was simply left to squint at the distant windows, the faintest movement of ruddy bronze on the other side of the glass giving credence to Elliott's assessment.

"Yes. And lucky us, it looks like he's home alone. You'd think he would at least have security stationed. Idiot."

"Lucky us," Niko muttered. "Let's get this over with, I guess."

He didn't have to see Elliott to feel the other man's gaze turn in his direction. "Is everything alright, Niko?"

"Yeah."

"Are you really that upset that I don't want to put this all on hiatus?"

"No," Niko said. "No, it's not that."

"Then what is it?"

*I just wish that I could give you something more than... all of this,* Niko wanted to say. Instead, he said, "When this is all over, we should come back here."

He felt the pause in Elliott, a beat of silence before he finally spoke again. Niko couldn't help but feel with a tinge of bitterness that some part of Elliott still somehow didn't accept that there would ever be an *after*. Elliott's voice emerged softer now, though, something cracked open and personal rather than the business end of a gun. "I would... really like that, Niko. That would be nice."

"Yeah. Me too."

Elliott crouched and drew his sniper rifle. Niko could barely make out what was happening; it was oddly easier to see him from the corner of his gaze than if he tried looking directly at the stealthed man. The faint outline of *Repartee's* long barrel distorted the air as Elliott set up his shot. He drew quiet and inward. Even his breathing shifted to something more conscious, controlled, and slow. Niko found himself subconsciously timing his breaths to flow with Elliott's. He briefly wondered if this was a meditative experience for him—to slow everything, to focus all his concentration and awareness to a single, masterful point.

Niko had never encountered a marksman with Elliott's efficiency in all his hunting days.

He watched a bronze limb—it was impossible from his vantage point to tell if it was an arm or a leg; Xermotl were always somewhat funny-shaped—shift in the distant window. Everything about this would be quick and quiet, an entirely different arena than Elliott's former insistence on crowded public events. Niko was all but useless here. There was nothing to protect Elliott from, no one to get in their way. It had been a good idea to switch it up.

Elliott seemed to have the same thought. "It's almost too easy like this," he murmured softly, letting another long, slow breath flow out.

Niko winced. "Don't jinx it. Please. The last thing we need is something coming in and fucking it up at the last second." He found himself casting a paranoid glance around, as though speaking the words would summon every Galapol agent to have ever enlisted and as many hungry bounty hunters as there were stars in the galaxy. But everything remained the same—the private beach and its mansion were tranquil, quiet. Empty, save for its sole resident.

And soon, even he would be gone, too, leaving only the two of them here.

Niko frowned, that realization giving him an odd and absolutely outlandish idea.

"What's the matter, Niko? You don't want to have a little bit of challenge in your life? Where's the fun in that?"

"Yeah, I think I've had enough challenge for now. I'll take this instead."

Elliott fell quiet. The air itself between them seemed to still, as though the fabric of the world were holding its breath too. Several long seconds later, a single gunshot tore through the silence. It was grim work, but always rather fascinating to Niko to see how incredible Elliott was at it. His aim was faultless.

The window was broken now, its glass spider-webbing in cracks around a central point. Cnrys's indigo blood spattered across it.

"Well," Elliott said. Niko heard him pull himself to his feet. "We should—"

"Check to make sure," Niko insisted. "Just in case."

They descended the wall and made their way toward the mansion, Niko doing his best to keep up with Elliott's swift pace. He could see the other man's footprints as they dug craters in the sand ahead of him.

It was hard walking on the beach. Its golden sands were uneven and unpredictable, and without any sense of feeling, Niko was losing his footing. When a particularly loose patch sent him crashing hard to his knees, Elliott paused, then deactivated his ORA.

"Elliott, we shouldn't—"

"I don't care," Elliott said. He held his hand out. "Give me your hand."

*I can do it.* Niko bit down on the thought hard, pushing it away. Elliott was trying to help, trying to show him kindness. Niko hated that he needed help at all. He deactivated his own stealth, then clasped Elliott's hand and let the other man pull him up, then steady him.

It proved much easier to stand with Elliott's help than the struggle to regain his footing on his own would have undoubtedly been.

"Sorry," Niko muttered.

"Don't apologize," Elliott said. "But be careful, Niko." He had a quiet warmth to his tone. Niko glanced away from him. They made their way—more slowly, to Niko's embarrassment—toward Cnrys's mansion, not bothering with stealth anymore. If someone were around to see them, they'd already have been long since noticed.

Up close, the white plaster of the mansion's exterior walls had small seashells and sea glass inlaid into it. The double entry doors were carved from oak and sported beveled, stained glass designer windows, their patterns forming an azure and purple landscape of oceanic creatures.

Elliott reached out and tried both knobs, but the doors were locked. "Hold on, I can—"

"Nah, I've got this," Niko said. "Get back." Once Elliott was out of the way, Niko took a few steps back, then ran full force at the doors, slamming them hard with his armored shoulder. They splintered around the lock and gave way, a rainbow of beveled glass shattering into crystalline rain around him. Elliott blinked at him.

"Sometimes I think you just like breaking things." He eyed Niko up and down. "Including yourself."

Niko grunted and rolled his shoulder. "Let's get this over with."

They stepped inside, guns raised warily, glass crunching beneath their feet. The house was empty and still. Elliott had been right—Cnrys would have been wise to employ some kind of protection—whether traditional security or mercenary. In the end, it didn't matter anyway. Elliott would have found a way through and around them, Niko knew.

The double doors led into an entry hall flanked with distinctly human decor—gilded mirrors, a marbled side table topped with a vase which sported some leafy thing Niko thought was probably called sage or eucalyptus. The hall opened up into a large, open kitchen dining room combo, with a big table for entertaining and glass doors facing the sea. A single framed and matted black and white photograph of Cnrys performing magic before several enthused human children hung in the dining room. Niko walked over to it and pulled it down, staring at the abomination, before tossing it aside like a frisbee. Its glass shattered as it hit the floor.

"So much for being quiet," Elliott murmured.

"I'm pretty sure your thundering gunshot gave away our presence, babe."

Just beyond the kitchen was a small, enclosed sunroom, which the tangled remains of Cnrys lay sprawled in, indigo blood painting a majority of the windows.

They stared down at the body, boneless, rubbery limbs flopped across the floor. The memory of the grotesque violations those floppy limbs had enacted on people made Niko shudder. Elliott stared down at Cnrys blandly, then nudged him with his boot.

"Well. He's dead," Niko declared.

Cnrys couldn't magic himself out of this one, it seemed.

"Good. Then let's get—" Elliott started.

"Actually," Niko cut him off. He glanced out at the kitchen behind them, the thought from earlier clawing its way back up now, urgent and insistent. It was a wild idea, and a stupid one. But he needed to do it. Niko's heart leapt into his throat at the realization that he was about to actually go through with this. "I want you to do a sweep of the perimeter."

Elliott's features drew into a confused, nervous frown. "What? Why?"

"I want to test something. I want to see if anyone really was here, waiting. Or if we actually caught the galaxy blindsided, this time. It's possible someone's still hiding out and just not acting on it. We can both look. It shouldn't take long. You can cover the expanse of private coastline here. I'll do a sweep of the house. Use the ORA. No one will see us even in a worst-case scenario. We can get out fast."

Elliott stared at him, scowling now. Niko swallowed, expecting him to see right through his bizarre and insistent request. "Is it really necessary to? If someone *is* here, we should just go, not spend time looking around. You said yourself if anyone else were here, they'd be quite aware of us by now."

"I know. I did. But there's also a chance some of his victims might be around too, you know? Since we're hitting homes now and not just big events. So, we should do a sweep for them, too."

That last part wasn't a lie. Niko prayed to any cosmic entity that might take mercy on him that they would find nothing even close to that.

It seemed to sway Elliott slightly. He could see something stubborn give way in the other man's eyes. His frown didn't let up, though. "Out on the beach, Niko? Let's just look in the house—"

Niko sighed in nervous frustration. He ran a gloved hand through his hair. "Just trust me, babe, okay? I won't ask anything like this again. I just want to see. I want to make sure nothing is amiss."

"Then we should do this together, not split up."

"We can cover it faster if we're split up. It's fine. With the ORA, we won't be seen."

Elliott shook his head. "This is a weird request, Niko—" Niko sagged slightly. It wasn't going to work. He was a shit liar, and always had been. "—but since you're so insistent, fine."

He perked back up. Elliott only shook his head at him again, but reactivated his ORA. Niko could hear his footsteps trailing back down the entry hall and outside of the house. He breathed out a long sigh of relief, then glanced around. To make this work, he'd have to move fast.

Elliott wouldn't be gone long.

He reactivated his own ORA and did a speedrun check through the house. He wanted to skip it entirely, but what he'd said might actually turn out to be true—if he missed a hidden assailant or victim in need of aid due to sloppy carelessness, Niko would never forgive himself. Each luxurious room of the house turned out quiet and empty, though, to his great relief.

Cnrys's bedroom made him pause at the threshold, unwilling to cross through the doorway. The huge room was as pristine and perfect as everything else here, but all of the Xermotl's horrific videos had taken place there. He backed out, leaving that one alone.

The basement proved host to an entire vintage alcohol rack, fully stocked.

*Score*. Niko grabbed some of the bottles, examining them, before quickly deciding on a champagne that would have probably cost a year of his bounty hunting salary. And he'd been paid quite lucratively when he had been active.

He hoped Elliott took his time on the beach. Maybe the other man's paranoia and attention to detail would be to his benefit this time around. Better yet, Niko hoped he paused for a quiet moment to himself to just actually take in the beauty and splendor of having a moment alone on one of the most beautiful beaches in the galaxy. He liked the thought of Elliott having a brief respite like that.

As he made his way back towards the kitchen, Niko paused and did a double take, mouth agape. Hanging on Cnrys's living room wall was the single greatest treasure in the entire mansion: a delightfully tawdry wooden sign.

*Elliott is going to fucking love this.*

He pulled it from the wall, feeling a little giddy at the anticipation of getting to gift him something.

His exploration revealed a few extra prizes along the way, too—a supply closet that had candles and a lighter, and a pantry full of fresh herbs and spices. He grabbed them all before rushing back to the kitchen.

Niko placed the candles along the grandiose dining table, then laid the sign across the seats, hidden away for a later surprise. Then he paused. There was one more thing left ruining this whole plan—rubbery, spade-tipped arms (or were they legs?) peeking through the doorway to the sunroom. He stepped inside and hastily pried the ornately woven area rug out from under Cnrys's body, then tossed it over him, so that all that remained visible was an awkward lump. And four walls splattered ceiling to floor with purple alien blood.

*There. Out of sight, out of mind. Kind of.*

It would have to do, and he didn't have time.

After that, he dug right into Cnrys's refrigerator, which seemed to primarily contain a mixture of various imported seafoods. Niko grabbed a fresh package of tilapia, thought on it, then snatched a few limes, an avocado, and sour cream. The pantry provided the touch of chili and garlic he needed to complete this.

It was time to cook.

He deactivated his stealth and threw the fish into a cast iron pan with a dash of olive oil and lime, and seconds later, it was already sizzling. Niko had briefly worked his first job as a line cook for a greasy mom and pop burger joint when he'd been in high school. Years later, he still knew how to cook quickly and efficiently under pressure. His heart hammered in his chest as he worked. Given the ORA, he'd be unable to see how near or far Elliott was, but hoped he could finish before the other man returned. Niko would be able to hear his eventual approach, at least.

With the fish underway, he got started on making avocado crema to drizzle over it. The kitchen was already beginning to smell like citrus and seafood now, a bright scent combination that had always evoked the essence of sunlight and warm places in Niko's mind. Once he'd made good headway on the crema and had flipped the tilapia, he moved back to the table and lit each candle.

It was almost ready now.

He was taking Elliott on a date.

# Chapter Eight

# CRÈME DE LA CRÈME

WHEN HE THOUGHT ABOUT it, the skirmishes he'd been in back when hunting Elliott were kind of—sort of, *vaguely*—like dates. Niko would spend the day preparing and getting ready to go out to meet him. He would wait with anticipation for those few moments when he finally encountered him. Then they'd have a thrilling bit of physical exertion, and Niko would go home utterly mangled and exhausted.

Totally a date.

He heard the sound of Elliott's footsteps approaching, the telltale weight of his steps and quiet whisper of his boots against the polished wood floor.

*Damn.* He'd hoped to be completely done before the other man had returned, but that he'd managed to get this much cooking accomplished at all before he had was a feat unto itself. Niko figured he could accept that.

"It's all clear," Elliott said. Niko glanced over his shoulder just in time to see him appear as he deactivated his stealth, *Repartee* held across his waist. He paused, staring at Niko in bewilderment, then took a visible sniff of the air. Then he looked at the lit candles on the table. "What's this? What are you doing?"

"I'm taking you out to dinner," Niko said. He finished up the crema with a pinch of sea salt.

"You're— I'm sorry, what?"

"We're having a candlelit dinner by the sea. I'm taking you on a date, Elliott."

Elliott blinked. He glanced around again, seeming completely displaced. "*Here?* I—"

"Why not?" Niko asked, plating the tilapia. Steam rose from the sizzling, golden fish. He topped it with the crema and a sprinkle of blushing chili powder. He eyed the plates, satisfied; they looked like they could have come from a restaurant. "You just checked the perimeter, and it's all clear, right? I looked around, too. And nobody knows we're here yet. They won't for a while. That's part of the beauty of striking unexpectedly and out of order like this. So, I'm taking you on a date. On Eanan."

He brought the plates over and set them on the table across from each other, then moved back to the bottle of vintage champagne he'd found. "Knife."

Elliott blinked at him again.

Niko held out his hand. "Elliott. Knife."

Elliott unsheathed the lucky knife and handed it over. Niko struck the neck of the bottle, slicing it and the cork clean off. It foamed all over the kitchen, but he didn't give a shit. He poured two crystal flutes brimming full, then brought them to the table too. The flames of the candles danced in their reflections.

He handed the knife back. "Come on. Have a seat." Behind the table was an entire wall of glass doors that looked out over the brilliant, teal ocean. Niko went over to them and pushed them open as wide as they'd go, the sounds of waves filling the room now. He could smell the salt of the sea.

Elliott sank into one of the chairs, seeming bewildered and cautious still. Niko figured he needed a little more convincing. "Look, this asshole was rich as fuck, and a total piece of shit. And now he's dead. So, let's use what his luxury bought and enjoy the spoils of his death."

"I— Alright. Yes, you're right. Why *shouldn't* we?"

Niko crossed the room and joined him, sinking down into the chair opposite of Elliott. It was a trooper, and only emitted a faint creak under the weight of his armor. He looked across the table at his boyfriend, two aromatic plates of fresh chili tilapia between them. Elliott was in his tactical gear, *Repartee* leaned against the table at his side now.

And all around them was beach house luxury that belonged to a dead man. Who they'd just murdered. Whose body lay tucked beneath his own probably ten thousand credit woven rug, growing cold.

Dinner was growing cold too, so Niko dug in.

They ate for a while in silence, the low sun above the sea and the dim candlelight their only illumination. It softened Elliott's features. Once he'd let himself start eating too, Elliott went nuts on the tilapia, as though he couldn't get enough of it. He licked the avocado crema off his fingers, making a mess. Niko took an embroidered cloth napkin and reached across the table, wiping a smear of pale green sauce from the corner of his mouth.

An emptied plate of pan-seared fish and flute of champagne later, Elliott seemed to finally be relaxing. He sat back in his chair, tilting his head back, exposing the column of his neck that Niko loved so much, then closed his eyes. He drew in a deep breath, seeming to savor the scent of the sea and the quiet of the moment. When he opened them again, Elliott looked straight at him with a bright feverishness that gave Niko chills. It was those very eyes that had made Niko crave returning to Eanan. He'd wanted to compare shades of teal.

The ocean was beautiful—breathtaking, even. Men paid billions of credits to have a private mansion here with a wall of glass that faced the setting sun over the water. But none of it compared to the sea-green of Elliott's eyes. Niko was the richest man in the galaxy.

He found himself smiling, and Elliott smiled back.

"This is... nice," Elliott admitted, finally. Niko reached over and refilled the other man's glass. He quickly took it and started sipping. "Thank you for the meal. It was wonderful."

"I wanted to take you on a date. A real date. I might have had to compromise a little, though."

"This is perfect, Niko."

"Just don't mind the body under the rug," Niko said.

Elliott's smile spread into an indulgent grin. His gaze flicked up, mischievous, toward Niko as he held the rim of his glass against his bottom lip. "Oh, I don't know. I think that might be the best part of this whole experience, personally."

"Sometimes I worry about you."

"Only sometimes?" Elliott drank indulgently now, until his glass was almost drained in a single go.

"Elliott," Niko said, looking at the handsome man across from him. The one who was, somehow, inexplicably, all his. "What was it like for you before this? What was a night out for you? What did you like to do?"

"*Oh*," Elliott said, his voice turning oddly whimsical, his gaze flicking down to the table. He propped his chin in his hand. "That was a very long time ago. A different lifetime."

"So?" Niko said. "I want to hear it. What did you do when you'd never even heard the word 'Honeybliss' before?"

"I wasn't very exciting, I'm afraid," Elliott said after a long silence. "I worked. All the time. I buried myself in my job. But in my spare time, I liked repairing things. I liked... going to cafes. Bookstores. Museums of technology. The occasional party with my sister and our mutual friends. Sometimes nights out for dinner and drinks. There was this incredible place I loved back on Delevia. They served the best sushi I've ever had." He paused a moment, before refilling his glass and taking another sip. When he spoke again, he seemed charmingly sheepish. "Every Friday night after I finished work for the week, I'd take Cleo there and treat her to as much sushi as she wanted. It was so small. The gesture, I mean. But it was my way of saying thank you for everything she'd done. It became our ritual. We'd go see a movie afterwards, usually. I always looked forward to Fridays."

"What kind of movies did you guys watch?"

Elliott shrugged. He took another drink. "Anything. Whatever Cleo wanted to see. I wasn't picky. I don't actually even like films much unless they're particularly cerebral, but I find most of them are made for... easier consumption. I hate having to turn my brain off and focus on a single thing in front of me, if that thing is going to be shallower than a puddle. I like complexities and concepts that stay with you. I'm rambling now. In the end, though, Cleo really loved movies and I liked that it made her happy. And that we got to spend time together. So I always went back."

"Yeah, plot matters, right? Don't get me wrong, I love me a good action flick with big explosions." Niko couldn't help but grin. "But honestly? My favorite movies are romances." He gave a quiet, self-conscious laugh. "I don't think I've ever told anyone that."

"Really?" Elliott said, looking shocked. "Romances? That's sweet, Niko."

"Yeah, heh." Niko picked at the expensive-looking table cloth. "I'm always drawn to movies that make me cry. It's stupid."

"It's not stupid," Elliott said. He peered at Niko warmly. "It's really rather endearing. I'd go see a romance movie with you."

"Would you actually enjoy it, though?" Niko asked. "I'd hate to just drag you along."

"'Cerebral' in my case refers to emotional intelligence, too."

Niko couldn't help but smile.

"So, what about you, Niko? What did you do before you met me?"

"Uh," Niko could feel his expression falling. "Not a lot, actually. I used to be really active but ever since I fell, I just sort of... kept to my apartment, I guess. I didn't do much. Just watched a lot of mindless TV. I tried to pick up a couple jobs to keep up on bills because I was living mostly off my savings. Data entry, shit like that. Where you didn't have to talk to anybody." He definitely wasn't selling himself as prime boyfriend material right now.

"I honestly can't imagine you working a desk job, Niko," Elliott said. He shook his head. "That's far too pedestrian for you."

"Eh, yeah. I really hated it. I had a couple of jobs like that but they never kept long. They wore me down hard and fast until I was so depressed I'd just quit on the spot. I was miserable. I really wasn't someone worth knowing, back then."

"I think you were," Elliott said. "I think you were just in a bad place and needed a hand. Why didn't you let yourself live a little? Enjoy things again?"

This conversation was heading down a rabbit hole Niko would rather avoid, but he wanted to be honest, too. "I did have a hand extended to me. Zann was there through the whole thing. He bought me the suit and even tried to encourage me to try hunting again eventually. He checked in on me constantly, tried to keep my spirits up. But I don't know. I think I was just struggling too much to adjust to, uh, how things were now. I think some part of me didn't want to let myself enjoy anything."

Elliott eyed him oddly. "So, a self-punishment."

"Yeah, I guess so."

"I've been there too, Niko."

They weren't so different. Elliott was digging into himself for not having done more, not having been able to save his sister. Niko knew the feeling well. To this day, he still felt he should have been able to prevent the deaths of his own family too. He hated that Elliott had to know that particular torment.

"You haven't done anything you should punish yourself for," Niko said, meeting his gaze. Elliott only stared back at him for a long moment. Then he refilled his glass and helped himself to another swallow.

The conversation lulled to a somber quiet that Niko hated. He didn't want to lose the light that had been held between them moments before, so he pivoted. "Before the fall, though, you know, I was a little crazy. I used to live for hunting. I felt the most alive when I was doing it. But between jobs, I hung out at a lot of bars and parties in Dainna, or places just like it. Got in a lot of fights that both resulted in me being knocked on my ass and knocking other people on theirs. Got a lot of tattoos. Drank a little too much. You probably would have hated me if we'd crossed paths."

"I wouldn't be so quick to assume," Elliott said.

"Yeah?"

"You're rather..." Elliott eyed him up and down. "Exciting. And sweet underneath all that hard armor of yours. You were just my type, actually. I go weak in the knees for sweet men. And I may have been craving some excitement in my life."

*Just not the kind you ended up getting,* Niko thought morosely. He wished they could have met before. That he could have spared Cleo and Elliott the painful fates they'd both met. He pushed the thought away; it was just another of many impossibilities he wished had turned out differently.

"I take it you didn't ever really go too wild, huh?" Niko smirked.

"Sometimes," Elliott admitted. He took another drink of champagne. "I got around a little. Everyone has needs, I suppose."

"Did you date a lot?" Niko asked.

"No. Not at all. The only person I ever dated before you was Liam."

Niko winced at having accidentally tread into a potential landmine there. Liam was a sore spot, he knew. He couldn't help himself, though—the words poured out of his mouth before he could change the subject. "Wait, what? You seriously never dated *anyone* else?" He couldn't imagine throngs of people not clamoring over one another to have a chance with both beauty and intellect like Elliott's.

"No. I slept with guys, but I just kept my distance. I did have a three-month fling with a lovely Gheroun man once, though."

"Did—" Niko had to ask. "Did he use his tenta—"

"Of course he did," Elliott said primly, helping himself to another sip.

"*Damn*. Nice."

This time, Elliott smirked at him. He looked Niko up and down. "And what about you? You must have gotten around the block a few times. Especially with looks like those."

Niko was thrown off balance by the compliment. He couldn't help but grin. It felt nice to hear Elliott found him attractive. "Actually, no." It seemed they'd both had assumptions about one another. "I dated around a bit, but I can't do one-night stands."

"What? Really? Why not?"

"I don't know." Niko shifted his weight. "It just doesn't do it for me, unless I have some kind of emotional connection with someone first. Like, I have to get to know them a little, at least. I have to have *something* there. I mean, don't get me wrong. I still find strangers physically attractive. But I don't want to have sex with them. If it's just a stranger, I have no interest at all."

Elliott swallowed down the rest of his champagne. "You seemed *quite* interested in me on Uula."

"Well, yeah. You weren't a stranger to me."

Elliott met his eyes and smiled, something both exceptionally warm and a little sensual. Wherever they were in this galaxy, when Elliott looked at him like that, Niko felt like he was home.

"Oh, hey," Niko said. He cleared his throat. "I almost forgot. I got you a present, too. You're going to love this. You won't believe what he had hanging in his living room. Like, seriously."

Elliott reached over and refilled his glass yet again. It surprised Niko. He was so used to the carefully controlled *Kestrel*—the assassin, the tactician—that he was fully unprepared for the ruddy-cheeked lush sitting across from him. Was this how Elliott had been, before any of this? Someone who drank a little bit too much? Someone who really let himself go, sometimes?

It didn't seem right, didn't match up with anything Niko had observed, nor what Elliott had shared about his past. There wasn't a drop of alcohol at the facility, save for what was in the first aid kits. And none of that had been touched, nor tampered with.

Maybe this was just a rare moment for Elliott to really feel safe and allow himself to let go a little, just once. The thought made Niko's chest warm.

He liked being able to make Elliott feel safe.

"Well?" Elliott asked, taking another swallow. "Are you going to just stare, or show me?"

"Right." Niko pulled the wooden sign from where it had been hidden from view on one of the empty chairs at the table. Three big, gaudy, painful words were carved into it:

***Live, Laugh, Love***

Elliott burst into laughter, sounding absolutely given to weightless delight in a way Niko had never heard from him before. "What a basic bitch!" he scoffed.

Niko couldn't help the grin that crept onto his face; when a little bit drunk, Elliott started sounding rather campy.

"Must have been easy for him to say, when he could piss credits and do whatever he wanted to poor people," Elliott continued. His words carried a mild, lax slur to their edges now.

"Yeah. Tell me about it." Niko turned the sign over in his hands and looked at it. It truly was a hideous and generic work of art. Cnrys must have seen this as the absolute pinnacle of human monoculturalism.

"This has to go in the Murder Room," Elliott said.

Niko was glad they were like-minded in that idea. "Oh, for sure. I was hoping you'd say that." He put the sign back down, laying it against the wall this time.

"Though, I might make a few modifications." Elliott swirled the remainder of his champagne around, but set the flute back onto the table, unfinished. "So," he said, sea-green eyes nowhere but on Niko now, his voice barely more than a breath. "You want me to fill that pretty mouth of yours? You made dinner, so I'll provide dessert. *Crème de la crème.*"

The collar of Niko's suit grew hot. He could already feel his pulse hammering in his throat, his whole body awake and alive. He could imagine it already—the taste, the texture of Elliott filling his mouth, his throat. He felt achingly empty, suddenly. Niko swallowed, lost somewhere between deeply disturbed and horny out of his mind. He glanced around before asking, "You really want that right, uh, *here?* In *this* place?"

"Why not? Why can't I kill him and then fuck all over his luxurious bed? Aren't we here to enjoy ourselves, like you said?" Elliott said, standing. Niko couldn't help but notice the faintest wobble as he did. "Come on, lover." He held out a hand to Niko and Niko took it, letting him lead him deeper into the house, toward the master bedroom.

Just as Niko had glimpsed before, it was huge. The bedroom was bigger than his entire Kaapra-19 megacity apartment had been. It had another wall of windows and glass doors that looked out toward the sea, a sizable balcony built off of them.

Against the room's far wall, flanked by two small marbled tables, was a king-sized bed full of frilly pillows and luxury comforters. One of the pillows had the audacity to say *Stay a While* in silvered embroidery with little seashell patterns.

A large, four-doored closet was covered in mirrors which reflected Niko as he was pushed back onto the bed by Elliott. He watched a surreal vision of himself as Elliott climbed atop him, one leg wrapped around either side of him, blond hair hanging in his face, expression a little lax from the rapidly consumed alcohol. Niko reached up to rub his hand along Elliott's thigh and the Niko in the mirror did the same.

"I want to fuck you," Elliott growled. "I want to fuck you until you don't know anything but me. Until you can't think of anything but me. *Until you can feel me days from now.*" He threw Niko's plea back at him from the last time he'd let Elliott top him and had lost himself. It stole Niko's breath away.

Elliott was ravenous, only of a single mind. He began unsnapping and prying the suit free, piece by piece. But something wasn't sitting right with Niko, and as Elliott leaned down to kiss greedily at him, he found himself turning his head away—both from the reflection and from Elliott himself.

Elliott paused immediately, going stiff. "Niko? What's wrong?"

"I—" Niko took in a deep, slow breath. His body was responding, deeply hungry for this act. And he'd wanted a date with Elliott, even if it had been in a dead man's house. But this room, this bed—he'd seen it in the videos. It was cleaned of any trace of the filthy, horrific acts Cnrys had engaged in then. The people he had harmed and ruined. In fact, the room was distinctly pristine, not a single thread out of place. But Niko couldn't get it out of his mind. This wasn't where he wanted to fuck or get fucked. Even if it was with Elliott. "Not here, okay, babe?"

Niko reached up and touched Elliott's wrist.

Elliott's expression darkened. He pulled back and sat up now. "You get weird when I say I want to fuck you. I wish you'd just be honest, Niko." His words slurred into one another slightly; he was clearly a little drunk, still.

"No— Elliott, no, it's not that. I *promise*, it's not that."

He slowly climbed off of Niko, then the bed, seeming deeply embarrassed. Niko noticed he wouldn't look his way now, nor at the mirrored closet. He took particular care not to meet his own reflection.

"It's not you," Niko insisted.

"Then why?"

"This room is just... horrible. All I can think of is what happened here. It feels haunted." He glanced around. "Don't you think so? I know what happened here, and I can't. I don't want to in this house at all, really."

After a moment, Elliott spoke again, barely audible this time. "You're the one who wanted to have a date here. You're the one who made me a candlelit dinner in a dead asshole's kitchen and said we should *enjoy his luxury*. You were fine with it all, until now."

"Because I—" It did sound a little hypocritical when put like that. Niko reached up and pinched the bridge of his nose. He was stripped down to only his clothing from the waist up. "I can't do that at the facility. When do we get a chance to do anything like this? I can't take you on a date in the same place we always are, day after day. And going out to a restaurant isn't going to work. I wanted to do something sweet for you."

After a moment, Elliott stooped to pick up the pieces of Niko's suit that he'd tossed to the floor and handed them to him, still not meeting his gaze. "...I'm sorry, Niko."

"Thanks, babe." Niko reattached each piece with a heavy snap. He wanted out of this room. Its pristine, luxurious walls pressed in on him like a phantom nightmare. The indicator on his wrist lit up, reading *CONNECTED*. "It's not you, Elliott."

"Right."

*I want to do that with you,* he wanted to say. *I want you to do those things to me. Just not here.*

Elliott spoke before he could get there, though. "I just want to—" He seemed at a loss for words. "To desecrate and destroy everything about these monsters. Their memories. Their homes. It's not even enough to just kill them anymore."

"Hey," Niko said, getting up and going over to him. He pulled him into a hug and was relieved when Elliott didn't try to fight against him. The words scared him a little, another slip down into somewhere darker. Elliott was losing his footing. "I know. I get it. I do. It's not fair that they get to continue hurting so many people like this, only to keep getting away with it. But we're making sure they don't hurt anyone ever again, okay? That's what we're here doing. Right?"

Elliott pushed his palms against his eyes. "I miss my sister. I watched her die. Oh god, Niko, I was—"

Niko cut him off quickly. "Elliott. Come on." This wasn't where he wanted this to go today. Today was for them. Not being drowned by the unspeakable cruelties of Honeybliss. Not being dragged down into the airless, lightless depths of a painful memory. He tugged at his hand. "Let's go out to the beach and watch the last of the sunset."

Elliott acquiesced with a nod, and Niko led him out of the house and down the private walkway to the beach. It was beautiful and empty, the scent of saltwater filling Niko's nose, the open breeze tossing his hair about. The last of the sun was glowing orange over the oceanic horizon, a scattering of the first bold stars dusting above them. The antitwilight arch painted the opposite horizon a dusky lavender, purple as a bruise, from which the gargantuan swell of the violet gas giant that Eanan orbited had begun to crest.

A flock of azure, mottled creatures Niko remembered from his last visit years ago but couldn't recall the names of flew overhead, letting out somber songs as they passed on outspread leathery wings, their long, spaded tails trailing behind them like kites. This was where he wanted to be, out in the open air beside Elliott, enjoying each other's company. Not in a bedroom where nightmares had been countlessly rendered.

Elliott peered out at the sea and the sliver of orange-golden arc that peaked above the water. His wild, blond locks were caught by the sea breeze, giving him the look of something ethereal. Niko pulled him against his side, wishing not for the first time that he could be free of the suit and stand beside him, skin to skin, feet sinking into the warm sands. The chair didn't do so great on beaches.

"What are you thinking, babe?"

"That I like it better out here too," Elliott admitted. He was sobering up, his words closer to their usual clarity now. "I don't know what I was thinking in there. I think I drank too much. I'm sorry."

"It's alright, Elliott. I wanted you to enjoy yourself. I wanted to give you something nice."

"This *is* nice, Niko. This is—" Elliott seemed to almost choke on the words, his body giving a shudder of emotion but his face remaining impassive, a veil to his thoughts. "This is nicer than anything I ever thought I'd get to see or experience again. And I get to be here with *you*. So... thank you."

Niko leaned down and kissed him on the hair. "The first time I saw you without your mask on, I thought of this place. Of Eanan. Your eyes are the same color as this ocean."

"You were on Vhesa station, waving a gun at me as corrosive melted the floor, and you were thinking of the ocean."

Niko laughed at the absurdity of it all. "Honestly? Yeah. I was. You were the most beautiful thing I'd ever seen in my life. I was so pissed about that fact."

"You shouldn't lie, Niko."

"I'm not." He pulled his glove off and reached over, taking Elliott by the chin, the golden light of sunset somehow managing to make the other man all the more striking, transforming his features into its graceful canvas. "You're the most beautiful thing I've seen."

"Kiss me," Elliott said. He closed his eyes. "Please."

Niko obliged. He leaned in, meeting Elliott's lips with his own. It wasn't fast, nor sloppy, nor hungry; rather, it was sensual and slow, a honeyed invitation. Elliott tasted a little of champagne, still.

"This is what I feel for you," Niko murmured. He leaned in and kissed him again, just as slowly, just as warm. "This is what I feel every time I look at you." He kissed him again. "This is how I feel when I think of you. This is how you make me feel."

Elliott let out a soft sigh, his breath warm. He turned his gaze up toward Niko's. "When I make love to you, I lose myself. You make me forget who I even am. That's how you make me feel," he said.

Niko smiled. He ran his hand up along the side of Elliott's face, gently caressing it, before twining his fingers around a few loose curls, capturing them from their dance in the sea breeze. "I make you forget who you are? Who are you then, when you're with me?"

"I'm someone that somebody could love," Elliott said.

Niko ached.

"You *are* someone to be loved, Elliott," he said, his pulse spiking suddenly at the realization of how close he was coming to admitting what he'd been afraid to say until now. "You deserve love."

"I don't know," Elliott muttered, turning away suddenly to watch as the sun slipped somewhere beyond the great ocean, leaving a pastel twilight in its wake. "Maybe."

Niko winced, knowing he was losing him, that Elliott was retreating into himself as he often did. It wasn't enough. He had to say it, had to go all the way. He wasn't one to half-ass things, anyhow.

He turned Elliott around to look at him again and leaned in, giving him another deep kiss, this one longer than those previous, his ungloved hand snaking up to touch at Elliott's face as he did. When they finally parted, Niko was breathless. They looked each other in the eyes.

"I love you, Elliott. I'm in love with you."

Elliott let out another shuddering breath. He seemed to be barely keeping himself together. After a moment, he closed his eyes, and said so quietly Niko almost missed it, "Can you say it again? Will you? I just want to hear it."

"*I love you, Elliott.* I'll say it as many times as you want me to."

"Even with everything that I am? That I've done?"

"Yeah. Even then. Especially then, maybe. I would never have met you, otherwise."

Elliott smiled at him, something that was both at once broken, yet resplendent.

Niko felt lighter, like gravity had no hold over him any longer. It felt as if were he to jump, he would never return to the ground. He'd finally said what had been sitting so heavy inside of him and now it was free, was inside Elliott.

Niko had spoken what he'd wanted to say, and now he wasn't afraid anymore.

Maybe, somehow, once this was all over, they could have this every day. They could have a life together to just enjoy one another's company. To call it tricky would be putting it lightly, but there were ways out there to make it work. Niko was determined to.

His phone rang.

The sound made them both flinch with such violence that it actually made Niko chuckle a little wildly. He was suddenly aware all over again that even here, on this private beach, they had never been *truly* safe. The police could have caught on somehow, some-one could easily have snuck up on them and ambushed them after a failed wellness check on Cnrys. The possibilities were endless and they'd been quite stupid. Niko didn't regret the time spent with Elliott, though.

Not at all.

He pulled up the caller ID hologram, and his heart nearly leapt into his throat at the name.

Lady Death.

Whatever she must be calling him about was undoubtedly important.

"Gotta take this." He answered. "Yeah?"

"Killjoy," Death said.

"What's up, Deleera?"

"I've made the stars align. Let's make this happen."

Niko paused and stared at Elliott. Elliott's face was what he could only imagine was a likely mirror to his own expression—eyes wide, mouth agape in shock. Then Niko's own mouth twisted into a grin. "Yeah?" he tried to ask without too much excitement creeping into his voice, and failed.

"Yeah. So, you'd better start working out whatever it is you intend to say. Because you'll only get one chance. I can't stress this enough. This is a once in a lifetime. How soon can you get your asses to these coordinates?"

"W-wait, like, right *now?*" Niko said, staring at Elliott still.

"Like right now. Give the word and we'll make it happen."

Niko looked to Elliott for consent, and the other man nodded enthusiastically.

"Alright," Niko said. He opened the coordinates she'd passed along in a new hologram. They appeared to lead to a major broadcasting station in the Luunvan system. "We're gonna be on our way. ETA six hours."

"Understood," Death said. "I'm going to pass that on. Six hours, Niko. Don't let *anything* stop you from getting there."

# Chapter Nine

# No More Killing

Niko sat with Elliott aboard the *Soñadora*, notepad holograms hanging in the air before them. Elliott had been scrawling his thoughts out with his fingertips. A glance at them made Niko wince—he couldn't make heads or tails of any of it. He himself had just stuck to typing.

Elliott paused, chewing on his thumbnail in thought. He scowled at his notes. "Niko. Take a look at this and tell me what you think."

Niko swallowed. "Uh. Do you think you could give me the gist of it, babe? Just read me a quick rundown?"

"You're being lazy," Elliott muttered.

*Sure. Lazy.* Niko could go with that. It was better than telling him his writing resembled a drunken Dvaab trying to piss a sentence onto a wall.

Elliott sighed. "Fine. So, basically, I'm thinking we should introduce ourselves and get straight to it. We won't want to waste time. Let's just tell people about our mission and that we aren't killing the others. We should mention the release of the online files too."

"Yeah, that sounds good," Niko said. "But maybe we should give a definitive list of the ones you *have* killed too, just so you have a claim to that work and anything else that you know or don't know about isn't linked."

"Yes. Good idea." Elliott scribbled something else down.

"So," Niko said, looking over at him. "Are you ready for this?"

"I'm more than ready."

"Good. You nervous?"

"Of course I am."

"It's going to be okay," Niko said. Elliott looked away from his notes, toward him. "It is. It's going to be okay. You're going to do great. We're going to do great. I'm here with you."

Elliott's gaze drifted to Niko's notes hologram. It had a grand total of three lines typed and was otherwise blank. They'd been at it for two hours now.

"Niko..."

He'd never been much of a planner. "I know, babe. But I think we know what to say, right? I'm just going to tell the truth of it all."

"I think we should be a little more organized than that, don't you?"

"I'm pretty good at just speaking from the heart."

"...You know what, that suits you," Elliott said, relenting. He seemed lost in thought for a moment, chewing on his lip before looking toward Niko again. "Some part of me can't accept that this is going to happen."

"It's going to happen," Niko said. "We're going to stop the copycat murders. And people are finally going to know what Honeybliss has done."

Elliott blew out a slow breath. When he looked at Niko, his eyes were a little brighter, a quiet determination in their sea green depths. "You're right. I'm... I'm finally going to do this. We're actually doing this."

*I can't imagine it anymore. I can't even hope for it. To hope for it and be let down again is going to make me sick*, Elliott had admitted to him back on Dainna. To hear that he was finally allowing that hope in made Niko smile, warmth lacing gently through him.

A thought came to him then, something impulsive. He wanted to celebrate with Elliott after, when they were back at the facility. He could use Death's supplies, cook him something special. The steak that he'd requested but had been saving. He wanted to see the joy in Elliott's beautiful eyes at finally breaking through and winning this. He could put Hayura and Kuliedi Taan on the intercom as they ate. He could finish what they'd started in Cnrys's bedroom on Eanan. Niko tried not to grin in anticipation at the thought of treating Elliott to something nice.

They were going to do this.

They were going to expose the monstrosity of Honeybliss to the public once and for all. Elliott had struggled for years to do so, again and again. They'd stolen his voice at every turn. They would never quell him again. In mere hours, Honeybliss would never again be able to hide behind their shroud of carefully curated silence.

Niko was ready.

They decided to utilize Elliott's cloaking modification on the ship, agreeing that they wouldn't be there long enough for it to excessively drain the battery. Niko landed the ship in an open, empty field behind the broadcasting station.

The station was a compact, gray building that seemed far larger than it really was, covered in over a dozen towering antennas, satellites, and communications beacons that strained up towards the sky like rigid claws. It stood somewhat isolated, surrounded mostly by fields of puffy, orange, alien flowers, with a scattering of commercial buildings in the distance.

Niko recognized a few of Death's people flanking the building, guns cradled at the ready. He and Elliott hesitated before deciding to approach with their stealth kept off. They were quickly waved inside.

Death had been waiting for them just inside the door, her hair in a thick braid that hung over her shoulder. She summoned her phone hologram which read one minute past the hour.

"You're late," she snapped.

"We got here as fast as we could," Niko said.

"Here. Have this for you, by the way." She held out a glossy, black helmet—a perfect copy replacement for the one he'd lost on Uula. Niko took it from her.

"Thanks, D."

"Come on," she said, turning and leading them down a thin hallway which was lined with doors and signs in Galactic Standard warning them from entering during live recording. Some of the doors were flanked by interior windows which granted view into the rooms beyond. One in particular was lined with Death's guards, their guns trained on a group of hostages kept sitting on the floor, whose wrists—or, in some cases, tentacles—were bound behind them, their mouths wrapped in tape.

"Whoa!" Niko did a double take. The guards glanced at him and Death waved him on.

"The staff," she said. "They're letting us *borrow* this place for a few minutes. Don't worry about it. Nobody's getting hurt. It's just until we're done here."

He exchanged glances with Elliott. "Yeah, okay."

"Here's how this is going to work," Death said as she held open a door for them and stepped aside. "In here. You're going to give your talk, say what you want to say. Keep it brief, to the point. The moment this goes live, my guys are going to publish your files online too. It's going to be chaos out there across the galaxy. Make it count."

They stepped into a recording studio filled with several more of Death's people. A familiar female Dvaab who Niko had used to be regularly demolished by in poker greeted them with a lazy wave. Some people present had no weapons on them and were instead fidgeting with recording equipment, including a deep blue Heenva Niko didn't recognize. He was adjusting some of the settings on the camera drone. They were all likely media equipment technicians or broadcasting specialists of some kind—just a few of many people who probably owed Death one favor or other that she'd come to finally collect on.

"I have no doubt we've had Galapol called on us, so that won't be long either," she continued. "We'll need to get out of here fast once you're done. Do you have any questions?"

"How long will we have?" Elliott asked.

"Can't say. Minutes," Death said. "Are you ready?"

"We're ready," Elliott said. Niko nodded his agreement, his anxiety suddenly spiking.

Death touched her fingertips to a small earpiece she wore and muttered under her breath. "Alright. You're going to stand over there. Right in front of the news desk. Yes. Just right there."

"A little more to the left," the camera technician said. They shuffled to the left as instructed. "Perfect."

Niko glanced around the studio. Ahead of them and out of view of the camera drone was a hologram along the wall that read OFF AIR. Sections of the room which weren't intended to be in view were covered in some sort of deep gray padding that Niko wasn't familiar with, but figured was for acoustics purposes or muffling outside sound. "Should, uh, I wear this?" He gestured to the helmet, currently nested in the crook of his arm.

"No. Everyone knows who you are now anyway," Elliott said. Niko nodded.

"This brings back memories," Death said, her expression briefly easing up a fraction.

Elliott gave her a small smile. "Having fun?"

"As a matter of fact, I am. Alright. Going live in one minute."

Niko took in a deep breath and looked at Elliott, giving him a nod. Elliott looked back at him. The other man appeared calm, but Niko knew better. He was likely drowning in anxiety right now. He resisted the urge to reach out and take his hand. The seconds crawled by as they waited, frozen and staring at the camera drone. A single red light on it indicated it wasn't currently recording. Niko realized he had been holding his breath and slowly forced himself to exhale.

His phone rang.

The sound cut sharp through the mounting anticipation of the moment. Elliott jumped, revealing the nervousness that Niko had predicted—and empathized with. Unease churned thick as tar through his gut. His phone was silenced to all but three numbers: Elliott's, Deleera's, and Zann's. And if Zann was calling, then something big had come up.

Niko quickly swiped the call away regardless, sending it to his undoubtedly full voicemail. He was a mess of nerves now, his hands shaking. "Sorry. Let's—"

It started ringing again.

"I—I think I need to answer this," Niko said. "I'll make it quick. Sorry. Can we...?"

Death spoke into her earpiece, already trying to buy them a delay. He could feel Elliott's gaze bore into him now, wild with nervousness.

Niko answered. "What's up? Can I call—"

"Oh god. Oh *fuck*," Zann shouted, almost incomprehensible. He sounded breathless. "Niko, *they fucking got him!*"

"G– What? Got who?" Niko knew who, but his brain struggled through denial to catch up with the icy, numb horror that had already begun pooling in his gut.

"*Dad.* Niko, he's gone. They got him. Fucking Honeybliss. And not just him, but Loolae too. Someone broke into his apartment and her fucking gym."

"*Gone?*" Niko could barely force the word out; it emerged as a whisper from his tightening throat. He glanced around the room, his gaze raking over the acoustic padded walls.

"Missing," Zann clarified. Niko was able to breathe again, but only just barely. To know they were potentially still alive was a comfort, though a pale one. Honeybliss having a hold of Oliver and Loolae—the Xermotl physical therapist who had trained Niko to utilize his suit—was harrowing, a terror that he felt in every cell.

He swallowed. "You're sure it's Honeybliss?"

"Pretty fucking sure. They are clearly targeting you now, Niko. They even left a paper note, just for you, in Dad's place. All it said was, '*Estrella. Drop this or they're dead.*'"

"Fuck. Oh, fuck." Niko tried desperately to think of a solution—any solution—that could fix this, make it better. He couldn't breathe, the horror of his reality strangling him. His gaze flicked towards Death in the background. "Can we, uh, can... Can we run some kind of handwriting check on it? Match it to anyone?"

"It's typed and printed," Zann said dully.

"What about security feeds? Galapol? Weren't they supposed to be watching him?"

"Whatever the fuck Honeybliss did got around it all."

"Cancel the broadcast," Elliott called out to Lady Death. "And the file distribution. We have to cancel."

"No!" Niko shouted, a new wave of panic coursing through him. "D explained it. This might be our only chance."

"Broadcast? What broadcast?" Zann said, his voice tinny and drowned in static through the phone. "Is that *him?*"

"Zann—" Niko felt dizzy, his pulse pounding in his temples and in the backs of his eyes. He couldn't breathe. "It's— I went to Lady Death and— The copycat murders—"

Elliott pressed in. "No, we can't go through with this. Not if it means your loved ones getting killed. This is over. It's not happening."

"*What broadcast?*" Zann asked again.

It was all too much. Niko wrenched his eyes shut, willing one breath into his lungs, and then another. He spoke as calmly as the slurry of panic, rage, and frustration allowed him. "Zann. I'll call you back. I need a minute."

"I really don't think you should be doing any kind of fucking broadcast right now!"

"*I need. A minute.*" He hung up on his brother, silence briefly heavy in the room. Every second that passed was strangling him tighter.

"We can't do this, Niko. I won't do it," Elliott said. His tone was deadly serious. The gravity of it only added to Niko's agitation. "Let's focus on getting them back. We have to."

"Can—" Niko turned his gaze up towards Death, who peered at him with a quiet sympathy through her remaining eye. He ran a gloved hand through his hair. "Can we postpone this? Delay it to another time?"

He already knew the answer.

"No." She pursed her lips, clearly unhappy to deliver the word. "I explained it. Too many strings were pulled to make this happen. We had to work in tandem across several different networking companies, and my contacts hijacked them and these stations all at once across the stars to make this possible. We can't pull this off again. Period."

"Right. Fuck." Niko clamped his hand over his mouth.

"It's alright," Elliott said. "We'll find another way. Or just keep doing what we've been doing."

"No." Niko groaned. "No. We came this far. We can't lose this. We'll never get this back. The public needs to know what Honeybliss has done. And innocent people are dying every day over this fucking bounty. We can't lose this, Elliott."

"Niko, your family might die if we do!"

They'd already had to push it back by several moments. The whole thing could fall through at any time. They had one narrow time slot to distribute this vital statement to people across the galaxy.

He had to make a choice. And he had only seconds to do it.

This broadcast would undoubtedly save countless lives. It would stop the copycat murders of innocent people from predatory opportunists pretending to be Elliott.

The distribution of the files would finally reveal the sordid secrets people of power and influence across the galaxy had kept successfully hidden away for years.

And it would also likely put his father and Loolae through an even darker fate than they were already facing down right now. It would possibly—*probably,* even—kill them. In a terrible, painful way. Their deaths would be on his hands alone if he made the call. Their suffering already was his fault.

Death pressed her fingertips to her ear, listening to some transmission. Her antennae flashed a bright blue. "We lost the Coroaan station. Galapol seized it back from my guys."

Niko swallowed, his breath emerging from him now in short, sharp pants. Sweat crawled over his body, underneath the suit, his nerves prickling in fear.

Every eye in the room was on him now, waiting, watching. Elliott, Death, her guards and militia. The recording crew.

Outside, he heard gunshots.

"It's now or never, Niko. But it's up to you," Death said. "This is your call alone."

Elliott looked at him. "Niko... Don't do this. Please."

Niko turned back to face the camera drone, his entire body trembling.

"We're going live."

A full minute of silence reigned over the recording studio.

"You're sure?" Elliott's green eyes bored into him, searching.

"Yeah," Niko ground out, sounding far more determined and confident than he felt. He wasn't sure at all. He fought himself to not give in to panic and renege on his decision.

"Niko," Elliott breathed out. "Do you remember what you said? To stop you if things start going too far?"

Niko looked away.

"This is too far," Elliott said. A heavy, tense silence hung between them.

"Elliott, this will save countless lives," Niko said quietly. He finally lifted his head and looked at Elliott again. "Thousands of people, maybe. We have to."

They stared at each other.

"We have to," Niko said again.

Elliott looked devastated. He glanced away, but didn't fight him on it anymore.

Death merely nodded, murmuring something into her earpiece, then listening to whatever voice was on the other side of it. "Going live in twenty seconds," she said. "Let's go."

When they got close to time, she indicated the last remaining seconds with her fingers.

*Three.*

*Two.*

*One.*

The light on the hovering camera changed from red to green. Behind it, the hologram on the wall blinked to instead read ON AIR.

A quick glance at Elliott showed any of the pain and struggle in the other man's expression had vanished, replaced now with a mask of perfect, stoic calm. He was a far better actor than Niko was. Niko tried to will his face to arrange itself into something more neutral, but he couldn't stop the trembling of his body.

They were live now, their faces and voices hijacking almost every mainstream channel across the galaxy, overriding whatever programs had been previously running. The two of them were now projected onto any TV hologram tuned to major and local networks. Living rooms, bars, businesses. Offices and phone cable live feeds.

They were everywhere now.

Niko opened his mouth to speak, but nothing emerged. Whatever words he'd once had inside him were determined to stay there, buried deep.

He stared at the camera, completely lost now as the seconds silently crawled by. Another muffled gunshot sounded from somewhere outside. Niko glanced nervously at the door, but Elliott stared straight ahead at the camera, unflinching.

He picked up where Niko couldn't, his cool outward persona present in his tone as he began to speak. His voice boomed, loud, crisp, and clear as a bell.

"People of Delevia. Of Yhanwe-ha. Of Haneen. Of all civilized worlds within this galaxy. Can you hear me?

"My name is Elliott James Kestrel. Beside me is Niko Estrella, and together, we are Starhawk."

He'd actually used the name. In any other circumstances, it would have brought a smile to Niko's face, but all he could do now was listen.

"I am responsible for the deaths of seventeen members of a vast but secretive network who call themselves Honeybliss. You may know these people as trusted leaders. As inspiring creators. As a force of good within this galaxy that you can trust. Unfortunately, that's only a hollow and carefully curated image that they want you to see. The real truth is something far darker. As I speak, years of data I've compiled on the crimes of these individuals is being published across the internet. It's not something for the faint of heart. But bringing these crimes into the light is necessary.

"For years, I've tried to get this information out. I tried to get anyone to listen to me. The Galactic Police. The press. I was ignored, silenced, and even painted as delusional and unreliable, again and again. The files I tried to share online were quickly wiped clean. Now Honeybliss can hide no longer. Their names and faces will be known and evident in the videos they themselves recorded for entertainment and titillation.

"Haaltha-se, the Prime of Ghalaecua. Nurun-Jia, Senator of Delan-6. Nadeen Navarri, philanthropist and heiress. Horu Duu'mari, film director. Essthessvia, the Grand Sovereign of Yhanwe-ha..."

Niko listened as Elliott listed, in chronological order, all the Honeybliss members he'd assassinated. He included Du-uru Orkan, even though in the end it had been Bubblegum who'd taken him down. Two more gunshots—this time closer than the first—sounded just beyond the walls of the broadcasting station. Niko tried not to turn and look reflexively. He partially succeeded, his gaze still shifting toward the door.

"...Starhawk takes direct credit for and condones those kills only. Any other murders of politicians, celebrities, Galapol officers, and other civilians that have occurred are the result of copycat individuals seeking to raise our exceptional, combined bounty in order to capitalize off of it as much as possible."

"Y-you—" Niko cut in quietly. He hated how shaky and unsteady his voice sounded. Speech class in high school had always left him near to pissing himself, and this entire mess was an even deeper nightmare beyond comprehension. "You should know that the bounty has become a, um, w-weaponized gamble that's only putting lives in danger now. It's doing far more harm than good."

Elliott glanced at him and gave him a subtle but solid nod of encouragement. Then he looked back to the camera. More gunshots sounded around them. They were coming more frequently, and closer. Whatever was going on had now broken into a straight up hot zone shootout, from the sound of it. Death glanced nervously at the door. Niko didn't like the look in her eye. Then she turned her gaze on the two of them and swirled her finger through the air, indicating *wrap it the hell up. Fast.*

"Cala'di Senth. Hathasa Velor. Meghan Friess. Daranu. Jayson Cohl. Angela Kelsa. Marco Fulari. Ssavissthrya—"

Elliott was naming the victims now. Niko recognized several of them from the files. His heart hurt. This hadn't been a part of Elliott's notes. This was a moment of passion. He continued on, listing the names of people who were forever erased from the galaxy, their lives cut short by monstrous cruelty. There wasn't enough time. There was no way he could ever get through the list of the forgotten and dead with the moments they had left. That he'd memorized every name was admirable to Niko, and touched something wounded and sorrowful deep in his chest.

Death gestured at them again, more harshly this time, but Elliott kept talking, the names rambled off quickly now, as fast as he could say them. His tone was growing into something frantic, faltering from the cool and collected veneer he'd projected moments before.

"Babe—" Niko cut in quietly. He looked sorrowfully at Elliott. "It's time. We have to go."

Elliott stopped, his list aborted now. He looked wounded. When he spoke again, it was in a plea to the camera—and whomever stood watching on the other side of it. "There are too many to name. Remember them. Remember the lost. Honeybliss took their lives because they didn't view them as—"

A scattering of bullets pinged loudly off the exterior wall, causing Elliott to flinch and finally look. Niko ducked, pure reflex.

"—as people."

"Let's *go*," Niko said. He grabbed Elliott by the arm, pulling him away, but Elliott fought him, straining and wrestling against him until he'd pulled free.

His expression turned to something desperate.

"Cleo... Cleo Kestrel. Because of them, my sister never came home."

An explosion somewhere nearby rocked the entire building and the lights flickered.

"Cut it," Death snapped, and the background hologram changed to read OFF AIR, the light on the drone fading from green to red.

"Backdoor emergency exit," Death said. "This way. Let's go."

They jogged out of the studio and down a long hallway, pausing at the very end before the fire exit. Death pulled them into a small side room that appeared to be a heavily fortified emergency and storm shelter, then closed and locked the door. She turned to Niko.

"We're okay for a moment," she said. "They're holding it back, but they won't be able to for long."

"We—we should help you," Niko said. He was dizzy, shaking. Nothing was making sense. "What do you need, Deleera? We'll protect your people."

"No." She shook her head. The word had the weight of a concrete wall, immovable. "Not this time. You both need to get out of here. We'll hold our own, don't worry."

Guilt crept through him, but he nodded.

"Take a second," Death said. "We have that."

Niko sagged into himself and laid the helmet on a nearby counter, the weight of two beloved lives crushing down on him now. He'd made the call to go live. He may have just killed his stepfather, and couldn't stop that thought from looping through his mind like a razorblade, tearing him to shreds. He couldn't think of a worse fate for the people he loved. Honeybliss had proven its cruelty again and again. He wanted to scream until his lungs gave out.

Elliott pulled him into a long hug that Niko couldn't feel through the suit. The degree of isolation, of separation it caused him was infuriating right then. He wanted to tear it off piece by piece, throw the damn thing, go sit on the cool tile of the floor. More than that, he just wanted to feel the embrace being given to him. He wanted Elliott, wanted the comfort and warmth of him, human to human. After a moment, he wrapped his arms around Elliott, a small wave of relief driving back the gargantuan, skin crawling panic a fraction.

"We'll get them back," Elliott murmured. "I'll find them. I won't let anything happen to your family, Niko."

Death came over to him once Elliott had pulled away and clamped a hand firmly on Niko's shoulder, then pulled him into a tight hug of her own.

"Listen to me. The moment you find where they are, point me towards them. My people and I will have your back."

He swallowed back a lump of emotion growing thick in his throat. Niko had allies. He had friends. He had people who cared, who were willing to fight for and with him. Maybe this wasn't the end. Maybe it wasn't all lost, after all.

He briefly wondered if Elliott had felt the same emotions once, waking up in Baouban's cabin with Niko at his side, granted another day of life at the compassion of another.

He felt more grounded now, if only marginally. He owed them both so much, in so many ways.

"Thanks, guys," Niko said, clearing his throat.

His phone rang again, shattering the moment. He stared at Zann's holographic contact photo, letting it ring through, unable to force himself to answer this time. The idea made him ill.

"It's alright," Elliott said again. "We'll find them, Niko."

A moment later, several chimes sounded as text messages began pouring in. Niko reluctantly opened them.

*Niko, what the fuck?*

*What was that? Starhawk?*

*You really did this right now? You couldn't wait on this?*

*What do you think this is going to mean for Dad and Loolae?*

*This was his fucking idea, wasn't it.*

He exhaled sharply in frustration. Niko was getting tired of Zann jumping to blame Elliott for everything that happened; the call to go forward with the broadcast, after all, had been his own and no one else's.

*I swear to fuck if my dad gets killed because of Kestrel's murdering ass I'm not taking this rolling over. Fuck him.*

That was too much, a line crossed. He knew Zann was spiraling into panic, lashing out. But he wouldn't abide the threat, either. This wasn't really the time to start texting, but he couldn't bring himself to let that one lie.

*No, Zann. This was my call. Elliott disagreed with me. Strongly. But we weren't going to get another chance.*

*And we aren't going to get another dad,* Zann shot back. The words made Niko ache. He was at a loss, with nothing more to say.

After a moment, Zann texted again. *Look, I'm sorry. I'm not being fair. I know why you did it. But I'm scared, you know?*

*I know,* Niko sent. *I am too. But we'll find them. I promise, Zann. If it's the last thing I ever do.*

*Make sure it isn't, Niko,* Zann replied. *I can't lose you too.*

Niko swept the texts away.

"Okay. It's getting ugly out there. You both need to haul ass. Don't let yourselves be seen," Death said.

"Are you sure—" Elliott started.

"Do you think I've lived this long to be taken down by some rent-a-cops?" Death cut him off. Then her tone gentled. "Go."

Niko glanced at her. "I owe you, Deleera. More than I could ever repay."

"Don't worry about that anymore, Niko. This is bigger than any one of us now."

Their ride back aboard the *Soñadora* was agonizing. The tiny ship felt like a cage, its metal walls pressing down hard on Niko. Minutes melted into a miserable hour. They still had several ahead of them trapped in here. The moment they'd gotten alone again, Elliott's brave facade had fallen apart entirely. He paced around the cabin of the ship, his expression crumbling further and further into despair. Niko sat in the pilot's seat, unable to look at him. Or at anything. The sound of his boots against the floor as he paced was wearing a hole through Niko's flimsy reserves.

Elliott paused in the doorway to the cockpit. Niko glanced up at him, but the other man looked on the verge of throwing up, his skin ashen and waxy, expression miserable.

"I— Niko—" Elliott's words came slowly, as though he were choking on them. His eyes were full of pain and quiet terror. "This—this is all my fault. I got your ex-lover killed. Now your father is— Honeybliss—"

It was too much. Niko wanted to shut him out. He couldn't handle it. He could barely keep himself and the horror of his situation together, could barely even keep drawing in breaths at this point. He'd possibly—had *likely*, even—made the call that would see his father and longtime friend dead. He couldn't handle carrying Elliott and trying to gather all his shattering pieces too.

Niko stared at him. The pain on Elliott's face made guilt and shame strike him hard in the gut. Elliott wasn't a burden. He wasn't too much. "Come here," Niko muttered.

Elliott hesitated, then sat on the edge of the co-pilot's seat. Niko clasped one of his pale, trembling hands in both of his own tattooed, bronze ones, then raised it to his mouth and kissed it. "Elliott. Look at me. This wasn't you. You had nothing to do with this."

"But I did. If you had never helped—"

"*I* made the call, Elliott. I did. Not you. It was entirely on me. You wanted to shut the broadcast down. I'm the only one who gave the go ahead. This is on me. I chose it. Just like I chose to help you in the first place. Do you understand?"

"But I—"

"Don't take my choices away from me, Elliott." They both looked each other in the eyes, pleadingly. Elliott was clearly feeling the same helplessness and misery he himself felt. He was just as scared. Finally, he relented, seeming to deflate a little before reaching out and wrapping around Niko and holding him tightly.

The remainder of their drive back to the facility, Elliott held Niko against himself. He cradled him, holding Niko's head against his shoulder and stroking his hair.

The warmth of Elliott's shoulder against his cheek was a gentle balm. Niko watched the star lines quietly drift by outside the *Soñadora's* windshield. They seemed to have a lazy, careless flow to their movement, yet in truth the ship was passing entire solar systems so quickly that they all blurred into lines of light. He drifted in and out of sleep, a vicious headache beginning to tighten behind his eyes.

"It's going to be alright," Elliott said. "We're going to get them back. I'm going to find them. I won't give up until I do. I promise you that, Niko. I'll do anything I can."

*We're going to get them back. We're going to get them back.* Niko let the words run through his mind like a mantra, a singular wall pushing back against the choking despair of knowing he might be the one to have ended his father's life.

*It's going to be alright.* The thought came delivered on Elliott's low, silken voice. And somehow that made it more tangible. It made it something Niko could reach for, try to believe in.

"No more killing until we find them," Elliott said. His fingertips brushed the shell of Niko's ear as he stroked his hair. "I'll bring your family back home."

Niko frowned, a new layer of guilt threading into the rest that already churned through his gut. He knew how much putting an end to Honeybliss meant to Elliott. He'd made that quite clear on plenty of occasions.

But Niko knew pausing was for the best. They couldn't afford to provoke Honeybliss even worse than they already had. This was his family.

He recalled the break in Elliott's voice when he'd finally spoken his sister's name. He'd been so insistent on getting it out—enough to overpower and fight off Niko's grip on him.

Niko couldn't save Cleo Kestrel. He was and would always be too late for that now. Nor could he save his own mother and brother, who both rested quietly forevermore in a cradle of dark earth. But he could, maybe, still save his father and Loolae.

If it wasn't too late for them, too.

"Okay, babe," Niko murmured, his voice thick and syrupy in his throat. It was hard to get any words out.

"No more killing," Elliott said softly, and leaned down to plant a lingering kiss in Niko's hair.

# CHAPTER TEN
# HOME

THE WALLS OF THE facility's hangar pressed in on Niko just as badly as the ship's had, despite everything being too big, too open, too empty. The fluorescent lights above hummed quietly as they bore down on him. His head squeezed tightly as a crawling pain inched its way, throbbing, along the left side of his skull. A migraine. He knew he had likely stressed himself into developing it.

"I'm gonna go lie down for a while," he murmured, even more guilt compounding into the rest now. He should be getting to work. Searching. Researching. Piecing together anything he could find. But the thought made his head throb even more, nausea beginning to reach its icy fingers up through him.

"It's alright, Niko," Elliott said. "Get some rest. I'll take care of this. I'll make sure they're found."

It was meant to be a comfort, but the words only speared more shame through him. He should be the one to be doing this right now. Niko turned his face away. "Yeah."

"Niko," Elliott said. He reached up and took his face in his hands, stroking Niko's cheek with his thumb. Niko looked at him miserably before closing his eyes. He reached up to rest his hands over Elliott's. "I mean it. It's going to be alright. I won't let anything happen to your family. I'll make sure you see them safe and sound again. I've got you."

"Thanks." It was all Niko could force out, the word gravelly and thick. He was torn between deep, humbling appreciation and gnawing guilt. Elliott leaned forward and kissed him on the forehead before pulling away, then made his way through the hangar and into the facility. Niko was left alone, the very air itself a relentless weight pressing into every inch of him. He wheeled his way to the bedroom they shared, sliding the door closed behind him. He climbed out of the chair and onto the bed, with its mess of blankets—and water bottles on Elliott's side table—and turned down the lights until only the holographic clock interface left its faint, eidolic glow over everything.

He felt most comfortable here, buried away in a tiny, familiar space where he could close his eyes behind shut doors and try not to think.

It was so like him to hide away.

The thought made bile rise in his throat, feeding the nausea that churned within him. Niko had liked to think of himself as some kind of—of what? A *hero?* The audacity of that word and that he'd thought of it made him cringe in shame. Someone who tried to make a difference, then, at least? The truth, he realized, was that he was nothing. When things got hard, he hid away and shut off. Sometimes for years. Sometimes for a lifetime. Now he was hiding under a layer of blankets while Elliott and, somewhere out there, Zann tried to save his father's life.

*Pathetic,* his mind hissed at him. *It's all you are and it's all you've ever been.*

His head pounded with a blinding pain so intense it, the nausea, and the emotional agony that coursed through him were all one and the same.

His father. Oliver. Why hadn't Niko tried to take bigger steps to prevent this from happening? Why hadn't he thought to get him more protections? Zann had said Galapol had him under their watch and care—but why had he ever accepted that it would ever actually guarantee safety?

Why hadn't he been smarter? Better? *More?*

Niko's thoughts wandered to Zann. Zann was still out there, probably still living on Kaapra-19. If he was clever, he would have switched up his residence to avoid being a target too, gone into hiding. But would it be enough? Would it ever be enough? Joining Elliott and fighting for his cause was something Niko had just *done*—like he tended to do anything else in his life. Unthinking, spontaneous. Stupid. Niko had been so drawn to him, like a moth to a flame. He still was.

Zann had been so close with what he'd said about Elliott—only there had never been any manipulation involved. There was never any needed. Niko would follow Elliott anywhere. He was simply that hopeless, that enamored.

But in doing so, he hadn't thought about how that would affect the people closest to him. He hadn't thought of the shockwave of horrific repercussions his family—and Loolae—were enduring. He hadn't even considered her, hadn't considered that even his physical therapist might suffer for his choices. She and Oliver were somewhere dark now, in the hands of the worst people the galaxy had ever vomited up. Ones with a known history of making cruelty their point. Their entertainment, just because they could. Zann had lost his job and good standing with Galapol. And now his life was at risk, too.

Niko couldn't leave him behind. He couldn't let his choices bring his only remaining brother down.

He forced himself to sit up, the room spinning as his headache roared, then climbed—slowly, carefully—back into the chair.

Then he made his way through the facility, looking for Elliott, until he found him sitting in one of the lounges, pouring over several open holographic screens of research.

Elliott looked up, his features drawing into a worried frown. "Oh. Niko. Are you alright?"

Niko knew he must look like shit. He pushed away the question—it wasn't what mattered. *He* wasn't what mattered. "Hey, babe, I was thinking."

"Yes? Come over here. You don't look well."

Elliott had a gift for understatement, it seemed.

Niko made his way over, glancing at the research on Elliott's holograms, then quickly looking away. Their blue light was too intense right now and threatened to send his nausea into outright throwing up. Elliott noticed and hastily waved them away.

"My brother is still out there. And he's at risk now too. I don't want him hurt or dead because of me."

"You're right," Elliott said slowly. "Alright. Let's find a place where he can lay low. Where they're not going to find him."

Irritation spiked through Niko, hot and sharp. Wasn't it Elliott who had just needled him not long ago over so easily trusting Baouban for shelter?

"No, Elliott, that's not going to work. I want to bring Zann here."

"*Here*," Elliott said, as though the word were difficult to chew. He reached over and picked up a bottle of water, uncapping it. Niko knew exactly what he was doing, but patiently waited as Elliott bought himself time through a few swallows. "Do you really think that's the best idea, Niko?"

"Where the hell else is he going to go? Maybe Baouban would be up for another call."

Elliott winced. "Well, no, of course not— I didn't mean—"

"Elliott, it has to be here."

"We could find an isolated place. Somewhere like Sunorrna."

"So, he's just going to be damned to living in complete and utter isolation from here on out?"

"What about Lady Death's compound? She's fond of you and seems quite hospitable—"

"Are you really fucking doing this right now? You really want to stick a former Galapol agent in Dainna? This is my *brother*, Elliott. This is my family. He's not safe."

Elliott winced. The guilt was obvious on his face—as was the squirming discomfort. Niko knew he must hate the idea, must absolutely loathe that he'd ever even suggested it at all. This was Elliott's sanctuary, where he'd meticulously worked from the shadows since before he'd even started killing. Where Galapol could never find him. Niko was asking him to invite in the very man who had been one of Galapol's lead investigators. Who Elliott clearly didn't trust—at best.

Not to mention, Zann had, after all, shot him too. Twice.

But none of that knowledge eased the deep irritation that clung to Niko at Elliott's resistance. Nor did it soothe the growing urge to call him an asshole. The migraine definitely wasn't helping.

"Niko, I just—" Elliott chewed over the words for a moment. "Are you certain he's not still with Galapol? That this isn't some kind of—"

"Some kind of what? Takedown? Trap?"

"Yes."

"It's not. He hasn't asked to come here. He's not doing anything like that. He isn't trying to stir anything up or insert himself—"

"That's not true."

"What? What do you mean?"

"He was clearly trying to convince you I'm someone you shouldn't trust, and that you should stay away from me. That I'm using you. He was trying to separate and isolate you from me, maybe even turn you against me. It was quite obvious."

Niko went still, a chill running through him. He blinked at Elliott. "How do you know that?" he asked quietly.

"I was there, Niko. I heard him say it."

*So, that's what I was feeling.* He remembered the eerie sensation of being watched on Celelast.

Niko stared at him. For a moment, his body went numb, no words to give. Then a deep rage flared through him, quick as wildfire, devouring every inch of him. It filled his lungs, making him clench his jaw. The pain in his head was agonizing now, but he paid it no attention. It only fed into his anger.

"You were there? You fucking followed me? I asked to do that *alone*, Elliott! I told you that! I told you I needed that!" Niko had started yelling. He couldn't help himself now, his pulse hammering against his skin. He was too angry to calm down. "*What the fuck?!*"

Elliott shrank away from him subtly. Niko's anger seemed to cow him a bit, the other man looking nervous, if not outright scared of him. Memories of what Elliott had told him about his father's shouting and abuse lanced through Niko's mind and a ghost of guilt crept inside him.

"You *were* alone. I stayed out of your way. Neither of you even knew I was there, until I said something just now," Elliott said quietly.

"That's not alone. I told you I needed that for myself. I *told* you that," Niko asserted, willing his volume to quiet to something marginally less aggressive now.

"Niko, I'm..." Niko thought he was about to apologize, but instead, he plowed right on. "I'm not sorry, if that's what you're expecting. The risk to you going out and doing that alone was just too much. What if he had been bait from Galapol to get to you? What if there had been agents there lying in wait? What if it had been something else entirely? Everything either one of us does now comes with an immense risk. I wasn't about to let you throw your life away by walking into what had a high probability of being a trap."

Niko was stunned. It was hard to breathe—somehow, the nausea had crept up into his chest, his lungs. "It doesn't matter, Elliott. When I ask you to let me do something for myself or by myself, I mean that I need that space. What the hell would you have done, anyway, if it *had* been a trap? Would you have just taken the headshot on my brother? Like he was one of your Honeybliss hit jobs?" He was getting too worked up now, his voice rising again.

Elliott flinched. "No. *Never*." He looked ill. "No, I was just going to make sure you made it back home to me."

Niko winced. *Home. Back home to me.* He hated this, hated that they were embroiled in conflict. But he was too far gone to stop it now.

"It's— This was deceitful, Elliott."

"You haven't been entirely truthful yourself, Niko, if we want to go there. You intentionally withheld context about your situation with Lady Death, because you knew I'd never accept reaching out to her if I knew the full, *real* story and the fact that you'd disappeared for years on poor terms with a lethally dangerous and influential bounty hunter.

"What *you* told me before that was *hours'* worth of feel-good stories about the Revolutionary of Sala taking you under her wing. What we both actually walked into was a situation you didn't even know was going to turn out even marginally alright. But I chose to trust you regardless, even after what was really going on came to light."

"Fuck," Niko murmured. Of course Elliott would never get caught in a fight unarmed. He pinched the bridge of his nose, willing himself to calm down. He was trembling, not from anger, but rather nerves now. He didn't want to fight Elliott, didn't want this to turn into something volatile and resentful.

And he'd had a point. Niko had lied to him too.

"You're right. I fucked up. I did lie to you, because we needed this so badly and I was scared. I knew you wouldn't take the chance if you knew the real risk. It was stupid of me, and it was wrong. And it could have gotten both of us really fucking hurt. So, I'm sorry, Elliott."

"I followed you to Celelast because I was scared too. I needed to know you were going to survive. I can't bear the thought, Niko."

In the end, Elliott had only been trying to protect him by keeping watch on Celelast—even if he'd done it in the most infuriating, insulting, and dickbag sort of way. It was all they'd ever done for each other, since they'd started working together instead of against one another. They watched out for and protected each other.

But regardless, it had still encroached on the privacy Niko had requested. He had boundaries and needed to reaffirm them. "I appreciate that you want to protect me, Elliott. I do. It means so much to me. And I want to do the same for you. But it's like we said before, we have to trust each other, or this is all going to fall apart.

"On our first mission working together, when you went out to set those EMP charges and I had to wait around hoping you made it back, all I wanted to do was go make sure you were okay, or go do it myself instead, or... I don't know. Take all the risk on by myself. But I get it. I wanted to interfere, but I didn't let myself. I had to trust you to work on your own and know what you were doing, because you'd told me to let you do that. I just want you to do the same for me when I request that you hold back, alright? I need you to let me have things for myself sometimes, even if it comes at a risk."

Elliott tilted his chin up, brows slanting down into a regal scowl. Niko knew he had to be working through the same internal struggle that he himself often did. Finally, he relented, the porcelain veneer cracking. He looked depressed. "You're right. I'm... I'm sorry that I was present when you'd asked me not to be.

That I heard what you hadn't wanted me to. I disrespected you. I couldn't bear the thought of losing you, and so I did the wrong thing."

Niko let out a slow breath. "Thanks—"

"But that still doesn't mean we should trust Zann being in this place. We can find a better solution. I have a lot of evidence as to why he's still likely Galapol's plant. It wasn't *you* they'd wanted—"

"Elliott—"

"—It was *me*. Or both of us, rather. But I'm the primary target; I've killed more. I'm the one who started this. So, they're probably using you to get to me and—"

"El—"

He wouldn't let Niko get a word in.

"Why do you think your father was taken when Galapol was said to have been surveilling them? How do you think it's possible that could happen and nobody knows anything about it? And that he was the one communicating to them about keeping an eye on him? Do we even know Honeybliss has them? What if it's actually a setup by Galapol to draw us out? Niko, this is all part of a complex plan and Zann's involved—"

"*Elliott.*" He kept his voice from rising this time, but pushed the name firmly. Elliott finally fell quiet. Niko hated how his last points had merit and weight—after all, he had found himself wondering, too, how Galapol had conveniently missed the physical therapist and Oliver's abductions. "It's not going to be like that. He's just going to stay here with us."

*Until this all blows over*, he wanted to say. But there was no blowing over. This was the rest of their lives now. Even if he and Elliott never spoke to nor saw each other again, they had imbued each other's fates and futures permanently, like two blazing stars colliding, their plasma spilling into one another. Once they'd crossed paths, it was impossible to ever separate again.

He was forever bound by Elliott Kestrel's gravity. And so was, unfortunately, everyone else Niko still loved in this life now too.

"Niko, I—I'm sorry. It's too much of a risk. He's too close to Galapol. Once he's in this place we can never undo it. We could be handing the keycard to our front door to the entire galaxy. We have to think of our survival first."

Niko hated how much he could see where he was coming from—the paranoia, cleverness, caution, and fear had all kept Elliott alive this incredibly far into his mission. He couldn't blame him.

But the cold rejection hurt, regardless. It hurt like a bitch. And it was a pain he felt in his chest, constricting the beat of his heart.

"He's my brother," Niko said quietly, any fight and energy draining from him as the migraine and its nausea surged even stronger. He was so weak, so flimsy. He could hear the exhaustion and surrender in his own voice.

He was failing. Again.

"I'm sorry, Niko. I'll figure something out," Elliott said. "I promise you." Niko didn't want to see the guilt on his fine features. He wanted to look anywhere but at Elliott. He turned and wheeled back out of the room, back to the bedroom-turned-cave, where he buried himself in blankets again, and lost himself to the lonely dark and blinding pain.

"Mh?" Niko woke to a sound. Dim light poured into the room through the hallway outside. Elliott sat on the edge of the bed, his body twisted so he could look at Niko. In the dark like this, he was all shadow and shapes, ephemeral form. Niko glanced at the clock, which read 7:09 p.m. It was useless to him anyway; he couldn't remember when he'd fallen asleep. It felt like he'd been down for a while. His headache still lurked, but it was a whimper instead of the raging roar from before.

"Niko," Elliott murmured. He reached out to touch the back of Niko's hand, but stopped himself, his fingertips hovering unfelt an inch above. Then he pulled his hand away. He scooted across the bed until he was sitting back against its plain, gray headboard now. "I'm so sorry. You were right. I was just afraid."

"I get it," Niko mumbled.

"This is your home too, now. Your brother can stay here. He deserves shelter too. And you deserve to keep your family safe. If you trust him, I'll trust him."

Niko hummed, turning over onto his back and stretching. He reached his hand out to Elliott, who, after a moment of hesitation, took it. His skin was cool to the touch. Elliott rubbed tiredly at his eyes with his free hand. Niko wondered how long he'd sat, scowling at countless holograms, trying to find the answers that would save Niko's family, all while warring with himself over whether to let a dangerous stranger into what was his last line of defense.

"Thank you," Niko said. He hesitated. "Listen, Elliott. I'm sorry he hurt you before. And that's something I should have acknowledged too. You have a pretty damn good reason for not wanting someone who shot you here. So... if—" It was hard to say the words, but he forced himself to. "—you don't want him here, we'll find another way. Okay?"

Elliott shook his head. "It's fine, Niko."

"It's not. Talk to me, *please.*"

"You and I both shot at each other with the intent to wound or kill. I understand why he did it. He wanted to protect you. And you were both working for Galapol then, trying to stop me from killing anymore."

Niko squeezed his eyes shut, remembering both times he'd tried—and failed—to convince Zann to side with them both and work against Honeybliss instead of Elliott. In the end, though, his brother's hands had been tied. But they weren't tied anymore.

"This is your..." Niko trailed off, searching for the right word. *Home* felt like a stretch when describing the sprawling, featureless halls of the facility. Yet, that was exactly what Elliott had called it twice now. Not just his home, but theirs. "Home. This is someone I know you don't trust. But he *is* my brother. He's my family. He might be my *only* family left now." The idea left him breathless. "I've already fucked up and gotten my father taken by them. I can stop it from happening to Zann too. In the end, though, I want your honest and full consent. If you don't want him here, I'll respect it. But if you do, I'll make sure he... uh, behaves, I guess."

"It's fine, Niko. Really, it is. You've given everything to help me and I want to do the same for you. I want to show up for you too. If you trust your brother to be here, then I accept. Though, I won't promise we'll be friends." He hesitated, and Niko could see how much he had to force himself to push out the next words. "Your father and Loolae, too. They can stay here once we liberate them. So long as word doesn't get out, no one will ever find them here."

"We'll take care of each other, okay? I won't let anything happen to you," Niko said, looking up at him. He ran his thumb along the back of Elliott's hand, tracing its contours. The idea of having everyone he loved—Zann, Oliver, Loolae, Elliott—here in one place, together and alive, filled Niko with a quiet, shyly blossoming hope. Even if it meant having them all exist in this oppressive, abandoned mining facility.

He just missed them, profoundly.

He wouldn't trade Elliott for anything in the galaxy, but the steep cost of being at his side had been a stunning sort of isolation. "You'll be alright, Elliott. I'll make sure of it."

Elliott smiled, though he looked tired. "So will you." He yawned. "I'm going to get back to it. I'm narrowing down who would be most likely to have the audacity, manpower, and ties to

Galapol to get through their supposed watch of your father. If they're not staging the whole thing."

"How long have you been researching?" Niko asked.

Elliott glanced at the clock. "Five and a half hours."

Niko winced. "Take a break with me, okay?"

Elliott looked uncomfortable. He hesitated. "I don't know. I really want to get back to this. I'd hate to waste a moment we can't spare."

"Yeah, but you need to take care of yourself, too. Just for a bit. Dinner and a nap with me. I'll wake you after an hour."

"I guess I could do that." Elliott didn't sound convinced.

"Come on."

They went to the cafeteria, where Niko began making tinga de pollo. He'd originally wanted Elliott to relax while he cooked, but a glance out from the kitchen to the table he'd sat at revealed he was taking the opportunity to get right back to researching, a dozen holograms spread in the air before him. Niko called him into the kitchen with the excuse that he could use help processing the vegetables.

They ate in contemplative silence, Elliott thanking him for the meal, then returned to the bedroom, where he held Niko as he drifted off to sleep, their bodies pressed together. Glimpses of things they could do whispered through Niko's mind—Elliott leaning in to kiss the back of his neck, buried wholly inside him as Niko lay face down on the bed, clutching the sheets tightly. The low moans Elliott would likely make in response. Niko felt himself grow hard, but the other man had already drifted off to sleep, his breathing growing shallow and slack against the back of Niko's shoulder.

Niko didn't want to wake him, especially after all he'd done for him in his hours of dedicated, tireless research. Instead, he leaned forward and planted a gentle kiss on Elliott's hand, then closed his eyes.

The gesture had woken him regardless, it seemed. Elliott shifted to wrap around Niko tighter, burying his face in the crook of his neck in a way that elicited a chill of pleasure.

"I love you, Niko."

The words left Niko breathless, goosebumps prickling along his skin in the surprise and delight of hearing them. Warmth trickled through him like sunlight glimmering on the surface of water. For a moment, he forgot about anything outside of Elliott. He craned his neck to look back over his shoulder at him.

Elliott looked at him sleepily, then leaned forward and met him in a kiss. Then he moved to Niko's neck and shoulder, his lips brushing softly against them, his breath warm on his skin. Niko's own breaths were coming in quiet, shallow gasps now. He wanted it so badly, wanted what he'd envisioned with him. Maybe now more than ever before.

"Do—" Niko started, barely murmuring. There was something he wanted to say, something he wanted to request. He wanted what he'd pictured. He wanted to feel Elliott within him, made a part of him. But even now, something sharp inside him snagged and kept him from putting it exactly into words. Instead, he wandered. "Do you want to...?"

Elliott responded with more attentive kisses to Niko's neck and jaw. He was quite obviously waking up again now. He combed his fingertips through Niko's messy hair and then down his side to rest along his hip in a way that drove him wild. Niko turned over to lie flat on his belly, his backside exposed for the taking now, all in offering to Elliott. He hoped what he couldn't say in words was clear enough through actions.

Elliott rolled over slightly so that he was lying on top of Niko now. The pressure and weight of him was dizzying and delicious. Niko heard him fumble through the bedside table drawer where they kept the lubrication, his erection and need pushing against Niko now, straining against the fabric of his pants. He leaned in and ran his hand along Niko's side and back, then bent down to kiss him along the neck again. Everywhere he touched bloomed with life, with sensation, like a painter gifting streaks of vibrant color to an empty canvas.

*"Please,* Elliott."

"I'll take care of you," Elliott murmured in his ear, voice dark, liquid, and lovely. He rocked his hips, needy erection grinding against Niko. "Lover. My Niko."

Elliott pulled Niko's pants and boxers down just enough to expose what was needed, then did the same to himself. Once he'd prepped them, he slid inside easily and Niko let out a soft, involuntary moan. He'd wanted this so badly.

Elliott buried his face in Niko's shoulder, leaving warm, sensuous kisses along it. He ran his hands along Niko, light as a dream. This wasn't vulgar. It wasn't fucking. It was something else. Making love, maybe. Only Elliott's breathing and the soft sounds of their joining filled the quiet room, until, with an electric thrill of both excitement and affection, Niko heard his breaths turn into low, lovely moans. They were his favorite sound.

Niko couldn't help the few soft sounds that escaped himself as well, so given to the moment. He wanted this forever with him, wanted it to never end.

But as all things, it was eventually over, Elliott sighing into Niko's mouth as they came together. Once they'd cleaned up, Elliott wrapped around him again, leaving quiet kisses along Niko's shoulder.

"I wanted to tell you for a long time," Elliott said, his words already hazy at the edges again with fatigue, "how much I've loved you."

Despite every harrowing thing that lay waiting for him beyond the shelter of Elliott's warm embrace, as he drifted off to sleep, Niko felt a peace he had never known before.

He was home.

# Chapter Eleven

# IT'S PERSONAL

"Zann," Niko breathed into the phone. His hands were shaking. He cleared his throat for the third time, trying to ease back some of the wild nervousness that had arisen in making this call.

"Niko. I've been trying to track down who the fuck could have pulled something like this. I've got a few possible leads, but I'm not getting far." His brother's voice grew gravelly with agitation. "I was supposed to be there with him, Niko. I was staying with him and making sure he was okay. And they ended up hitting while I was out on a fucking errand. Getting Ch'ua's fucking piece of shit chicken. I wish I had access to Galapol's fucking files. If I could get their data—"

"I don't think that's a good idea right now," Niko said, slowly. "They were supposed to have eyes out on him, weren't they? What if they're in on this?"

Elliott may have had a point.

Zann hissed out a sigh, the sound staticky over the phone line. "I know. I know that. But I still wish I had access to everything they know. Cut off from their database and left to try and figure all this shit out on my own feels like I'm stuck doing it crippled."

Niko was silent for a moment. "...Really? Zann?"

The silent horror that was likely running through his brother as he realized his fuckup was almost tangible. "Shit. Fuck, sorry. I didn't mean— I wasn't thinking— Look, I haven't slept since any of this started."

Niko shook his head. "Where are you staying right now?"

"I'm still on Kaapra-19, but laying low. In an old shit hotel in District Twenty-One, where you can pay in cash and don't have to register your real name."

"Hey, so I wanted to propose something. You probably aren't going to like it, either."

"Well, add it to the pile, then. Let's hear it."

"I want you to come stay here."

The gentle hum of the call's background filled the air before Zann spoke. "Here. Where, exactly, is here?"

"Uh, to where Elliott and I have been staying."

"What happens if I go there?"

Niko sighed, shifting to try and get more comfortable in his wheelchair. He looked up at the ceiling, where fluorescent white lights glared down at him. "What happens is you come here and lay low instead. It's not safe out there anymore. If they got Dad and Loolae, they're probably turning their gaze your way too. It's just a matter of time now. You'll be safe here, though. Nobody knows about this place, and if we're careful, they're not ever going to."

He could imagine Zann's mannerisms—chewing on his full lips, dark eyes glancing about in thought. Turning a pen over and over in his hand, fidgeting with it. Or maybe it was an unlit cigarette now.

"And does your murder boyfriend know you're asking this? He cool with this?"

"We, uh, talked a lot about it, yeah. He knows. He's okay with it."

"So, you think I'm safer there with Serial McKiller than I am out here? You know, the same guy who we both know has been manip—"

"Zann," Niko cut him off. "You know why he's been killing them. *I'm* killing them too. They're monsters, and nobody gives a shit that they are. He's not just murdering anyone he fucking comes across. They killed his sister. It's personal."

An odd beat of silence fell across the phone line before Zann spoke. "I mean, technically... Eh, sure. You could put it like that. Fucked him right up, too."

"How could you be anything but fucked up, after seeing any of that sick shit happen to the only family you had? Those videos were even worse than the recording of Mom and Ryen. I don't know how I'd stay sane, seeing the footage he did if it was someone that close to me in it."

"...You watched *all* those videos, Niko?" Zann said slowly. "Every one?"

"I did. Listen, he isn't going to do jack shit to you. In fact, you're the one who tried to straight up murder him. You shot him point blank. Twice. Remember that?"

"So, he's really going to love me being there, then."

"Look, Zann. We talked about it. He says it's okay. I'm asking a lot of him to do this. I'm asking *everything* to let you in here. This is a show of trust. And stop fucking saying he's manipulating me. You think he's pulling my strings and he's convinced you're a Galapol plant."

Zann honked out a laugh. "Galapol plant? I mean, that's *exactly* what I was, up until they fucking fired me!" His voice grew into a half shout and Niko winced.

"Well, he's convinced you still work there."

"Yeah, I wish I did. Then maybe I could make some actual useful progress on finding our dad."

"Listen. Are you going to come here, or not? I can't keep you safe if you're not here, Zann. We can work together again. I—I miss you."

Zann was quiet for a moment. "Yeah, I miss you too, Niko. Everything's really hit the fan lately." He seemed to hesitate a moment, before adding, "You know, it's not that I don't feel for the guy. Believe me, I *do*. I just—"

"I know, I know. You don't agree with what he's— What we're doing."

"Yeah. This is a dangerous game, Niko. The most dangerous in the entire galaxy. But— You know what? Fine. Yeah. I'll go with you. It *is* a matter of time before I'm next. I'm only here out of sheer, dumb luck. If I'd been at my apartment or Dad's place at the time, it would've been me too. These fuckers took him. And I said I wanted to help you with Honeybliss. So, let's do it. No more fucking around. But there are a few things I need to take care of here first. Give me a day."

Warmth spread through Niko's chest at knowing he'd see his brother again soon—and that they'd get to work together like they always had. The thought washed a buoyant brightness through him, granting a brief respite of normalcy against the backdrop horror of his situation. "Yeah. A day. We can do that, Zann."

"You going to come meet me somewhere, or am I going there?"

"No, we'll come pick you up. Meet at Celelast again?"

"That works. Hey, have you been watching the news since your broadcast stunt?"

Niko tensed. "No, actually. I've—" *Been hiding away like a coward.* "Been preoccupied."

"Sure. Check it out, though. Everyone's going nuts. It's all the news stations are talking about, day and night. You had some real shit timing with that whole thing, but you guys actually got through to people. I think they might actually cancel the damn bounty." He sounded surprised.

Niko let out a long, slow breath, the air that flowed from him seeming to carry the crushing weight and tension he'd been carrying with it. "That's great. That's... Wow."

"Yeah. Take a look. Anyway, I'd better get to it. See you soon, Niko."

It felt good to have a victory.

Niko closed his eyes and smiled. "See you soon, Zann."

Niko wheeled back into the lounge that Elliott had planted himself in again while he researched. He couldn't help the grin that spread its way across his face, and felt a prickle of goosebumps at the anticipation and excitement of being able to share the good news with him. He knew Elliott was going to love this—if he didn't already know about it.

Elliott paused in his research, gesturing a cluster of holograms away, his green eyes focused on Niko now. He frowned, but it was something light and quizzical, rather than the nervous one he usually wore. "What is it?"

Niko made his way over to Elliott's side. "Have you been watching the news?"

Elliott hesitated, glancing away. Niko could swear he looked a little sheepish. "I— Ah, no. No, I've been busy with this."

Niko's grin only grew. He knew what Elliott was doing. He'd been avoiding it.

"Why? What happened?" Elliott prodded.

"I'm not going to tell you," Niko teased, parroting Elliott's earlier presentation of the *Soñadora's* new stealth system. "Instead, you'll have to see." He opened a new hologram from his phone of live newsfeed. On it, two Gheroun reporters were excitedly trying to predict if the bounties on Elliott and Niko's heads were going to be dropped. They speculated on the name of Starhawk. Their chatter was spliced with various replays of clips from the footage Elliott had gathered—with the victims' faces and certain anatomy all blurred out—and clips of him speaking from his live statement. From the view of the camera, he was serious, composed, professional. He spoke articulately.

Beside him on the broadcast, Niko looked painfully nervous—miserable, even, his eyes unwilling to directly meet the camera far more than he'd realized at the time—and stayed clammed up, aside from his single, stuttering debut.

He'd only just learned devastating news, though. It was all he'd been able to do to keep himself together. He just prayed nobody would start trying to suggest he was Elliott's hostage, or something. That would be the last thing they'd need.

Niko looked back at the Elliott on the newsfeed, his heart swelling with pride. This was his boyfriend. This was the man he'd chosen to believe in. He felt so in love, brimming full with it, the sugared sensation of it threatening to spill over.

"Not to mention this footage itself," one of the reporters continued. "Awful, awful stuff. The link to those files has so much more than we can even show on television. It's all pretty damning. A lot of people are going to be in big trouble now."

"This is something that's shaking up the entire galaxy, folks," the other Gheroun said, blinking her three wide, golden eyes. "Coming up after this break: is Elliott Kestrel, once feared and detested across the galaxy, actually starting to gain *fans*, instead? Stay tuned to hear about how some people have begun to express sympathy for Galapol's number one most wanted."

The broadcast cut to a sports drink commercial and Niko swiped it away, silence filling the room again now. He looked at Elliott, unable to take his eyes off him. He wanted to kiss him senseless, until Elliott couldn't think anymore. Until they both forgot who they even were. The jubilant grin from before made its way back across Niko's face as he watched the man beside him.

Elliott sat, stunned and frozen, his skin turned a shade paler. His expression was profound—eyes wide with a mixture of shock, pain, and hope. His lips were parted slightly. For a moment, Niko thought he might actually cry. But instead, he seemed to snap out of it, composing himself again, and looked back at Niko.

Elliott swallowed. He was starlight made tangible, all of it contained in the radiant reflection of his eyes. "*Niko.*"

Niko's grin widened. He was smiling so hard now that his face was beginning to hurt. "I know, babe. Zann thinks they're really going to cancel the bounty, too."

Elliott shivered, a subtle thing. He absentmindedly snaked up a hand to tug at the collar of his turtleneck, long fingers playing at its edge. "Niko, I—I've tried to get this out for years. I thought it would never change. I thought no one would ever listen."

"I listened, Elliott," Niko said. He couldn't help himself, reaching over and taking the hand that still played at Elliott's collar, and held it tightly. "Even if no one else did, you had someone who heard you and believed you. And now you have the entire galaxy listening. *We did it, Elliott.*"

"Niko." Elliott cupped his cheek with his free hand and leaned forward, kissing him deeply once, twice, several times until they were lost in each other. Niko couldn't help but smile again once they finally parted, and reached up to comb at his wild blond tresses. "Thank you. For everything. For listening. For being here. I... I couldn't have done this without you."

"Yeah, well, none of this would even be possible without *you*, Elliott. You're the one who was brave enough to stand up to them."

Elliott searched his gaze with his own, his sea of green vivid and passionate. He looked alive and free in a way Niko desperately loved seeing, like something from his case photographs, back from before Honeybliss had ever taken his sister away. It was unspeakably precious, something so rare and wonderful that Niko found he would do anything to bring that look back again and again.

And then, just as quickly, it all fell away, replaced with a somber shadow.

"I can't afford to celebrate right now," Elliott muttered, seemingly more to himself than Niko.

"I think you deserve at least that much, babe," Niko said.

"No." Elliott turned away from him now, summoning his wall of holograms back to hover before him. Documents, portraits, and political histories filled Niko's vision in harsh blue. "Not until your family is home safe. Not until I know that they're alright. We need to find them."

Niko hesitated. He wanted to give Elliott his moment in the sun. But the man had a point, and thinking about it slammed Niko back onto the ground under the harsh press of gravity. "Okay, Elliott," he said, finally. "We keep going." He paused, before adding, "Hey, um. Zann said he's going to come, but needs a day. I'm going to pick him up in Celelast. I can go by myself or—"

"I'm coming with you," Elliott said quickly. Then he added, a little hesitantly, "If it's alright with you."

Niko smiled again, though it was only a mere ghost of the celebratory jubilation from before, this time something fond, subtle, warm. He was grateful to Elliott. Grateful for the selfless grace he'd exhibited when he'd pushed to cancel the broadcast that had meant everything to him to instead protect Niko's family. Grateful that he'd agreed to let Zann stay. And grateful that he was being mindful now with Niko, respecting the boundaries he'd communicated before.

"It's alright, babe. I want you there with me. In the meantime, let me help you with the research. Whatever you need. You don't need to try and do this alone. We'll find them."

"We'll find them," Elliott said. "Let's get to work."

Zann stepped onto the *Soñadora*, glancing around its cramped interior. In his hands were two dark, heavy duffel bags, so overstuffed that angles jutted out from their sides at random intervals, making them into abstractions. "Been a while since I've seen the inside of this thing."

"Well, get used to it," Niko said. "It's going to be a four-and-a-half-hour ride back."

Zann's gaze then landed warily on Elliott. Niko could almost feel the electric tension in the air between the two men. Elliott stared back at him, expressionless and watchful. Zann smirked. "Hey there, killer. Long time no see."

"Oh, yes. Not long enough," Elliott murmured.

This was going to be fun.

Zann's smirk only grew. He set his bags down, then sank into the co-pilot's seat, the one Elliott typically sat in now during their travels. Elliott stood in the tiny cabin of the ship, arms crossed tightly over his chest. Niko rolled his eyes, then shut the door to the ship and sat down in the pilot's seat. He punched in the coordinates for the facility, the ship beginning to ascend.

"Sit down, babe," he murmured to Elliott. There were no other seats, so the other man simply sat on the floor in the cabin, clutching tightly to a support bar along the wall. "You good?"

"I'm alright," Elliott said. Niko hated having him sit on the floor, but it felt a little weird to eject Zann from the seat, and even Niko had enough wherewithal to know asking Elliott to come sit in his lap right now probably wouldn't go over well.

All three of them were jostled to and fro as the ship shook, resistance from Celelast's atmosphere pushing back against them. Then they were in the quiet dark of open space, rising slightly from where they sat before Niko switched on artificial gravity and set the course back to RM-9832642G.

"So," Zann said, releasing the position lock on the co-pilot's chair and spinning back and forth in half circles. "I brought you some presents."

Niko eyed him warily. "You did?"

"Yeah. Got some shit from Galapol's archives."

Niko sat up straight as a rod, opening his mouth, but Elliott beat him to the punch, speaking first. "How did you get that?"

Zann smirked, spinning another half circle, then swinging back around again. "It's probably better I spare you the details."

Elliott shot Niko a sharp look, clearly on edge. Niko could hear the words in his voice without them even being spoken. *He's with Galapol, Niko. This was a horrible idea.*

Niko sighed. "Zann, how the hell did you get anything from the archives?"

"So, you remember Naanu Kiit?" Zann asked.

"The Toliai secretary from Logistics?" Naanu was, in fact, hard to forget. Toliai were rare as white-collar workers and the department had scrambled to accommodate her thirteen-foot tall, scaly, four-legged self by installing a customized chair and desk. She was also, unfortunately, one of those types of people who mistook any sort of professional politeness as potential romantic interest, so Niko had kept a cordial distance when he'd had to speak to her.

"Yep. She works graveyard shift. I still had my ID badge, though it doesn't work for shit since they disabled it. But she had no idea I got fired since she's in an entirely different level of the building. I played up that the research division check-in systems were being overhauled and that I brought the old version of the badge by accident. You know how she is. I just flirted her up for about fifteen minutes and she let me right through. Helps that I remembered her favorite latte flavor and brought it too. And that I'm very aware of when the door cop takes his smoke breaks every night."

Niko blinked at him. "You— No. You flirted with the Toliai secretary and she just. Let you walk right in with no badge. To Galactic Police Station Twelve. And then let you into their archives."

"No, no. All she did was get me inside," Zann corrected, wagging a finger. "Getting to the evidence archives was all *me*. That was a hell of a wild half hour trying to avoid anyone who recognized me."

"You're shitting me, Zann."

"Nope."

"You don't actually believe this, do you, Niko?" Elliott ventured.

Niko had no words. If anyone else had told him this story, he *wouldn't* believe them, straight up. But this was Zann, and Zann was staring at him with squinted, dark eyes, looking quite pleased with himself.

"No fucking way," Niko said.

"*Yes* fucking way. Anyhow, I made it quick. Grabbed some shit and got out fast before anyone realized what was going on. I figure it'll help us get some answers. You're welcome, by the way."

"Zann," Niko mumbled, anxiety webbing throughout his chest.

"I figure Chief owes me big time anyway for replacing me with that slimebag douche-freighter, Fourier. Dude had such an obvious hard-on for murder," Zann said. He glanced back at Elliott over his shoulder. "No offense, or anything. I know your ass has an extra-strength prescription for murder boner enhancement."

"Only when I'm in the special mood for it," Elliott purred.

"Which is pretty much all the time, if your track record is any indication. Anyway, I haven't had a chance to go through most of the data yet, but I got a lot of classified files. Copied them onto a blank hard drive," Zann continued. He held up a tiny, translucent data chip, looking at Niko. "Maybe now I can figure out how the fuck Dad managed to get taken when they were supposed to be watching him. Because, curiously, Galapol didn't seem to have answers to give me."

"Are you surprised?" Elliott asked.

Zann spun in his chair to look at him. "Yeah. A little. But I have a feeling whatever I find in here is going to tell me I shouldn't be."

"I can tell you the same, without even having to look."

"We'll see. Oh, and I got you this thing, Niko," Zann said. He pulled one of the bags over and started rifling through it, until he procured a familiar looking orange orb with two spindly arms and an old Lord Fukkaho lyric sticker that read FUKK YA NOISE ORDINANCE, FUKK YA HOES pasted to its backside.

*Tina.*

"Figured you missed it," Zann quipped, clearly knowing Niko was doing anything but. He tossed her at him without warning, and Niko caught the little bot reflexively with both hands.

"What is that?" Elliott asked, perking up.

Niko groaned. "An old disability assistance bot he got me years ago."

"You love that thing. I know you do," Zann said.

"Yeah, sure," Niko grumbled. Yet, peering down at the deactivated little bot, Niko couldn't help but feel an unexpected pang of nostalgia. His life felt normal for a brief moment at the sight of her, the little clueless and bumbling bot who'd become a constant background presence to his shut-in days. She'd been the closest thing he'd allowed himself to a friend. He could almost picture her hovering around his apartment still, tiny engines whirring, cleaning up the depression messes he'd always left lying around.

Yet nothing was normal anymore, and she sat unresponsive in his hands, cheery virtual interface gone dark, parts clearly removed from her for data capture.

He felt an utterly pointless pang of guilt for having left her behind.

"Maybe you can... do something with this," Niko said, handing her off to Elliott. "Zann, I can't believe you broke into the Galapol archives to get a fucking assistant bot."

"Nah, I just saw it lying there all dejected and dead looking and thought of you. The real treasure is in these files," Zann said.

Elliott puzzled over T1-N4, turning her over in his hands. "An old T1-N4. Second generation, after they'd ironed out the primary bugs, but before more advanced AI capabilities were iterated. This is, ah, *quite* a basic model. See how the arms don't have full rotational functionality?" His eyebrows rose, unimpressed, when he found the sticker. Then he pried open a small panel on her side and fished around inside it, before glancing at Zann. "The tracking module is missing."

"Yeah, I'm not an idiot."

"Astounding. But did you think to check your phone?"

"Destroyed my old one. I have a burner phone with tracking disabled. Anything else you want to try asking?"

"Yes. Though, I doubt you'll be honest. Are you working for Galapol?"

Zann laughed. "I fucking wish I was. I had a pretty nice job there, you know? Had great dental."

"I had a nice job too, building more sophisticated versions of things like this," Elliott said coolly, "before Honeybliss destroyed my life."

"Yeah? Niko said they doctored your files. So, did you ever actually work at LaraTech making fancy robot AI, or was that their lie too?"

Niko flushed, realizing he'd never taken more time to actually ask Elliott more about the truth of his life versus what had been in those files. They'd been so caught up in just *surviving*.

Elliott narrowed his eyes. "I worked at LaraTech, yes. Design engineer of the robotics division. I didn't program machine AI, but conducted root-cause failure analyses on the physical models."

Zann whistled. "So, you really were a smartypants, huh? Makes sense, with all that irritating assed tech you have."

"If my technology irritates you, then I consider it a success."

Niko sighed. "Okay, okay, guys. If you're going to be like this the entire time, this isn't going to work out."

The ship fell into a tense silence, his brother and boyfriend regarding each other warily. Niko shook his head. He peered out at the star lines flowing past them, entire solar systems there and gone in the blink of an eye.

His attention drifted back to Zann, the telltale blue of holographic display catching his eye as his brother began to fish through the files he'd gotten.

"There's some interesting shit in here. I wasn't able to grab much; I only had a few minutes. But I think I might have found something on your little asshole unlicensed hunter, and I grabbed a whole bunch of shit on Fourier."

"Really?" Niko asked. He leaned in, trying to see the details. Elliott grudgingly moved a little closer too, though kept a notable distance from Zann, T1-N4 still clutched in his arms.

"This your girl?" Zann asked, bringing up several holographic mugshots that Niko instantly recognized. Bubblegum looked a few years younger there, possibly in her late teens, her hair its natural black, with a respectable shiner on one cheek. She wore an insolent smirk, her narrow, dark eyes fixed defiantly on the camera.

The numbers behind her had the top of her head barely reaching the five-foot-two line.

Beneath her photos read: CLAIR SUZUKI.

"Yeah, that's her."

"I recognize her too," Elliott said.

"Yeah. Looks like she's been in and out of jail several times for piss poor behavior. Assault, theft, something to do with running an illegal fighting ring," Zann said.

"That tracks," Niko mumbled. A chill went through him upon seeing her face, the memory of over a dozen Galapol agents dead or quickly dying around Elliott and himself, shards of glass pouring down onto them all like wicked rain. "I'm surprised Galapol was willing to work with her at all."

"And that's where it gets interesting," Zann mumbled. "Take a look at this."

At that, Elliott seemed unable to help himself, standing and making his way over to peer—cautiously—over Zann's shoulder at the information. Niko looked too, his eyes skimming over some internal notes about her meeting with a particular officer to collect bounties.

*Primary contact*, it read, *Agent Fourier.*

"Fourier?" Niko said, leaning back. Another chill crept its way up him.

"Yep," Zann replied. "The one and only. Looks like these two probably had some back-alley deals going on. Interesting she chose to waste him in the end, huh?"

"Why turn on him?" Niko asked.

"Still haven't figured that one out," Zann said. "I haven't gotten to delve into his file much yet."

"Can I see that?" Elliott asked. Niko and Zann both paused, looking at him.

"I'm not done looking through it," Zann said coolly, though after a moment, added, "but, here." He swiped the hologram over towards Elliott, who wasted no time immediately thumbing through the information there. He looked to be speed-reading it, much like he had before with the Galapol files on him.

"Those are classified files, you kn—" Zann started.

"No. No more of that bullshit," Niko cut him off. "I don't think Galapol is friends with anyone on this ship right now. Am I wrong?"

Zann hesitated, then seemed to deflate. Niko got it. Old habits died hard, and digesting that your life was now entirely changed forever was difficult, at best. He'd been there himself before too, and still was trying to make sense of the repercussions of his own choices made months ago. "No. You're not."

"We might be the only friends we have from here on out," Niko said. "So, let's start acting like it."

"So," Zann said as the ship descended toward the icy, dark surface of RM-9832642G, its frozen spires curling and bowing into one another under the moon's gravity. "This is the place, huh?"

"This is the place," Niko said. He guided the *Soñadora* through the entry gates to the hangar, then landed it. Once the engines were killed, heavy silence pressed down into the ship's interior. Zann craned his neck to peer out the windshield at the hangar as it cycled in replacement oxygen.

"Huh," he said, glancing over at Elliott. Niko looked at Elliott too; he was outwardly calm, but Niko knew his tells well enough now that the stiff set of his shoulders gave away a deep, latent anxiety.

"It's gonna be okay," Niko murmured to him.

Zann picked up his duffel bags and glanced to the exit door of the ship as Niko started the procedure of getting out of and charging the suit. "So, you have this place trapped to hell and back?"

Elliott hesitated. "No."

"Really?" Zann eyed him. "Nothing at all?"

"No. I relied on no one being able to find it in the first place."

A chime sounded, followed by an announcement in Quwa-quay, signaling the oxygen cycling had concluded and giving the all-clear to exit the ship. Zann opened the door and stepped down the ramp, into the giant, empty hangar. Niko and Elliott were briefly left together on the *Soñadora*. Elliott shot him a dark, intense glance that all but said *I don't trust him.*

Niko sighed. "I know," he muttered, moving himself into the chair and stripping his boots off. "We'll talk about it, okay?"

The scent of burning tobacco drifted into the ship as Niko wheeled his way out and down the ramp.

Elliott emerged shortly after him, a death stare affixed on Zann as he took a drag off his cigarette, one hand shoved in his coat pocket. "Mind if I smoke?"

"Zann. Don't be an asshole," Niko said.

"What? I waited until we weren't in that little tin can anymore. Or would you rather I step outside?"

"It's a nice night out," Elliott said flatly. "You should go for a walk."

Zann only grinned at him. "Sure. You want to show me around out there? You go first. I'll follow."

Niko was beginning to realize the grave mistake he'd made. He was going to have to be the adult here.

"Alright," he said, moving toward the main entrance to the facility proper. "Facility is this way. It's where we've been staying. There's a lot of empty rooms, so you can take your pick of whichever one you want—"

"*Not* next to ours," Elliott interjected. "Unless you want an earful."

Niko nearly choked. "Wh— Uh, yeah. There are a lot to choose from anyway, like I said. So." He made his way up the ramp and through the doors, the footsteps of the others following shortly behind. "I'll show you around the place. There are a few bathrooms, so you can pick your own too. There's a cafeteria with a kitchen and food storage. I've gotten a few extra ingredients since we saw Lady D. She put in a supply order for us."

"Huh," Zann marveled.

Niko glanced back at him and saw him sweeping his gaze across the empty control room, dark eyes wide as they took in the strange lifelessness of the place. He wished he could ask what he thought about it, and entertained the idea, but then pushed it away. That was probably best for another time, especially with the underlying tension brewing between him and Elliott. The last thing he needed was for Zann to start shit-talking the place when Elliott was already on the defensive.

"There's an intercom system hooked up if we need to make any kind of long-distance announcements."

"Don't abuse that. In fact, don't use it at all," Elliott interjected again. Zann only gave him a wicked grin in response.

Niko sighed. "*Anyway*," he continued, moving now into the hall.

"I'm going to get back to searching," Elliott murmured, slipping off ahead of them down the hall before Niko could protest otherwise. Zann watched him go, then paused, looking down at Niko.

"Told you he wasn't going to be a fan."

"Are you fucking serious? You've done nothing but antagonize him since you got on the ship. 'Hey, killer?' 'Murder boner prescription?' Are you even trying right now?"

"We've got a history. It's going to take time to be besties with him."

"For fuck's sake, Zann," Niko snapped. "Stop acting like a toddler. Come on."

He continued down several long and winding halls, giving the grand tour to Zann. Niko tried to inject a little more enthusiasm and emotion than Elliott had espoused when he'd shown him around. It was hard, with how desolate the whole place still was. It was bizarre to Niko that he'd started to think of these featureless halls with the ever-present buzz of their fluorescent lights as his residence now.

For his part, now that Elliott wasn't nearby, Zann seemed to have mellowed out, taking in the sights and directions, nodding and peeking around curiously. He chose a room respectably far away from the one Niko and Elliott shared, merely giving a "Hell no, I don't want to hear that shit" when Niko cast him a glance.

When, at last, they reached the Murder Room, he asked, "What's this?"

Niko sighed, anticipating the inevitable commentary. "So this is, uh, the hub where we do most of our strategic planning. It's kind of come to be dubbed the Murder Room."

Zann barked out a laugh, peeking inside. Elliott had already been by, it seemed; T1-N4's lifeless body lay atop an island counter. Zann gave a chuckle at the sight of the two tacky signs that hung along the side wall. "Cute."

Joining **This is Where the Magic Happens** was now **Live, Laugh, Liquidate**, as since doctored by Elliott. Zann peered around the room, at all its half-assembled tech and weapons racks, at its grid of x-ed out portraits of galactic luminaries. Finally, he turned and looked at Niko, eyebrows raised.

"So, this is a hell of a thing, Niko."

"I—I know. But at the same time, is it? We've done stuff like this before, Zann."

"No, not on this sort of scale. Never on this scale."

"No. But we did exactly what he's doing now, just... quieter. We're just lucky nobody saw us."

Zann shook his head. "So, this is how it's going to be from now on, huh? This abandoned alien mining facility. Are you even okay, Niko? This place is a fucking shitshow. It's a big empty nothingness. On a fucking airless nothing moon. In a lost solar system no one else has even heard of. And it's just the two of you living here."

"Uh. Yeah. I'm alright, Zann. I mean— No, I'm not. That's a lie. I haven't been okay since I heard about Dad and Loolae. It's been... hard."

"Yeah. Well, I'm going to find them, Niko. One way or another. Especially now that Galapol so kindly lent me their data."

"We've been looking too. Day and night. Elliott doesn't stop. He isn't even fucking sleeping."

Zann frowned. "Is that what he meant by 'searching'? I figured he meant for your next victim."

"*Yes*, that's what he meant. We're not doing any more hits until they're found. I know we probably poked the hornet's nest with releasing the files and doing that broadcast, but—"

"No, you straight up dropkicked the fucking hornet's nest, Niko. Every fucker in Honeybliss right now is going to be in panic mode. And really, really pissed off. Even more than they already were."

Niko winced, and rubbed at the back of his neck. "Yeah. ...Yeah."

Zann sighed. "He find anything yet?"

"He has a couple of potential leads but is still struggling. I—You know, maybe you guys could try working together. Combine your knowledge and all that."

"Yeah. Maybe. Sure."

*I don't regret it*, he wanted to tell Zann. The words were urgent, insistent on the tip of his tongue. *I don't regret it at all.*

*I don't regret him.*

But Niko stayed silent. It was too cruel a thing to say, given the situation. And all the consequences it had led to—and might potentially still.

Instead, he said, "Why don't you get situated into your room, and I'll get some dinner started."

"TV dinners?"

"No, I was thinking carne asada, actually."

"You're cooking again, huh? Been a while."

Niko shrugged. "Yeah, I guess so." He had motivation to start cooking again, something he'd once loved doing. It made a difference that he had someone to cook *for* now.

It was easier to take care of and treat Elliott than it had been to take care of himself.

"Sure, Niko. Carne asada sounds amazing," Zann said, pushing off the side of the island. He walked by Niko as he exited, pausing to look down at him and place a warm, firm hand on his shoulder. His clothes still held an echo of stale smoke, and the nostalgia of it oddly made Niko crave the old vice. Or maybe it was just the stress of everything getting to him. "Hey. I've got your back, now that I'm here. I'm gonna look out for you."

Niko sighed. He reached up and placed his hand over his brother's. "Zann." He appreciated the vigilance and care being offered, but it wasn't necessary. "Will you trust me? It's not what you think it is. He's not a bad person. And he's not manipulating me. He gave me information, and I came to the conclusion independently on my own to help him in the end."

"Gave you information and a pretty saucy jackoff pic. And apparently a little bit of tongue on Uula."

Niko groaned. "Okay. Uh, yeah. Maybe. But honestly, all of that was just trying to fuck with me."

"Oh, you mean like *manipulation?*"

"Err. It's not—"

"Not like that?" Zann finished for him, grinning again. "Sure, Niko."

"Whatever," Niko said. He was too tired for this right now. "I'm going to go make dinner."

On his way to the cafeteria, Niko stopped by the lounge he knew he'd find Elliott in. He paused for a moment, merely watching through the open doorway at the wide spray of dozens of holograms, Elliott's face morose, mouth drawn in a tight line, his pale skin washed in spectral hologram blue. The sight had become so familiar that Niko almost forgot how he looked these days when *not* tinted azure.

"Hey," Niko said, making his way in.

"Oh. Niko."

"How are you doing?"

"I might be making progress. I'm trying to look into Kuuru-um Tolu. The duke of Orddin, on Thoro. He has strong ties with family in Galapol, and could have likely pulled strings there to get them to look the other way. Or maybe even help."

Niko sighed. It was hard to get a straight answer from Elliott sometimes about how he really was. "No, I mean, with everything today. With Zann. I know he's been prickly."

"I wouldn't expect anything else," Elliott said. "And I know he's your brother, Niko, but I really don't think you should trust him. I know you're going to just shake your head at me and argue, because of the connection you have with him. But I think you need to hear this. There's something more to this whole thing going on. It's too convenient that they took your father when they did. Galapol was supposed to be keeping an eye on them. Your brother was the one who asked them to. Then they get taken anyway, and no one has any explanation as to how. And now, that same brother managed to waltz right into Station Twelve? I don't believe it, Niko. I'm sorry, but I can't.

"I know you won't like hearing this, but I think bringing him here was a mistake. Now he—and probably Galapol—know exactly where to find us. We're sitting ducks. If they decide to act, we're just fucked."

Niko ran a hand over his face. This cycle of distrust was never-ending, pressing down on him from both sides.

"I'm sorry, Elliott. I'm sorry you can't relax in your own home, now that someone you don't trust is here. I'm still going to say it, though. Zann isn't with Galapol anymore. There probably is something more going on with this whole thing, you're right. But whatever it is doesn't involve him anymore. And he never asked to come here. It was my idea."

"It was your idea, Niko, but you should also be aware of the possibility that he might be manipulating—"

Niko huffed out a tired laugh.

"What?"

"...Nothing, babe. Listen, I'm going to go make dinner. Let's just take this one day at a time for now, okay? You and he have the same goals. All three of us do. We're trying to find two missing people. And Zann, before he got fired, was a hell of an investigator. Maybe you could actually work together."

"I— Maybe."

His tone was clear that by *maybe,* he meant *not a chance in hell.*

"Consider it, okay? I'm thinking carne asada tonight. Does that sound good to you?"

"Carne— *Steak?* Do we really have the ingredients for all these meals? Especially with a third person here now."

"I may have requested a metric fuckton of kitchen shit when Deleera ordered from market."

"That explains why you had me haul so many boxes in there."

"I love you, Elliott, but I have a side fling, and it's called 'food that doesn't taste like cardboard.' Really, though, don't worry. Just enjoy it. You'll actually get to have flavor in your life again that's not canned chickpeas and green beans. You're welcome."

"Ah. The depths of my eternal gratitude are boundless. Thank you, savior of my tongue," Elliott quipped.

"Better watch what you say," Niko warned, as he turned the chair to exit. "I might just have to make use of that title."

# Chapter Twelve

# FIFTY-FIFTY

Niko had outdone himself, and he knew it. The scent of tender, grilled meat coated in tangy chili, garlic, and lime, draped in a cradle of corn tortilla and cheese, permeated the entire enormous cafeteria as the now three inhabitants of RM-9832642G sat down to dinner.

"Oh damn," Zann said, looking awed. "Just like Mom used to make."

That compliment meant more than Niko wanted to let on, a warm sensation webbing through his chest. "I tried."

Zann dug in, heaping mouthfuls of carne asada taco into his face. Niko helped himself too, trying to outdo Zann in how much he could consume in under a minute. Elliott seemed hesitant to join them, glancing at them both and leaving his food untouched.

"Whaffa madder, babe?" Niko asked through a mouthful of meat.

"Don't tell me you're a vegetarian, or something. That's an irony I can't fucking take," Zann said.

"I'm not a vegetarian." Elliott narrowed his eyes.

"So, it's the company you don't like, then," Zann said.

"Fvann—" Niko warned with a full mouth again.

"No," Elliott said. He picked off a small piece of garlic and ate it. "I just— We're going to burn through supplies quickly now. Maybe we should keep meals simpler, more pared down—"

"You can eat it," Niko said. "We're going to have a lot more meals like this. We'll get more supplies from Lady D."

"Are you sure, Niko?"

"Yeah. You don't need to worry about food shortage anymore. Even with another person here."

Elliott finally dug in now, eating just as ravenously as Niko and Zann had. It seemed he'd needed permission of some kind to enjoy the experience—whether from Niko, or himself, Niko wasn't sure. Maybe both. The three of them collectively destroyed the food before them.

"Speaking of Lady Death. What's going on with her these days?" Zann asked.

Niko reached for more food, his fingertips dragging instead along the last tragic crumbs of meat and cheese. How had it disappeared so fast? "She's still doing her thing. Same old. She, uh. She killed Aleksi."

"*Whoa.*" Zann sat back in his chair, eyes wide. "Wait, what? When? Why?"

"When we went to see her, he tried for our bounties. He ended up ambushing us—"

"Unfurprivingly—" Elliott interjected around his own mouthful of food.

"Unsurprisingly, yeah. Unfortunately, too. I... hadn't wanted it to end that way. But you know how she's always been when her people try and pull one over on her."

"Shit," Zann said. He still looked stunned. His gaze crept over toward Niko, eyeing him a little warily. "Did you see it happen?"

"We did," Elliott said flatly.

"...You, uh, okay, Niko?" Zann stared at him now. There was a lot Niko wanted to say about it. The truth was, he wasn't entirely okay. Aleksi's death was something he still wrestled with sometimes, when he had quiet moments alone.

The man had brought it on himself. He knew that—and reminded himself of it repeatedly, like a mantra. But if Niko hadn't crossed paths with him again, he'd still be out there, living his life, running goods to and from Dainna. He'd died for something as useless as greed.

Niko could feel Elliott's gaze on him without even looking. The last thing he wanted to do was stir up the other man's self-loathing again with painful wording. He knew he still blamed himself for all of it too. The whole thing had been a blow below the belt to them both.

"Yeah, you know, it's— It sucks. But I'm alright."

"Yeah?" Zann asked, silence falling between them for a beat. "Just making sure."

"Yep. I'm okay, Zann. He chose his path."

"Hey," Zann said, his tone changing as he sopped up a dollop of tangy chili lime juice with his last scrap of tortilla. Niko envied that he still had a bite left. "So, the past few hours, I've been combing more of those files. Found some real interesting things in there about Station Twelve. In Fourier's in particular."

Niko sat up a little more. "Yeah?"

"What did you find?" Elliott asked.

"So, get a load of this. Uru Taal, of all people, has been making generous donations to Station Twelve for the past two and a half years."

"Ever since you gave them the files," Niko said, looking at Elliott.

"Wanna make a guess who was in charge of the fundraising and donation outreach effort?" Zann continued.

"Not Fourier," Niko said, his brow furrowing. "He didn't even start at Station Twelve until a few months ago. Right?"

"Right. But here's the thing. He ran this whole big donation drive with the funds disbursed to three stations in particular. One he worked for at the time, and two he didn't. The Ouriaus Station on Vhesria, Twelve on Kaapra-19, and," Zann flicked his gaze toward Elliott, raising his eyebrows, "the South Althiss Station on Delevia. That fundraiser got significantly high donations from some big people. With the highest contributor being Uru Taal."

"Those—" Elliott's eyes were wide. "Those were the three I directly sent files to."

"Taal was paying them off from circulating or investigating your shit. Through Fourier."

Niko could see the muscles in Elliott's jaw strain as he ground his teeth. He watched him in silence.

Zann shook his head. "This piece of shit Toliai prince has been nothing but bad news. He's got his fingers in everything."

"I'm not convinced he isn't the primary head of Honeybliss," Elliott said. "At least unofficially. They're not terribly hierarchical, but I find more and more that he's the one making things happen in the shadows."

"Yep. My thoughts too," Zann commented. "It gets worse, though."

"Of course it does," Elliott muttered.

"I actually got a glimpse into some of Fourier's old personal finances too. Taal's been wiring him dark money under the table for years before that, even. And the dates of each transaction seem to line up with a history of shit Fourier pulled in other stations before he'd transferred. Investigations into people. Arrests. Even potential disappearances. I'm still trying to match it all up. Fucker was a straight up Honeybliss clean-up mook."

"Shit," Niko murmured. "I hated that guy from the moment I saw him."

"Yeah. Greasy little sleazeball," Zann muttered. "I thought when he'd first shown up that maybe I'd give him a chance, but now I wish I'd tossed his ass straight in the trash compactor. See if Uru Taal could bail him out of that. Wonder how many other cops he's personally gotten killed for looking too deep into it all, too. Fucker's worm food now anyway. Good riddance."

Elliott sat in silence, his gaze lax and fixed on nothing in particular, lost somewhere deep in thought.

Something began to dawn on Niko, and his skin crawled.

"Wait. If Galapol had all these records of his personal finances on file, were they—?"

Zann smirked, joyless, harsh, and sharp as a knife. "Yep. Looks like they knew all along. Chief knew too. They just didn't give a fuck. But even more than that, it meant they *condoned* it. After all, they chose to rank him up as my replacement. Being wary of Honeybliss is one thing, but actively helping them do the shit they do is a whole other level of fucked up. And for what? Station funding? Fucking *fundraisers?*"

It hurt. Niko had believed in the police for so long, had worked alongside them to keep people safe. Had it been a farce all along? Only *some* people were worthy of keeping safe? Only *some* were extended protection? If the right person was the one to inflict the hurt, were you just shit out of luck as Galapol helped them sweep your ruination under the rug?

It seemed that way.

How many other young, hopeful officers, investigators, and bounty hunters on the right side of the law were beginning their careers now too, with no idea of the corruption that ran rampant through the very system they'd devoted themselves to, like a deeply rooted cancer?

Zann seemed to hold the same sentiment. "I gave those bastards years of my life. I worked hard for them. Day and night. Overtime. Weekends. I gave so much to them, and in the end it's all just bullshit."

Elliott eyed Zann quietly, his attention focused on the dark-haired man now. He stayed silent, whatever thoughts swimming through him now held deeply within.

"I know," Niko agreed. "But in the end, it wasn't for *Galapol*, really, was it? It was for Mom. And Ryen. It was for all the people out there who needed help. It was to try and protect *them*. People like— Like Cleo." He glanced at Elliott. "Those were the people I worked hard for and still want to continue working hard for, Galapol or not. I don't think any of that was a waste."

"Yeah," Zann said. "You're right. Of course you're right. But it still fucking smarts."

"I wish," Elliott finally spoke, his tone quiet, "that I had met you before any of this." He looked at Niko as he said it, their gazes locking for a long moment.

"Yeah, Elliott," Niko said. He ached. "Me too."

Another thought crossed his mind, goosebumps pricking up his arms and neck. He glanced back at Zann. "Do you think, if he has that kind of reach into Galapol, that Taal could be the one who has Dad and Loolae?" Niko asked.

A cold quiet descended over the table. Elliott looked sick.

Zann eyed him. "Yeah, I sure fucking hope not. Not that any of those other fucks would be much better. I'm going to look into him, though. See if there's anything we can find."

"I'll help you," Elliott said.

Zann stared at him for a moment, pressing his lips together. "Yeah, sure. I'll take all the help I can get."

Niko was relieved. He realized he'd wanted the two of them to like each other more than he'd been willing to admit. *Like* might still be too strong of a word, but seeing both men willing to set aside their differences and unite against their real enemy was a start.

He could accept a start right now.

Niko yawned. Having to play chaperone to the two all day had worn his energy reserves low. As well as days of endless research and not knowing if he'd gotten two people he loved killed.

"Why don't you get some rest, Niko? You look like you haven't slept in a week," Zann said.

Niko felt Elliott's gaze jump to him instantly, and for a brief moment, they both eyed each other. "No," he started warily. He trusted his brother fully, but knew Elliott didn't. To leave them alone together would be too cruel. "No, I should be helping—"

"It's alright." It was Elliott who spoke, which shocked Niko. Especially at the firm, inarguable line drawn in his tone.

"But—" Niko started.

Elliott only clamped down tighter, more forcefully. "It's alright."

"I don't bite," Zann said.

"No. Just shoot," said Elliott.

"Oh, that's rich, coming from you."

Niko sighed, then after another long, wordless exchange with Elliott, relented. "I'll get this cleaned up, then, and grab a quick nap. Then I'll join you guys and we can hit it hard."

"Sure, Niko," Zann said, rising from the table. "Nice job on dinner. I missed your cooking."

Elliott stood too and walked over to Niko, leaning down to plant a brief, chaste kiss on his temple. It was the most affection he'd shown since Zann's arrival. Niko could feel his brother side-eyeing them, but paid him no mind.

"Are you going to be alright?" Elliott murmured.

"Yeah, babe," Niko said, reaching up to touch his hand. "Are *you?*"

"There's a fifty-fifty chance I'll survive this."

"Nothing's going to happen." Niko gently squeezed his hand.

"After you," Zann said, gesturing toward the exit.

Niko watched as the two turned and left the cafeteria side by side, Elliott murmuring something about using one of the lounges. Something raw and painful tugged inside of him at the sight of them together. He wished things had been different. He wished everything had been. Maybe this could be the start of a new direction.

In their absence, the cafeteria suddenly took on an entirely different feel now. It seemed somehow stranger—more colossal, each angle sharper, colder. Even the fluorescent light seemed to press down on him. How Elliott had lived here alone for so long, Niko had no idea.

He cleaned up the dishes and kitchen, then went back to their room and laid down for a nap. The bedside clock read 8:13 p.m. He could sleep for just an hour or two, then join them.

If they didn't erupt into outright open warfare by then.

Elliott lowered himself into one of the cushioned, gray lounge chairs. He kept his back straight and stiff, every muscle tight with nerves. He chose a seat between Investigator Delamar and the door, back kept against the wall. He was more athletic than the lanky Galapol agent, and he trained almost daily. If it came down to it, he could be out of the room and down the hall in under seven seconds. Let Niko deal with him.

To say Elliott wasn't thrilled about Delamar's encroachment into his territory was putting it lightly. But this was Niko's family, and there was no way he could deny Niko. He could no sooner deny the galaxy its bejeweled, hanging stars. The deep pain in the other man's soulful eyes when Elliott had tried to reason with him dug deeper, hurt more than any physical blow could ever aspire to.

Besides, Niko's family was only in this nightmare because the man had chosen to help him. The same creatures who had taken Cleo from him and stained his life with a trauma that would never wash away now had Niko's father too. He hoped that whoever it was, it wasn't Taal.

*Please don't let it be him.*

Not that any of the other swine were a much better option, but that was too much. *Would they—?*

Elliott winced at the thought. Niko wasn't even in the room, but he fought against turning his face downward in shame. How much was Elliott even worth being around, when it came with so many horrific consequences? In how many ways could a person inflict pain on another, while only ever loving them?

It would have been a kindness if Niko had listened to him before, had left the facility—and him—behind.

Delamar cleared his throat, sinking into his own chair and glancing around. He made himself at home, leaning back and even propping his feet up on a nearby table. It grated against something hard in Elliott and he fought to swallow a protest against the gesture. *How ridiculous,* he chastised himself. *To act like this place is precious and needs to be kept pristine.*

But it was more than simply insulting the facility itself. The gesture was clearly meant for Elliott. The man had the audacity to actually flex on him.

"So," Delamar started, eyeing him, then taking in the lounge. "Nice murder fortress you got here. Real homey."

Elliott didn't grace him with an answer. There were plenty of things he could say—wanted to say—but every one of them would somehow wound Niko too. Sometimes it was better to keep quiet. Instead, he began to sift through what infuriatingly labyrinthine research he'd amassed so far, gesturing one hologram after another into the air between them with several flicks of the wrist.

Behind the transparent haze of blue, Delamar's eyebrows rose. "Straight to work then, huh? Not even going to go around the room and say three interesting facts about ourselves first?"

"I suggest we don't waste time," Elliott said curtly. He was unable to help the dig that came from his mouth next—though he wasn't sure if it was aimed at Delamar, or himself more. "So your father doesn't have to spend another moment suffering."

*If Delamar isn't in on it all too.* He'd worked so closely with Galapol before. He had been the only one to conveniently be out while any of this had happened. Niko seemed to accept it all just fine, but the man often had a blinding belief in others. He trusted, he gave his heart too easily. Elliott wanted to protect him, to melt around him like a second, stronger, more durable armor and shield him from every opportunist bastard.

But the smirk or quip that Elliott braced for didn't come. Instead, Delamar's face shifted to what appeared to be genuine discomfort. In that moment, the wince of his dark eyes could have been a mirror of Niko's. Elliott tried to push that thought away.

"Yeah. Yeah, you're right." Just like that, the other man sobered up, playtime over. He pulled his feet from the table and hunched over it instead, beginning to bring up his own holographic research and notes.

They were both here for a common reason, and though neither trusted the other (which was quite clear by the way Delamar constantly kept Elliott in his visual periphery, and had since he'd stepped aboard Niko's ship, eyes sharp and wary), for Niko, they would both behave and work together. After all the pain and problems he'd wrought for Niko and his family, it was the very least that Elliott could do.

He wouldn't screw this up too. Even if it meant swallowing both his pride and paranoia.

"I've managed to rule out a few of them," Elliott said as a tentative peace offering. "And I have a list of potential suspects, but it's... long." He hated how lost that last word sounded. He hadn't made the progress he'd been hoping for. It had been all he could do to focus on the task at hand the last few days and not turn against himself in an angry frenzy. He wasn't good enough. He wasn't doing enough for Niko.

Not that the beautiful man would ever think to accuse him of that. In a way, it only made Elliott's disdain towards his own incompetence burn even hotter.

"Yeah?" Delamar said, glancing his way. He was buried behind his own wall of case files, criminal records, and notes now. All likely gifted from Galapol—or stolen, if the man could actually be believed. "Send them my way. I'll send whatever we had on these fuckfaces, too."

*We.* The word reverberated energetically through Elliott's mind. It danced. *He still says 'we.'* Either the man was slipping up miserably, or he was sincere. A skilled actor would be sure to put clear distance between himself and Galapol. A masterful one would instead muddy the waters, appear sentimental, married to habit.

"Do that." After a moment, Elliott added on a, "Please."

Once each man had exchanged his files, the two of them got to work. What information Delamar and Galapol possessed matched up quite well with Elliott's own research and files, mixed with a few surprises—most of them unpleasant.

As the hours wore on, Elliott found himself relenting more and more, opening up, and inviting Niko's brother into his research—murmuring questions and insights both, and providing explanations when the investigator puzzled over his notes.

Fatigue began worming its way into his mind after several late-night hours of endless research. If this was a trap, he wasn't certain which direction to step to evade it anymore.

His thoughts had long since begun to slow, until they were straight-up sluggish. The realization made him nervous; more than any physical skill, Elliott's mind was his truly greatest weapon. And it had been intensely dulled by another sleepless night. He glanced at the time. It read 2:03 in the morning.

Niko had never come back.

Paranoia reared its head again, hazy thoughts churning through him now. Perhaps Delamar had drugged his own brother at dinner to get Elliott alone. No, that didn't make any sense. Niko had been the one to prepare the meal and serve the drinks. And Elliott and Delamar had been working together now for hours, making what felt like genuine progress. He forced down a sharp sigh.

Delamar gestured a set of Elliott's notes closer toward himself, then enhanced them so the words were magnified and filling half the room. A sour scowl crossed his features like he'd just unexpectedly bitten into something gone rancid. "You know, you have the shittiest handwriting I've ever seen." Elliott scowled back, but Delamar continued on, regardless. "They invented typing for assholes like you. Come here."

He hesitated.

"I'm seriously not going to fucking bite you. Or shoot."

Elliott reluctantly sank down into the chair nearest Delamar. He folded his arms tightly across his chest, as though trying to keep his wildly racing heart trapped inside.

"This," Delamar said, circling an entire paragraph. "What the actual fuck does *any* of this say?"

Elliott huffed out a sigh. It was obvious what it said, if anyone knew how to read. Niko never seemed to have a problem with it. "It's details of Iincha'cul's schedule. He goes to visit his second family, every Monday. He never skips it."

"Why even write any of this down? You were aiming to take them all out at big events, right?"

"It's good to have a backup plan. And I knew they'd eventually get smart about it."

"Yeah? Like Seiiren and Alexopoulos."

"Precisely, yes."

He wondered if Delamar knew that Giannis Alexopoulos had been intentionally left by Niko to die, rather than Elliott's own doing. And even before they'd technically partnered up. The words were on the tip of his tongue, but he stayed silent.

"You know," Delamar began. He leaned back in his chair, swiveling it back and forth in the same obnoxious way he had on Niko's ship. His eyes met Elliott's own, and for a moment, both men stared at each other, gazes locked intensely. Elliott felt a chill creep up his spine, the hair on his arms rising. "You're right."

He nearly choked. "What?"

Elliott hadn't expected that.

"Yeah, you heard me. Every one of these fucks? They have what's coming to them, and have for a long time."

Elliott said nothing.

"I just think you went about it in the worst way possible," Delamar continued. "You went and made enemies of everyone."

"Niko said you'd had a similar situation, once."

"Yeah. But we were smart about it."

Frustration crested in Elliott, his mind swimming to keep up as he fought back an awkward, ill-timed yawn. "I *wanted* everyone to know. To see. I wanted to—"

"Send a message. Yeah, I know." They stared at each other. "But to who? Not the countless people who were witness to the violence and had no idea why it was happening. Honeybliss would still have figured it out if their numbers started thinning."

"I wanted—" Elliott started. "I wanted to show the ones who could get away with these things—who have always been untouchable—that they're actually small. So small that they're nothing. Their fame is their shield and their power. So, I'm taking them down in their own public, adoring eye. Right where they feel safest. I want them to know, this time, that there's no way out of it. Not even for them. That, just like all the people they've killed, they can die too. I want them to feel despair. To *feel* it."

"Like they made you feel," Delamar said.

Elliott looked away. "Like they made *Cleo* feel."

Silence fell between them, heavy and full of ghosts. Shared research looked back upon them from every angle in hologram blue. Something in Elliott had cracked a little. He was letting his guard down.

Probably, he was just slipping up from exhaustion.

He leaned back in his chair, blinking against the bleary text. Staring endlessly at the glow of holographic data had made the perpetual tension headache he'd been nursing since their broadcast worsen. He rubbed at his eyes, trying in vain to work out some of the pressure. When he looked back at the text, it was in a blur. Too many countless hours staring through a rifle scope, staring at hologram text. Squinting at the fine details of blueprints. If he survived this whole ordeal somehow, he would probably need glasses. Did Lady Death peddle in those, too?

Delamar was watching him. He always was. He opened his mouth to speak. *Here it comes.* "You look like shit. Not used to pulling all-nighters, huh?"

*I'm fine* was on Elliott's tongue, vying to get out. He clamped down on it and swallowed. It was no use denying it. Station Twelve's lead investigator clearly saw the clues of fatigue and struggle written all over him.

"No, I am," he admitted. "But I didn't sleep much the night before, either." *Nor the one before that.*

"Coffee?"

"I—" Elliott glanced around. "I don't have—"

Delamar raised his eyebrows. "I mean, do you want to go get some? From the cafeteria? You do have coffee there, right?"

"Oh." Elliott felt himself flushing with embarrassment at being so daft. *Don't show him how much you're lagging. You need to keep a clear head.*

Caffeine would help that.

"Yes. Sure."

It felt good to move around, to stretch his muscles. Once they were back in the kitchen, with a packet of instant coffee warmed for both of them, Elliott took a long drink of the rich liquid. It was bitter and bright on his tongue. He hoped it worked quickly. He gazed out the narrow serving window, into the empty cafeteria beyond, some part of him hoping to see Niko there.

Beside him, Delamar sipped from his own cup, leaning back languorously against the counter. He seemed to be hesitating, working out something he wanted to say.

"Just say it," Elliott said.

"Hey, look. I'm sorry I shot you. That was pretty fucked up."

"It was a tense situation. You were just trying to protect your brother. I understand."

"Still. Doesn't make it better."

"It makes it understandable."

"Eh," Delamar grunted.

"I never wanted your family to be caught up in this and hurt, either. Or Niko." After a moment, Elliott added, "I'm so sorry."

"So, do you actually give a shit about him?"

"Would you even believe me if I said I did?"

"I'm listening." Delamar looked over at him.

Elliott hesitated. He could barely think straight, his thoughts a tangled mess of ephemeral, illogical fragments that led to nowhere, then looped back around again. He was long past needing sleep. Wherever this conversation was heading, he knew he should be having it with a clear head. But instead, he found himself speaking. "He— Niko means more to me than anything."

"Yeah?" Delamar probed. "Even more than this whole murder spree mission of yours? More than your revenge? Your message?"

"You think I'm just using him."

"Yeah. Maybe I do," Delamar said. "Can you blame me?"

"No. But you're wrong."

"Am I?"

"I—I told Niko to recuse himself from hunting me, and to go live his life. I told him he was only going to get himself hurt if he kept it up, kept insisting on trying to help me get the word out about Honeybliss."

"Yeah, that's Niko. He doesn't listen," Delamar said, blunt and certain. He gave a loud yawn, not bothering to cover his mouth as he did. Then he eyed Elliott up and down. "So, you care about him. A lot. Would you call it love?"

His heart jolted in his chest as he realized what he was admitting to this dangerous stranger. This was something deeply *private.* Elliott's tone quickly pivoted to something cold, closed off. "What does that matter?"

"So, you don't, then?" Delamar pressed.

"I didn't say that, either." Elliott was bristling now.

"You don't always have to say something to get the idea across."

"I just don't know why it matters. In fact, I don't even know why I'm telling you any of this." *Finally*, he scolded himself. *Some sense.*

Delamar spread out his hands, coffee cup still clutched in his right. "We're just talking."

"You're interrogating me," Elliott said flatly.

"You still think I'm a Galapol plant?"

Elliott said nothing, so Delamar continued. "Look. I know why you're doing all this. You made that pretty clear, already. I just want to know where my brother stands in any of it." Elliott's gaze flicked up, meeting the other man in the eyes that were so uncannily familiar, yet those of a stranger. "Are you using him to keep yourself alive through this?"

Elliott ground his jaw, a pang of white-hot anger lancing through him. It was hard to think straight, hard to keep himself in check. The insinuation that he was merely using Niko, like a tool, insulted him. It was egregious.

And yet. He couldn't help but see where Delamar was coming from. He probably would have had the same concern about Niko, were the situation flipped.

As the two of them searched each other's gazes, Elliott found no maliciousness there. He found only, instead, concern.

This was a man genuinely worried for his brother.

If Delamar had wanted to send Galapol after them, he'd be pointlessly wasting his time for not having done it by now.

This wasn't a trap. This, Elliott was almost loath to admit, wasn't a ploy to take them down.

He relented, letting out his anger with a long, slow breath, some of the tension slipping out of his shoulders. "Why are you here?" he asked instead, ignoring Delamar's own question.

"Isn't that obvious?"

"You want to survive. Of course. But there were other lo-cat—"

"I wanted to see Niko. I wanted to make sure he was alright."

*And not being used by you.* The unspoken words hung in the air between them. Elliott raised his mug to his lips, drinking away a few precious seconds to gather his crawling thoughts. The coffee had begun to cool, the liquid tepid and coating his tongue now.

"And he told me you could help me find our dad," Delamar said.

Elliott paused.

"Look. You were the biggest pain my ass has ever had to suffer," the other man continued. "For *months.*"

"You weren't my favorite either," Elliott muttered. "Anyone from Galapol."

"Yeah. Yeah, I can imagine. But we're both here now, and everything's fucked. And we both have a chance to try and make it right. So... Maybe we should try to start over, yeah? And make it right."

Elliott hesitated. "I just have one question."

"What's that?"

"Why didn't they take you, too?"

All expression dropped from Delamar's face, replaced with something heavy and haunted now. It was a raw moment of honesty. "I've been wondering that since it happened. It seems too convenient, right? I thought that too. Is this planned somehow? Was it intentional? Or did they really just fuck up that badly? It was just a day. A normal day. I went out to get some fried chicken for us for lunch. When I came back, he was just..." Delamar waved his hand, his next words coming louder, sharper, a stiletto stabbing into the silence around them. "Fucking *gone*.

"And then there was that note. And the back door was smashed open. Glass everywhere." His gaze turned out into the empty cafeteria. "The fucking TV was still playing. It was a car commercial. I remember it. The stupid one with the... with the— The fucking jingle about 'journey over destination' that they play all the time. I don't know why I remember that, but I do. The world was falling apart and that *fucking jingle* was playing—"

"It's..." Elliott began. "...Alright."

Delamar looked at him, eyes laden with guilt. If he were an actor, his skills far surpassed even the best movie stars Cleo had once adored.

Elliott knew guilt. He'd made a home in its pain. He hadn't been able to save Cleo from everything that had happened.

This was real.

"They were supposed to be watching him." This time, Delamar's voice came smaller, quieter. They both remained silent for a moment, likely sharing the same unspoken thought: Galapol had never been something to put their trust in.

"It's alright," Elliott said again softly, knowing it was anything but alright and that his words would never reach the core of that guilt.

"I don't know why they picked right then. I think about it all the fucking time. I can't sleep because I think about it. I wish they'd just taken me, and left him the fuck alone. He's never hurt anyone. He's never done anything. I—" Delamar paused, running a hand over his face. For the first time that night, he'd begun to look fatigued, worn down to the bone. "Fuck. I—I hadn't really been good to him, you know? I sort of stayed away for a few years and let Niko deal with all the bullshit, instead of manning up. And now he's... He's gone. He's *gone.*"

"I'll get your father back," Elliott said. "And your friend. Loolae. I won't let..." *What happened to Cleo happen to them.* "Anything happen. We'll find them before that." He swallowed, finally forcing more of the long-held tension out of his body, and set his empty mug down on the counter. "I have plenty of reasons not to trust you, if we're being honest. And I know that you don't trust me, either. But even if you can't trust *me*, please at least trust that I would never do anything to intentionally harm your brother." He battled with one last resilient splinter of hesitation, before finally offering his hand out to Delamar. "I'm willing to start over."

*For Niko.*

Delamar chewed his lip, before grasping Elliott's hand in his own and giving it a firm, brief shake. "Yeah. Me too."

"I'm ready to get back to work now," Elliott said, "if you are."

# Chapter Thirteen

# DESPERATE DREAM

Niko's head swam as he woke, groggy and heavy, his thoughts slow. He glanced at the clock again.

4:26 a.m.

*Whoa. Shit. That was a hell of a nap.*

A slurry of guilt, shame, and nerves coursed through him as he forced himself to sit up, rubbing his hand across his face. Beside him, the other half of the bed was empty, not a single wrinkle of sheets disturbed. Elliott had never come to bed. They'd been researching all night.

Or had killed each other in a double murder-suicide. Either was equally possible.

Niko made his way into his chair, then down the long and winding hallways toward the lounge Elliott had mentioned. The door slid open for him, revealing at least two dozen different holograms hovering across the room, and two very tired looking men awash in pale blue light.

"Uh, hey guys."

"Aw, look who it is," Zann teased. "You get enough beauty sleep, Princess, or do you need a few more hours?"

Even Elliott smirked at him—though he looked exhausted, dark circles under his eyes, his gaze unfocused.

"Yeah, yeah, I know. I have no idea how the hell I slept that long." Niko wheeled into the lounge. "You guys should have woken me."

"Nah, I know how you get when you don't have enough sleep. I don't want my head bitten off," Zann said. "Besides, there's no way in hell I'm going into that bedroom. Probably some kind of freaky ass sex dungeon in there."

Niko rolled his eyes, then turned to Elliott.

"Morning, babe," he said, a tinge of sheepish guilt in his tone. "You good?"

Elliott yawned. Niko only now noticed two big, emptied mugs of coffee sitting by both men. "Niko. I'm... good. We've made some progress tonight. Do you want to get some more work done with us?"

"You look pretty tired, actually. Why don't you get some rest? You've been at it all night. You too, Zann. Right? I can take over from here."

"Nah, I'm good for at least another hour, maybe two," Zann said. Niko believed it. His half-brother had a practiced history of all-nighters doing obsessive research or combing over new evidence for a hot case, when he'd worked at the station.

"I can stay too—" Elliott began, but Zann cut him off.

"No, you go on ahead. Niko and I can pick it up for a while."

Elliott hesitated, glancing at Niko, but the unfocused look in his eyes told him everything he needed to know.

"Zann's right. It's okay. Go get some sleep."

"Alright." Elliott stood and gave him a kiss on the hair, then slipped out of the room. After a long moment, Zann turned to eye Niko.

"Maybe he's not using you."

"For fuck's sake. He's not. I've been telling you."

"I said *maybe*."

Niko sighed. It was the best he was going to get for the moment. But it was another step in the right direction.

"So how is it?" Niko asked. "Working with him."

"Utterly fucking surreal," Zann admitted, leaning back in his chair. He picked a stylus up from off the small, white table beside him and began turning it over in his hand. Then he started tapping it against the tabletop. "Past several months of my life have been spent investigating Elliott Kestrel. Never imagined I'd be doing an investigation *with* him."

"Life's weird, sometimes," Niko muttered.

"Guy's sharp as a tack, though," Zann grumbled, maybe a little begrudgingly. "We've been making more progress tonight than I had the entire time I was working on my own from that nasty-ass motel." After a pause, he added, "He's not a bad person. I know why he's doing the shit he does. I just... wish it had all been different somehow, you know?"

"Yeah. Me too." Niko wished Galapol had listened, had tried to help. Had, in fact, done anything but actively work to silence Elliott. Their lives all would have been very different if even that much had changed.

But it meant Niko would likely have never met him, either. The thought made him ache, a tide of guilt flooding in with the sting of it. He didn't want Elliott to have to suffer. He didn't want him to have to go through everything that he'd had. But Niko was grateful he'd gotten to cross paths with him because of it.

In the end, he pushed the thoughts away. There was no use feeling guilt over them—he couldn't change reality, nor the past. Galapol had been callous monsters and none of that was on Niko.

"Well, let's get to work," he mumbled. "If you're still good for another hour or two."

"You bet I am," Zann said. He rolled his head back and forth across his shoulders, his neck emitting an audible set of pops and cracks.

It felt good to work alongside his brother once more. It was something Niko thought he'd never have the chance to do again.

Maybe everything might actually work out for them, after all.

The next four days went more or less the same, with the three of them working diligently on piecing together research, sifting through files, trying to follow paths of logic. Sometimes all three worked together, and sometimes only one or two as the others slept or took a break. No one gave each other shit for needing a few hours to recoup and just be a person or rest. There was a mutual and unspoken understanding of the necessity of breaks between them.

Niko provided the cooking—chilaquiles in the mornings, slow-cooked tender barbacoa ready for dinner, and much more. He found he'd really missed cooking, and to be able to provide for the two people he loved had become far more than any kind of chore. It was a delight.

Sometimes they stayed silent over meals, too lost in thought or burned out by endless research. Other times, they talked a lot, Zann probing Elliott with questions and Elliott throwing them back at him. The two of them seemed to be tentatively co-existing, even if it came at a grudging effort.

Over meals, Elliott spoke of his years in university and how he'd graduated early thanks to a uniquely tailored, advanced program. Zann said he'd never had the chance to attend, but had graduated high school as class valedictorian. He'd had to work his way up the hard way through Galapol, without a degree to fall back on.

He then embarrassed Niko with old stories about him growing up, and Elliott, in turn, shared memories of Cleo from happier times, including a surprise sweet sixteenth party she'd planned for him that had ended in pure chaos and had somehow involved an ostrich.

Elliott spoke, too, about his previous romantic life—which truly only amounted to Liam, and an escapade of briefly-acquainted lovers before him—and, after a generous handful of goading, Niko finally got Zann to admit out loud that he'd been both married and divorced twice, by age twenty-five.

That information prompted Elliott to describe Zann as 'speed-running the milestones of an apocalyptic midlife crisis,' and Zann retaliated by calling Elliott a 'dandy little murder-twink who thinks he knows everything.' A fight nearly erupted between them that Niko was forced to referee back into uneasy peace.

And thus, their mealtime chats were over, Zann sulking and taking his food to his room instead, after that.

On the evening of their fourth day, Niko checked up on Elliott, needing a brief break of his own from the endless research. He'd been at it for the last few hours with Zann, while Elliott had left to take a few personal hours.

Niko found him in the Murder Room, where he stood now at the island with T1-N4 pieced apart and an assortment of tools and circuitry lying scattered on the countertop. Niko couldn't help but laugh.

"You're actually going to fix her up, huh?"

Elliott shrugged, not glancing up from unscrewing a tiny component from her side panel. "Why not? This is a project. This is fun. And I think... I needed a break. I couldn't think or see straight anymore, from doing so much reading. I wasn't contributing much at that point."

Niko winced. "Yeah, staring for hours at holograms will do that to you." He made his way over to Elliott's side. "How are you holding up?"

"I'm—I'm alright."

"Yeah? How's working with Zann been?"

"Not... horrible. It's strange having people here, though," Elliott admitted. He pried the small part from T1-N4 and turned it over in his hands, examining it before setting it on the countertop.

"Yeah? I can imagine."

"It still messes me up a little sometimes, though."

Niko frowned. "What do you mean? Messes you up?"

Elliott stared at T1-N4 another moment, not answering, before looking over at Niko. "I was alone here for a year and two months. Complete isolation does not do kind things to a human mind."

Niko was at a loss for words this time, a quiet dread snaking into his gut. He remembered the cafeteria and how it'd transformed once he had been left alone in it, too vast and full of strange angles that were somehow both too spread out, yet suffocating. "Yeah? It must have been really hard for you. I honestly don't know how you did it."

"Mostly, it was just that I didn't care anymore. I was so... lost that I just didn't *care*. I buried myself wholly in my mission and in preparing for it any way I could. Training, obsessive target practice, learning as much as I could. But it still hurt. It hurt a lot. And after so many weeks, and then months, my mind started playing tricks on me. I'd be working on something in here, just like this, or lying in bed, and suddenly the silence was broken. I'd hear footsteps clear as day. Someone walking down these halls."

"Holy shit," Niko murmured, goosebumps pricking along the back of his neck at the chill of imagining it.

"Right. So naturally, I imagined every scenario there was. Honeybliss had found me. Galapol had. I thought maybe one of the original Quwa-quay workers was still here all along, hiding away. After a while, once you'd started showing up in my life, I had a paranoid thought that you'd found me. I even heard your voice once."

"Wait, what? Really?"

"Yes. I couldn't make out what you were saying, though. Just something about... 'peacefully.' I figured you'd wanted me to surrender."

"Elliott..."

"When it all first started, I couldn't sleep. I'd get up and go look around. I *had* to. I couldn't just lie there and pretend I hadn't heard it. I couldn't reason myself out of it. But no one was ever there. Everything was still, and quiet. Again and again.

"Then over time, it got worse. I'd hear things crashing, like something falling over, or off of a shelf. Someone messing with something. Clear as day, and loudly. I could never find anything that had fallen over, though. Eventually, I'd confuse myself too. I *knew* I'd left something in a particular place, but then it would just be gone. I'd find it somewhere else entirely."

"So, are you saying this place is haunted?"

"No, Niko, of course not. I was just unwell. It was slowly driving me into an awful state. The worst was when I started having nightmares. I—I heard—" He paused and took a deep, slow breath. "I heard Cleo's voice, once. I didn't want to get up for that one. I just laid in bed. And when I finally fell asleep, I dreamed she was here, wandering the halls, lost. Looking for me. Coming to finally take me with her. I started wearing my earbuds more and falling asleep to music every night after that."

It was too much. Niko swallowed, trying to take it in. The sheer horror that Elliott's isolation and his own breaking, lonely mind had wrought on him made Niko ache so deeply it stole his breath away. He'd had no idea Elliott had truly been so close to falling apart and losing himself completely. Niko reached up and touched his sleeve.

"You're not alone here anymore. We're here. If you ever see or hear anything and need to question it, you can ask me, okay?"

"I know that. But sometimes, hearing him walking around out there, or coughing, or talking to you... It reminds me. And some part of me still instinctually wonders if it's real. Any of this. Like I just dreamed you up because I was so desperate." He hesitated. "I was that way when you first arrived here, too."

"You didn't dream me up. I'm really here, Elliott. It's not going to be like that anymore. You'll never be isolated like that again. Okay?"

Elliott nodded. He picked up a small, transparent chip and inserted it into T1-N4's side with a little bit of jury-rigging. They fell into a deep silence before he finally spoke again, pulling Niko out of his wandering thoughts. "Speaking of Zann, though, and your original question," he started, haltingly. "Did you... believe anything he said?"

Niko frowned. "Don't listen to him. He's an asshole and was just trying to get under your skin—"

"No. I mean on Celelast."

"No, Elliott. I didn't. Honestly."

"He seems very adamant I'm just using you, and nothing more," Elliott said. His tone was distant and detached, his eyes somewhere far away, lost in a thought unreachable to Niko.

"He can be adamant all he wants, Elliott," Niko said. "I know that's not what's going on. Besides, he recently admitted that he doesn't really think that anymore."

"In the end, it's not so important what *he* thinks." Elliott met his gaze now. "I just wanted to make sure you didn't actually think it too."

"I don't, Elliott. I never did. Not even for a minute. I believe in you. And I always have."

For the first time since Niko had come to check on him, a small, sincere smile graced the other man's lips.

*"Niko!"*

Niko twitched, glancing up from the game he'd been play-ing on his phone hologram as two voices called his name in unison. He sat on the bed, looking now at a pair of excited, urgent faces peering back at him from the doorway. Even Zann had come, though he hesitated awkwardly at the threshold of the bedroom, refusing to enter.

"We figured it out," Elliott said, his tone hurried and breathless. "We were finally able to piece it all together."

"It wasn't Taal. Or even Galapol. It's Khaathra," Zann said.

Niko's blood turned to ice water as he stared at them both. His brain vaguely registered the game over music playing from his phone now.

Imperator Khaathra.

He remembered not long ago, Elliott had wanted to finish what he'd started and take her down. He himself had argued against it.

This whole thing could have been avoided. Niko had only gotten in the way all over again.

Elliott must have seen it on his face, his own expression shifting into a worried frown. "Niko. This isn't your fault. We had no way of knowing."

All Niko could do was nod.

Over the past few days, the three of them had pieced together that it was likely someone else who was particularly desperate and would have it out for Elliott, narrowing down their list signifi-cantly. Imperator Khaathra had already had a straight up attempt on her once, so she was one of their prime suspects, along with Iincha'cul, Uru Taal, and three others for various separate reasons.

"Kestrel's actually the one who figured it out in the end," Zann said.

"Well. Only because Zann started piecing it all together."

The two of them paused, glancing at each other and seeming to awkwardly regard one another. Niko shook his head, but in truth it made him relieved—and as marginally happy as the situation allowed—to see. He'd always known if they could overlook their differences and put both their brilliant minds together, that they would accomplish incredible things.

And now they had.

"Kestrel managed to finally find and hack into some private security footage from that parking garage across the street from Dad's place."

"And Zann ran facial recognition on one of the assailants as someone who'd done work for Khaathra in the past."

"Good job, guys," Niko said, and meant it. "Now, we just need to get there."

"Right. Let's not waste any time," Elliott said.

Zann glanced between them. "I'm going with you guys."

"Uh." Niko paused. Elliott froze, too.

He hated the idea, hated Zann being out there with him. Especially knowing the kind of preparation Khaathra undoubtedly had awaiting them. "I don't know that that's a good idea right now."

"What? You think I can't do it? Don't insult me, Niko. I may not be a big dumbass linebacker-slash-bounty-hunter like you, but I've been an officer of Galapol for just as long as you've been doing this shit. I know how to work a gun and how to handle active situations. Besides, this is my fucking dad. I'm not going to sit on my ass while his life is in danger."

"No," Niko started uneasily, "I know you're capable. But Zann, I think it's best you lay low for now. Nobody knows you're with us right now, and I'd like to keep it that way. You can still come back from all of this. We can't. You can still return to society and have a normal life if nobody associates you being with us. They probably still think you're just laying low somewhere."

"It's Dad."

"I promise we'll bring him back, Zann," Elliott said, making Niko do a double take. "I won't let any harm come to your family. I'm the reason they're even in this situation. I'll make sure they come home to you."

Zann eyed him, worrying his bottom lip with his teeth. He looked ready to argue, when Niko stepped in again too. "It's okay, Zann. He's right. We'll get them. We're just going to be in and out. I'm calling D's people in for backup, just in case, because it's probably going to get messy there. But I need to know you can still have a life outside of all of this. Okay?"

"Fuck," Zann muttered. "Fine. Okay. But only because you said you're bringing backup. Don't do anything stupid. I mean, *unusually* fucking stupid." His gaze flicked to Elliott. "Same goes for you, asshole."

"We won't," Elliott said.

Niko had a phone call to make.

# Chapter Fourteen

# WEAKNESS AND STRENGTH

NIKO AND ELLIOTT MADE their way under stealth through the Imperial Hunting Woods of Haneen, the name given to a bizarre "forest" of dense and hardy alien foliage, the same kind that had straight up taken an explosive shot from Niko on Uula and stayed standing. Their wide trunks tapered into thin spirals which sported rubbery, vermillion leaves. Gravel and broken rocks covered the ground, from which tenacious and thick new growth sprouted. It quickly became a trial to both make brisk pacing and avoid tripping.

Beyond the Hunting Woods lay the grand city of Zaaka Narai, the heart of the Gheroun Empire. Its conical buildings stabbed up toward the sky, cradled in a mountainous valley and all awash in mottled, faint green sunlight that filtered through swift-moving clouds. The sharp silhouettes of the city reminded Niko of the jagged teeth of a great maw, ready to mangle them all and spit out the remains.

It didn't escape him that the last time they'd been here, it was for the Starlight Awards, where everything had quickly fallen apart.

He, Elliott, and even Zann had spent several of the previous hours coordinating with Lady Death over the phone to piece together a course of action. The plan that had begun coalescing was intimidating, complex, and involved several moving parts.

Niko and Elliott would sneak into the Gheroun Imperial Palace under stealth, utilizing labyrinthine and enigmatic tunnels uncovered from old blueprints. This was something even Elliott and Deleera hadn't been able to secure data for, but Zann had come through, and produced rare and dated files from Galapol's archives showing the hidden old routes used by the Gheroun imperials for centuries. Niko only hoped they still applied.

Lady Death and her people would run heavy interference to keep the attention of the Imperial Army off Niko and Elliott's backs.

And the Legend, the aged bounty hunter who had tried—and failed—to bring Elliott and him down after coming out of retirement was, according to Death, going to join them, donning his own armor and playing a decoy of Niko.

Niko balked over the phone when she'd mentioned him. "Wait— The *Legend*? I'm not sure this is the best idea, D."

"He's with me," Death had replied blandly. "And he's going to behave himself, as far as you're concerned."

Elliott had worked diligently to create spare copies of the ORA, one for Oliver and Loolae each to use in getting them out unharmed.

The visor of Niko's helmet displayed a holographic map of the secret corridors of the Gheroun Imperial Palace as they trekked through tangled alien overgrowth. That he was even *in* a place like this, let alone embarking on what they were about to do was dizzying to him.

The leader of the entire Gheroun Empire had taken his father. Khaathra wasn't just the leader of one nation or planet; rather, she headed multiple worlds and galactic outposts. And it had been a hard-won position. She'd had decades of experience serving as a commander in the Gheroun Imperial army, before ascending to leadership of their people.

One of the most powerful and dangerous players in the entire galaxy had Oliver's fragile life in her tentacles. And she was anything but kind. He couldn't bring himself to watch her videos again, knowing this time it was his family and friend who were there to suffer her wrath. But the images from the first time he'd watched still haunted him, creeping through the corridors of his mind and taking up unwanted residence. She was, apparently, a woman who bore a lot of unbridled rage. And took it out on others behind closed doors.

He couldn't let a repeat of history happen. He just couldn't.

This had been his fault—all of it. Oliver should have been at home right then, settling down for the evening and watching his favorite sitcom or movie rerun. He shouldn't be facing down his own demise. Yet he was, and it was all because Niko had so carelessly assumed he would be safe.

This was the reality that Elliott had long known. This was the reality that he'd had to face every day since his sister had been taken. Since she'd been killed and never came back home. Elliott had lived Niko's worst nightmare. It wasn't a fear anymore for him; it was simply his life now.

Niko shook his head. Sinking into the abyss of these dark thoughts would do nothing to help him. They had a mission to see through. He would get his father and Loolae out.

They would be fine.

They were fine.

They had to be.

"Here," he muttered, heart leaping into his throat as he nearly stumbled over another curled, unyielding sapling. It was dense as an aged root. "Just ahead past this small hill and these, uh— Trees?"

"Trees," Elliott confirmed. "They make up ninety-one percent of Haneen's foliage, actually."

"Neat," Niko grunted out. He shifted from one foot to another, his entire body craving action. He just needed to get to his loved ones, to see that they were alright.

They resumed moving in the direction that Galapol's data indicated was the hidden entrance to one of the ancient palace passageways, Niko slightly in the lead, antsy to get a move on. When he crested the hill, he froze. Almost two dozen figures no larger than ants crowded around where the secret entrance lay, half obscured by curling trees. "Guards."

He magnified his visual of them through his visor, an unsettling realization turning his skin to ice beneath the suit as a familiar symbol came into view on each figure's armor.

"Those aren't guards," Elliott confirmed, his tone turning a shade darker.

Several elite Galapol special ops agents stood around the area, their bodies clad in thick armor as impenetrable as Niko's own. Niko tripped, the world around him suddenly spinning, but Elliott's hand shot out to grab his arm, steadying him. The other man must have heard his stumble.

They'd talked about this with Zann. Galapol had sold their dignity at the cost of lives.

But to see it here, to see the same people—and the same insignia he'd once proudly upheld and defended with his brother—guarding Imperator Khaathra, and supporting her cruel captivity of Niko's innocent loved ones was a shot straight through his heart. And it wouldn't stop bleeding.

Galapol knew. Galapol had let it happen, had let his father's life be put in the hands of an abuser and murderer. They'd, likely, even worked with Khaathra to set a trap for himself and Elliott. Even knowing what she'd done. After Elliott had sent them everything, nearly three years before. And even after Deleera had released to the public at large all the rancid footage Elliott had painstakingly gathered.

They didn't only just know that Khaathra had taken Niko's family. They weren't trying to recover them. They were, in fact, here helping her.

If Oliver and Loolae were even actually here. All of this could be for nothing, throwing their lives and the lives of Lady Death's loyalists into harm's way for two people who could be anywhere in the galaxy.

A deep rushing, rhythmic pounding filled his ears. It took a moment to realize it was his own pulse.

"Niko," Elliott said quietly. "Are you alright?"

Niko hated the lack of surprise in Elliott's tone. Of course he wouldn't be surprised. Elliott had been trying to tell him this entire time, had tried to show him the truth that lay bare before him now.

"Yeah— I—" He fell quiet at a loss for words.

"Niko... We can take a moment, if you need," Elliott offered quietly. But Niko shook his head. He couldn't bear the thought of his family in there still. He swallowed down his own agony, filing it away to approach at a later time. They needed him right now, and he wasn't about to fail them again. Death's group was relying on them too; he could hear the staccato ring of gunfire and commands on his headset. They were holding their own just fine, but in an operation as particularly dangerous as this one, right in the heart of the Gheroun Empire, even someone as resilient and seasoned as Deleera or the Legend only had so much time before they would be outnumbered.

"No." After a moment, he spoke again. "Do you think they're actually in there? I mean. Maybe this is all just a trap—"

"Of course it's a trap, Niko."

"No, I mean— With another layer to it, where—"

"I think they are," Elliott said. "We saw people distinctly linked to Khaathra taking them on that footage I'd found. People she has a history of trying to hide her ties to. Not Galapol. They likely just figured it out quicker than we did and wanted to use it to their advantage, or she outright tipped them off."

Niko blew out a sharp breath, briefly fogging up the visor of his helmet. He willed himself to try and calm his trembling body. He didn't know if it was more a relief or curse that his family was likely here after all, in the clutches of a known monster, rather than the unknown. "How are we getting around them? I can try to make a diversion."

"No, I don't think that's going to work," Elliott said flatly.

Niko had no choice but to relent. For all Galapol knew, the two of them were out causing havoc in the streets, with the Legend as a decoy of himself. Yet, this particular group still hadn't so much as budged. They were undoubtedly under strict orders to remain planted if even the Legend's ruckus couldn't draw them away. He sucked in an unsteady breath, his lungs burning with uncertainty. They'd have to do this the hard way. They couldn't afford a fight.

"Yeah. We'll have to sneak past them."

"Mmh," Elliott acknowledged. "That's going to be... hard. They're crowding that hidden entrance tightly."

"You've done it before, right? Plenty of times."

Elliott said nothing, and something sharp snagged at Niko's insides. He knew what Elliott was leaving unsaid: *I've done it. But not you.*

"Elliott, let's go. I don't want to waste any more time. D's waiting on us. If Dad's in there, I don't want to leave him at their mercy for another minute—"

"I understand," Elliott cut him off. "You're right."

Niko started forward, his heart hammering. It was so loud in his ears it matched the muffled gunfire on Death's end of their connection. It was so loud he feared it alone would give them away to Galapol.

After a moment, he heard Elliott's steps fall silent, and knocked into the back of him, nearly losing his balance again. He clenched his jaw to keep from snapping out of unbearable stress, his patience barely restrained. Everything was pressing down on him, crushing him under its weight and urgency. "What's up?"

"Niko..." Elliott's voice came slow, calm, and careful now in a way he didn't like. He was suddenly transported back in time ten years ago, a Galapol officer at their front door, explaining in that same careful way that his mother and brother were never coming home from their shopping trip again. "I need you to listen to me."

"Yeah?"

Elliott paused to consider before continuing. "I think that I should go in there alone."

"No." The word ejected itself from Niko's mouth before Elliott had even finished speaking.

Elliott took it in stride, continuing in that same calm, delicate tone. "It's a minefield up ahead. Galapol is littering the entrance. Getting through them is going to require not giving *anything* away."

"You think I can't do it—"

"Listen to me. Please. I just want to make sure, more than anything, that your family gets out. You're not as used to working with stealth yet as I am."

The memory of brilliantly failing their hit against Skeevy Larry burned through him, a hot shame. He felt sick. His father was in there, and Niko was going to hang back and let Elliott take all the risk. Let him walk—alone—into the Gheroun Imperial Palace, through a cluster of hostile Galapol agents and however many trained imperial soldiers and guards lay waiting inside.

This whole thing had been a trap, and he was about to send Elliott alone into it.

Elliott, who had taken on the lion's share of researching who'd even abducted them. Elliott, who now was going to be the one to put his life at risk. Who was going to be the one to—with any luck—save the lives of Niko's father and friend while he stood around and hoped for the best.

Niko was truly useless.

"You'll have to get back out, too. You know, Dad— Dad and Loolae have no experience with stealth, either—"

He heard Elliott's slow, shaky intake of breath as the other man searched for what to say. *I can work with them. I can't, with you.* He didn't even have to say it.

Inappropriate, awful rage surged up through Niko. It choked him, nearly blinded him. Every breath he took was thick with it, an anger aimed at everything, at everyone. At Elliott, at Khaathra. Most of all, at himself.

If he hadn't ever gotten injured, if he were able to ambulate with the careful steps and quietude of Elliott—

"*I can do it.*" He spat the words, pushing on ahead before Elliott could protest, each step matching the anxious and rageful pounding of his pulse.

"Niko—" Elliott began, but Niko barreled right past him. He couldn't see the other man, but felt the impact and heard the quiet, sharp exhale as they collided. After a moment, Elliott's voice came again, somehow shouting and yet only a hissed whisper at the same time. *"Niko!"*

Niko didn't stop. He wasn't going to sit this one out, wasn't going to stand back and be incompetent while all his allies did the heavy lifting for him. Something jerked him back by the arm and Niko stumbled, nearly losing his balance yet again. Elliott had grabbed him. He shrugged free, spinning to face the other man. When he did, Elliott was barely visible at all, merely a faint outline, a distortion of the air.

"Stop," Elliott warned. His tone was dark, a command that left no quarter. "I'm not done talking to you."

"I told you I can fucking do it! There's nothing to talk about!" Niko turned to continue on, when he was grabbed once more. He wrenched his arm away harder this time, and with a pang of guilt, felt—rather than saw—Elliott stumble back from the force of it.

For a brief moment, Elliott paused, quiet and still, a dark storm brewing in the air between them. Then something heavy and hard slammed into the side of Niko's helmet, eliciting a solid, reverberating *thud* that made his ears ring.

It wasn't enough to be felt through his thick armor, but the impact had been so unexpected that this time, Niko was knocked off balance and couldn't recover his footing. He crashed against the ground so loudly that he and Elliott both briefly froze, but the cluster of agents was still far enough away that none of them even looked in their direction.

It didn't take long for Niko to put the pieces together.

Elliott had punched him.

He heard the other man step closer, boots crushing the gravel beneath them. Elliott bore down over him. Even without having a visual right now, Niko could sense the cold rage radiating from him.

"You're not listening to me, Niko. You're going too far again. You don't know when to back down, and it's going to get us killed. If any of those agents sense a single thing is off, we're done for. We can't take that many on. Look at their armor. It's like yours. We can't get through them by force. Not to mention they'll probably sound the fucking alarm. We'll be swarmed in seconds."

"I can do this—"

"We just spoke about this, right? About staying back when asked to?" Elliott's voice finally softened. "Let me do this for you. Let me get your family back safely to you."

Tears stung the corners of Niko's eyes, behind his closed visor. Every muscle in his body was taut with pent-up frustration, with agony and rage directed, now, only at himself. Even now, he wanted to argue. Even now, knowing every word Elliott had aimed toward him was right.

In the end, making sure they all got out of this alive was the only thing that mattered. Far more than his own ego. Far more than feeling competent.

"Niko," Elliott said. "Give me your hand." For a moment, Niko merely stayed as he was, before finally reaching out. The two of them found each other's hands, and Niko wished he could feel the warmth of Elliott's through his gauntlet. Elliott helped pull him back to his feet.

Humiliation and sorrow washed through Niko, a cold, congealing oil that replaced all the anger that had once filled him to the brim.

"Listen to me. There are so many things you excel at that I can't do," Elliott continued. "I never would have made it this far without you. I'm *alive* because of you. You told me we need to work with each other's strengths. This is my strength. Not your weakness, but my strength. So let me do what I do best for you. Let me return the kindness you gave me. *Please.*"

"I—I—" Niko relented, hanging his head as he let out a long breath. "Alright, babe. Yeah. Please, just…"

"I'll be careful. You can trust me, Niko."

"…Thanks, Elliott."

"I love you. More than I have words for. I hope that you know that."

He did know that. It was what made Elliott going in there alone for him all the harder. Niko ached.

With that, he heard Elliott slip past him, then the other man was gone, the forest around them silent and still as though he'd never been there.

Niko kept watch over the hidden entrance, breath held for what felt like moments at a time. His visor's tech allowed him to magnify his view of the entrance and the agents there. They kept their tight formation around it, gazes pointed warily towards the columns of smoke rising from the faux Niko's onslaught of Zaaka Narai. His breath caught every time he thought about Elliott having to maneuver through the cluster of them.

Niko waited for the moment when Elliott would slip inside, to look for any telltale giveaway—the stirring of gravel, a brushing up against gnarled foliage. He was especially grateful for the distractions wrought by Deleera's group and the Legend, hoping if there were any small slip-ups, that the explosions and chaos in the city beyond would be enough to divide and keep the agents' attention. But Elliott was so skilled that as the time crawled on,

Niko realized he'd likely already gotten through and he himself hadn't even noticed.

He tried to swallow the slurry of discomfort and shame that crawled through him. He was both ashamed at the tantrum he'd thrown—the mission here on Haneen was one that only allotted precious little time and had lots of moving pieces that put dozens of lives at risk, including Oliver and Loolae's—and that they'd even had to go there in the first place.

Elliott had been right. They needed to balance one another out. He needed to relinquish control and let Elliott take the reins sometimes. But he wished he hadn't had to.

He fought against pelting Elliott with inquiries over their comm line *(Are you okay? Everything good? What's going on in there?)* and tried to remind himself that if the other man wasn't reporting anything back, he was either at risk of being overheard or nothing was going wrong that needed reporting.

Today had been a lesson in restraint.

Instead, Niko reached out to the others to try and quell his restless anxiety. "How's it going out there? Death? Legend? Elliott's inside now."

*"Not you?"* Death asked. Niko faltered, looking for how to answer, when she pushed on anyway. Her responses were peppered with gunfire in the background. *"Fair on my end. You guys need to work fast, though. Gheroun Imperial Guard is right pissed and the Galapricks just joined the party, too."*

The Legend's staticky chuckle sounded through Niko's earpiece, an explosion of some kind on the other end making him wince. A second later, he heard its real-life echo booming in the distance to the west. They weren't too far from him now. *"Havin' fun, old girl? I sure am. Been a while since I got to have a day this wild."* Another rocking explosion sounded, followed by a cackle. *"Oooh, you shoulda seen that one. Guy's head just yee-hawed right off his damn body. Giddyup, assholes!"*

"Uh, sounds like you're having a good time, at least," Niko said. He glanced out towards the city proper, the sounds of sirens blaring now as columns of wispy, dark smoke rose into the air. "Wait. 'Old girl?' You're one to talk."

*"Hah, she's older'n me,"* the Legend said. *"Just gots a better skin care routine."*

*"And Heenvan longevity,"* Death quipped back flatly. *"Alright. They're going to expect you heading further west, so why don't you pivot south down one of the back alleys and we can start making our way over to get you. We need to wind this down soon."*

*"Yes ma'am,"* the Legend said. *"Whatever you say, ma'am."*

*"Niko? Elliott? You need to work quickly. We won't have much longer."*

"Right." He bit down again on reaching out to Elliott. If the other man could speak, he would have. There must be undoubtedly countless guards inside to navigate through. Maybe even traps.

The thought made Niko lightheaded.

A moment later, his salvation came, carried through barely a whisper over their line. It was the most beautiful sound he'd ever heard. *"Got them, Niko. They're okay, as far as I can tell. We're moving fast, though. Had to neutralize the guards where they were being held and it won't take long for someone to figure that out."*

"Okay, babe," Niko managed, heart tightening in his chest. He hated how clunky the words emerged. There were so many things he wanted to say. Elliott was alright—so far. And his father was there with him, recovered and safe. And alive.

So far.

"I'll be waiting at the spot we were before, unless you need me somewhere else," he added.

*"No, stay there. We shouldn't be long. I'm going to have to go dark again, though."*

"Yeah, I get it." *Be careful* died on the tip of his tongue. Instead, he settled on, "Love you, babe."

He didn't get a response.

For the next few moments, the only change came in the form of more explosions and gunfire throughout the city, perforated by occasional status updates and coordination over the comm line between Death's group and the Legend. Niko could see and hear Gheroun reinforcements arriving, as well as the telltale flash and sirens of Galapol's crafts moving onto the scene. Their voices slowly began to turn strained over the frequency, Death's commands coming more sharply and briskly. They didn't have much longer left. Above him, the gargantuan, lavender crescent of Uula pressed down on the city and all its ongoing struggle and chaos from above in glimpses awarded between thick, veridian cloud cover, ever looming.

"Come on," Niko muttered under his breath, turning his eyes back on the secret entrance and cluster of agents.

Seconds later, Elliott's voice filled his ears again, this time louder than the whisper before, and from just ahead of him. "Niko? Are you still here?"

"Yeah, I'm here, babe."

"N-Niko?" a hoarse, frightened, and deeply familiar voice called out. Niko couldn't see anything of them but faint distortions as they closed in, but hearing his father's voice choked him up so badly he could barely bring himself to respond.

"Dad," Niko said, his own voice catching on the lump that sat heavy in his throat. *"Dad."*

"Niko. Oh god, Niko. I missed you."

Niko swallowed back a hearty swell of emotion, all tangled with guilt. "You alright? Did they—? They—?"

"I'm okay. We're both alright."

"Loolae?"

"I'm here," another familiar but haggard voice sounded, Loolae's translator chip conveying her fatigue. He'd never heard her so worn down.

"Niko, we need to keep going," Elliott said.

"Let's go, then," Niko said. "Straight to the ship. Run. But watch the ground. Lots of overgrowth to trip on here."

Niko kept to a slower jog for Oliver and Loolae. He didn't know what kind of shape they were in, and it was their first time operating under cloak of stealth. He knew from experience how far too easy it was to trip over the back of someone's heel or knock into them. Or even just lose track of those around you.

"It would be nice to take care of the Imperator too, since we're paying a visit," Elliott muttered.

"It's too risky, Elliott." He hated that the beast called Khaathra would be spared a second time, but his priority would always be his family. "Let's just get out of here."

The other man relented. "Right. I know. You're right."

*"Killjoy? What's your status?"* Death's voice crackled through their earpieces. Niko winced at the tension in her voice. Her words came sharp, cutting into his ears like jagged shards of thick glass. His mind assaulted itself with macabre possibilities—whatever was going on out there, he knew they didn't have long now. Lady Death may have taken on a planetary government before, but one's luck and skill only ran so far. Even when they were as exceptional as the Revolutionary of Sala.

"We got them. Heading back to the ship now. ETA, five minutes tops."

*"We don't have five minutes."* Gunfire erupted through their frequency. Niko's breath caught in his throat as he heard someone let out a gurgling scream close enough to Death to be picked up on their call. Was it someone he knew? People were dying for this. For him. For all his choices and mistakes.

"We can make it in three," Elliott asserted over their line.

"Dad, Loolae, I'm gonna need you to pick up the pace. Think you can?"

"We'll be fine," Loolae said. "Right, Oliver?"

"Right," the older man assured.

Niko broke into a full run now as Elliott kept pace beside him, evidenced by the soft pounding of his combat boots against the gravel below.

"*I can probably do three.*" Death's voice rose to a commanding shout on the other end of their line. "*Alright! Fall back! Let's start planning the retreat. Where's Esteban?*"

"*Got pushed back to, uh, Esaarai Street. Things is gettin' a little dicey over here,*" the Legend called back, followed by a nervous, wheezy chuckle. Niko nearly did a double-take. He'd never even heard the man's actual name in all the years he'd known him. "*Think they're boxin' me in. Can't get around to you.*"

"*Shee'ylata,*" Death cursed in her native Sala-Heenvan. "*Esaarai's a long way out. Niko, get to the ship and get your people out of here. Now. We're going to try to swing around and intercept you, Esteban, but they're making a chokepoint in your direction.*"

"*Well, I'll just keep doin' my thing, then,*" the Legend replied.

"Shit," Niko muttered under his breath. Whatever was going on out there, it was rapidly becoming untenable. He knew all too well how quickly a mission could fall apart.

They were nearing the *Soñadora* now; he could see the cluster of dense tree trunks that they'd parked behind, even if the ship itself was invisible. The sight of being so close to getting out of this alive pushed him all the harder. Half a minute later, and they were there. Niko slowed and called out to the others.

"Stop. We're here."

"Here...?" Oliver panted out. He sounded further behind them than Niko liked.

He heard Elliott begin stomping around against the gravel, until his boot collided instead against the ramp, the solid *clang* of metal ringing out. "Here. Come on."

They began the awkward process of getting Oliver and Loolae up what was essentially an invisible, ascending walkway, where they couldn't even see their own feet.

To his credit, Oliver only paused momentarily at its base, disoriented. Niko didn't have time to gentle the man's first time using stealth tech the way he would have liked, though.

"Everybody inside. Let's go, let's go!" Niko grasped for his father, until he clumsily found his arm and gently guided him up onto the ramp. Loolae was close on Oliver's heels, taking the dizzying ascent much better. Elliott started halfway up after them, when their comms crackled again.

*"Shit,"* Death's voice cut through Niko's helmet. He had never heard her so unnerved sounding. *"Fuck. I— Esteban, we... We can't get to you."*

The Legend gave another wheezy chuckle, defeated and tired now. *"Well, ain't that a heapin' bucket of Toliai shit. Eh, no worries."*

*"I..."* Death started, her voice trailing off into a miasma of uncertainty that made Niko's stomach churn. This wasn't supposed to be happening. Lady Death had always been such a towering, strong figure in his life. So had even the Legend once, before time had forced the old man to his knees. His heroes were breaking

around him. They had reached their limits. And it was all because of trying to help him.

Niko froze, standing just before the transparent base of the ship's ramp.

"Niko?"

When he didn't respond, Elliott temporarily deactivated his stealth, appearing halfway up the ramp. His eyes scanned Niko's vicinity, trying to pinpoint him. "Niko, we have to go. Now."

*"Hey, kid? You there?"* the Legend asked, his words punctuated by more gunfire.

"Y-yeah? I'm here," Niko said.

*"You get your family out?"*

Hurt lanced through his chest. "Yeah. Yeah, I did. Thanks, uh, Esteban."

*"Good. Did what I came here to do, then."* After a pause, he added, *"Sorry about before. Had to try, with a bounty like that. But I ain't what I used to be. You put up a good fight, though. I'm glad for it. Yer gonna do just fine."*

Niko deactivated his stealth and backed away from the ship, his heart pounding in his ears. He raised the visor of his helmet, gaze locking onto Elliott's own now.

"What are you doing?" Elliott breathed, something hysterical edging at his words.

"I—I have to try," he said slowly.

"Try what?"

"To help him."

Elliott blinked several times, incredulous. He glanced around nervously, before stepping down the ramp toward Niko. Niko readied himself for the onslaught that was coming. "Niko, I'm sorry. I'm so sorry. You can't. It's far too dangerous. Even Death's group can't get to him now."

"I have to try. He's here because of me."

"He chose to be here. And he tried to kill you, if you don't recall?"

"I tried to kill you too, Elliott. It's in the past. Look, I can't keep talking. I'm running out of time. I have to do this. I have to at least try."

Elliott's eyes searched him for a moment. Finally, his shoulders sagged and his face contorted into something miserable; he must have seen something there in Niko. Something unmovable. "Then we should take the ship—"

"No. I need you to stay here with Dad and Loolae. I'm relying on you to keep them safe and get the ship out of here if I don't make it back."

"If you don't— Is this about earlier? I..."

"No, Elliott. It's about helping the people who helped me. If they hadn't come here and risked themselves to make a distraction for us, this would have gone a lot worse. I'm asking you to trust me, this time."

"I fucking hate this," Elliott seethed. In that moment, he reminded Niko of someone more boyish than a man in his mid-twenties. Niko had probably come off the same not so long ago himself, he figured. "Niko, you need to make it back."

His own voice softened. "I know, babe. I will."

"Promise me."

"I promise."

Elliott pulled him into a long kiss, desperate, passionate. Niko reluctantly pulled away, all too aware of the passing by of precious seconds he couldn't afford to lose.

"Take this with you," Elliott said, unlatching and then handing him his own ORA and shield generator.

"Elliott…" Niko began warily, but the other man shook his head.

"He might be able to use it. I'll be fine. I'll be in the ship."

Niko took them, then forced himself to step back again. "Hey. I love you." A small, sad smile crept onto his lips. "More than I have words for."

"I love you," Elliott said. "I'll keep your family safe."

"I know, babe. I trust you." Niko lowered his visor, reactivated his stealth, and turned towards the deadly, winding streets of Zaaka Narai, which spread before him for miles upon endless miles, its maw open and waiting.

Then he stepped into the fray.

# CHAPTER FIFTEEN
# THE FRAY

ELLIOTT WATCHED HIM DISAPPEAR, anxious nausea clenching in his gut. The audacity that Niko possessed, trying to save the life of an old, toothless bounty hunter—who'd outright begged them to kill him in their last encounter—made Elliott want to spit his name in a curse. But that was who Niko was. Selfless, brilliant, radiant. And it was why Elliott had fallen so hopelessly in love with him.

Niko had also had every reason to let Elliott himself die back on Neema, not all that long ago. To earn his bounty and lifelong prestige, and keep his own family safe and at peace. And far, far away from any sort of nightmare like ending up in the Imperial Palace of Haneen had been.

But he hadn't then, either.

Elliott paused, gaze scanning the dense forest around them, the sharp, conical spires of the palace they'd just fled from on the eastern horizon flanking the city, a sobering reminder of the real danger not far from them at any given moment. An eerie chill settled over him, creeping along each vertebra, making him shiver.

*Best get in the ship.*

It was armored, it was stealthed—both qualities he was painfully lacking at the moment. And he could get it airborne in mere seconds if the need arose.

*If I don't make it back...*

Niko's words haunted him and he felt sick. He swiftly swallowed the thought. He wouldn't go there, wouldn't allow himself. Elliott couldn't imagine continuing on without Niko now. He didn't know if he would have the strength—or sanity—left to.

He needed to check on Niko's family. To see if the thing called Khaathra had done anything more to them than they'd initially let on in the chaos and rush of getting them out safely. They could be wounded and he hadn't fully realized. He hadn't had the time nor luxury to assess them further.

He turned to ascend the ramp into the *Soñadora*, when silver flashed by the corner of his vision and ricocheted off the invisible side of the ship, where it tumbled across the gravel before skidding to a stop. A second later, his cheek began to sting, something warm trickling down it. Elliott reached up to touch it, stunned.

Blood.

*No. No, no—*

He stared down at the offending object on the ground. Five protruding, wicked points, one still tipped with a smear of fresh crimson, told him immediately what it was. A Gheroun star knife.

He spun on his heel, trembling hands struggling to aim his rifle in the direction it had been thrown from. He was entirely exposed and vulnerable.

Then he saw her, emerald tentacles wrapped tightly around several more star knives.

Imperator Khaathra.

"Where do you think you're going?" she asked, her three eyes far too wide, her teeth bared in a predatory grin. "This ends here. And I'm going to *enjoy* every second of breaking you."

Elliott's heart leapt into his throat, veins turning to ice. It was instinct to flee—he almost always chose survival. But he didn't even have the time to—she'd managed to move quietly enough through the forest to catch him unaware. She was on him in an instant, bearing down on him before he could even get a shot in or flee back up the ramp. Her tentacles were everywhere, some twining tightly around his wrists and legs, others doling out vicious, quick slices with five-pointed knives that he barely dodged in time. They laced around his arms like boa constrictors, tightening him in a vice grip so painful he was forced to drop *Repartee*. Already, he was being quickly overwhelmed as she tangled him in herself.

He'd been so stupid before, deactivating his stealth to talk to Niko. Or maybe she'd just sniffed them out from their trail of all but neon breadcrumbs of footprints and trampled foliage leading back to the ship.

Elliott's pulse hammered in his chest, his throat, his ears, so hard that it ached. No matter what happened, he couldn't afford to let Khaathra get through him and into the *Soñadora Despierta*. He wouldn't let her take Niko's family back. Elliott knew exactly what animals like her did. She wouldn't be so "kind" a second time around. Her videos showed she worked a well-hidden rage and aggression out on helpless, unarmed people, forcing them to engage in a sadistic mockery of a fight against her.

It always ended the same.

The lives of Niko's family, more than ever, were in his hands now. If he failed here and fell to her, it wouldn't just be himself suffering. He would fail Niko. He would let the people he loved most meet the same repulsive fate that Cleo once had.

He couldn't let that happen. He wouldn't.

A memory bloomed in the back of his mind, even as Khaathra wrapped herself around his limbs, constraining them. Cleo had been his defender once. She'd taken their father on, the towering goliath that he'd been at the time. She'd gotten in his way, had been the wall, the barrier that had cut off the drunken man's access to hurting Elliott. She'd pushed back. She'd taken the hits and bore the hurts, instead.

Words, once spoken with defiance and desperation, echoed through his mind.

*Dad, leave him alone! I won't let you hurt him!*

*Stay back, Ellie. I'm going to handle this.*

*You'll have to go through me first. Come on, then!*

She'd saved him.

She had always been his hero. Cleo had taught him bravery.

*Breathe in,* he told himself. *Remember what you've learned. Apply it. You still have options.*

He willed himself to meet the monster who had come for them all. She was a violent, hateful creature, and when she'd said she would enjoy hurting him, Elliott knew she had meant it. He wouldn't let her through, wouldn't let her near the ship which was the last bastion of safety for two vulnerable civilians who never should have had any part in this. His fight had never been theirs.

A preternatural calm fell over him then. Elliott was going to best the Gheroun Imperator. He would win. There was no other choice. There was no other option. Dying here wasn't a possibility, because he wouldn't let it be.

"You're right," he said. "This ends here. How kind of you to make it so convenient for me. And you didn't even bring your guards. It's a wonder your keepers let you out all by yourself."

His words were more than just a taunt; it was something he really needed to know. If she had the backup the head of an empire would normally have waiting out among the trees, he'd quickly be in over his head. He twisted his left wrist at an angle that sent a sharp and shooting pain up his forearm but made it difficult for her to keep her grip on him, and managed to just barely slip it free. Then he wasted no time, grasping for the knife at his hip.

"I don't need them here to put you in your place, you little parasite," she said. "What I'm going to do to you isn't for civilized eyes."

She'd really shown up alone. His lucky knife had brought him good fortune, after all.

*Time to test that luck again.*

He pried it free of its sheath and engaged in the single best way to shut down a Gheroun in close combat: he jammed it into the tentacle that gripped his other wrist and ripped the blade straight through.

With an anguished shriek, Imperator Khaathra's appendage came partially free, the end dangling off now as ultramarine blood spurted from it. It didn't stop her onslaught though; the madwoman was an experienced, honored fighter among her people. And Elliott knew from her dirty little secret that she more than craved the violence.

But it was enough to free his right arm.

He didn't let up against the Imperator either, pushing back into her tangled form and slicing for another tentacle, while narrowly dodging her own attempt to behead him with a furious swipe. She prioritized Elliott's knife, grappling desperately to try and wrench it from him. He twisted his arm again, though, this time in the opposite direction, and in a swift, fluid maneuver, brought his blade arcing straight through another tentacle, severing it clean off.

Cleo's voice wove through his thoughts once more, a thread of light among the tumultuous horror of the fight he was in now. Time and time again, she'd shown up for him, had protected him, had risen to the challenge of someone bigger, stronger. After each hit, she'd gotten up and faced their abuser again.

*He's your son! He's just a child!*

*You're an absolute monster. You treat everyone like they're beneath you!*

*This isn't love. This isn't family. This is just your ego wanting to lash out against the people who depended on you!*

Elliott had mourned the loss of the avian costume mask she'd gifted him. It had given him the illusion she was still with him, a phantom watching over him through the worst of it. But he didn't need the mask anymore to feel that. It was never what had mattered.

*Know your place, you stupid bitch,* their father had once slurred at her, in a rage and riled up when she'd refused to back down after he'd become aggressive toward Elliott for taking apart their grandfather's watch.

*No,* she'd replied, head held high. *I know my place, and it will never be beneath you again.*

Khaathra tried to send him to the ground, grabbing him by the leg and jerking to the right. He predicted her though, using the momentum to half-spin and carve into another one of her assaulting tentacles.

*Breathe,* he willed himself. *Just like you trained. Move to the left. Drive the knife into her right. Match her on the right. Defend. Push into it, shift with her and flow. Left kick to the abdomen. Use her unbalancing against her. Exploit the advantage.*

"Where'd you learn to fight like that?" Khaathra hissed, tucking what remained of her severed tentacles against herself as she kept on him. It seemed he hadn't been the only one taken by surprise in this encounter.

When Elliott had set out to teach himself hand-to-hand, he'd favored the Gheroun method—which served him well now. It relied on evasion and fluid motion, twisting and meeting one's opponent in a dance that rarely halted in movement. It had worked well enough on keeping certain tenacious bounty hunters at bay.

And now it was proving surprisingly effective against the head of the Gheroun people herself.

She'd chosen to take him on alone. She'd decided to do it in melee combat, likely just to prove she could.

Elliott wanted to hurt her where she was most vulnerable—her ego.

He felt the grin spreading across his lips now, something lupine. "I taught myself. Do you like it? Do you like that I can take you on? Or does it infuriate you that I'm going to win?"

"No one wins against me. Especially not someone like you."

He was vaguely aware of voices filling his ears now—the desperate back-and-forth of Niko's and Lady Death's parties. He couldn't pay them enough mind to pick up on the specifics of their communication, but the panicked tone of their voices was enough to tell him about how much they were struggling.

Khaathra took another swing for his neck with a jagged star knife. Elliott met and deflected it with his own blade, sending her knife clattering to the ground. Her tentacles were too slicked with blood now, making it nearly impossible to keep a grip on him. He slipped away from her, finally free, and took several steps back.

Then he laughed. "You're pathetic."

She answered with a violent laugh of her own, a manic, too-wide grimace splitting her face. Elliott could hear the crack of her teeth under the strain of how hard she clenched them. "Making me work for it, are you? The ways I'm going to break every one of you..."

"No. You've broken enough people," he said. "We know our place, and it will never be beneath someone like you again."

"You're no one," she seethed. "You're nothing. You just got lucky you made it through this little game of yours this far." She began screaming her words now, somewhere between rage and desperation, spittle flying. "I'll string you up and hang you from the palace wall, where everyone can come desecrate your worthless corpse for entertainment!"

Elliott could see the emerald of her skin had begun paling now, her features turning sallow, her wild and angry eyes appearing sunken into her face. She was weakening. Yet even now, she wouldn't capitulate.

Not that Elliott would let her. She was a blight on the galaxy that needed to be put down. She'd abused her power and influence for too long.

He had already won this—it came down to a matter of time, now. He could wait her out, keep the fight going until she bled out. But he needed to make this quick.

A fragment of Niko's voice crackled over his comm lines. *"—trying to get there, D, but it's not looking good over here. They have us completely surrounded now."*

It was time to end this.

He beckoned her toward him with a wave of his knife. "Come on, then."

Khaathra leapt at him, her tentacles shooting out and attempting to bind him again, but he spun to the side, evading her, and buried his knife hilt-deep in her sternum, right where her primary heart lay. She coughed out a spatter of thick blood—a gesture so disturbingly familiar that even now he had to glance away—before stumbling back and finally sinking to the ground.

It was slow. Even defeated and bleeding out, the Imperator of the Gheroun Empire refused to die. Her remaining tentacles still snaked up him sluggishly, weakly attempting to entwine themselves around his arms and legs. They strained to get at his knife again and again. He shrugged out of her grip with ease and took a step back. She sagged into herself, her breathing ragged now, and tilted her head to gaze up at him.

*"You... killed me,"* she whispered, astonished.

"How many people have you killed, just because they couldn't fight back?" he spat, staring down his nose at her. "It was only a matter of time before someone could. You did this to yourself."

Khaathra didn't answer. She merely sat, her three unseeing eyes still open, blankly pointed towards his own. No one was behind them anymore.

She disgusted him.

Elliott bent, panting, and retrieved *Repartee* from where it had tumbled to the ground. His entire body trembled from exertion, adrenaline, and fear. He had actually bested her. He'd taken on the head of an empire today to protect Niko's family... and had won.

Somehow.

Cleo had been with him today. He could almost imagine glancing over his shoulder to see her grinning at him. Would she have been proud?

*"Status, Niko?"* Lady Death's voice over the comm line tore him out of his reverie.

*"We're gonna try to make a go for it,"* Niko responded. *"But they're bringing in more reinforcements. Lots of them."*

The fear in his lover's voice snapped Elliott back to the matter at hand. His job wasn't done yet.

He stumbled away from Khaathra and turned back toward the ship. Oliver Delamar peered out nervously at the aftermath of their exchanged carnage. Despite everything, the bizarre sight of the man appearing to peek out from a doorway suspended in the air made Elliott emit an exhausted snort.

He didn't have time to think any more about it, though, already halfway up the *Soñadora's* ramp now.

"Niko."

*"Elliott? Hey, babe, I... Things aren't going so great out here. Think we might have gotten in over our heads, a little."* After a pause, he added, *"It's really good to hear your voice, though."*

"Hang on just a little longer," Elliott insisted. He made his way toward the pilot's seat, glancing toward Oliver and Loolae, who watched him with uncertainty. "Find something sturdy and hold on," he instructed them as he passed. "This might be a bit of a wild flight."

*"Wait, what?"* Niko interjected. *"Listen, I—I'm gonna need you to take Dad and—"*

"No. We're all making it out of this alive." Elliott sank into the pilot's seat, ready. "Do you still trust me, Niko?"

The city of Zaaka Narai was a labyrinth of tangled, winding streets that looped in on themselves and then back again, circling grand and towering cone-shaped buildings. The Gheroun people, it seemed, had a particular aversion to corners and straight lines, and it made navigating a city built by alien minds all the more confusing to Niko.

He kept a map hologram projected on his visor at all times, his only savior in being able to make good time navigating the shortest path that led to where the Legend had gotten cut off from Deleera's group.

Despite the size and grandeur of the city, its streets were eerily empty and quiet now, belongings left scattered and spilled across the ground, vehicles left parked haphazardly, their doors open, their engines left running.

The Imperial government must have called for a hasty evacuation of this sector.

On every horizon, the lights of Gheroun Imperial Guard vehicles flashed and glimmered like furious purple and gold stars. By the minute, more and more blue and red lights of Galapol crafts joined them.

It was a sight that would have comforted Niko once, not all that long ago.

His lungs burned from having run so far. His legs sent ominous pangs of electricity burning up through his spine. With Elliott's ORA, he'd managed to keep up a good pace and reach the Legend's location more quickly than would otherwise have been possible.

Seeing the old bounty hunter again was shocking and surreal. They'd custom painted his armor to be a respectable replica of Niko's own, glossy and black. The sight of him—rifle out and crouching down behind an alleyway dumpster for makeshift shelter—was like looking in a mirror.

"I have visual of you," Niko said. "Coming in from six o' clock now. I'll be approaching in stealth."

*"Kid!"* the old man lamented over their line. *"Damn fool is what you are. The young ain't supposed to die for the old."*

"Nobody's dying here today," Niko said. He closed in behind the Legend, and the old man instinctively spun, waving his rifle vaguely in Niko's direction.

"It's just me."

"Thought it was another one of those drones. Damn things have been the worst part of this." Above them, a Galapol drone sped past, delivering a series of shots that sent both men crouching behind the dumpster for shelter. The Legend took aim at it. "Speak of the devil. They keep sendin' these things and I'm just about outta—" He pulled the trigger, but his rifle gave a useless click, the chamber empty. "Yep. Well, shit. You came just in time."

"I've got it," Niko said, and raised his own rifle. Seconds later, the drone ruptured into flaming shards from an explosive round.

"Listen, I have some things you need to use if we're going to make it out of here," Niko started, crowding in closer. He briefly deactivated his ORA to avoid the awkward dance of trying to exchange items while in stealth. "Take this. We have to move quick." He handed the old man the shield generator, explaining how to work it, then Elliott's ORA.

"So, you see that switch there on the top? You'll need to hit that and—" He watched as the other man completely vanished, only a faint outline of himself remaining. "You got it."

"Eh? Stealth, huh?"

Another drone came flying their way, hurtling straight for Niko on a collision course and visibly laced with explosives. He took it out mid-air with a quick shot. This time, the drone exploded with such force that the windows lining the alleyway shattered and came raining down on the two of them, tinkling loudly as they struck the dumpster and their armor, then the ground.

"Pain in my goddamn ass," the disembodied voice of the Legend muttered.

Niko quickly reactivated his own stealth. "I'm going to need you to stick close to me, but we won't be able to see each other. So, we'll just have to rely on saying where we are, and where to go. Follow my directions."

"Got it."

*"You're with him now, Niko?"* Death asked.

"Yep. We should be good to go, D."

*"We're going to start pulling out, then."*

"Stay safe."

Yet another pair of drones rounded the entrance to the alleyway, then sped toward their location. Niko's hands twitched; it was instinct to try and shoot them down. But the drones passed right by, not noticing them anymore.

"Damn, this shit's useful," Esteban mused. "Dude coulda just sold this for a fortune and had it made, instead of this whole murder thing. Retired on a yacht on Eanan."

"Uh, yeah, well, things are a little more complicated than that. Listen, we need to make a run for it. And we need to do it now." Niko stood, stray shards of glass falling from his suit. They cracked beneath his boots as he started forward. "Let's go. Head down the alley and we're going to keep to Naiaa Avenue for a while. I'm gonna need you to keep up."

"Don't patronize me, kid," the Legend said. "I do my cardio."

Niko broke into a swift jog, praying the old man could keep decent pace with him. They made their way back through the alley the way he'd arrived, but were forced to halt in their tracks.

An impenetrable, building wall of blue and red lights and wailing sirens cut off their path back to the *Soñadora* now. Even in stealth, there was no easy way around them, and though the ORA helped, it was all too easy to be spotted if one got too close or careless. Niko had been forced to face that reality not even an hour ago with Elliott.

To get back out of this, he and the Legend would need to make a go for Lady Death's ships.

"Change of plans. Are you still on the ground, D?"

*"Yes, but not for long."*

"We're gonna need to try and make it to you."

*"Niko, I don't know how much longer we can hold out,"* Death pressed, her voice carrying a gravelly fatigue and strain that shaped every word. She hesitated, before asking, *"How soon can the two of you make it to Hannua Park?"*

"We're going now. We should have a clear shot straight through to you."

*"Make it happen, then. Our time is up."*

"Alright, this is gonna suck," he grunted out. *May as well be honest about it.* "We're gonna need to go faster."

Both men backtracked, breaking into a run now as they made their way back into the alleyway, this time heading toward the opposite exit. They emerged into an open, circular plaza full of abstract sculptures and littered with more hastily abandoned possessions. A wall of Imperial Guards wielding tower shields had formed a living barricade and were closing in on the alleyway, dozens of special ops Galapol agents behind them in armor as impenetrable as Niko's own.

Another minute spent in the alley and they'd have been done for.

Niko spotted a gap to the far right of them in the open plaza. "Keep right!" he called to the Legend, maintaining a healthy distance from the hostile forces. "Still with me?"

*"I'm with you!"* the other man responded over their comms.

*"Niko, I need you to go faster,"* Death pressed.

"We're going as fast as we can!" He consulted the map. Ahead of them, a major throughway led straight past Hannua Park, where Death's group was holding out at. "Straight onto the highway," Niko directed the Legend.

*"Hey! What're those drones doing?"* the old man called back, his tone wary.

Niko couldn't afford to stop. He spared a brief glance over his shoulder, nearly tripping over a curb in the process. Dozens of Galapol drones had risen high into the air, spreading out into a quickly widening circle. He magnified his view of them through his visor. Each was carrying something he couldn't quite make out, some heading straight in their direction.

"Shit— Esteban—"

It was too late. The drones dropped what they were holding all at once, the nearest to them releasing a glint of silver that tumbled through the air and down into the city streets below. Niko instinctively crouched, bracing himself for an explosion, but instead, a shockwave tore through the city block, killing all the nearby traffic lights and holographic ads, and instantly darkening the windows of the conical buildings around them. The quiet hum of still-running abandoned cars and other machinery fell to an eerie silence, only the distant explosions and staccato gunfire in Death's direction and his own heavy breathing echoing through his helmet filling the vacant quiet now.

EMP explosives. They'd been willing to shut down entire sectors of their own city to get at him.

"Aw, fuck," the Legend said, mirroring his own thoughts.

Niko glanced down at himself, his body quaking now with a new kind of fear. The glossy, dinged and dented black of his suit was plainly visible, his stealth and shield fallen away.

But they'd protected him from the initial hit. His suit still functioned.

He could still run. He could still fight.

Niko rose out of his defensive crouch and glanced back at the old man, a mirror of him in his own dark armor, also visible again now.

*"GO!"* Niko shouted. Already, he could see Galapol agents pointing his way, turning their weapons on them. "Stick close to me!"

He shoved the Legend forward again, both men audibly panting from pushing themselves so hard. He knew the older hunter had to be in agony; he himself was. But it didn't matter. They had to keep going, or they were dead.

Shots pinged off the back of their armor, causing Niko to stumble.

"The hell's your armor made of? Mine's good, but not *that* good."

*Shit. He's not going to hold up through this.* Niko positioned himself beside Esteban to try and form a barrier between him and the hail of gunfire assaulting them now. "Stay behind me. I don't want you getting hit, if that's the case." He twisted, taking a few shots back at the guards, who deflected them with their own fortified shields.

*Assholes.* Only a Gheroun was able to wield two-handed firearms and massive shields at the same time—the benefit of having ten limbs. It was particularly inconvenient for Niko.

He kept the two of them pressing forward, continuing to use himself to shield the other man from the unrelenting onslaught of bullets. The sound was nearly deafening as each impact rang through his suit. Though they weren't able to penetrate his armor, they still jolted him again and again, but he held his ground, firing back into their ranks and trying to keep them at bay. If they could just keep going, just keep closing the distance between themselves and Deleera's getaway ships—

Niko halted to a sudden stop, grabbing the other man hard. "Oh, shit."

Before them was another line of Imperial guards fanning out across the throughway, cutting them off from being able to reach Hannua Park now.

Just like during his and Elliott's last foray onto Haneen, it was all falling apart. He was grateful this time Elliott was safe with the ship—as was his father and Loolae.

But he wasn't ready to give up yet.

*"They have fucking EMPs. Are you holding up?"* Deleera called.

"We're trying to get there, D, but it's not looking good over here. They have us completely surrounded now. They cut off the path to you."

*"Where are you?"*

"South of Luuvoa Plaza, moving onto Palnna Way. But it's blocked."

*"Try Frieseba. It's a detour down here to the park."*

"On it. Come on," he shouted to the Legend, shoving the old man ahead of him as they ran. After a moment, the other hunter slowed, and Niko nearly collided with the back of him.

"Got bad news, kid. Frieseba's cut off too. Galapol's joinin' the party over there. They know where we're tryin' to get to, and they don't want us there."

*"Status, Niko?"* Lady Death pressed, her words painfully desperate now.

Niko readied his rifle, drawing in a breath that became strangled in his throat. They could try to use brute force, push their way through the gathering resistance on Frieseba Street. He could, at the least, buy time for the older man to get through. He'd done what he'd come to do, had gotten his family out. Deleera and her people could still make a clean getaway. Elliott was safe, back on the ship and hidden in its stealth. His father and Loolae were with him now. Niko could try to act as a distraction, could get the Legend through to make a final run for Deleera. It would have to be enough.

"We're gonna try to make a go for it. But they're bringing in more reinforcements. Lots of them."

*"Niko,"* Elliott's voice rang out over his intercom. A mournful pang of affection pooled in his chest at the sound of the other man saying his name.

"Elliott? Hey, babe, I... Things aren't going so great out here. Think we might have gotten in over our heads, a little." He exhaled slowly, trying to keep himself steady, to not stop and think about the reality of his own situation. "It's really good to hear your voice, though."

*"Hang on just a little longer."*

The words frightened him. They weren't a plea; they were a command.

"Wait, what? Listen, I—I'm gonna need you to take Dad and—"

*"No. We're all making it out of this alive. Do you still trust me, Niko?"*

He wanted to lash out, wanted to fight against that question. The last thing he wanted was for Elliott to dive into this chaotic ocean and drown alongside the rest of them in another heroic but ultimately tragic rescue attempt. He didn't want a repeat of the Starlight Awards. And this time, Elliott had Niko's family with him.

But.

They'd discussed this already, hadn't they? Elliott had pleaded for Niko's trust, and when he'd given it, the other man had come through. Maybe he could afford them the break they needed to all make it home again. Maybe Niko could let go, and trust him in his darkest hour once more. Fully, and without reservation.

Niko was at a crossroads now, and both options were full of pain.

"Yeah, babe." He swallowed, nearly knocked off his feet by a poorly aimed grenade which went off to their left. "I trust you."

*"I'm on my way. Where are you?"*

"We're stalled at Frieseba Street. We're surrounded and can't make it to Deleera anymore."

*"On it."*

Niko flinched as another grenade exploded nearby, the sound making his ears ring with a tinny, high-pitched whine. More reinforcements were arriving now—Galapol vehicles and ships, even an armored Imperial tank. The sheer number of them made Niko's heart leap into his throat.

The ground beneath them began to lightly shake. Niko spun, trying to see if another tank was approaching from behind, but only a wall of Imperial Guards stood behind them. Confusion briefly pricked at his brow; it wasn't an earthquake. He could see some of the guards breaking their stoic formation as they began to glance upward in bewilderment.

Seconds later, something large and swift-moving tore low through the air above their heads, causing the ground beneath them to rumble in its wake. Niko glanced up instinctively, but only caught a glint of distorted air before it was gone.

The *Soñadora Despierta*.

*"Now* what the fuck is goin' on?" the Legend bemoaned, head tilted toward the sky as well. Before Niko could answer, shots began raining down from seemingly nowhere, the ship's artillery laying down double trails of rapid-fire assault. Niko watched,

breathless, as they ran a wide circle around himself and the Legend.

Each shot's impact let out a deep, shuddering *wump, wump, wump* that vibrated through Niko's chest cavity as dirt, concrete, and other debris were launched into the air. Elliott knew what he was doing, though—his shots looked sloppy, but Niko knew they were intentionally so. He wasn't aiming directly at any Galapol agents, nor the Imperial military. Niko could see the trail of tiny craters always kept just in front of their forces, pushing alarmingly closer to those blocking access through Frieseba Street. He was creating an impenetrable no man's land with the gunfire, forcing the guards to give way. He was clearing a path for them.

And it was working.

"Elliott..." Niko murmured under his breath, his heart skipping a beat.

Beside him, the Legend let out a sharp whistle as the *Soñadora* made small craters in the streets of Zaaka Narai. "Whoo-wee! Now *that's* what I'm talkin' about! It's finally gettin' good."

Some of the Gheroun and Galapol forces switched focus to the *Soñadora,* one of the tanks raising its gun and firing into the air, but in the chaos and confusion of trying to hit a heavily armored, fast-moving, and invisible target, none of their shots connected.

Seconds later, the ship circled around and roared by overhead again, the wind stirred up in its low passage sending abandoned and scattered trash flying. Elliott laid down another series of ground-shaking shots.

*"Niko?"* he called over their line.

"Uh— Yeah, babe?"

*"Run."*

Niko grabbed the old man by his heavily armored bicep. "Come on! We have to go."

"Ain't gotta tell me twice, kid."

Together, they ducked their heads and continued booking it for Hannua Park, Elliott aggressively forging a brief path for them straight through the heart of enemy offense, as fresh chunks of stone and concrete were sent airborne by his calculated shots.

The old bounty hunter finally began lagging behind, the demands of the day clearly wearing on his aged body. Niko was grateful that, despite his age, the guy could run as hard as he had been.

*"Niko, we're being overwhelmed,"* Death spat. *"We have to get out. We're done for, if we don't go now. I'm sorry."*

Niko swore under his breath and winced. They'd almost made it home free. He drew in a breath to reply, his lungs burning from constant running, but Elliott cut him off before he could speak.

*"That's fine. Get your people out of here. I've got them now."*

*"You're sure?"* Death asked.

*"Yes. Go."*

Niko wracked his brain for what to do, when a dangerously unhinged idea came to mind.

But it just might work—and when pursued through the heart of an alien empire's capital city as its number one enemy, beggars couldn't afford to be choosers.

He fumbled for the grappling gun at his toolbelt. "Elliott, think you can circle past us low and slow? Let the wheels down, too. I'm going to try and hook onto one with the grapple."

*"I'll do my best."*

He was going to have to do this literally blind. But it was the only way they were making it out of this mess and back to the ship now.

"Okay," he told the Legend. "I need you to hold the fuck on." He quickly sheathed his rifle and turned, pulling the old man tightly against himself, chest to chest.

"What is this, Free Hug Day at the Galaxy Peace Parade?"

"You want me to leave you here? Let you deal with Galapol and their friends yourself?"

It seemed that idea wasn't particularly appealing to the grizzled old bounty hunter, even if it meant he had to hug his way out of Zaaka Narai. He wrapped his arms around Niko tightly, clinging to him.

"On your mark, Elliott."

*"Coming over you in five... four... three... two... now."*

Niko fired the grappling hook. It sailed into the air and knocked against what must have been the smooth underside of the ship, ricocheting off and falling back to the ground.

*Fuck. Fuck, fuck.*

*"Niko?"*

He scrambled to reel in the cable for another try. "Didn't work! I hit the underside. Can you come back around?"

*"Coming."*

The *Soñadora* let out another series of shots, the windows of nearby buildings shattering from their intensity. Elliott targeted one of the tanks that had begun launching heavy artillery fire into the sky, his shots connecting. It wasn't enough to outright destroy the armored vehicle, but damaged it enough to stop its impending assault and decommission it. The years Niko had spent pouring income into modding the ship instead of upgrading his tiny apartment were finally paying off.

*"Heading your way again."*

"We're ready." Niko held his breath and tried to steady his mind and body the way he'd seen Elliott do countless times. *Focus. Fucking focus. He does it. So can you.*

His heart hammered in his chest as he willed away all distractions. Nothing else existed now but his target and focus. He envisioned the ship he loved and knew so well in his mind's eye, picturing where its wheels and landing gear lay. He imagined its swift approach, and his previous error suddenly occurred to him.

Elliott began the countdown. *"Five... four... three—"*

Niko released the grapple early this time, just before Elliott was due to be over them.

*"Now!"*

The shot connected, the hook vanishing as it passed the cloaking boundary of the ship. Then Niko and the Legend were yanked violently off their feet. It was all he could do to hold on to the grapple and the old man at the same time.

Esteban and his full armor suit were heavier than Elliott had been.

*"Did it work?"* Elliott asked.

"We're on! Pull up now. *Now,* Elliott!"

Elliott guided the ship sharply upward, and Niko's legs barely missed crashing into the tip of a pointed building. Soon, they were soaring above Zaaka Narai, the entire city and all its oddly curling and curving streets growing smaller and smaller beneath them. Flashing red, blue, purple, and gold lights spread in every direction. For a moment, Niko was dumbfounded at just how many Gheroun military and Galapol agents were flooding the city now.

Along the far eastern horizon, the last of Lady Death's ships departed, pursued by more flashes of red and blue.

*Good. Get the hell out of this nightmare city.*

He struggled to keep hold against his own weight and the other man's, his arm burning from the strain. To his credit, the Legend managed to hold on tight to him as well. Niko could only pray he had half the old man's strength and endurance if he made it to his age.

"Elliott, I need you to find an open space and get low. We need to get inside the ship."

*"I've got you."*

They soared above the city, the strength in Niko's arm rapidly waning as his muscles shook and shuddered now from the strain.

His grip on the grapple gun slipped, both men getting a violent jerk that sent Niko's vision turning black at the edges. He clung on tighter, his entire body drowning in a cold sweat. He refused to let go, holding on out of sheer stubborn willpower. After everything he'd just gone through to get the Legend out, he wouldn't deign to let them both pointlessly fall to their deaths now.

He was grateful they were both armored, despite the added weight of their suits. The raw, biting wind against bare skin at this speed would have undoubtedly lacerated them.

*Need to thank Zann for—*

*"Here. There's a vacant outcropping west of the city that I'm going to stop at. Be ready,"* Elliott warned.

"We're ready."

Soon, the city and its sharp buildings fell away and they entered the foothills of mountainous terrain, which Elliott carefully navigated. Then Niko felt the ship slow—to his great relief—and begin to descend.

*"Now, Niko."*

He saw the uneven, rocky ground of the outcropping approaching fast from below and tried to meet it foot first, but without feeling or a sense of when to push himself into standing, his legs instead buckled beneath him. The grapple gun finally slipped free of his grip, sending the older bounty hunter and himself both tumbling. He pulled himself back up quickly.

"Rough landing there," the Legend grunted as Niko helped pull him up off the ground. "But coulda been rougher."

The *Soñadora*'s stealth deactivated, Niko's beloved ship appearing once more in his sights now. He reeled in the grappling cable and hastily ascended the ramp, following the Legend.

Esteban whistled. "Nice little ship you got here. It's cute."

"It's more than cute," Niko muttered. He was exhausted. "It just saved our asses." Once they were both inside, Elliott brought the ship back into flight. Niko watched the outcropping begin to grow smaller through the still-open door, the ramp not even fully retracted yet. He slammed the side of his fist against the door control. It slid closed with an agonizing sluggishness.

"Niko..."

Niko looked over to see two faces that panged at his heart. His father was back in their protection, as was Loolae. They were here. They were real. They were alive. They'd both managed to survive this nightmare. He wanted to pull them into an embrace, but needed to talk to the one who'd gotten them out of this mess first.

He made his way to the front of the ship, where the sight of beloved, familiar gold cowlicks greeted him. Elliott turned to glance over his shoulder back at Niko, casting him a brief but sincere, exhausted smile.

He was covered in teal, alien blood.

Niko frowned, his heart skipping a nervous beat. He opened his mouth to ask about it, when Death's voice cut him off through the comm line.

*"I'm sorry, Niko. Esteban."*

"Don't worry about it, D. I'm grateful for everything today."

"Eh, yer good," the Legend added. "Though, maybe you owe me a drink."

*"I'll take you up on that. I'll owe you the whole damn bar stock,"* Death said.

"Nah, no need. Buy these two kids a couple of drinks and we'll call it even. Actually," he eyed Niko. "Next time yer on Dainna, I'll take you out for drinks myself, after you risked your ass for me. Least I can do."

"Sure," Niko said.

Deleera continued. *"Police channels are reporting that Khaathra's dead."* She sounded as bewildered as Niko now felt. *"Was that you?"*

"What?" He blinked. "No."

Niko turned to stare at Elliott. Silence fell over both the ship and their comm line while the other man guided the *Soñadora* up through thick cloud cover, then finally broke through the atmosphere of Haneen, the dark of space surrounding them as the planet slowly began to fall away. He switched on the artificial gravity.

Then he spoke, his voice quiet, though Niko could see the satisfied smirk as it crept across his lips.

"It was me."

# Chapter Sixteen
# A Fair Fight

After they'd gotten a good distance from Haneen, Niko and the others were caught up on everything—Khaathra tracking them down and trying to get revenge, Elliott taking the head of the Gheroun Empire on in hand-to... well, tentacle combat, and the flight of the *Soñadora,* from his perspective.

It had all rendered Niko, the Legend, and Death equal parts stunned, terrified, and deeply impressed.

Once they'd both showered on the ship, then met up again with Deleera's fleet in an asteroid field, they exchanged the Legend back to her and finally returned to the facility, where Niko hooked the *Soñadora* up to recharge. The ship's power had apparently dipped down to sixteen percent due to staying stealthed for so long, something Elliott had monitored closely, but initially kept quiet about to avoid adding to everyone's panic.

Niko gave the grand tour of the facility to his father and Loolae, remaining in the suit for now, just to get around quicker and help move any furniture or supplies they might need.

That they'd managed to get them back, mostly unscathed, was a blessing Niko would be grateful for until he took his last breath.

He both hated seeing the two of them here now—in these endless halls with their fluorescent, softly buzzing lights and gnawing emptiness—and loved it. Niko had tried not to think of how he'd probably given up ever seeing his father again by choosing to save Elliott's life. Now, in an ironic twist of fate, Elliott had saved Oliver's.

Niko had fallen into the role of caretaker for the older man as he'd sunk deeper into the mire of grief over the years. Maybe going forward, even here in this place, he could watch over him again.

Zann was here now, too. Stuck in the same facility with their father, the other man could no longer avoid him or push his own grief down somewhere in the dark anymore, like he'd slowly begun to as of late. Maybe the two of them could finally reconnect. Or maybe they already had been, in Niko's absence.

After everyone had gotten settled in, Niko checked in again on his father in the bedroom he'd chosen. He pulled Oliver into a tight embrace, and both men held each other. It felt so unfathomably good to hug his father. A cold, sickly chill ran through him at the thought that he'd come so close to losing him forever.

Especially after Honeybliss had gotten their tentacles on him.

"*Dad.*"

"Niko. Niko, I'm so glad you're alright. I didn't think I'd get to talk to you again. I—I missed your birthday."

*Why? Of all details, why that one?* It made Niko ache. He held his stepdad tighter, before finally letting go of the other man and taking a step back.

"We'll be together for my next one. And yours. All the ones after. Okay?" Niko said.

Oliver nodded. "Alright."

"Dad..." Niko started, scared to ask, but knowing he had to. He could feel his brow draw heavy with sorrow, with guilt. A bruise and shallow cut ran along Oliver's left cheek, reminders of the sobering reality of what he and Loolae had been put through. "Are you really alright? Did they—"

"I'm alright," Oliver said gently. "Really. Loolae too. They could have been a lot worse to us than they were. Mostly, they roughed us up a little, but otherwise we were just tied up and left alone. I think they wanted to use us as a negotiating piece, so we were spared worse treatment." After a moment, he added, "Loolae and I did a lot of talking. To pass the time. She's a very strong woman. She helped keep me in good spirits."

"Yeah?" Niko asked. He needed to talk to her. "Well, I'm glad you guys had each other. Though I wish neither of you had ever had to be there. Dad, I'm so sorry. I'm so, so sorry. For everything."

"No." Oliver shook his head. "Please don't blame yourself for the cruelty of others. I don't blame you for any of this, and neither does Loolae."

*You probably should,* a bitter part of Niko thought. He tried to swallow it down. "I'm just glad you're alright. I'm never going to let that happen again. To either of you. Okay?"

Oliver nodded. "Okay, Niko."

Niko let out a long breath. "So, I guess I owe you a huge explanation of what's been going on. I'm not sure how much Zann told you, before this."

"He just said there was more to it than what the news was saying, and that he couldn't talk about it yet, but that you weren't just killing random people out of cruelty. The Imperator kept mentioning Honeybliss when we were there, though. Does that have to do with this?"

"Yeah." Niko proceeded to tell him as much as he could—about Honeybliss, about Elliott. About how Niko had been called back in by Zann to hunt him, only to find out nothing had really been what it'd originally seemed. He told him about Lady Death and their broadcast, and about how Elliott and Zann had worked tirelessly together to find who'd taken them.

Niko tried to be sparse on the details of Honeybliss. His father had been through enough and didn't need that kind of horror stuck in his head. The man had always been of a gentler make than himself or Zann. There was no part of him that had ever even longed for vengeance toward his own family's killers. He didn't have an aggressive bone in his body. That both his sons had gone into risky law enforcement jobs had only ever stressed Oliver out. "I'm sorry I didn't call you, or text," Niko finally added. "I didn't want to somehow make things worse for you."

"I had no idea," Oliver said quietly, his gaze somewhere distant as he was lost in thought. He finally glanced up at Niko. "About, um, Kestrel."

"Elliott, Dad. Please."

"Elliott. Right, sorry. The news really did paint him as someone rather unhinged, didn't they?"

"Yeah. That was all part of a smear campaign by Honeybliss. Their final attempt to discredit him."

"The news had started being quite unkind to you as well."

Niko nodded. He could only imagine.

"Is he, ah," Oliver seemed to search for the words. "Is Elliott your ally, or is he... someone a little closer to you?"

"You mean like— Do I have a thing for him?" Niko asked, blinking.

"Yes."

"...Yeah, Dad. I'm in love with Elliott."

"Oh," Oliver said. "Is it, ah, mutual?"

Niko couldn't help the smile that found its way onto his lips. "Yeah, it is. We're a thing."

"Oh, good. I'm glad. I'm glad you're not alone anymore, Niko. You deserve someone to keep you company. To keep you happy. Does he make you happy?"

Niko's smile only widened to an affectionate grin. Warmth spread through him, golden and luminous. "He makes me really happy, Dad. I know it might be weird after everything you heard in the news, but I hope you and he can get to actually know each other." He paused a moment, before adding, "He could really use a family, I think."

"I'd be honored to talk to him," Oliver said. "After all, he saved our lives. I won't ever forget that."

Niko smiled again, something softer this time. Elliott was incredible. It both hurt and warmed him to know he'd risked everything to go get his father and Loolae out by himself.

He needed to talk to Elliott about it.

His smile faded a bit as reality came crashing back down on him. "I'm sorry you're stuck here with us, Dad. I know this place can be, uh," he paused, searching for the right word, "oppressive. It's just an abandoned Quwa-quay mining facility. It's definitely not Kaapra-19."

"Don't worry about any of that, Niko. Really."

"If you need anything at all, though. Or to talk to someone. If it's getting to you. Please, *please* come talk to me or Zann, okay?"

"I will. Thank you, Niko. Honestly, I'm just glad to be here with my sons again. You two are my home, not Kaapra-19."

Niko pulled him into another tight hug. "It's gonna be okay, Dad."

"Niko?" a familiar, handsome voice called from behind him. "Sorry to interrupt. I was just—"

"Hey, no, it's okay," Niko said. He turned to look at Elliott, who stood tentatively in the doorway. Niko held a hand out to him. "Come here."

Elliott seemed to hesitate.

"Elliott, come on." He finally acquiesced, crossing the room toward them. Niko wrapped an arm around his waist and pulled him over against his side. He leaned in and planted a long kiss on Elliott's cheek.

Elliott got a sheepish smile and glanced at Niko, then Oliver, his cheeks darkening. "What's this about?" he murmured under his breath.

"I just wanted to formally introduce you two. You know, when we aren't all trying to fight for our lives, or recover on the ride back here. Dad, this is Elliott. My boyfriend."

Oliver extended a hand. "It's my pleasure, Elliott. Thank you again for helping us."

Elliott stared at his hand for a moment, seeming almost dumbfounded, before clasping it in his own and shaking it. "Likewise, Mr. Delamar."

"Please, call me Oliver."

"Right."

"Hey, babe, what'd you need?" Niko asked.

"Oh, ah—" Elliott hesitated. "I just wanted to know if you'd like to come have a drink with me."

"I'd love to. Dad, go ahead and get settled in. Let me know if you need anything, okay?"

"I will." He smiled. "Enjoy your time, Niko."

As they left the room together, Niko couldn't help but think how different this place felt now. With each new person who walked its halls, it was a little less abandoned, a little less pressing in its silence.

They were building a community. Even if it was one born from situational necessity and desperation.

"So, he's doing alright?" Elliott asked as they made their way to the far lounge that he'd told Niko he had drinks waiting in. Niko was surprised how well he'd taken to Oliver and Loolae being here. There were no growing pains to their addition the way there had originally been with Zann.

"Yeah. Khaathra and her goons didn't hurt them much, after all. Apparently to keep Galapol happy."

"I'm glad."

"Yeah, me too," Niko said. He hesitated. "Hey, Elliott... I wanted to say thanks for what you did back there. And sorry for all the trouble I caused. Getting them out wasn't about me, but I made it that way."

Elliott smiled at him, his thin lips curled upward in a warm grin, his eyes sly crescents. "You didn't make it about you. I understood. I would have done the same in your shoes. I never would have been alright staying back, if it had been Cleo. I would have given you ten times the hell you gave me." His smile widened a fraction. "I hope you know, Niko, how much your happiness means to me. If I'd had to choose, I'd rather they made it home, instead of me. I'm glad they're safe now."

"Hey." Niko took his wrist, interrupting him as he reached up to open the lounge door. "*You're* my home. I'm going to make sure you make it back to me, every time. I'll never leave you behind."

They locked gazes for a moment, something intense and profound in the depths of Elliott's eyes now. Something Niko couldn't put words to, but felt intrinsically. The unspoken language, old as time itself, that bound two souls together.

Then Elliott turned, opened the door, and slipped into the lounge, Niko dutifully following. On one of the small, round tables was a bucket of ice, atop which lay a chilled bottle of champagne and two wine glasses. Niko grinned at the sight.

Elliott took the bottle, its glass semi-opaque with a layer of clinging condensation. He unsheathed his lucky knife and tried his hand at slicing off the top. It took him a few attempts, with Niko giving gentle pointers on how to angle it. The neck of the bottle broke cleanly on his fifth try, champagne fizzing out onto the floor. "I liked your method of opening these. It's very... dramatic."

He poured two very full glasses, then handed one to Niko.

Niko unlatched his gloves and tossed them onto one of the nearby chairs, then took the glass. The liquid was bright and shimmering. It matched the light in Elliott's eyes.

"We did it," Elliott said. "We got your family out safely."

"Yeah." Warmth bubbled up through Niko, matching his own glass of champagne. "We did it."

Elliott raised his glass for a toast. "To you and me."

Niko clinked his glass against Elliott's. "To us." He tipped his head back and swallowed down the entire glass in one go. Elliott laughed, then followed suit. They looked at each other, smiles on their faces.

"Come here." Niko said, pulling him over against himself. He leaned in and met Elliott in a sensuous kiss. "You taste like champagne," he mused, his voice turning into a low murmur.

"So do you," Elliott murmured back.

Niko was lost in his eyes, in the beautiful, living green of them. He leaned in and kissed him again, fingers wandering the wilds of the other man's hair. Then he moved back to the table and poured them both another glass. Elliott laughed again, and this time they drank more slowly.

"You know..." Niko started. Something came over him then, a joyous impulse born, perhaps, from being a little bit tipsy now. "We'll have to think of a way to celebrate, when this is all finally over." He set his glass down, then grabbed Elliott and swept him up off the ground suddenly. Elliott gasped. "Because I want to have a hell of a celebration with you."

"Niko..."

"You like that, babe?" Niko grinned down at him. Elliott was laughing in his arms. It was oddly familiar; Niko remembered carrying him when he'd been bleeding out and unconscious on Neema. It felt so good to be able to carry him now, like this, instead of during any kind of dire situation where Elliott had been wounded and Niko was running for both of their lives. He held him a little tighter.

"I'd like it more if you kissed me," Elliott said.

"Yes, sir." Niko leaned down and met him again in another kiss, Elliott draping his arms around his neck now.

"Mmm. Let's fuck. Right here in the lounge," Elliott purred in his ear, breath warm. "I'll make it good for you." Niko swallowed, heat flushing through him at the thought.

"Can I take a raincheck?" he said, groaning. "I should probably check in on Loolae first, make sure she's settling in alright, too, after everything."

Elliott sighed. "Fair point. But I very much intend to collect on that later."

"Come with me?"

"Where else would I rather be?"

Loolae wasn't in the room she'd picked, so they went poking around the facility for a while, eventually finding the Xermotl in the training room, where she was inspecting a set of dumbbells.

"Wanted to get a better look at your setup here," she explained when they approached. "We didn't have time earlier to do much more than glance around."

"Yeah. Look around all you want. This might be your home for a little while. I, um, wanted to introduce you guys more formally. Elliott, this is Loolae. My friend and physical therapist. She's incredible. She helped me get back to myself after I fell."

Loolae waved a spade-shaped hand flippantly. "Flatterer. You're the one who did the work, Niko. You're the one who showed up for yourself. I just helped you through it all."

"I admire that," Elliott said.

"Well, regardless, I'm grateful that you kept kicking my ass until I could get back up again. I really needed that. I don't know that I could have done it without you. Loolae, this is Elliott. My boyfriend. You probably know him better as 'the Kestrel.'"

Loolae laughed. She turned her four-eyed, golden gaze toward Elliott. "I think they dropped the formal '*the*' a long time ago. But yes. Kestrel seems to be the colloquial name everyone's using. Anyway, it's a pleasure to meet you in a more peaceful situation this time, Elliott. Thank you again for helping us."

"The pleasure is mine," Elliott said. "If you need anything, just ask."

"I will, thanks."

"Loolae..." Niko started, deep guilt flooding through him. "About Destination: Reclamation... Don't worry about your studio. We'll get you back to it—and your life out there—soon." *I hope,* he didn't add. "We just need you guys to lay low for a while until it's not dangerous for you anymore."

Loolae sighed, her patterns fading to blue, briefly. "I appreciate that. I've put a lot of work into that place. But don't worry about it right now. I'd spoken with my brother's wives before, and they both said they'd take care of it if anything ever happened to me. I'm honestly just grateful for your help. In the end, that everyone here is alive is what matters."

"Thanks, Loolae. And thanks for keeping an eye out for Dad in there. I think he'd be a lot worse off if you hadn't been there to talk to him and keep him calm."

The Xermotl's patterns briefly flushed green, before fading back to a neutral yellow. *Was that a blush...?* "Don't worry about it. The truth is, your dad helped me a lot too. He kept me calm as well. He's really a very kind and thoughtful man."

"He is," Niko agreed.

"It's too bad I didn't get to meet him other than once in passing before any of this," Loolae said. "He's quite enjoyable for conversation and has a big heart. Especially when it comes to you and your brother."

Niko had no idea the two of them would have even wanted to chat, let alone hit it off as friends, or he would have tried to introduce them earlier. His father had been so lonely, stuck in a self-perpetuated isolation driven by his wife and son's deaths. Having a regular friend certainly wouldn't have hurt.

"If you ever want some training while we're here, Niko, let me know," she said. "This room is perfect for physical therapy."

"Thanks. I'd like that." It would be good to get back to regular therapy sessions, but Niko had a feeling the offer would help Loolae just as much as—if not more than—himself. Especially with the loss of her practice and livelihood.

"Well, I'm going to go bug Zann. It's been a long time since he ever bothered to come say hello, even before all this happened. It's been good to meet you, Elliott." She wandered out of the training room on strong, rubbery legs, leaving just the two of them in there now.

Niko looked at Elliott.

Elliott moved closer to him, head tilted. "I was thinking. I want to hit Enva'ruu next. Tomorrow."

He blinked. "That's pretty soon. You ready for that after what we just went through?"

"Of course I am," Elliott said. "Are you?"

"Yeah. I can handle it."

Elliott eyed him, then glanced around. "Speaking of training. It might be a good idea to prepare. Since we're in here and you're still in your suit, do you want to?"

"You mean, like, spar?"

"Why not?"

"Sure," Niko said.

They sparred together for the better part of an hour, training different hand-to-hand techniques against each other, offensive and defensive both. Niko couldn't help but find the whole thing rather mechanical and bloodless. This sort of play-by-play sparring and training had become routine for them in their down time. It was growing stale.

"Sometimes I actually miss the old days a little," he admitted once they'd paused for a break. "When it was me against you. There was something electrifying about those moments."

"You miss hunting me, Niko?" Elliott wiped sweat from his brow.

"I mean, don't get me wrong. I prefer what we have now, by far. But despite everything, didn't you have a little bit of fun every time we met?"

Elliott grinned now, something wild and indulgent. "Oh, I did. You pissed me off. And were always getting in my way. But you're right. There was something about those moments. I just really..."

"Felt alive," Niko finished for him.

"Yes," Elliott said. They looked at each other for a moment. "Let's do it again."

"Fight? Isn't that what we've been doing?"

"No. More than that. I want you to pretend you're still hunting me."

Niko shifted his weight from one leg to the other, feeling a little awkward. "You mean, like some kind of roleplay thing?"

"That's exactly what I mean, Niko. I want to experience that again. The thrill of it. Don't you?"

"Yeah. Okay. Well, what do I get for kicking your ass, then?"

Elliott laughed. "Should I even bother answering? I'm going to kick yours. As I most often did."

"No, I think it went a little differently," Niko said. "Besides, I held back with you. A lot."

"Oh? Did you? I don't recall that ever being a thing. You seemed *quite* exhausted by the time I was done with you on most of those skirmishes."

Niko grinned. "Trust me. I could have gone a lot harder. But I didn't want to break you. If I win this..." Something about the whole thing brought out a feral side of him. Even a reminder of the lightning-strike energy they'd once had between each other as adversaries did something to Niko. His voice emerged low now, a shade darker. "I want you. I dreamed about doing that. About catching you and then fucking you senseless."

He didn't need to share the direction that fantasy had eventually shifted to, with Elliott being the one to pin him down instead.

Elliott looked at him for a long moment, something unreadable in his eyes as he studied Niko. Niko suddenly felt sheepish and stupid. *Shouldn't have admitted that. Probably took this in a weird direction.* Elliott was likely going to laugh at him for it.

Instead, the other man stalked over to the door and locked it. Niko hadn't even known the training room possessed a lock. Then Elliott made his way back over. "*When* I win, I want to take you. I want to make you submit to me. I'll have you begging for it."

Niko swallowed, an illicit thrill running through him at the idea.

It didn't matter.

He wasn't going to lose. He wasn't going to let Elliott best him, this time. He glanced again at the locked door. They were really going to do this. "So. Uh, something like this might get a little too much, if we're really going back into that mentality. I don't want to do something stupid that accidentally really hurts you in some way."

"Neither do I."

"Maybe we should have a safeword thing, in case... I don't know. It goes too far."

"I agree. I was going to suggest the same. Especially for what comes after. You pick the word."

"Me? Ugh." Niko was horrible at these things. There were millions of words at his disposal that Galactic Standard was comprised of, yet trying to search for a single one now, his mind went blank. Naturally.

He searched Elliott's face, his gaze falling on the sea green of his eyes. "Ocean," he blurted out. But Elliott only laughed.

"In the middle of a fight, Niko? It sounds far too close to 'oh, shit.'"

Niko couldn't help but laugh too. "Oh, shit, you're right."

Elliott smirked.

"Uh, okay, then, what about... sailboat?"

"Sailboat it is, then, lover."

Niko let out a long breath. "Okay, so, whenever you're ready, let's—"

Elliott took the advantage, darting in before Niko could finish speaking. He aimed a hit between the armor plates, sending Niko's adrenaline spiking. Niko immediately jumped back, putting wary space between them now. "...Do this. Asshole."

*So, you want to fucking fight dirty, huh?* he thought. *I can meet you there.*

It wasn't any different than how their actual altercations had gone.

"You're really the best Galapol could do?" Elliott teased. He wore a wicked smile. "They're getting more desperate by the day. I've outsmarted dozens of bounty hunters before you. What makes you think you're any different?"

"I'm not here to chat with you," Niko said, throwing himself toward Elliott, hoping to overpower the other man. Elliott was frustratingly fast, though, slipping just out of his way before Niko could get a grip on him. This was all so familiar, that it actually felt nostalgic.

Niko loved that it did. He knew Elliott was loving it too—especially by the cocky grin on the other man's face. Fighting with him was a little bit like dancing with him.

Niko knew he should probably reevaluate his romantic standards. That, or speak with a therapist.

"Why not?" Elliott asked, moving in quick again and feigning a punch to Niko's left. Niko tried to deflect it, but Elliott used his folly to slip around his right instead. Niko was ready for him now, though, too wary to let him try anything tricky again. He spun quickly and deflected another hit, shoving him back hard. Elliott managed to keep his footing and narrowed his eyes. "This 'fight' is boring me. Either make a real attempt, or at least entertain me with conversation if you're going to just waste my time."

Niko ground his jaw. He may have forgotten how easily and often Elliott had gotten under his skin during their old encounters. This time, he tried to bait Elliott into a trap, throwing a sloppy punch. Elliott dodged with ease, but Niko predicted it, snagging him by the wrist and pulling him against himself. Elliott struggled against him, but Niko got him roughly turned around and trapped in a rear bear hug.

Elliott threw his weight into Niko hard, bucking against him several times, which Niko barely managed to keep his balance through. Finally, Elliott threw himself to the side and it was too much for Niko's unfeeling feet to keep up with. They both went down, Elliott still pinned to him as Niko held tight.

They wrestled on the ground, Niko trying to keep a solid grip on him, Elliott too infuriatingly slippery to ever get pinned down for long. He kicked his long legs and squirmed against Niko below him. "You know," Elliott ground out between panting breaths, "I'm starting to get the feeling you aren't even trying to actually bring me in. You just want to get close to me."

"You mean, cop a feel?" Niko asked. He couldn't help himself, sliding a hand downward to fondle Elliott's crotch. "Maybe."

It wasn't as fun as he'd hoped it would be, unable to feel anything through his gloves. And especially when Elliott elbowed him hard in the side for his attempt. Somehow, he always managed to find the miniscule soft spots right between the armor plates. Niko grunted in pain.

"I'm not interested in letting you feel me up like a fumbling, drunk teenager at his first party." Elliott finally slipped out of his grip and sprung up, turning around quickly to face him. He narrowed his eyes. "*If* I were interested in going there, I'd want a *man* who actually knows how to use his hands."

Niko hastily got to his feet, irritation grating through him. It was all a game. But he couldn't help but want to show Elliott just how much of a man he really was.

This time, he let Elliott strike first. The other man was almost too quick, nearly dancing around him to try and get a kick in at the back of Niko's knee. Niko sidestepped just in time and turned to grab him, then slammed him back against the wall, finally able to pin him there with his body weight. Elliott gasped, the air knocked sharply out of him from the impact.

Niko seized his wrists in an iron grip. "How's this for using my hands?" he taunted.

Elliott began struggling, his face twisting into a mixture of rage and frustrated panic. For a moment, Niko thought he might actually use the safeword, but the other man stayed silent.

Niko kept him pinned against the wall, a rush of victory and pride coursing through him. He'd done it. He'd bested Elliott. He had won.

If anything inside him was somehow disappointed, he pushed it down and refused to dwell on it. He'd won, and decided to relish in the thrill of it.

He leaned in and whispered in the other man's ear. *"You're mine now."*

Niko bent to plant a greedy kiss on Elliott's jaw when the assassin twisted under his grip, in a sudden surge of strength. Then he pushed into Niko, delivering a sensual, forceful kiss of his own against his lips, his tongue penetrating him. It was all so familiar. He could be back on Uula again, the wind in his hair, the taste of Elliott on his tongue. The man had tried the same tactic once before.

Only now, there was something else, too. This time it wasn't a handcuff. A sharp pinprick, cold and hard as steel, pressed against his neck where it was exposed above the suit's collar. Niko opened his eyes and pulled away.

"Elliott?" he asked uncertainly. "Isn't that, um, kind of cheating?"

They'd never technically agreed to a no weapons rule, but Niko had thought it was a given.

Elliott held his lucky knife to Niko's throat. Niko locked gazes with him in silence.

He looked up at Niko, eyes hard and sharp as the dagger he wielded now, all dogged cleverness and determination. There was a wilderness there, a danger. Elliott had the blade he'd murdered with before to Niko's neck. A single flick of the wrist and he would be gone before he'd know it.

"This was never a fair fight," Elliott said, deadly serious. "I was always going to make you mine."

# CHAPTER SEVENTEEN
# SAILBOAT

"GET ON YOUR KNEES," Elliott said, a victorious smirk tugging one corner of his mouth upward now. Niko stared at him for another silent moment. "I'm collecting on my raincheck."

There was a long, odd pause between them, something electric and deeply tense. Elliott had made this more real, had crossed a line into something dangerous by bringing the knife to Niko's neck. Yet he wasn't hurting him with it at all, either. He hadn't pushed it far enough to draw blood. And they'd discussed the safeword to stop this roleplay if he wanted to. *Especially for what comes after*, Elliott had said. He'd made it very clear that exit still applied now. Niko searched his eyes, and Elliott did the same, merely waiting.

Niko realized what he was doing now—granting him a moment to put a stop to this if it was too much, if he were too uncomfortable. The question hung silently in the other man's eyes, and he even saw Elliott's eyebrows quirk up, as though to ask: *Well?*

Niko would play along. He acquiesced, giving the other man a subtle nod and slowly sinking to his knees. Elliott still held the knife to him, though more loosely this time, the blade no longer even touching his skin. He reached out and stroked Niko's hair, then slid his hand down along his jaw to cup his chin. He gripped it firmly, forcing Niko's attention and gaze fully up on him now—as though Niko had anywhere else he wanted to look right then.

"You're going to do something for me, hunter," Elliott purred. "You're going to pleasure me until I'm satisfied. And then I'm going to fuck you until you can't take it anymore. Does that sound good to you?"

Niko swallowed. He was dizzy, both fully immersed in the roleplay and separately aware of what it was—pretend. The mere idea of this ever really potentially happening drove him wild. He wished, on some level, that it had, absurd as it all was. The idea of Elliott besting him like this in their former cat and mouse games and then taking it further—using him as a fucktoy—made him salivate. He knew Elliott saw it, too. It must have shown in his expression; the other man's lips curled upward wickedly as he gazed down at him now.

"Good boy," Elliott said.

Niko let out a sharp breath, looking away. Those words were too much. He felt his body turn to liquid inside the suit. All but one part, which remained hard as a rock.

Elliott pressed the flat end of the knife against Niko's cheek and gently directed him back to face him again. "No. I want you to look only at me while you do this."

Niko couldn't even speak. He barely nodded, hoping it got his agreement across adequately.

"I'm going to be rough with you," Elliott said, tilting his head. "Because I think you can take it." His fingertips wandered the length of Niko's jaw again, before settling into and running through his hair. Then he tightly grabbed a fistful of it, and wrenched Niko's head back. Niko grunted at the handling, but instead of any sort of complaint, he found he loved it. It spoke to everything his body craved right then, to every anticipating need.

"Unzip me," Elliott said.

Niko's gaze dropped from the other man's face to rest on his crotch instead. He was eye level with it, perfectly positioned. Elliott was clearly just as much into this as he himself was—if the bulge that strained against his dark jeans was any indication. Niko reached towards him but hesitated, thick, armored gloves still covering his hands. He began to unlatch one, when Elliott pressed the knife toward him again. "I didn't say you could do that."

Niko froze in place, briefly at a loss. "It's going to make it harder to—"

"Ask me, then."

A flare of defiant rage shot through Niko, white hot as fire. But with it came something else, too—he felt absolutely drunk with desire in a way he never had in his entire life. He warred between telling Elliott to go fuck himself for trying to control him or deferring to the command he'd given. It certainly hadn't been a request.

He finally glanced up at Elliott, hoping the intensity of his scowl communicated some of the disobedience he felt. "Can I," he said flatly.

"Can you what?" Elliott snapped at him.

*Asshole.* Niko ground his jaw, biting down on lashing out at him. He felt feverish—a bizarre mixture of stubborn frustration and utter delight that made for a wild combination. "Can I remove my gloves so I can unzip you?"

"Since you asked so nicely, I'll permit it," Elliott said.

Niko unlatched the gloves and tossed them aside. They landed on the ground with two solid *clanks* and rolled slightly before coming to a stop. He half expected Elliott to chastise him for overstepping by throwing them, but the other man said nothing, except, "Well?"

Niko reached towards his fly and unbuttoned, then unzipped it slowly. He wanted to be ornery back at him, wanted to take his sweet time. Like he didn't need this so badly it made the very marrow of his bones feel aflame with ecstasy. Like he didn't feel the desire might consume and kill him.

"Pull me out," Elliott said.

Niko just as slowly slid his hand beneath the elastic waistline of Elliott's underwear and pulled him free. It was hard to breathe now. He felt so good in his grip. He wanted to pump and stroke him until Elliott came on his face—an impulsive need. He started doing just that, letting his hand grip and work Elliott's cock, when to his surprise the other man batted his hand away sharply.

"No."

"*Elliott*," Niko protested before he could even think better of it.

"Elliott *what?*" He looked down at Niko now, gaze displeased, regally cool. It was a rhetorical question—Niko searched for any sort of comeback that wouldn't make his situation worse than it already was, but fell silent instead. On his knees and with an assassin's lucky knife to his throat, he was hardly in a position to argue.

He found he liked it that way. In spite of everything he thought he'd known about himself.

"Open your mouth for me."

Niko knew exactly where this was going. A chill of exhilaration and pleasure rippled up his spine and webbed through his whole body. He opened his mouth slowly, his gaze rising to meet Elliott's own.

Elliott gripped him by the hair again, prying Niko's head back, then pushed himself in.

All the way in.

Niko choked on him. There was no building up to it this time, no preparing himself or relaxing his throat—Elliott wasn't fucking around when he'd said he was going to be rough with him. Then he showed Niko mercy, pulling himself free again. Elliott's cock glistened with his saliva, and Niko wanted it back inside him.

"You can take it, Niko. I've seen you do it before. You were so good at swallowing my cock." He pushed himself in again, relentless, before Niko could answer. He tried to brace himself this time, but still gagged slightly. Elliott thrust again and again into his mouth, pushing the entire length of himself in before pulling out, pausing only occasionally to give Niko a few seconds to gasp for breath.

Soon, Elliott's own breaths were emerging from him as his telltale, soft, low moans as he used him. A visceral, electric thrill jolted through Niko at knowing he was enjoying himself so much.

Niko was enjoying himself, too.

"Mmm, like that," Elliott groaned, his voice low and silken, given to his pleasure now. Then he said it again. "You're being such a *good boy* for me."

This time, Niko let out an involuntary moan, the sound strangled with his mouth taken up completely. Goosebumps covered every inch of his skin. He wanted to melt into Elliott. He'd never felt like this, not in his entire life. Not in any other experience, not with any other lover.

He would have never let any other lover come close to doing this to him, either. Not by any chance in hell.

It felt so fucking good, though, Elliott filling him again and again, making him take it all, making him choke on his cock while he gripped him roughly by his hair. He did it hard, and he did it quickly. It bordered on too much—but that was what Niko liked most about it. His body responded reflexively, gagging on him until his eyes brimmed with tears and Elliott pulled out, a string of glistening saliva connecting them as he gave Niko another few precious seconds to recover.

Niko wanted none of that. He reached up and wrapped his arms around Elliott's hips, planting his hands on his ass, then pulled the other man forward to force him all the way back in, greedy to swallow the entire thing. He needed it, couldn't get enough.

Niko was starving.

Elliott emitted a breathless moan. "I didn't say you could—"

Niko grunted his answer, unable to speak. He could feel the seep of tears dampening his cheeks now, all involuntary bodily reaction. He wanted—*needed*—to touch himself, but was stuck beneath the thick armor. He knew Elliott probably wouldn't let him anyway.

It didn't matter. He liked everything about this so much—to be used, to be sloppily face-fucked, existing in that moment only to serve Elliott however he wanted it—that the next time he took in the other man's full length after pausing for a breath, he began to panic and reached up to grip Elliott's leg tightly. He pulled away from him, then turned his head to the side, wiping saliva from his mouth.

"S-sailboat."

"What's wrong, Niko?" Elliott asked. He quickly tossed the knife aside. It clinked against the floor, landing near the discarded gloves. His voice was hoarse and worn thin from his own exertion, though his tone was laced now with sincere concern, very much the opposite of how he'd spoken moments before. "Are you alright? Was it too much? Niko, I'm sor—"

"No. It's not that," Niko said, clearing his throat. It ached slightly and he mourned the emptiness of Elliott's absence. He could taste him still along the back of his tongue. "I just needed a minute. I was going to fucking come if you didn't stop."

He would rather be caught dead than let himself go prematurely again like he had during their first time together.

Elliott paused, his expression betraying blunt shock for a moment. Then he smirked, head tilting as his eyes narrowed. There was something deeply ravenous but patiently restrained in them now. "Just from that? From servicing me? You liked it that much?"

"Yeah, I— Yeah," Niko mumbled. His face was hot and he knew he was flushing. He wiped his eyes and palmed at his damp cheeks.

"So, you want to keep going." It was half question, half statement, Elliott's tone toying but laced with probing caution.

"Uh. *Yeah.*"

"Then, maybe I should reward you for holding back so admirably," Elliott purred at him. He was right back in character now—or maybe this was just how he was. Niko didn't know and didn't care. He was into it. "By letting you come when I fuck you."

"Mmh," was all Niko could manage.

A tinge of wary concern crept back into Elliott's voice, deadly serious. This time, he outright asked. "Do you still want that?"

Niko might just go crawling over to the tossed knife and murder Elliott himself if this all stopped now, before reaching its climax. "Yeah, babe. I do."

"Good," Elliott said, his tone back to its silken taunt again. He reached out and stroked Niko's hair. "Because I know you've been dying for this, ever since you started trying to earn my bounty."

He was definitely back in character. Probably. Even if what he said was pretty much the truth.

In the end, the only characters they were playing in this game were themselves—just a fantasy version of their past, if things had gotten a little carried away. The dangerous, slippery man who wielded a knife and face-fucked Niko until he cried *was* Elliott. Which meant the pitiful man on his knees brought almost to rapture just from being used by Elliott was, truly, Niko too. He couldn't hide behind the idea of a character, that this was a *different* Niko somehow, or maybe a different bounty hunter altogether, anymore.

They were both only exactly what they wanted to be.

Niko felt the familiar swell of discomfort and humiliation as the thought began to rise, so he pushed it all away. It was easier not to think about it.

Elliott crouched down, eyeing Niko in thought. Then he reached out and stroked his cheek with such tenderness and warmth that Niko felt himself involuntarily leaning into his touch. He then realized with a tinge of embarrassment that his cheek was still damp, and that Elliott was wiping away the last of his body's reflexive tears for him.

"That's better," he said. "Now. I want you to take your armor off for me. I want what's underneath it."

The lightheadedness from before struck Niko anew. He found himself reaching up thoughtlessly to unsnap his shoulder pads, then chestpiece, as he sank back onto his ass. He could feel every distinct beat of his heart, each pulse vibrant through his body as it carried his blood where it needed to be. Finally, he was down to only his clothing.

Elliott stared at him expectantly, but said nothing. Niko thought to strip it too, but hesitated, remembering the chastisement from before. "Should..." he started, tentatively, "should I take this off too?"

The other man's lips curved upward and he narrowed his eyes. "You're learning. Good. Yes, you can do that. It's in my way."

Niko did so, starting with his t-shirt, then awkwardly adjusted himself to pull his pants and boxers off. His legs were numb to the temperature, but his ass was painfully aware of how ice cold the simple metal floor of the training room was against bare skin. He couldn't help but shiver a little.

Elliott stood suddenly and stalked off across the room, pausing before the locker Niko kept his duffel bag in when they weren't out on a mission. He dug through it, then came back, the near-empty bottle of lubrication in hand. Then he sank to his knees, pushing Niko gently back to lay down. The floor was just as shockingly cold against the bare skin of his back. Elliott moved between Niko's legs, pushing them so they were spread wide. Niko felt dizzy all over again and swallowed.

Elliott then bent forward and ran his tongue slowly up along the length of Niko's needy, aching cock in one, long, sensuous lick. Niko shuddered, barely able to keep himself from reaching out to grip the other man. Then Elliott slowly swirled his tongue around the head of his cock, licking up the pre-come there.

He pulled away, sitting back up as he stared down at Niko. It nearly killed Niko not to beg him to give him more. To not leave him like that. But he knew that was exactly what Elliott wanted, and the stubborn, defiant side of him wouldn't allow the other man the satisfaction.

Instead, Elliott said, "Do you want to touch yourself, Niko?"

"Yeah." More than anything.

"I'm not going to let you."

Niko bit down on another pang of anger. Of course Elliott was going to torment him. Yet, it all drove him into an even deeper, more urgently wild place. He felt feverish.

"In fact. I have something I want you to try on," Elliott said. Niko watched as he held up the pair of handcuffs—he must have swiped them from the duffel bag. Niko froze again. This was, somehow, even more terrifying than the knife had been. The knife had just been a prop. This was something more. Anxiety coursed through him suddenly at the mere thought, his breath quickening.

Without the suit or chair, he couldn't get around, couldn't move his legs. And now, Elliott wanted to take the free use of his arms, his hands. It nearly sent Niko into a panic thinking about it. He would have to rely completely on Elliott and whatever he chose to do with—and to—him. He'd never given that sort of utter and complete power, nor profound trust, to anyone in his life. He had never planned to.

Elliott looked at him calmly. There was no pushiness in him, no insistence. He had given to another long, patient pause that Niko recognized again. He was letting him think on it, letting him be the one to decide. He was giving Niko the unspoken power, in that way. Niko could utter the stupid word again, could end this decisively before it went somewhere that was too much. He trusted Elliott to honor it—he had, after all, immediately stopped what they were doing and changed up his entire attitude in concern the moment Niko had spoken it before.

Or he could try it. See where it took him. He still had their safeword, even after agreeing. He could still say it any time. He could stop it any time at all. He searched Elliott's eyes, which, despite their current positions of submission and dominance, held nothing but a quiet warmth. There was no threat in them.

Part of Niko wanted to push back against his gnawing fear and let Elliott have complete control over him in any way he wanted. Something buried deep inside him outright ached for it—to give everything he had to Elliott. To be owned by him, at the mercy of his whim and want. It was the same feral desire he'd had back on Dainna. The same impulsive need that had driven him to ask Elliott to take over and face-fuck him during their first night together. Niko swallowed again, frozen for another moment, before barely nodding for him to continue.

"Yeah."

"You're sure?" Elliott murmured, barely audible. They were still in their characters-which-weren't-characters roles, and Niko had given him consent, yet Elliott still paused to double-check and make sure. Appreciation and affection spread thick and warm through Niko's chest, where his heart resided. He loved Elliott profoundly in that moment—wholly, truly.

And he trusted him.

"Do it," Niko said, confidence and warmth overcoming most of his fear. "I want you to."

Elliott took Niko's left hand in both of his, trailing his fingertips along its contours, scars, and calluses, then down along his wrist. Then he brought Niko's hand to his mouth and pressed a long, soft, sensual kiss to it. He wrapped one cuff around his tattooed wrist and sealed it closed with a click that immediately brought Niko back to the alleys of Uula, bewildered and freshly kissed by his enemy. And wanting so much more.

"Yes?" Elliott said quietly, looking to him again for consent. Niko nodded. He wasn't afraid at all, anymore.

"Yeah."

Elliott took his right hand and kissed it too, then pulled Niko's arms up above his head. He looped the handcuff chain around a thin metal pipe that ran along the wall—probably part of the electric or heating systems. Then he slid the other cuff around Niko's wrist and clicked it closed. A brief, light prick of anxiety rose in Niko again as he tried to pull his arms back down and found he couldn't anymore, but he willed himself to keep calm.

Elliott watched him again for a moment, as though checking to see that he was alright. Niko nodded to him again.

Elliott ran his hand through Niko's hair lovingly, then down his chest and stomach. "You're being so good for me," he murmured, and Niko's insides felt like melted honey. Then Elliott poured a few drops of lubrication into his palm and began gently stroking Niko's cock in an achingly slow rhythm. Niko grunted, turning his face away.

Elliott could do whatever he wanted to him now, use him however he wanted. It was agonizing, overwhelming. Absolutely delicious.

"Niko. Look at me."

Niko forced himself to look back at Elliott as he worked him with his hand. "I want you to look at me the whole time. Only me."

Niko swallowed. "O-okay."

"Okay." Elliott squeezed another generous helping of lube into his hand, then applied it to Niko's opening. Just the touch of him alone was euphoric. He slid his fingers inside him. Niko knew he was tense, wound up by the handcuffs. He forced himself to take a few breaths in and out, then relaxed his body. He wanted it badly.

Elliott smirked at him. "You're all ready for me, aren't you?"

"Mmh. Yeah."

"So perfect, Niko."

He positioned himself over Niko. The very anticipation of the other man penetrating him drove Niko wild. He didn't care what Elliott did to him at this point. He just wanted—*needed*—to be touched. Elliott took hold of Niko's legs, pushing them up and holding them against himself. Then he entered, still fully clothed, except for his cock. Niko felt every inch of him, and a long, pleasured sound escaped from between his lips that made him flush with shame.

He hardly recognized himself.

Once he was fully buried within Niko, Elliott paused for a moment to let them both adjust. Then he began moving, sliding in and out of him in a torturous, leisurely rhythm. He was taking his time. He looked at Niko, locking gazes, his own gorgeous eyes half-lidded, given to indulgence.

Niko fought himself. He clamped down on asking. He would do anything but beg him. But as the moments passed, Elliott kept his slow, gentle cadence within him, reaching out occasionally to trail his fingertips along Niko's needy cock, before letting them drop again.

Niko knew what Elliott was doing. He found himself speaking regardless, before he could think to take it back. "El-Elliott."

"Mmh? What's that, Niko?"

"I—I need you to fuck me harder than that. I need it."

"Then why don't you ask me?"

Niko couldn't even be mad about it anymore. It all fed into something extravagant inside him. Something he never knew he'd needed. Now that it was here, he craved it like air. He liked that he had to ask. "Can— Will you please fuck me hard? I need you to, Elliott. *Please.* Will you let me feel you?"

Elliott smiled at him, his eyes narrowed and clever as a fox. He leaned forward and gave Niko's neck a long, indulgent kiss that turned into sucking and lapping, still fucking into him slowly all the while. Niko realized Elliott was the one marking him this time. Then he moved to hover inches above Niko, his breath warm against his skin. He leaned down and met him in a long kiss, tongue against tongue, his hand reaching up to touch Niko's chin. Niko wished he could pull him down into a possessive embrace, to hold Elliott's body against his own.

Elliott smiled at him again. He closed his eyes and nuzzled his cheek affectionately, then whispered so quietly it gave Niko goosebumps, *"Since you asked me so sweetly, I'll give you what you want."*

He leaned back, taking hold of Niko's legs again, then began railing him—fast and hard, rough and wild now. Desperate and so, so hungry, not unlike he'd been when taking Niko's mouth. It was sloppy. He was giving Niko everything he was worth.

It hurt, and it felt extraordinary. It was everything Niko wanted. In that moment, he knew it, and couldn't deny it. Elliott fucked him so hard that his blond hair dampened with sweat from the effort.

Niko's whole body shook with each hard thrust. He was left with nothing to do but take it. The inability to touch Elliott, to touch himself, to respond in any way only drove Niko to a deeper, wilder delirium. He couldn't help himself. He closed his eyes and tilted his head back until it touched the floor, his neck arching.

He was emitting sounds now unlike he knew he was even capable of, something akin to agony—half whimpering, half moaning. His entire body was on fire with feeling, with vibrant life. He felt Elliott everywhere, in every part of him, every cell.

Elliott's soft moaning soon joined his own loud cries. With his eyes closed, fully under the control and will of Elliott, he fell into an almost meditative experience. It was something transcendent.

"Niko," Elliott panted out. He didn't stop in relentlessly fucking him. When Niko didn't immediately respond, eyes wrenched shut, he tried again, insistent, commanding. "*Niko.*"

"Mmh— What?"

"Open your eyes and look at me. I want you to see who's doing this to you."

It was hard, but he finally forced his eyes open and turned his gaze toward Elliott. The other man was completely flushed now, golden hair hanging in his face. Sweat trickled down his cheek. He gripped Niko's legs tightly, digging his fingers in as he pushed his knees up into a bend, fucking into him hard again and again and again.

He locked gazes with Niko as he did. "Who's fucking you good, lover? Who's taking care of you?"

It was hard to formulate words. Niko had forgotten what they even were, had discarded them somewhere along the way, with all the other unnecessary things. "Y-you are, Elliott."

More words surfaced then, something from deep inside him, something thoughtless. He didn't have to ask, didn't have to beg for this. But he wanted to, now.

He wanted Elliott to grant it to him.

"Please, Elliott. Can... Can I come?"

That earned a particularly indulgent moan and shiver from Elliott. He seemed to like that very, *very* much. Niko thought the other man just might lose himself then and there from what he'd asked.

Elliott's voice emerged breathless now. "Let go for me, Niko. Show me how much you like my cock."

"Not just." Thoughts floated hazily through Niko's mind. "You, Elliott. All of you."

He could do nothing but oblige, too lost now. Niko felt it everywhere, something uncontrollable and inevitable, an electric riptide mounting and coalescing in his lower belly, in his balls, begging for release. When it came, he cried out again, the sound unlike anything he'd heard come from himself. It was filthy. He sounded like he was dying. Maybe he was.

Elliott emitted a low, breathy moan as well, his thrusts turning more erratic until he pulled out. He knelt over Niko, finishing himself by hand. Niko longed to help, his handcuff chain clanking against the utility pipe as he strained thoughtlessly to reach for him.

"You were so good for me today. Such excellent service," Elliott panted out, "deserves a reward. Don't you think?"

He came on Niko's face. Niko let out a low groan as one last whisper of pleasure rippled through him from the sheer thrill of it.

He was spent after that, his body exhausted. Every nerve glowed, swimming in a sea of ephemeral bliss, his mind eviscerated and emptied. *That's one way for an assassin to finish you.* The thought came randomly, nonsensical. Niko gave a single, tired huff of a laugh. *Don't bougie people call it the little death, or something?*

He lay on the floor, trying to catch his breath, the warm sensation of Elliott's come still dripping down his cheek and chin.

A whispering mantra repeated through his mind in time with the pulse that hammered in his ears, perhaps indistinguishable from it.

*Elliott, Elliott, Elliott.*

"Here," Elliott murmured, his voice just as breathless sounding. He hastily took the small key meant for the handcuffs from his pocket and unlocked them, setting Niko free. Niko was grateful, massaging his wrists, taking the opportunity to flex and move his arms and test his regained freedom.

Then Elliott got up and went back to the locker, and quickly wiped himself clean with a rag before tucking himself away back in his pants. He made his way back to Niko and knelt beside him, gently wiping his face and body clean for him. Niko was exhausted, too tired to even sit up.

Elliott smiled down at him, warmly. "How was it? Are you alright, Niko?"

"I—I don't even know what to say," he started, mind still lost somewhere, but then realized that wasn't at all a satisfying answer, and that Elliott might perceive it as him not being fully okay. In truth, he felt euphoric. High. He was stuck on the metal floor, yet he was flying. "I'm alright. I'm... more than alright. I've never experienced something like that. Fuck. It was— It was incredible. I can't even move. I've never felt like that with another person. I've never felt like this before." He laughed at himself a little mockingly, flushing as the familiar shame crept back in at the memory of his own pleading mewls that had emerged so unlike him.

"Good," Elliott said. "I know what my good boy likes." He bent and kissed Niko chastely on the cheek, smiling at him again. Even now, the words sent another electric buzz trilling through Niko. "Here. Let me help you." He extended a hand to pull him up.

Niko groaned. He closed his eyes and turned his head away. "Do I have to? Can I just lay here for the next... seven or so hours?" He felt like he was going to need days, maybe weeks, to recover from whatever the hell had just happened to him.

"I mean, if that's your preference, you're welcome to. But I don't think it's going to be very comfortable."

Niko grunted, draping his arm across his face, ready to settle in for the long haul. *This is my life now, I guess.*

"Niko. Come on. I'll take care of you." Elliott stood over him still, hand outstretched. He was wearing a smile, something easy, warm, and full of affection.

*Who's taking care of you?* Elliott's voice stuck in his head.

Now that Niko was beginning to come down from their sloppy roleplay sex, he was quickly becoming acutely aware of himself again.

Painfully so.

Laid out on the ground, wearing nothing. Having made sounds that were akin to wordless keening. Begging permissions and praise from Elliott, like a subservient, helpless thing. And now, unable to get off the floor without the armor he'd tossed aside in careless pieces. He didn't want to be taken care of. Something stuck inside him like a shard of glass, the familiar wound.

It washed over him all at once, a plunge deep into icy water. Niko was pathetic. He felt ashamed.

"I've got it," he mumbled, ignoring Elliott's hand, and sat up. Elliott paused for a moment, but let his hand drop. His smile dropped too. He went to the pieces of Niko's armor and began picking them up for him.

*I said I've fucking got it*, Niko wanted to snap at him. He didn't want his help, didn't want to be awkwardly pieced back together into something semi-functional. He suddenly wanted to be alone, seen by the eyes of no one.

He clamped down on the slithering anger that snaked tightly through him now. He didn't want to snap on Elliott. It was the last thing he ever wanted to do. It wasn't Elliott he was pissed at, anyway.

It was himself.

Niko reached for his clothes and pulled them on as quickly as he could, making a conscious effort not to appear awkward. He accepted the armor pieces as Elliott handed them to him, keeping his mouth firmly shut and doing his best not to straight up wrench them from his grip. It was stupid. Stupid to act like this, to be so full of dangerous and aimless rage.

He didn't know what was wrong with him.

Elliott looked at him. He was too good at reading him. "Are you really alright, Niko? Did I do something wrong? Was this too much?" His voice was quiet, a tinge of fear to it.

It tore something in Niko apart, but was exactly what he'd apparently needed to finally calm his misplaced anger a fraction. He looked up at Elliott, fastening his gloves back into place with the rest of his armor. He could stand again now, but hesitated to. "No, Elliott, I—" He paused for a moment, wanting to navigate this carefully. "I always love being with you."

Elliott crouched on the floor before him, meeting his gaze on a level field now. His expression was full of concern, worried that he'd done something harmful. It was a bullet straight through Niko to see it. He hated that he'd caused it, that he was ruining the moment. "Then what is it, Niko? Something's wrong. Please talk to me."

He was right. They needed to talk about this. Niko had pushed it away for too long. But it was easier to keep shoving away what he couldn't even begin putting into words. "I was just, I guess, thinking that maybe from now on, we should do things the other way around," Niko said. The words came out wooden and stiff, all wrong. "That's how I like it best."

Elliott only stared at him, his brow drawing into a shadowed frown. "Is it, Niko? Really?"

"Yeah. It is."

"You're lying," Elliott said simply. "Why?"

"No, I'm fucking not," Niko asserted, rage spiking through him all over again. This time, at both Elliott and himself.

"You love it when I fuck you," Elliott said, his tone coming out like a sultry dagger, taking a stab. "I can tell the very idea always excites you. You go crazy when I even talk about it. You like it *far* more than the other way around."

"No. I've never said anything like that to you before. I've never said I like it more that way."

"'*It was incredible*,'" he said, repeating Niko's own words. "'*I've never felt like this before—*'"

"*Don't*," Niko snapped at him. He got to his feet. "Don't... fucking throw it back at me like that."

Elliott rose as well, slowly, and stared at him, utterly perplexed seeming. "Like what? And even if you didn't outright say it, you don't have to. It's like night and day. It's in the way you respond. It's in your expression, your eyes. The way you let out that shaky little breath, like you're barely controlling yourself. The sounds you make when I take you—"

"Stop."

Elliott stared at him a moment, before speaking again. "So, would you rather be my sub top, then?"

"No. I—" Niko folded his arms tightly across his chest. "Not like that either. I don't want to be—"

*Soft. Weak.*

"Be what, Niko?"

Niko said nothing.

Frustration began to creep into Elliott's voice. "It's so plainly obvious how badly you want it, but won't often let yourself go there with me. Why are you denying yourself?" After a pause, he added, "Are you ashamed?"

Niko wanted to be anywhere else right now. "I'm not ashamed of anything. It's just that everything you're saying right now is utter bullshit."

Elliott looked unimpressed. "Niko, I know a submissive man when I see one."

Niko nearly choked. A flash of anger, white hot as lightning, gripped him. He laughed bitterly. "Excuse me? What the fuck is that supposed to mean?"

"I think we both know what it means. I think you like being topped, and I think you like it when another man dominates you, even more. You like what you like, Niko. And it's alright if you do. Why are you acting like this?"

*I don't know*, he wanted to say. He was all agitation and tangled energy now. Instead, he snapped, "Because you don't get to tell me what I like. You don't even fucking know what you're talking about, saying all this shit, making assumptions about me. You're trying to make this all about me, but— You just say I like it and want it like that, because it's how *you* want it. *You* just want to dominate somebody, so you want to push me into the receptive role." Submissive. He couldn't even say the word, pivoting to *receptive* instead. "You're just— This is just you using me for what you want. And trying to justify it."

It wasn't what he'd wanted to say. Any of it. He was never like this. But he felt strangely cornered, like an animal. He was taking a verbal swing at Elliott now, looking to wound. All because the other man had been trying to reach into and explore what Niko only wanted to push back down into the dark and neglect again.

Niko was in agony. He wanted to unspeak the words, take them all back, start the conversation over. He was losing himself to the grip of something that was half blind rage, half utter panic.

Elliott looked at him like he was a stranger now.

Niko had clearly fucked up badly, had wounded him with what he'd said. The other man merely stared at him, as distant, cold, and closed off as he had been the first time Niko had ever seen his face. The depths of pain it elicited in Niko were boundless.

He wanted to apologize. He couldn't apologize. He didn't know if it would even matter at this point.

Niko hated himself.

"Right," was all Elliott finally said. He walked past Niko and out of the training room. Niko choked on calling out his name, swallowing it down by force. He ran his trembling, gloved hands over his face, trying to calm himself down. It didn't work.

"What the fuck is wrong with me?"

No one was there to give him an answer, anymore.

Niko banished himself to a spare bedroom that night. He couldn't bear to lie next to Elliott, stewing in awkward silence. Not after the hurt he'd inflicted on the other man. Not after he'd made Elliott look at him with such cold contempt.

He didn't want to trouble him any more than he already had.

Sleep wasn't coming to him. Niko hadn't really expected it to, anyway. The bed he'd picked smelled of dust. He'd sequestered himself away, not bothering to wash the sheets first, in case he ran into anyone in the halls or laundry room. Worst of all, however, was that it distinctly *didn't* smell of Elliott. His boyfriend's scent had become such a balm to him. It made him sleep easier than any medicine, alcohol, or drug ever had.

And alone, in this room, there was no one to hold.

Or be held by.

This was three years ago, all over again. This was hiding away from himself and everyone Niko had cared most about.

He may have come back to hunting again, but the cowardice in him still hadn't changed.

Nor had the loathing—a weapon aimed nowhere but at himself.

# Chapter Eighteen

# Another Buyer

They still had work to do. Enva'ruu, the Dvaab business mogul. Niko was up dutifully to his phone alarm, waking with at first confusion and then dread, as the memory of what had transpired returned gracelessly to him. He'd barely managed to sleep at all and his sore and sluggish body felt every repercussion of that now, an electric fire crawling through his legs from how hard he'd pushed himself back on Haneen.

This time, Elliott wasn't beside him to massage them.

He was scared to leave his room, but knew he had to. When he reached the bathroom, he pointedly ignored looking at his own reflection after glancing at the dark and passionate bruise Elliott's mouth had left on his neck. He took a long shower, buying himself an extra few moments before making his way out to the cafeteria. The scent of freshly cooked eggs, bacon, pancakes, and coffee filled the expansive room.

The empty and eerie quiet of RM-9832642G was slowly eroding away now. Zann stood leaning against the serving counter to the kitchen, engaged in conversation with Loolae. Smooth lounge jazz played over the intercom system, clearly Zann's pick. Elliott had finally permitted him to use it, it seemed.

In the kitchen, visible through its slim serving window, were Oliver and Loolae, both working together to make breakfast for everyone. Loolae laughed at something Zann said. Niko was grateful they could still laugh, that they seemed to be recovering well enough from what they'd been put through.

Seated at one of the tables was Elliott, a scattering of holographic maps and blueprints of Enva'ruu's home before him, a mug of steaming black coffee on the table.

Niko froze when he saw him. Elliott undoubtedly felt his gaze and paused from his research, looking up too. Their eyes met for a brief moment—until Elliott's brow furrowed into a subtle, displeased frown, and he looked back to his blueprints as though Niko were nothing of note.

Elliott may as well have shot him. The sting of it stole his breath away. Niko glanced away from him too, and wheeled his way over toward Zann instead.

"Hey."

"Niko. Morning."

"Smells good in here."

"Yeah. Kind of reminds me of Ch'ua's breakfast platter special. I could go for one of those right now."

Niko salivated at the memory. The loss of Ch'ua's Chicken was perhaps the most profound of all his severed ties to society. Both brothers were feeling it, it seemed. "Shit. Me too."

"Oh, hush," Loolae chimed in. "That food was greasy trash. It had no nutritional benefits whatsoever."

"Besides, a home cooked meal is far superior, in my opinion," Oliver quietly added.

"Fair point," Zann relented. "And I'm pretty sure they were adding jhiinrax spice to it. Which is highly addictive. And illegal on Kaapra-19."

"Explains a lot if so," Niko muttered.

"So." Zann turned to look at him now. He eyed Niko up and down. "Heard you guys are already going back out."

"Yeah, uh." He glanced vaguely in Elliott's direction, but willed himself not to look at him. "Elliott wants to hit Enva'ruu next. The Dvaab—"

"Yeah, I know who he is," Zann cut him off. "Seems kind of soon, don't you think? Everybody only just got back from Khaathra, and all."

"Well, the longer we wait at this point in the game, the harder it's all going to be. People are going to start disappearing, going into hiding. Strike while the iron's hot and all that, right?"

"I guess so."

"Besides, we were, uh, kind of taking a hiatus to focus on finding Dad and Loolae, and everything. Didn't want to stir the pot any more than we already had."

"Speaking of 'the pot,'" Oliver said, "breakfast is ready." He chuckled at his own joke.

They filled their plates, and everyone sat down together to eat at the same table Elliott had sat at. Then they dug in, not talking much for a while, too busy concentrating on the indulgent home-cooked meal provided.

"This is great, Dad. Loolae." Niko swallowed an entire mouthful of bacon. "Thanks."

Oliver smiled. "I'm glad you enjoy it. It was nice cooking with Loolae." He glanced at her.

Loolae's patterns turned a pleased magenta. "It was mostly you, Oliver. I still struggle knowing how to prepare human meals, sometimes. One of the most bewildering things I encountered when I first moved from Valaevanas was that food needed to be cooked."

"You guys eat everything raw down there?" Zann asked.

"Most of it, yes. Try cooking underwater."

"This is especially excellent, then," Elliott said. "Thank you for making it."

"My pleasure," Loolae said. She blinked curiously at him. "Elliott, can I ask? How did you acquire food supplies after you'd started your... work?"

"Moft of defe are from Lady D," Niko mumbled out around a mouthful of fluffy egg.

"She meant before you saw Lady D, dumbass," Zann said.

Niko glanced at Elliott, who was quiet for a moment, obviously choosing his words carefully. "I pre-planned how much I would need for a mission this long, and added in two surplus months just in case anything went wrong or was delayed. I already had everything I needed, before I ever started taking them down."

"So, what about after?" Zann said, staring at Elliott. Niko shifted uneasily, but didn't jump in to help him. He didn't think Elliott would appreciate it right now.

Elliott took a long drink of coffee, his Adam's apple shifting as he swallowed several times. It was the old trick Niko knew well by now. He was buying himself a moment to think, to navigate with care. He set the mug back down. It clinked softly against the scuffed, gray tabletop. "I hadn't thought that far out, honestly. I was too focused on doing this."

It was a lie, and Niko knew it. Elliott never overlooked details as big as that. The lack of life-supporting supplies after his work concluded wasn't an oversight; it was the intent. His mood soured a little. Breakfast suddenly didn't taste so good.

"So, you didn't think you were going to survive til the end?" Zann asked. Niko cast him a wary glance, but Zann's attention was honed in only on Elliott now. This wasn't really a conversation to be had over pancakes, but Zann had been an excellent investigator and sometimes, even in their personal lives, struggled to switch it back off.

Elliott started to reach for his mug again, but stopped himself. "I don't know, actually. Part of me did, and part of me didn't. It's why I'm saving Uru Taal for last. It's been my primary motivation for survival."

To Niko's surprise, Zann actually grimaced. He leaned back in his chair, the pressure suddenly dissipating from Elliott now as he turned his gaze upward toward the fluorescent overhead lights instead. "Shit. That's some real restraint. I'd have fucked him up, first thing. I don't know how you couldn't."

Elliott impaled a piece of pancake with his fork, then dragged it slowly through a puddle of golden syrup. It glistened beneath the lights. "I'm savoring it."

"Zann," Oliver chided gently. "Maybe this isn't the best conversational topic over breakfast."

Zann grunted. He seemed mildly cowed though, casting a guilt-ridden glance around. When he met Niko's gaze briefly, Niko only shook his head at him. Zann shrugged back, then hunched over his own plate and helped himself to it.

The remainder of breakfast went, to Niko's relief, relatively peacefully—ignoring the fact that he and Elliott had barely even exchanged glances all morning. When they were finished eating, Niko helped his father clean up the dishes, before getting ready to head out on their next strikethrough of Honeybliss's roster.

Aboard the *Soñadora*, he and Elliott sat together in the pilot and co-pilot's chairs, Niko clad in the suit. He ached. He wanted nothing more than to push away what had happened, and go back to his usual banter with Elliott. To reach out and touch his hand or hair or face. But he also knew trying to do so would be an even deeper blunder. It would be doing Elliott a graver disservice than he'd already inflicted. Niko knew he'd harmed him with his words, but didn't know yet how to face it, how to apologize. Apologizing meant having to give recognition to what sat uncomfortable inside him. And it wasn't ready to come out yet.

So, instead, they stayed quiet, a cavernous distance between their two seats.

"Here," Elliott said. He sent Enva'ruu's coordinates to the ship console and a moment later, Niko had it programmed in, the course set.

"ETA, three and a half hours," Niko murmured.

Elliott only nodded. He didn't even look in his direction. He pulled up his phone hologram and began going through the newsfeed, then paused on a video. Niko couldn't help but be nosy, his gaze sliding over toward it as two unfortunately familiar faces filled the screen. He realized it was a live broadcast.

Elliott played it.

Mary and Johann Kestrel practically glowed, their faces seeming to have somehow de-aged by a good several years in a matter of months since their initial interrogation at Station Twelve. Johann wore a beige suit and Mary had a deep blue, asymmetric dress on. She had trimmed her brown hair into a short pixie cut. She'd apparently gotten her eyebrows and nails done, too.

They stood surrounded by ravenous reporters, up behind a podium which bore the municipal government seal of Althiss City, Delevia.

"—and do not condone the actions of our son, Elliott James," Mary said. "Regardless of the reasoning or context behind his chosen targets, murder is never something that should be excused, nor accepted in civilized society."

"Elliott has taken upon himself to be judge, jury, and executioner," Johann added in. His face bore a tragic expression that made Niko want to punch him. This had been the same guy who'd gladly told Galapol about Elliott being a broken and violent child, only to have been the one to actually dole out drunken violence on his family instead. "We don't accept those actions and, as Mary said, we don't condone what he's done and continues doing."

A reporter mumbled something and Johann shook his head. "No. We're not in contact with him in any way. We haven't been in years."

The press was practically climbing on top of one another now, frantically crowding in to try at a chance for getting a statement. An elegant and veiled Quwa-quay won out, asking, "Do you have any thoughts on the rapidly growing support across—" Niko couldn't make out the rest.

Johann and Mary glanced at each other. "No, we have no comment," Mary said. "We've made our statements. We don't condone murder, regardless of the reasons or any public sentiment."

A Gheroun woman desperately shouted for their attention from further back in the crowd. Niko could only make out fragments of what she said. Something about a bounty hunter, Starhawk, and the word 'babe.' Mary listened before shaking her head adamantly. "No, I don't know anything about that. I never met that man. I have no comment."

Elliott swiped the feed away, and the ship fell into heavy silence.

"They're being paid off, still," he said. "Their clothes are designer. They never had the money for that sort of luxury before. They're too stupid to even try hiding it. I recognize the dress. It's an authentic Danaala Vessce. She has a very distinct style. It's ironic. Cleo used to love her work."

"Elliott..."

"They know exactly what happened to Cleo, now. They're accepting money from the people who raped their daughter and ensured she never came home again. They're buying her favorite fashion designer's dresses to wear with it."

It was sickening. Even thinking about the elder Kestrels and the complete disregard they had for the lives of their children made Niko's skin crawl.

And it wasn't fair. Elliott had given a home and safety to Niko's family; they played music over the intercom, filled the halls, worked out in his training room, cooked breakfast in the kitchen. Yet, Elliott's own parents were deplorable pieces of shit who, somehow, still continued to only betray the memory of their fallen daughter and wound their living son. Again and again and again.

*Be part of my family,* he wanted to blurt out. The words were on the tip of his tongue. *We'll take care of you.* But it felt wrong, felt disingenuous or cruel to say when Niko himself had wounded Elliott too. He needed to do something about it.

Even though the words were still so tangled up in the pit of his stomach, wrapped in dread. He didn't know how to address what was so misaligned inside himself.

But maybe he could try.

"Elliott, listen—"

Elliott stood. "I'm going to go take a nap. I didn't sleep well."

"Do you want me to go with you?" The words fell from Niko's mouth before he could even think about it.

Elliott froze and narrowed his eyes as though he'd heard something unpleasant. "No."

Before Niko could say anything more, the other man left the cockpit.

Niko had definitely fucked up. Why was it so hard to talk about? Why was it so hard to even acknowledge? Even the idea of discussing what they'd done between each other was daunting and sent his pulse hammering. He missed the days when things were easier, when he didn't rely on tech-suits and chairs. When he could shove his lovers against the wall and take them roughly, or have them while they were down on their hands and knees for him, sloppy and uncomplicated. He didn't have to think about it then. And they'd all been happy enough with that arrangement.

Why did Elliott have to come in and shake it all up?

And why had he had to insist that this was exactly what Niko wanted most? As though the other man were some sort of omniscient god who could claim to know what Niko felt inside.

His chest tightened with frustration and an anger he didn't know where to direct—Elliott, himself, or maybe something else entirely—all over again.

No. He wasn't ready to apologize yet. Not until he was able to approach this more calmly. Even thinking about the subject got him riled up again, defensive and pissed off like a porcupine putting up its spikes. If they went there right now, he knew he'd probably just lash out once more. He might be a fucking mess at the moment, but he at least knew not to try and make things even worse for Elliott by panicking and doubling down all over again, driving the knife deeper.

Today's job was going to be hard.

They landed the *Soñadora* back behind Enva'ruu's mansion, which resided on a private and generous amount of acreage on Neema. The skies above them were a deep, thickly-clouded azure. Enva'ruu's land was filled with wild foliage, all indigo-tinted and feathery to the touch, with—to Niko's awe—a few bioluminescent, gently glowing flower cups scattered here and there. They decided to keep the ship's stealth on. With any luck, they would be in and out fast. Another quick job, just like Cnrys's had been. Elliott wasn't much in a talking mood and neither was Niko, a sea of unspoken words churning between them. When they did talk, it was short and to the point.

All business.

"There's a back entrance," Elliott said, "that I saw on his blueprints. It should lead in through the kitchen. It will be easier to keep unnoticed if we go that way. He might have guards here keeping an eye out that we'll have to be careful of. Especially now that I tattled on him all over the internet."

Niko nodded. "Alright. Let's make this quick."

"Yes. Let's."

They made their way under stealth to the back door, exactly where Elliott had predicted it to be. He seared straight through its lock with the small laser he carried, opening it softly and slipping inside. Niko tried to follow as quietly as he could, though the suit would always make it a challenge. Both it—and he—would never be built for stealth.

They traversed through an ornate and elaborate kitchen with pale, marbled counter tops and arching windows, and into an open foyer with a grandiose chandelier and polished floor, whose tiles formed a spiral pattern not unlike the image of a galaxy. The mansion had to be huge, even bigger than the Xermotl magician's had been. Niko couldn't help but wonder what people even did with houses this big, other than throw parties. There would never be any need for possessing seven bedrooms and four bathrooms. And Enva'ruu had no family; his wife had been dead for over a decade and he'd never remarried. Niko wouldn't be surprised if the man had actually killed her. His videos had shown a particular aggression and torturous violence that, unlike most of Honeybliss, had never strayed into anything sexual.

There were no guards or security staff posted, the entire estate silent and still. Nor were there any Galapol agents waiting them out, like they'd been at Khaathra's. But there was something heavy in the air that gave Niko pause.

"Master bedroom's upstairs, to the left," Elliott said, taking a step toward the spiraling, central staircase. Niko lashed out an arm and quickly grabbed for where he thought Elliott's wrist was. He'd aimed true and gripped it tightly, stopping the other man in his tracks. They were slowly getting better at functioning under stealth, it seemed. Elliott froze, before subtly trying to pull his hand away.

It hurt. Niko let him go.

"What is it?" Elliott said, sounding tense now.

"I... don't know," Niko admitted, swallowing. Inside the helmet, he could hear the click of his throat. The rest of the mansion was eerily silent. "Something's not right, though." He couldn't pinpoint it, but it was that electric tension in the air, something uncanny that he'd sensed before on jobs. Something was off about the entire place that made Niko's skin crawl, pressing down on him. He wasn't even sure what had set him off—a sound, maybe, so quiet and subtle it could have been imagined. But *something* had sent every alarm in him blaring now.

They weren't alone, and it wasn't welcome company.

His heart was pounding now, a survival instinct, something primal. He could feel his pulse in his throat.

"Elliott—"

The world around them exploded suddenly in a flash of bright, caustic green that hung in the air. Niko instinctively grabbed Elliott against himself. He realized their energy shields had been triggered by and were drenched in bog-theun toxin. It hung heavy on them, eating away into whatever force Elliott used to power their barriers.

"Oh shit, oh shit."

Niko pulled them over behind a tall, thick, white pillar near the base of the stairs. Seconds later, they watched in helpless horror as the protective barriers around them faltered, glitched, then fell away entirely, followed by their cloaking.

"Hi there, Paycheck," a familiar voice sang out. Bubblegum. "I missed your pretty face. Why don't you come out and see me?"

A spray of bullets pelted the column they hid behind, chunks of plaster flying around them.

He could hear Elliott's breath emerging in shaky, sharp pants beside him. "Are we bugged?" he murmured. Then, he called out louder, "How the fuck did you know we were going to be here?"

"There are only so many of these dipshits left at this point," Bubblegum said. "So it was a matter of guessing. I knew you'd be coming here sooner or later, so I've been waiting. Today was my lucky day. You're pretty sneaky with your stealth shit, but tweedle-fucking-dumbass over there gave you away with his heavy steps."

Niko winced. Elliott had definitely made the right call before, on Haneen.

Enva'ruu had fled long before they got here. Their work was going to be like this from now on. They'd had a massive victory in getting Elliott's files out, but it had come at just as profound a cost. Nothing would ever be easy again—if any of their missions before could have been classified as easy. Bounty hunters, Galapol, traps, and empty houses with vanished Honeybliss members were all that awaited them now. Niko wondered if they'd even be able to track down everyone who had fled.

He missed when things were quieter, like they'd been at Cnrys's beach mansion. It had been almost too easy, then. But being superfluous to Elliott's work was better than being blindsided.

Niko leaned around the side of the column and fired on her several times, trying to take her down quickly before this unfolded into an even bigger problem. Bubblegum ducked around a corner, the bullets peppering the wall she'd disappeared behind. The stairs beside them groaned and began collapsing in on themselves, kicking up wood dust and the bitter scent of burning timber and tile, strong enough to smell even through the helmet. She'd cut them off from accessing the second story now.

A moment later, another grenade came soaring their way.

"Run!" Niko barked, shoving Elliott ahead of him. He heard its explosion behind them as they beelined for a door which led into a study full of bookcases, a marbled desk, and a bust of some deeply-pontificating, solemn Dvaab Niko didn't recognize. A flurry of bullets trailed them, and Niko turned to fire back before ducking around the corner.

"Shit."

"This isn't going to work," Elliott muttered, huddling down beside him.

"Told you I'd be back to collect," Bubblegum said. "And with your cute little broadcast, the bounty's about up. This is as high as it goes. So, it's time. I'm cashing in."

"You don't even know if they'll be good for paying it," Niko called out. It was a long shot, but maybe if he could target her greed, he could make her reconsider. "Galapol is a fucking mess right now, and the whole thing's being renegotiated anyway."

"Oh, they'll pay. And besides, I found another buyer, too," Bubblegum said. "One who's willing to tack on an extra two billion on top of your fat bounties to let me... lease you to him for a few hours, first."

Niko and Elliott glanced at each other, Elliott's gaze sharpening with rage now.

"Who?" Niko called out. His skin crawled. He knew who. But he wanted to hear it.

"Prince Uru Taal. He's pissed, too. He wants your little blond buttlicker. And he wants to hurt him real bad." Niko could hear the smirk in her voice. "*Again.*"

Beside him, Elliott seethed. Niko saw his jaw clench as he ground his teeth together, the color draining from his face. His body stiffened, and he sprung up suddenly to try and fire on her.

Niko grabbed him before he could, wrestling with the other man and pulling him back behind cover. A scattering of shots splintered the plaster around them.

Elliott strained against him with everything he had, but Niko was stronger. He wasn't used to seeing him lose his cool like this. Elliott was panting hard, his clenched teeth bared.

"Elliott. No. She's trying to rile you up."

"It's fucking *working*," Elliott snarled. He was trembling in Niko's grip.

"Ignore her. Fuck her. She's not getting out of this alive anyway."

"Right." That seemed to calm him some. Elliott let out a few panting breaths before finally steadying himself. Niko nodded at him and released his grip, and Elliott nodded back. "Sorry."

"Keep your head in the game, Elliott," Niko said. "That's how we win this."

Niko knew it was a lost cause to waste the words on Bubblegum. This had, after all, been the same unlicensed hunter who had been perfectly willing to cause both civilian and police casualties to get at Elliott in the past.

But he had to try.

"Clair, do you really want to work with him?" he called out. "Honeybliss destroys families all the time. They hurt and kill innocent people who've never done anything wrong and have no part in any of this. Is that really who you want to ally yourself with right now? Especially now that public scrutiny is building against them?"

"I don't give a fuck about any of that," Bubblegum said. *Yep. Lost cause.* "I go where the money is, and right now he's willing to pay me more than anyone else is. So, I'm gonna feed your golden dick-sleeve to him with glee. Then, after that ugly Toli-ai motherfucker chews him up and spits him out, Galapol and every government that you've pissed off can have the sloppy seconds."

He felt Elliott tense up again beside him.

"Alright," Niko muttered under his breath. "She's fucking dead."

"The sooner the better," Elliott ground out.

Something exploded against the wall they'd been using as cover. Seconds later, Niko could smell the same acrid burning, the entire structure of the estate groaning as the plaster, wood, and insulation of the wall began to dissolve under bog-theun toxin.

"Shit. Elliott, get *back!* Now!"

Elliott flinched and quickly threw *Repartee* to the floor. Its long barrel began sizzling where droplets of green corrosive had caught it, the scent acerbic and nauseating. He couldn't even imagine how much Elliott had to be suffering without a helmet of his own to block out most of the smell.

They both took off running deeper into what Niko saw now was an entertainment room of some kind, full of Dvaab cultural games and marble tables topped with little carved figurines. Behind them, the wall they'd been near sagged, then completely collapsed into itself, burying what remained of Elliott's damaged rifle with it. The ceiling above the rubble groaned and started sagging downward as well. Its ornate plaster cracked and rained down in chunks.

"Fuck," Niko murmured. "Another couple of these things, and she's going to bring the entire house down. We don't have long now."

"That's part of the plan. Drive us out where there's no cover."

"Shit. We're going to have to meet her head on, then."

"We should split up," Elliott said. Niko paused, looking at him. "We have a distinct advantage over her, in that there are two of us. Distract her. And I'll go around from the back and get her."

"How are you going to do that, Elliott? You don't have stealth or a shield. You don't even have your gun, anymore."

"I don't need it."

"Fuck. I don't like this. Getting close to her is dangerous."

"Then we'll just let her push us around the house, until the whole fucking thing collapses!" Elliott snapped. "Maybe I should just handle this myself. You can go back to the ship and wait until it's over." He was still shaking. Niko watched him force himself to calm a little, letting out a long breath. "I—I'm sorry."

"Elliott..." Niko had never seen him so aggravated since they'd started working together. Elliott had been taunted and insulted plenty of times in his work before. Every time, he'd gracefully matched his opponents in verbal blows, dancing circles around them. He was clearly getting sloppy now, letting his emotions get the best of him. And Bubblegum's particular brand of assholery certainly wasn't helping, threatening Elliott with the very tragedy that had befallen his sister.

Or maybe it was Niko who had gotten under his skin.

He should have apologized before they'd started this.

Niko sighed. "We need to talk after this."

"Oh. Do we?" They both ducked behind a solid marble Dvaab Julakkanerr game table as another spray of warning bullets perforated the wall behind them. Carved game figurines rained down around them as they were caught in the gunfire.

He ignored Elliott's snipe. If they couldn't get their shit together quickly, they weren't going to make it out of this alive. "Fine. If anyone's going to get close to her like that, though, I should be the one to do it."

"Why don't you try trusting me, Niko? Didn't we have a whole talk about that, a while ago?" Elliott said, his tone still scathing. "Besides, one of us is going to need to pull her attention and keep her occupied. And you're the one with the bulletproof armor."

Niko ground his jaw, swallowing down an argument. They were running out of time to act, and Elliott had a point. He wasn't going to make it into another fight, like he had on Haneen. Especially when Elliott was so obviously already hurting right now.

"Right. Yeah, fine." After a long moment, he added, "I do trust you. I just don't know what I'd do if you got hurt."

"Then distract her well enough, and I won't be." Then Elliott added, his voice finally softening a bit, "But don't get hurt either, Niko. Be careful. *Please.*"

*Right. No pressure at all, there.*

They looked at each other and Niko nodded to him. Elliott slunk off across the room, crouching to keep out of sight and behind the game tables. Niko took the opportunity, peeking up above the table and firing on her, then just as quickly ducking behind it as she fired two more shots, one missing and the other pinging off his arm.

*Really fucking need to thank Zann for this suit.*

He was protected from her gunfire with the armor—and especially thanks to the replacement helmet Death had gotten him—but that wasn't what concerned him most, anyway. Her arsenal of corrosives made it so he may as well not have even been wearing armor at all. A splash of bog-theun toxin, and it would be over. It would keep eating away at the protective material of his suit until either he stripped it and was left vulnerable, or it ate away into his flesh and kept going.

Neither was a particularly pleasant option.

He willed himself not to glance in Elliott's direction—doing so would only draw attention to the fact that the other man wasn't still behind cover, next to him.

Niko had to distract her. He had to keep her talking.

"So, why'd you kill your buddy?" he called out. "Fourier? Wasn't he useful to you?"

"Oh, that Galapol microdick? He outgrew his little panties and decided he was going to cash in on Paycheck himself. So, I decided to remind him of his place. Which is face down. In the fucking dirt."

"You know, I've always thought unregistered hunters were shitty wannabe hacks. You're only continuing to prove my point."

"Don't care," Bubblegum called back.

Niko took another couple of rapid shots. Maybe he'd get lucky and actually hit her, and Elliott wouldn't have to worry about taking her by surprise. But she was too good, ducking back behind her own cover—another thick, white support pillar. She returned fire.

"What's even the point of any of it? Money's great and all, but it'll only take you so far in life. If you have to trample and hurt everyone in your path to get it, it's not worth it anymore."

"I didn't come here to get lectured by you," Bubblegum said. "And I don't care about your high ground moral bullshit."

He could see Elliott now, creeping along in the background behind her, crouched and silent as a stalking cat. His green eyes were intense, fiercely focused nowhere but on the back of her. He'd already pulled the knife out. It glinted in the light as he gripped it tightly. Just a few more feet, and he'd have her.

Niko let out a shaky breath. They had this. They could do this. He fired several more times on her, leaning heavily into making sure her attention was focused on him now and nowhere else. He could see her reaching for another grenade as she ducked behind cover.

It wasn't enough.

"Where's blondie?" she ground out, her own hunter's instinct too infuriatingly good. A fresh surge of icy adrenaline spiked through Niko's veins at her question. "It's been a while."

She turned on her heel just as Elliott sprung for her with the knife. It wasn't the stealthy, clean cut to the neck he'd obviously intended for.

She fired point blank on him.

For a moment, Niko couldn't breathe, the air caught in his chest as ice jolted through his body. Then he realized that somehow, miraculously, Elliott's brandished knife blade had caught and deflected the bullet instead as he'd plunged it toward her. Even Elliott seemed briefly stunned, pausing for a beat to process before driving the dagger toward her face this time.

Niko would never question its luck again.

She dodged and swung out a heavy fist, connecting hard with his side. "I know your tricks by now, you little bitch."

Elliott grunted and briefly folded into himself, but recovered admirably, grabbing her tightly and trying to get her into a bear hug not unlike Niko had pulled on him in their mock fight the day before. Bubblegum fought him hard, twisting fiercely in his grip.

Niko aimed on her but couldn't fire—it was too risky with both of them fighting for their lives now. He could just as easily hit Elliott.

*Shit.*

She knocked the knife from Elliott's hands. It clattered to the ground, bounced, then disappeared into the gaping chasm beside them that bog-theun corrosive continued eating away at. Its luck and good fortune had, it seemed, finally been exhausted.

Elliott was on his own for once, truly, no tricks left at his disposal now. He had no tech, he had no weapons. He wrestled with her, trying to keep her in a tight grip against himself, but Bubblegum was determined. She threw her weight around and bucked, making it difficult to hold her. She got an arm free, and started driving her fist again and again into Elliott's exposed side. He cried out in pain.

It drove Niko into a frenzy. He glanced at the doorway Elliott had exited through. He'd have to circle around through several rooms while the house was beginning to collapse on top of them. It would be too hazardous now, and take too long. Elliott was struggling against her and as she dealt him damage, he was clearly beginning to lose. Niko had a mere minute at this point—maybe even less.

He stared out at the ever-widening gap in the floor between them. He could make it. Maybe. He could try to get to them. He'd jumped farther distances back on Uula. Probably. But those had been *down* instead of *across*. And the widening gap before him only revealed to Niko what he didn't want to acknowledge.

He couldn't make it.

Elliott cried out again in agony as Bubblegum managed to get a good hit in now on his right eye, her fist connecting hard with the socket. Niko had to get there fast, one way or another.

At any cost.

*Think*, he willed himself. *Fucking think!*

The grappling hook. He hastily sheathed his rifle on his back, then grabbed it from his utility belt, looking upwards. The structure of the mansion was already unsteady, the ceiling groaning and bowing down in a way Niko didn't like. His added weight to it might bring the whole thing down on top of them, ending this struggle swiftly and permanently for all three of them. But he couldn't afford to wait. He'd have to risk it.

He aimed it at an ominously swinging and shuddering chandelier that consisted of a downward spiral of glimmering crystals. The thing wouldn't hold him for long, and if Niko ended up falling through the widening hole below, he would be fucked six ways from Sunday. And so would Elliott. He had to try it—Niko had no choice. Not when it came to keeping the other man safe.

He released the hook. It latched onto the light fixture with a *clank*, a few of the delicate crystals falling into the growing pit below. Then he took a few steps back and broke into a full run, launching himself off the edge as close as he could get before his boots made contact with bog-theun corrosive. He held on tight, heart in his throat.

The grappling cable held taut as Niko swung across the dark gap of floor.

Until it didn't.

He felt and heard the chandelier give way above him, the cable snaking into something horrifically slack in his hands.

*Nononono. Oh fuck.*

He'd barely built enough momentum to make it to the other side. But now the ceiling was going to collapse around them all. He'd brought an entire second story down on their heads. He'd just killed Elliott himself—

Niko missed his landing, and tumbled across the floor as an icy flush of adrenaline seized up his body. Around them, the chandelier smashed against the edge of the hole, splintering into glinting shards. It snapped off several floor tiles and broke the supporting planks beneath them. Niko waited for the worst, waited to be buried under tons and tons of rubble—but it never came.

A glance upward showed the ceiling still held, though barely. It didn't look great, a sizable hole gaping straight up into the second floor where the chandelier had been. The ceiling bowed in and creaked more than ever as the walls and house itself shifted around them, slowly eaten away from the inside out. Deep cracks ran across it as a fine rain of plaster chunks and dust filled the room.

He wasted no time, scrambling up and sprinting towards Elliott. Bubblegum threw her weight backwards, tripping him up. Elliott went down, landing close—far too close—to the widening edge of the hole in the floor.

*I've got you.*

Niko slammed into her hard as she tried to recover, tackling her to the floor. She scrambled and fought him too, her eyes wild with animalistic survival instinct. He tried to give her the *Larry Special,* struggling to get a grip on her head to wrench her neck into a break, but she managed to get a leg and arm out from under him and pried his arm away from her.

Niko grasped for his rifle as he fought to keep her pinned down, finally unlatching it. He aimed it right for her face and fired.

It clicked, out of ammo.

*"Oh, fucking seriously?!"* Niko shouted.

"Get bent, you tin can asshole!" Bubblegum reached down now, and he could see she was attempting to get another explosive loose. Niko slammed the butt of his rifle down against her hand and heard the cracking of bone.

"Niko." Elliott's voice came from his right, weak and quiet. He was still down on the floor, struggling to gain purchase. "Here."

He rolled a neon green grenade toward him—the very same corrosive she'd wielded against them. Elliott must have managed to nab it off her before she'd thrown him off balance.

This wasn't going to be pretty. But it was going to be effective.

Niko grabbed up the grenade, nearly losing his grip entirely on Bubblegum in doing so, then ripped the pin out as he straddled her. He shoved the thing down against her face as he struggled to keep her held down, before calling out. "Elliott, *get the fuck back!*"

He had to time this right. Too soon, and she'd slip out and get too far away from it. Too late, and he'd get sprayed with it too.

*Three.*

*Two.*

*One.*

Niko let go, springing up off Bubblegum and hurtling towards the door. Elliott was already halfway there, moving sluggishly and clutching his side. Niko heard it go off behind them, followed by a watery scream that dissolved into something broken and awful that would haunt that cursed place in his brain for the rest of his days, alongside all the horrors of Honeybliss. Niko didn't dare to look back at her, but Elliott paused and stared.

The mansion gave another shuddering, ominous groan as though yearning to fill in the silence that terminated her dying sounds.

They had to go.

Now.

Niko scooped Elliott up off his feet and made a run for the *Soñadora*.

"I can walk," he protested, but Niko ignored him.

Once they'd gotten inside the ship, he sat Elliott down on the edge of the bunk, then went to the first aid kit and pulled the whole thing from its latch on the wall. When he turned back to Elliott, the other man was drawn into himself, head bowed, one arm wrapped around his side. His breathing was ragged, full of quiet, sharp little gasps. It killed Niko to see.

Niko knelt before him. Elliott's face was startling, the entire cornea of his right eye blood red where she'd struck him, a dark bruise already purpling the outside corner of it. He looked depressed and worn down, his anger turned to sorrow.

"*Baby,*" Niko murmured, breathless. He reached up and wiped gently at a small cut at the side of Elliott's eye.

"Niko, we need to go," Elliott said quietly. "We should get the ship into space, at least."

He was right. The explosions, the estate slowly collapsing in on itself. It was undoubtedly going to draw attention. They'd be swarmed in minutes. "*Fuck,*" Niko hissed out. "In a— Just give me a minute."

"Do we have a minute?"

"For you? Yeah. It's stealthed anyway. So that buys us some time. Here." Niko gently lifted Elliott's shirt up. What he saw was harrowing—his right side was already painted with a dark, ruddy bruise that ran from hip to mid-rib.

Niko pried open a topical numbing wipe and gently touched it to Elliott's side, before trailing it down the bruise. Elliott hissed in pain, his body stiffening, but otherwise he said nothing.

"I should have gotten there sooner," Niko said.

"It's not... really that bad," Elliott said quietly. "It's not even the worst I've ever been through."

Niko paused, the implications of that sinking into the marrow of his bones. He wanted to do more than punch Johann Kestrel now. He wanted to throttle the life out of the man. The thought of him in his expensive new Honeybliss-bought suit drove Niko's blood pressure spiking.

"Yeah, well, I'm going to make sure this never happens to you again," Niko ground out.

"It's okay, Niko." He sounded tired. "You should have seen the other guy," he mumbled, aiming, it seemed, for a bit of levity. "Or girl, I suppose, in this case."

"Yeah, well, good fucking riddance. We won't have to worry about her anymore." Niko gently cleaned and numbed Elliott's injuries. "I think we're lucky in that most of these are fairly surface level wounds. It's going to hurt like a bitch for a while and you have some internal bruising, but I don't think anything is seriously damaged inside."

He'd had to give himself a trial-by-fire crash course on basic first aid, simply due to the number of injuries he himself had often sustained in past years of hunting.

Elliott nodded.

"How's your eye?"

"Blurry. Hurts. But otherwise, fine."

"No blind spots in your vision? Blood?"

"No."

Niko dabbed at the corner of his eye.

"I lost *Repartee*."

"I know. We'll figure something out. I can talk to D about getting another."

"No. They're custom modded. I have one remaining, but it's the last. That one's called *Banter*."

That statement felt far more ominous than Niko wanted it to be. He paused, a chill creeping up his spine.

If a cat's longevity was measured through its nine lives, Elliott's was measured through his uniquely named guns.

"Yeah," Niko said. They both fell silent, an awkward fissure hanging between them as Niko gently dabbed at his wounds. After a moment, something in Elliott's expression shifted, a cool shadow coming over his features.

"You don't need to do that anymore. I don't want you to. I'm tired. I'd rather just go home."

"Elliott, I—"

They were interrupted by a startling explosion that rocked the entire ship. Niko stood and glanced out the windshield to see open air and only one wall standing where Enva'ruu's mansion had been just moments before.

As much as he hated it, Elliott was right.

It was time to go.

# CHAPTER NINETEEN
# LET ME

ELLIOTT HAD NAPPED THE entire ride back. Niko thought several times of waking him to talk, but figured it was best to let him sleep off the exhaustion of his injuries. When they'd arrived back at the facility, everyone greeted them in the control room with genuine concern and worry for Elliott. It gave Niko, despite everything, a quiet blossom of warmth to see. Elliott, for the most part, seemed a little bewildered by the attention, as though not sure what to do with it. Loolae inspected his bloodied eye and Oliver nervously fawned over him, asking several times if he was okay and even once if they should take him to a hospital.

Even Zann stood off to the side, arms folded across his chest, his brow knotted with worry. He cast a glance at Niko, raising his eyebrows, but Niko only shook his head. "He wasn't even there. Got ambushed by Clair Suzuki, instead."

He got the others caught up on what had transpired, and eventually Elliott slipped off somewhere further into the facility, claiming again that he was tired.

Niko had been so stupid. He had been unthinking. He'd taken Elliott for granted, had assumed the man would always be here. But this last failed hit and subsequent ambush showed just how horrifically close he'd come to losing Elliott Kestrel forever. If Niko had taken only a few seconds longer to reach him, he would have.

And the last thing he would have ever done before he had was reject, accuse, and scorn the other man, just because Niko had been too afraid to let himself be vulnerable around him.

The deep anguish and grief of that thought stole Niko's breath away. The shame it brought him made it hard to even move. But he had to. He had to make this right. He'd let the wrong things matter. He'd let something so trivial in the face of it all get between them. He had to confront the pain that lay tangled inside himself.

He had to talk to Elliott. He had to apologize.

Niko wheeled through the facility until he found him alone in one of the lounges—not the one he'd usually haunted when researching for Niko's missing family, but one far deeper into the facility, full of scattered chairs. Elliott sat in one, long legs stretched out and feet propped up on another chair. He had a single small hologram hovering in the air before him. This time, it wasn't a wall of Honeybliss files, but rather a simple newsfeed cast from his phone. Niko glimpsed one of Elliott's commonly used old professional portraits on it. The old photo's trimmed and maintained hairstyle, dress shirt, and bland smile—free of injury, free of exhaustion—were a harrowing contrast to the Elliott before him now.

"Elliott, hey," he started. The blond man merely stared over at him with the same cool expression he'd taken to lately, the cornea of his right eye a shocking crimson still. The bruising along the corner of it had spread and darkened. It pained Niko to see. "I—I wanted to say I'm sorry. I was an asshole. I shouldn't have said what I did about you after we— What we did. It was wrong."

Elliott remained silent for a moment, before speaking. "You're right. It *was* wrong. I don't appreciate that you went there."

Niko huffed out a nervous sigh, casting his gaze around. He nodded.

"Is that really what you think I've been doing with you, Niko?" Elliott continued. "Forcing you into something just because *I* like it that way?"

"No."

"Do I like being the one to top you? I do. Do I like it when you let me dom you? Even more. But that's not why I try to do it. Or *only* why. I do it because I see that you love it too. That we have compatibility in what we both want and need. It actually works out quite well—when you let it."

"Mh," Niko grunted out. He stared at the floor, unable to meet Elliott's gaze. From the corner of his eye, he saw Elliott swipe the phone hologram away, then sit up a little straighter, pulling his feet off the adjacent chair.

"You had a safeword. You could have used it at any time if you were uncomfortable, and I would have stopped. You *knew* that."

"I know. I, um, I wasn't uncomfortable. I just— I was just ashamed, afterwards. Not of you. Of myself." He'd finally said it out loud.

"Why are you so ashamed of that, Niko? Of being with me like that?"

Niko wanted to leave. Every instinct told him to turn tail and get out of there before he had to talk about it. There was nothing worse than *talking* about it. Acknowledging it. But the only way out was through.

"I—I don't. Actually know," he finally ground out.

"There has to be something driving this," Elliott said. "You won't let yourself be vulnerable with me. Even in private. You struggle. You fight it. Even when it's obvious how badly you want to. There's something that always stops you. To the point where you're lashing out instead, lately."

"I—" Niko tried again. He needed to be open with Elliott, even if he didn't know what he'd find if he was. He spoke slowly. "I think it's a lot of things. I think it's my old bounty hunting job and the black market I spent a lot of time in— You had to be tough, right? You had to push everyone around to get respect. You had to be more powerful than everyone else, or they'd eat you alive the moment you showed an ounce of weakness. None of that shit survived there. In a life like that, you aren't allowed to be vulnerable."

He paused for a moment, his thoughts turning to, of all people, the delicate and graceful Xermotl hidden away in Deleera's compound. *I'm not weak*, she'd protested, pleading for anyone present to listen. Maybe he and Sweetheart actually had a lot more in common than he'd ever wanted to admit.

"But it's more than that, too," he continued. "It's— I think it's my accident. Um, the fall, I mean. Not... really an accident. It's tied into that too. It's why I disappeared, why I didn't answer anyone's calls anymore. I didn't want them to see me as weak. I can't stand anyone helping me. I can't stand anyone even acknowledging it. The way I am now. I can't let any limitations hold me back. I'll push myself until I break. I'll push myself until I fucking die." He said it with complete sincerity. "I'd do that before I ever let myself rest, or let someone take care of me, or acknowledge that I might need help sometimes. I want to provide for people. I want to be the one everyone can rely on. I want to be the one who can do everything.

"The one thing I cannot do in this life is be *helpless*. I can't fucking stand it, Elliott. I can't stand sitting back and letting someone else take on my risks or burdens or—or take care of me, or have to pick up my slack. And when you ask me to let go and be your—" he glanced away, unable to look at Elliott when he said it, "—submissive lover, some part of my brain goes crazy and thinks that it's not what I should be doing. That I'm being weak, somehow. Even if—if I like it. It's so hard for me to keep calm when you do things, like, just... I don't know. Massaging my legs, or having to go pick up something across the room for me. Even though I fucking appreciate and love when you do! I'm such a fucking mess."

He pushed a hand through his hair. It was all coming out now, apparently. Years of what he couldn't put words, nor even solid thought to. This was something he knew he probably should be working through over several deep sessions with a therapist, rather than pelting it all onto Elliott. Especially right now. "I think it all goes back even further than *that,* though. It goes back to when they killed my family. I was so useless and helpless. I wish I had been there. I wish I'd been able to change it, prevent it. Do something. Keep them safe. Anything. I wish I'd been able to help my surviving family more, afterwards— I tried to be strong, tried to take care of Zann. Tried to take care of Dad. Dad was falling apart, and I couldn't even help *him*—"

"Niko," Elliott interjected softly. Niko fell quiet, and Elliott reached out to gently take his right hand in both of his. For a brief moment, Niko stiffened, wanting to reject the comfort and compassion, even now. He wasn't worthy of it.

Elliott sensed it. "Are you going to pull your hand away from me?" he asked, patiently.

Niko swallowed. He didn't want to do that. He didn't want the walls that he himself had erected again and again like a fortress. The same he had stubbornly reconstructed, every time a nail came loose. He wanted to melt into Elliott, to just *let* himself accept the love given. To hide away in the arms of his boyfriend for days, until it didn't hurt so much anymore. "No."

"Good. Niko. There's a lot to unpack here."

*No shit,* Niko thought.

"But I want to do that with you," Elliott continued. "Thank you for being honest."

Niko nodded. He couldn't look at him, so stared down at Elliott's beautiful hands instead. He'd missed him.

Elliott fell quiet for a moment, thinking. "Okay. I'm going to start back at the beginning of what you said, and go from there. You've spent years in places like Dainna. You had to hunt people down, fight, prove yourself and your reputation over and over. You had to put on an air of toughness, because anyone who appears weak gets picked off or destroyed in one way or another, right?"

"Yeah."

"I want to deconstruct something for you, then. The preferences you have in private sexual relations have nothing to do with being weak or strong. They—"

"I *know.* I know that," Niko cut him off.

"You might know it on a surface level, Niko, but I don't think you really feel it or agree with it. There's nothing inherently weak about submitting yourself to your partner during sex. It doesn't mean anything outside the two of you. It doesn't make you lesser in any way. You might know that, but I think it might also help you to hear it, too. Many submissive men actually tend to be particularly powerful or influential outside of the bedroom. It's a *release* to be able to just let go, to be controlled and told what to do for a little while, instead of having all the weight on their shoulders and everyone looking to them for the answers."

Niko glanced up at him.

"Did you know that?" Elliott asked.

He shook his head.

"I think that might apply to you a little bit too. You're someone who carries a lot of power in your line of work, and in what you're capable of. And you're someone who carries the burdens of any person in need around you. You try to be everything to everyone. You put so much pressure on yourself that you're going to collapse, Niko. Why not let me be an outlet for you? Why not let yourself forget about all of it for a while with me, sometimes? You can give the weight to me. And let me take care of you in the bedroom. There's no shame in that.

"In fact, I think it's healthier to. It keeps you sane. It's *good* for you, Niko. Think of giving yourself that indulgence as letting yourself recharge. It actually helps you continue to help the people who depend on you."

"I—" Niko glanced at him again. "I hadn't ever really thought of it that way, I guess." He'd always thought of letting himself go there as something shameful, something that had somehow meant he wasn't actually strong enough to carry others. But in truth, maybe it meant that he would be more capable than if he'd continued to deny himself what he really wanted. Who he really was.

Elliott nodded at him, his bloodied gaze searching Niko's face for a moment. "I'm going to move on to something else now, too, and I think you're going to struggle with it."

Niko chuckled nervously. "Fuck. Okay."

"I really think you don't like yourself much, Niko."

"How'd you know?" He couldn't help the sarcasm.

"Honestly, we're similar like that. I don't like myself much either, for a lot of reasons. But it hurts me to see you feel that way about yourself and—"

"Well, I feel the same way about you," Niko interjected. Elliott paused and got a ghost of a smile. Niko knew he was still hurting from what he'd said to him before.

"I know you do. But my point is—" He paused again, drawing in a deep, slow breath. "This is what you're not going to like hearing, Niko. But the reality of your life is that you're a man who has to learn to live with a disability. That doesn't just mean in a physical way. You can clearly get around and take care of yourself just fine, whether it's with your chair or suit. But you just admitted that you'd push yourself until you broke or even died rather than... what? Take a break? Appear weak, somehow?"

"I—" Niko swallowed. "Yeah."

"I imagine there's more to adjusting your life to accommodate a change like that than just learning how to navigate the physical world again. It's emotional, too. It's mental. It's *here*." He reached out and gently touched Niko's chest.

Niko stayed quiet.

"I can't speak for you, Niko. I'm privileged in being able-bodied. I can't view the world the same way you do, or experience the same challenges you do—inside and out. But I can only tell you what I see in front of me. And that's that you're in denial of yourself, even now. Even years after the event that changed your life forever. You seem embarrassed or angry, any time it's perceived or acknowledged. You want to hide it away, somehow. I'll say it plainly, Niko. You still won't accept that you have a disability."

It hurt. It stole the breath from Niko's chest. It was a raw, stinging sort of pain, like having sea salt rubbed into an open wound.

It wasn't where he'd expected this conversation to go when he'd started it.

But everything Elliott had said was true. Niko couldn't deny it. He couldn't even begin to.

"Niko. I wish you could see everything that you *are,* and stop focusing on what you're not. You're one of the strongest people I've ever known. You saved my life... in more ways than one. You helped save the lives of your father and Loolae. That wasn't just me. You saved the life of your friend, when he was falling behind and no one else was willing to try. And you were the one who did what I couldn't. You made sure the Honeybliss files finally got out.

"You're so resilient. You make up for so much of what I lack. I meant everything I'd said, back on Haneen. We're a team. We're equals. We make up for each other's struggles, and lift each other up.

"You... are such a beautiful, extraordinary person. You are. You take my breath away. I love being around you. With you. I love talking to you. I love being your boyfriend, your lover. And I love sex with you. I love the way you look at me when you let me inside you. I love *you.* You're compassionate. You're funny. You're a great cook. You're the whole package. You're my *dream,* Niko.

You don't need armor and tech to be that way. Just you, as you are. You're so beautiful. And I just wish you could see what I see.

"I wish you could love yourself the way that I love you. And just allow yourself to be taken care of, sometimes. To be loved, and cherished. Just because you need help sometimes, or let yourself be a little soft with me hardly makes you helpless. Nor weak. I wish you would trust me enough to let yourself be vulnerable with me. I wish you would let me love you. Will you do that, Niko? I want to. I've been reaching out to you, and you're only pushing me away."

That hurt, too. Niko glanced away, swallowing back a lump that was growing in his throat, blinking back something that stung in his eyes. He'd had to be strong for so long, for everyone, in everything, that he hadn't allowed himself the grace of simply being Niko Estrella. A man who was sometimes scared, sometimes lonely, sometimes vulnerable. Someone who needed help sometimes, too.

Someone who, underneath the layers of bulletproof armor, really liked being taken care of and loved.

And now Elliott had said the plain truth—Niko was breaking what had begun to grow so beautifully, so perfectly between them. He was made for Elliott in every way. Even down to their sexual compatibility—something that was incredibly rare. He wanted to put himself in Elliott's hands and give him control. He wanted to let go with him in a way he wouldn't with anyone else.

He was being given love. Selflessly, wholly, without reservation. And he was pushing it all away, because he couldn't love nor accept himself.

He was pushing Elliott away.

Niko wiped his eyes. "I'm sorry." His voice emerged tight and hoarse, laden with pain.

Elliott stood, then knelt before him. He looked up at Niko. He took Niko's hands and kissed the backs of them, slow and gentle, a deeply affectionate gesture. Then, he reached up and took Niko's face in his own hands, and wiped at the tears that had finally begun to fall. Elliott didn't mock him, didn't tell him to toughen up. Niko was falling apart and Elliott accepted him, even now. Elliott, who was injured. Elliott, who was the one who probably needed comforting most. He gently brushed at Niko's cheeks, looking up at him with nothing but a sweet, searching love. Niko had never felt such profound connection and need for another person in all his life. Not like this.

Elliott left him humbled.

"Let me love you, Niko," he said again.

Niko nodded. "Please. I love you. I love you so much, Elliott."

"Then you need to love yourself too. You need to let me in. Will you let me take care of you, like you've taken care of me? Will you let me help you carry your burdens? Will you let me see what's underneath the armor?"

Niko brought a hand to his mouth. He was trembling now—from emotion, from overwhelm. It was all he could do not to break down. He'd never felt like this before. He nodded wordlessly. "I'm sorry I hurt you, Elliott. I'm so sorry. I should never have accused you of that. It's not like that. You're not like that. You never were. It was me. I don't want to be like that to you.

I don't want to accuse you of something like that. Everything you said was true. I'm *sorry.*"

Elliott gave him another warm smile, something a little freer this time. "I know, lover. Take care of me, and I'll take care of you."

"I will. I'll do anything."

"Then, what more could I ever ask?"

Elliott stood and climbed into his lap. Niko wrapped around him, holding him tightly around the shoulders, mindful of his injuries. He clung to Elliott as though he were something ephemeral, just on the precipice of slipping through his fingers at any moment. After a long while, he finally, quietly said, "I don't want to lose you."

"We're okay, Niko."

Niko combed his fingertips through Elliott's hair. "How are you feeling, babe? How's your side?"

Elliott was quiet for a moment. "It hurts. But I'm alright. I'm doing much better now, actually." The relief in his tone wounded Niko as he realized Elliott had felt the weight of emotional pain from their rift even more deeply than the physical injuries he carried now. He vowed to never take this man for granted again. To never let his own fears and self-loathing become bigger than the love he carried for Elliott.

Then Niko remembered something that he'd meant to say. "Hey, Elliott. I want you to know... you have a place in my family. We'll take care of you. And care about you. Dad will, I know. Zann's an asshole, and a little surly, but I can tell he's opening up already. I don't think he minds you, actually. Loolae seems like she's stuck with us now, too. And if you stick around, you can get to know everybody more. You have a home here with us, if you want it."

"*Oh*," Elliott murmured, the sound quiet, surprised, breathless. Reverent. There was the depth of an ocean in that sound. For a long moment, he didn't speak, something deeply, profoundly pained on his features. "I— That's— I would really like that, Niko."

"You don't need…" He searched for the words. "Those people on the news. You don't need them anymore. You can have a family here, around you. One who actually cares if you're okay. One who loves you."

Elliott's whole body trembled. His breath emerged, shaky. For a moment, Niko thought he might cry. But he kept it, as always, tightly sealed away. Elliott nodded. When he spoke, it was only in a whisper. "*Please.*"

Niko kissed him in his wild hair, then combed his fingers through it again. "Hey, babe. Why don't you let me give you a trim?" Elliott looked over at him, then nodded. He got up and came back a moment later with his comb and a pair of scissors, then settled down into Niko's lap again, his back to him.

Niko was no hair artisan, but he could at least help clean Elliott up a little. He combed gently at the unruly cowlicks he loved so much, then started trimming them back, little by little. He could hear Elliott's soft breathing filling the silence of the room. Little golden wisps and curls fell around his shoulders, and Niko brushed them away.

Twenty minutes later, Elliott resembled the man from his old photographs a little bit more. He was still bruised, and still looked tired. His eye was still damaged. But he looked a little less far gone now, a little less let go. It was strange how a simple haircut could sometimes be a tether back to something civilized. Niko leaned in and kissed him on the shoulder. "Better?"

"Yes. Thank you. I'm grateful."

"What do you say we go out there and spend some time with the others? You don't have to interact if you're not ready."

Elliott nodded. "I think... I would like that very much."

Niko and Elliott made their way into one of the lounges where the other three were gathered, watching a holographic newsfeed of some kind. Oliver gave Elliott a warm smile upon seeing him.

"Hello again, Elliott. I like the haircut."

"Thanks. It was all Niko."

"Are you doing alright?" Oliver ventured, gaze wandering Elliott's face.

This time, Elliott got a tiny smile, glancing away. "I'm alright. My eye looks worse than it is."

"You look like shit," Zann helpfully commented. "Like you got put through a garbage disposal, then ran over by a truck, then—"

"Dude, Zann. Really?" Niko cut in.

Zann eyed him defensively. "I'm just saying. The hair does look good, though." He glanced at Elliott. "*Are* you okay? Really? This isn't any of that macho shit Niko tries to pull?"

Elliott gave a soft laugh. "I'm alright. Really. It's something that should heal on its own. It just hurts a little."

"You should take it easy for a while," Loolae said gently. "Get some rest and ice up the bruises, if you can stomach it."

Elliott's smile grew by a fraction.

"Hey," Zann said. "Speaking of all this Honeybliss shit. Did you hear the news?"

Niko froze, glancing instinctively at the newsfeed in the background, but the volume was down and he couldn't yet tell what the reporters were saying. Aerial footage of some city on Thoro, the Toliai homeworld, was playing.

"Somebody tried to go for Taal."

"What?" Elliott said. He looked absolutely destroyed, the smile eradicated completely from his face now.

"Yeah. He's been hospitalized. Someone tried to take him out, though. They got the guy arrested. It wasn't a copycat thing, this time. Guy outright said Taal deserved it, and that this was for you."

Elliott blinked, his mouth gaping. Niko stared at him too, at a loss. This was certainly something he hadn't expected. He could see the war of emotions on Elliott's face: shock, hurt, rage, then something sorrowful.

"For what it's worth, the fucker survived," Zann muttered. "Toliai are like that, though. You'll still get your chance at him."

"He's *mine*. I'm going to kill him," Elliott murmured, his voice trembling.

"Better get on that, then," Zann said, raising his eyebrows. "Because there's an outright line forming at this point. All in your honor."

Whoever had done this had been trying to do Elliott a favor. But they unknowingly were only getting in his way. Niko could only imagine the internal war the other man was enduring, torn somewhere between scathing hatred for Uru Taal, and a sickly relief that his sister's tormentor and killer was actually still alive.

"He's yours, Elliott. I'll make sure. We'll finish this and get him before anyone else does," Niko said. He was fully on this roller coaster ride, committed. If he'd had any reservations before about eliminating the remaining members of Honeybliss, they were long gone now. He would follow Elliott to the ends of the universe. Niko would do anything for him. "Fuck Uru Taal. Prick made his biggest mistake the day he killed Cleo Kestrel."

Niko felt every eye turn his way. A heavy and charged silence fell over the room.

The hair on the back of his neck rose. *What the hell? Did I say something weird?* Maybe he'd been too forward. He should have been more considerate towards Elliott, and not tacked on that last part.

"Sorry. Uh, maybe I shouldn't have—"

"I thought you knew." Elliott's voice was strange, distant. Something was wrong.

"Knew what?"

"...You told me you watched the videos I sent. You've said that, all this time."

Niko blinked at him. "What? I—I did!"

"Then why do you keep saying Taal killed her?" Zann asked.

Niko blinked again in shock, looking back and forth between the two of them now. "Wh— He did. ...Right?"

"*Holy fucking shit*," Zann muttered under his breath. He rubbed his mouth.

"Well— I mean—" Niko was stumbling over his words. "I watched every video, except, um, for Cleo's. It was too hard, with— She was your family—" He looked at Elliott. "I only watched the beginning of hers. Is there something...?"

Elliott said nothing. He looked like he'd been slapped.

Niko glanced from each person to the next, utterly bewildered and begging silently for context, for anyone to fill him in. Zann shook his head. Loolae gazed at him with pity, as did Oliver.

No one, for some reason, was willing to give him the grace of an answer.

"Guys? Elliott? Zann?"

Everything had pointed to it being him, especially Elliott's particular vengeance and disdain for the Toliai crown prince. He'd been the one in the video, clearly abusing Cleo. Again and again, Elliott had referenced what Taal had done to her.

He'd said it was why he was saving him for last.

"You really didn't know?" Zann asked. "This whole time?"

Niko looked back at Elliott, panic hammering its rhythmic pulse in his neck and chest now. He was terrified. He'd only just mended his fuckup with the other man, but the look in Elliott's eyes had become something altogether unreadable. "If it's not Uru Taal, then who?"

Elliott pushed off the wall he'd been leaning against. The color had drained from his face. He wouldn't look at Niko anymore, and swiftly left the room.

"Elliott—"

He was already gone.

"Wh— *Zann?* What the fuck?" He looked back at his brother again in pleading bewilderment, but Zann only shook his head and raised his hands in defense.

"Nah, don't look at me. You'd better see this one for yourself instead, Niko."

Niko gaped at the others. Oliver only cast him a sad, sympathetic smile before bowing his head.

Then Niko looked to the empty doorway that Elliott had exited through. He ached. They'd been fighting together, side by side, a team of two against an entire galaxy, and all this time, he had missed something immense.

Something *vital*.

He wanted nothing more than to pursue Elliott. To talk to him, to hold him. But it wouldn't feel right until he'd forced himself to watch what he had avoided all this time. Zann was right.

He needed to see Cleo's files.

# CHAPTER TWENTY
## STILL ALIVE

NIKO WANTED TO BE alone for this. He'd made his way out to the *Soñadora* and sat in the cabin. The ship was quiet, the silence of the giant, empty hangar beyond pressing down on him. He could hear the whisper of his heartbeat in his ears, warning him away from what he was about to undergo, speaking its dread.

He opened her folder. Niko didn't want to see this. If it had been difficult to force himself through watching the other victims' videos, this was nearly impossible. He'd never gotten to meet Cleo Kestrel, but the abundance of devotion and feeling Elliott had for her had spilled intrinsically over into Niko as well. Elliott had loved her deeply, so Niko couldn't help but love her too.

She was like his own family now, yet someone he would only ever know through her living proxy. He'd become acquainted with her smile and natural, bright charm through the myriad photographs in Elliott's case files. He had nothing but admiration for her through Elliott's stories of a sister's selfless love.

She had rescued Elliott in so many ways. She'd taken the hits for him, standing up to their cruel, pathetic excuses for parents.

She'd taken him away from their abuse and given him a real home. She'd worked hard to put him through school, so he could have the best chance possible for a good life. She had never expected anything in return.

And, above all, she had *loved* him—a gift that was painfully rare, Niko was finding, in Elliott's life.

Niko had made a promise to her that he would carry on her legacy of watching over Elliott. They shared a posthumous bond through that oath.

And now, he was going to watch her die. He was going to watch her suffer. Every part of him rebelled against it. In some ways, it was worse than even facing down the security footage of his own family's deaths. Theirs had decimated him, had scraped his heart out from its chest cavity, leaving only a gaping wound behind. But their deaths had been clean, and quick, too.

He knew Cleo's wouldn't be.

But he owed it to Elliott to see what he'd had to, all on his own. To witness the final cruelty of the Honeybliss files. To find who had really killed Cleo Kestrel.

He played the first video. It started the same as before, with Cleo at every disadvantage, tied up in a large warehouse, Uru Taal looming over her, grotesque as a monster. Niko kept looking away, but not looking didn't stop it from happening. Not looking didn't mute the sounds of her pain and pleas, either. Someone was filming it from their phone, a Heenva with a telltale blue thumb that occasionally blurred the corner of the video with sloppy filming.

The video ended, and she was left still alive.

Niko felt ill. It was hard to even breathe. It would take a lifetime to recover from what he'd witnessed in that ten-minute video. How Elliott had ever sat through this, he couldn't fathom. He didn't know if he could move on to the second and final one. He felt like he needed days to heal between them. But he didn't have that grace available to him. So he opened it, too.

This one was longer, and appeared to be possibly days later. Cleo was bound against a far wall, looking worse for wear. Uru Taal was there again, as well as his son, Duuru Orkan. The same clumsy-handed Heenva was filming, his amused chuckle occasionally coming from behind the camera as though something was quite funny to him. Niko had no idea who he was.

All around them in the warehouse were emptied bottles of alcohol, drugs, and various weapons, as though it were a makeshift seedy compound. No—that's exactly what it was. Niko's grip tightened on the arms of his wheelchair as he watched.

The camera shook wildly as the Heenva stepped forward and drove his boot down hard into someone Niko could now see had been kneeling on the ground, previously out of the shot, hands bound behind him. A second captive and victim. The figure fell forward before moving to right himself—

All the air left Niko's lungs. He paused the video.

A familiar mess of pale gold crowned the head of the kneeling man. He would recognize it anywhere.

*Elliott.* Elliott was there.

Niko had never known. He had never realized. He'd never even thought that he could ever have been there, too.

He'd never watched the video.

And Elliott hadn't mentioned being there, not even once. It was probably locked so deeply inside him, so wildly, searingly painful that he *couldn't*. He'd likely just assumed that by giving him the files, Niko had known what he wasn't able to say.

Everyone else knew it.

Everyone but his idiot, fuckup self. Lady Death's quiet conversation with Elliott. Zann's perplexity at Niko's ignorant comments. Even fucking Bubblegum had known, with her cruelly aimed taunts that had wormed their way beneath Elliott's skin.

This very video was out online now. Everywhere. It was all around him, and had always been. He was the only one in an entire galaxy who hadn't known what his own boyfriend had endured.

Elliott had never just been avenging his sister's death.

He'd been a direct victim of Honeybliss, too.

The edges of Niko's vision turned black, and he had to force himself to take in one breath, then another.

Several minutes passed before he had managed to calm down enough to continue the video. It resumed, the Heenva laughing as Elliott struggled to sit up again.

Uru Taal stood beside him, his disgusting form towering partially out of the shot. He reached out and stroked Elliott's hair, and Elliott flinched violently at the touch. Niko was going to be sick. He wanted to kill Taal himself. He wanted violence, craved it like air.

Uru dropped his arm and gazed over at Cleo in the background.

"Let her go. *Let her fucking go!*" Elliott yelled. His voice was hoarse and broken.

"Are we gonna have fun with him too? He's pretty, like his bitch sister," said the Heenva.

"This one has been whining," Uru said, his voice a deep grumble. "He won't shut up about the other one. But since I'm generous, I'm going to give him a chance."

Uru moved away from Elliott and made his way—unhurried, leisurely—across the warehouse space toward Cleo. Elliott screamed in wordless rage, straining against the ropes binding his wrists and trying to stand, but the Heenva gave him another hard kick. Niko wanted to break the arms of his chair, break the Heenva.

Uru hunched down and took Cleo's hand, Elliott defiantly screaming his fury at him the entire time. It was ignored. He stroked the back of her hand with his own thick, clawed, scaly thumb, then plucked a delicate ring from her pinky finger.

Then he stood and hung the ring on a small peg, just above where she was chained. It was so tiny that it was hard to see; Niko had to enhance the video. Then Uru just as slowly made his way back to Elliott and the cameraman. "I'm going to give you one chance, because I'm so benevolent."

The Heenva snickered.

"If you can shoot her ring off the wall, your sister gets to go home and you'll take her place, instead."

"No. No, no no no! Please! Don't do that to him, please! Don't hurt him!" Cleo wailed from the background. "Please don't. Ellie, don't do that. I don't want you to take my place. Please, just let him go home instead, I'll do anything—"

"I'll do it," Elliott said.

The Heenva gave another snicker, and Niko had never been so blindly enraged by a sound in all his life. He would rip those lungs out, if he could. Maybe he would still get the chance to.

Uru reached into the weapons pile and drew out a sniper rifle. The sick irony of it made Niko's stomach churn. "There's one bullet in here. You get one chance. You hit that, and she gets to go live her life again. If you try to shoot me or my friends here, we will break both of you. I'll kill her first in front of you, and then you die. Do you understand?"

Elliott nodded, his whole body trembling.

"Say it, you fucking worm," the Heenva said.

"I understand," Elliott ground out.

Uru took a switchblade and cut through the ropes restraining Elliott's wrists. Niko could read him, could see the way he hesitated and thought as he rose to his feet, the way he considered if he could take on Uru. But Uru was a Toliai—even bullets did nothing to them. Even if he'd managed to get through Uru somehow, the second Toliai and Heenva—and anyone else not caught on camera—remained.

Elliott took the sniper rifle, his hands shaking. Niko couldn't bear it. He held the thing oddly, like he didn't know what to make of it, what to do with it, how to even hold it. It was so vastly unlike the Elliott that Niko knew now, intimately familiar with a sniper rifle like it was an extension of himself, his aim unmatched, his work frankly masterful.

"Take your time," said Uru.

Elliott looked at Cleo.

She shook her head at him pleadingly. Tears streamed down her bruised and dirt-stained cheeks. "Ellie. *Hi*, Ellie," she said, and the heartbroken affection in her voice even in the midst of such suffering broke Niko's heart to pieces too. "You don't have to do this. I don't want you to take my place. I'd rather you go home, okay?"

"Nobody said anything about him going home," said Duuru.

Elliott said nothing. He raised the rifle, peering through the scope at the ring hanging above her. It pained Niko to see him do it—he was so awkward, so wrong on how he positioned himself, on how he gripped it, like it was something alien. He stood for a long moment, lining up the shot with as much care and focus as his trembling hands would allow him.

"*Boo!*" the cameraman yelled, and Elliott jumped violently. Niko had never been so infuriated at anyone in his life. Not even his family's killers. Not even Uru Taal.

Elliott recovered quickly though, lining up his shot again. Niko could read the determination in him, the willful, meditative calm in spite of everything happening around him. He stayed like that a long while in silence, then pulled the trigger.

Nothing happened. Both Duuru and the Heenva howled in laughter.

"Safety's on, you dumb idiot," Duuru said.

"Hah, yeah, Honeybliss'll love this shit," the Heenva said.

Cleo let out a soft sob, her slim shoulders shaking. "I love you, Ellie," she said. Her voice broke on the words.

Elliott was trembling so badly now that he seemed barely able to hold himself together. It was quite apparent he'd never utilized—nor even been near—a gun before this. He examined the thing in silence until he found the safety selector and switched it off. Then he readied himself again, lining up his single, pivotal shot that would send his sister home—if Uru Taal and his piece of shit friends were to be believed.

He stayed like that, everyone around him silent now as the seconds ticked by.

Elliott fired.

The ring hung, untouched, on the wall.

A spot of deep crimson bloomed quickly across Cleo's chest. She discharged a choking cough and wet gasp, blood dribbling down her chin. Then she slumped forward slowly into herself, head hanging, her entire tattered shirt stained red now.

It was too much. It was all too much. Niko's body was numb with horror, with agony.

The sounds that came from Elliott were animalistic. He lost himself. He turned the gun on Uru Taal and fired, but it was empty, as he'd been warned. Then he flipped it in his hands and struck the Toliai with the stock as hard as he could, driving the metal down against Uru's scaled hide. If Uru had been a human, it would have been hard enough to kill him instantly, hard enough to crush bone.

But he wasn't, and it did nothing.

Uru easily wrenched the rifle from the hysterical man hard enough to spin him, then knocked him clean to the ground with it, the blow landing hard on his right shoulder blade. Exactly where that single, deep old scar still was.

All the while, Duuru Orkan and the Heenva laughed. They were having the time of their lives.

The video ended.

Niko found him in their bedroom, lying on his side, eyes closed and earbuds in. Even from across the room, he could hear the glittering pop music and lilting voices. He wheeled to the open side of the bed and pulled himself onto it from the chair, then laid down beside Elliott. Niko reached out to touch him on the back and he flinched.

He pulled his hand back, a caustic mixture of barely controlled rage and sorrow flooding him. Niko wanted to destroy everyone responsible, everyone involved. To know how much they'd hurt Elliott was unbearable. It had taken everything within him to force himself to calm down enough to seek Elliott out to talk. The other man's well-being trumped any sort of violent penchant Niko had for exacting revenge on his tormentors.

Niko merely stayed with him, lying on his side as he stared at Elliott's slender back. He watched the rise and fall of his breathing and found he'd begun to time his own breaths to match Elliott's.

After several moments, Elliott stopped the music, the gentle, tinny sound of it abruptly falling silent. Then he pulled the earbuds out and set them on the bedside table. He lay there, still not turning to face Niko.

"Hey," Niko said, voice quieted to barely a murmur.

Elliott was reticent a moment before speaking, his silence heavy and deep and full of swimming, restless behemoths. "I thought you knew. All this time. I thought you knew. I thought you'd watched it."

Niko ached. "I'm sorry, babe. I watched everything else. I didn't want to see that happen to her, though. Knowing what she'd meant to you. I thought I had an idea of how it went. I'm so sorry. I've seen it now."

"Now you know," Elliott said simply. "What are you going to do about it?"

"Do?" Niko asked, shifting on the bed. It creaked beneath his weight.

Elliott said nothing, so Niko spoke again. "I'd really like to hand those utter shitstains their own assholes, if you're asking."

"No," Elliott said. "Are you going to leave?"

Niko blinked. "What? Why would I leave?"

"Liam left."

Niko remembered the subtle downturn of Elliott's mouth upon reaching his ex-boyfriend's interview in Zann's files, the way it had been the only thing to crack his carefully blank veneer.

*Elliott was a piece of shit, yeah,* Liam had gladly offered up.

Another asshole to add to the list of people Niko wanted to feed their own teeth. Everyone in Elliott's life had truly forsaken him. Everyone except the fiercely loving sister who he'd been forced to kill.

And Niko.

"Well, I'm not Liam. And I'm not going anywhere, Elliott."

Niko watched his shoulders and back untense, sagging as he let out a long breath. Elliott turned over in bed to face him, finally. The unspoken pain in his eyes drove Niko wild with the need to try and fix it for him, to take all his suffering away.

"Hey there," Niko said again instead, giving him a sad smile. He tentatively reached out and brushed his hand against Elliott's pale brow, and the other man closed his eyes again, though only briefly.

"You told me you thought I killed her, back on Uula," Elliott said. "You asked why I'd kill my sister." His voice sounded hollow, far away.

Niko winced. He looked away instinctively, shame thick as molten lead searing through him now. He'd taunted Elliott with it all once, trying to goad him out of hiding. He'd intentionally tried to injure him with it.

He had to look this in the eyes. He had to look Elliott in the eyes. He forced himself to meet his gaze again, to meet and accept the pain he'd caused that hung deep and wounded in Elliott's sea of green.

"I know, " Niko said, swallowing. "I did. And I'm sorry. It was different then and I—I thought you were someone you're not."

"But you were right, " Elliott said. "I k—" He choked on the word.

"You don't have to say it, Elliott," Niko said gently.

It only seemed to summon a renewed, spiteful fight within the other man. Niko could see as he wrestled himself to work the words out. "I killed my sister."

"It wasn't you," Niko said. "They—"

"It *was*," Elliott spat, cutting him off. He drew sharply into himself, wrapping an arm around his own waist. Niko could see he was rapidly descending down into the inwardly destructive self-hatred he had seen take over before.

He needed to stop it before it got worse. Niko reached out and gently took his hands. Elliott flinched again at the touch, but Niko held on firmly now, rubbing his thumbs into Elliott's palms. His hands were cool and clammy, a reflection of the agonizing anxiety he must have been enduring. They shook in Niko's grip.

"Listen to me, Elliott. It wasn't you. It was them. You may have had to pull the trigger, but it was their game all along that they'd forced you both into. They knew what they were doing from the start. They knew how it would end, too."

He seemed to be getting through. Elliott closed his eyes for a moment. Niko saw him draw in a deep breath, and then another, before opening them again. When he spoke, it was without the icy edge that had begun to creep in. He sounded, now, worn down. "I know. I know that. I tell myself that a lot."

"It's not your fault, Elliott," Niko said again. "And I know Cleo wouldn't think so, either. The last thing she ever said was that she loved you."

A brief, wounded sound escaped Elliott's throat, before he clamped down tightly on that lid again.

"You were just as much a victim as she was," Niko continued. "As anyone in those files was." The heavy, horrific realization of it made Niko nauseous and enraged. He couldn't handle it. It was too much, knowing all along Elliott had suffered just as all the lost souls captured in those haunted videos and images did. All this time, he'd been among their ranks, had suffered directly at the hands of Honeybliss. Every video he'd had to collect and see must have been a special kind of hell, reliving his own trauma again and again through them. It hadn't ever just been Cleo. It had been both of them there, together. But Elliott had been the only one to make it back out alive. Niko's heart began racing at the mere thought of it.

All along, Elliott had championed the victims of Honeybliss. He'd compiled meticulous files, had researched and organized. He'd named every victim and every tormentor. He'd said he was doing this for them. For his sister.

But he'd quietly erased himself, passing over the misery that he had undoubtedly endured. There were no files labeled *Elliott Kestrel*. His presence was merely a recorded accessory to show the fate of Cleo. It made Niko ache in a way he'd never encountered before.

Every other person who had been taken by Honeybliss had died—or had been destroyed inside, ground down into ruin. Elliott was the sole survivor, a revenant out to avenge the silenced.

"Elliott," Niko began haltingly. He reached up and stroked at Elliott's cheek. "How did you get away from them? Everyone else—"

"They forgot about me," Elliott said, the words trailed by a breathless, wild little laugh. "After he was done with me, they threw me in what I believe was a utility closet for supplies and spare parts. It was in a derelict factory, and full of old machinery. It was pitch black in there, though. I managed to finally break the lock with a pipe wrench I'd found digging around in the dark on the top shelf. It took me hours. It was a relatively simple, brute task, but I was nearly delirious from dehydration. And weakened by injury. And. ...And grief. It's funny how survival instinct carries on, even when there's nothing left for you.

"When I eventually got out, everything was quiet and still. The weapons and drugs and supplies were all gone. The lights were out. No one else was there. No one. I later matched Taal's schedule with that timeframe, and he must have gotten called back for an emergency address regarding the flood fatalities from the hypercane on Thoro.

"They'd killed everyone else. There had been at least six other people in there with us. Victims, I mean. I don't consider Uru Taal nor his ilk people. They discarded the bodies somewhere. My theory is they dissolved them in hydrochloric acid. They'd had large barrels in the back of the warehouse that were missing later. Even her ring was gone. If they hadn't forgotten me in a fucking closet, they'd have actually been impressively careful in covering their tracks.

"...Unfortunately for them, I'm a simple oversight that has since proven to be their downfall. How sloppy."

Niko was breathless, his heart tightly constricting in his throat. He'd heard everything Elliott had said, but his mind had latched onto a single, chilling implication.

*After he was done with me*, Elliott had said. The words spread out and filled his brain, seeping into every thought like an oily poison. *Done with me.*

The very thought of it was too much, to think that they'd hurt him in that way on top of everything else. Maybe they'd only wanted to use him for their games with Cleo. Maybe—

He had to ask. He had to know. Niko swallowed, the words unable to dislodge themselves from his throat. When he finally spoke, his voice emerged thick and hoarse. "Did— When they were still there— Did they— Did he—?"

Elliott stared at him, his gaze hollow. "Rape me?" he asked, the words cutting through the air and plunging deep into both of them like a knife. "Yes."

It was a grief Niko felt in every part of his body. He closed his eyes and couldn't speak.

"It's why Liam finally left," Elliott said.

"What?" Niko whispered. He opened his eyes.

*How could he? How could he?* It was unfathomable.

"He—" Elliott took a steadying breath, before continuing. "He was already spooked by everything I'd told him about. Cleo, the crown prince of Thoro. I'd started researching and putting things together. I learned more about Honeybliss. I tried to build a case against them, and he started getting scared over it. Scared about what kind of backlash we'd face for it. That *he'd* face. And I was hospitalized for over a month from where my mental health had gone. But when I finally admitted to him what had been done to me... that's when he got really uncomfortable. He... didn't want to touch me after that. Like I was sullied. Or too much."

"You're not sullied," Niko said quietly. His heart was breaking. "You're not too much."

After a pause, Elliott added, "He was just. Different." His gaze was distant, staring off into some memory inaccessible to Niko. Then he smiled, though it was all broken, all wrong. "I even started begging him. I just wanted to feel normal again. I was so pathetic, Niko—"

"*No,*" Niko said, taking his face in his hands. "No, you weren't pathetic. You're not pathetic. He's—"

Niko couldn't think of vocabulary strong enough to convey the mired trenches of disgust he felt for Liam Soren then. Not in Galactic Standard. Not in any language.

But Liam himself had found the words that would have to suffice.

"He's a piece of shit," Niko seethed.

"Maybe."

"Can I ask you something?"

"...Ask whatever you want, Niko." His voice emerged flat, lifeless. He looked tired.

"Since we first talked, you've been telling me about the things Honeybliss has done. But all your focus was on everyone else they hurt. And your sister. Even in your files. But they hurt you, too. You were just as much a victim of them as any of those other people. Why did you erase yourself from it all?"

"Because I'm not the one who matters. *She* mattered. They matter."

"Why not you?"

"Niko, the only person I ever truly mattered to all my life is dead. And I'm the one who killed her."

Niko looked him in the eyes. "You matter to me. You'll always matter to me. I love you, Elliott. I would die for you in a heartbeat. Do you understand that?"

"I don't want you to die for me. I don't want anything like that."

"I know you don't, but it's the truth. That's how much you matter to me. I need you to know that."

"I would die for you too," Elliott said, his voice turning thin and quiet, his gaze lost now somewhere far unreachable to Niko. He looked pleading, in pain. "I—I wish I had died there, instead of her. I wish they'd killed me, instead. Or killed me after her, too. I don't know why I was left behind. I don't know why such an extraordinary person had to suffer and die, and I just got left behind to be useless waste. To be her murderer. I deserved everything they—"

*No.*

"No. No, no. Elliott. We're not going there. You're not going there, okay? I don't want to hear that from you. Not ever. It's not true. You're not useless, and you're not waste. You're far from it. You've never deserved anything that they did. Not any part of it." He paused. "Is that what this is? ...Are you punishing yourself for what happened to your sister?"

Elliott choked. "I— *Yes.*"

"Babe. Baby, listen. Elliott. I need you to listen to me right now. You're not responsible for what happened to her."

"But I *am.*"

"No. You're not. That was their cruel game. That was their cancer on this galaxy. You only ever tried to protect your sister. You were trying to free her, Elliott. You were trying to save her from that suffering. It was clear as day. You were trying to give her a chance to get out of there. Hell, you were trying to *take her place,* for fuck's sake."

"But it doesn't matter! She's fucking dead. She's dead. She's *dead!* I killed her! I fucked it up—"

"*Elliott.* No. They put you in a game you could never win. It had impossible odds. You didn't even know how to handle or shoot a gun like that. And they knew it. They knew it was an impossible shot. There is nothing you ever could have done to have changed that. You *never* deserved to be in that place. Cleo never deserved to be there. Neither of you deserved the... things they did to you both. You don't deserve punishment. You deserve kindness, and compassion. You deserve to be heard. You deserve to be believed. And instead, they just kept gaslighting you year after year as you tried to appeal for help. Elliott, you're a good person."

Elliott shook his head.

"You are," Niko insisted. "You're the most incredible person I've ever met. You leave me in awe."

"No. No. I'm a murderer. I'm a piece of shit. I'm fucking *garbage*."

It stole Niko's breath away. Elliott had paid attention. He'd listened to and quietly collected every insult hurled his way. Liam had called him shit. Niko had once called him garbage, before he'd understood. He wondered where *waste* had come from—perhaps an archaeological relic unearthed from the years spent around his piece of shit parents. Every name stuck with him, a deep and quiet pain. He cared far more than Niko had ever thought he would.

"You're trying to protect people, Elliott. You're killing the ones who take, and take, and take, and will never see consequences. You said it yourself. They'll never see justice. You're doing this to make sure they don't hurt anyone else like they did you and your family.

"And you know what? I'm right here with you. I hear you. I *see* you, Elliott. I know everything now, the full truth of it. And I'm not going anywhere. I don't want to. What happened to you isn't something you should be ashamed of, or feel guilty for. I'm not Liam. I'm not your parents. I'm here with you. And I'm going to see this through to the end with you. We're going to win this. We're going to erase them from the galaxy.

"Look," he added, "I don't believe in superstition, or anything, but you said you don't know why you were the one left alive. I think you still have so much more left to your story. But maybe part of that story is doing this. So you could be the one to tell the stories of everyone they've silenced. So you could be the one to finally put an end to what was never going to stop. And maybe that night on Yhanwe-ha, I was meant to be called back into service, after years of accepting I'd never hunt again, so that I could meet you. So I could help you see it through and help you finally get all those files out there. Maybe we were meant to be here. You're still alive. So am I, after surviving a fall that should have killed me. Let's make the best of it together.

"From the very beginning, I've been drawn to you, Elliott, and I couldn't turn away. I think I was meant to love you."

"Why do you love me, Niko? Why do you even *like* me?"

It hurt to hear. Especially after Elliott had just so beautifully and patiently given such profound love and kindness to him, when he'd been only breaking everything due to pointless fears and insecurities. Elliott had pieced him back together, gently and with care. He had built him up until Niko felt like someone who had value, worthy of love.

But he still couldn't see any of that value in himself.

"Because I see you. I see every part of you. Every facet, every potential. Your brilliant mind, your capability, your kind heart. Your protectiveness, your care. There's no one else in this galaxy

I'd rather be next to, right now. I—" Niko had to say it. The word was resonating in his head again and again, a stain. "I'm sorry I didn't see it sooner. That I didn't listen. That I was trying to stop you. When I called you garbage, it was my ignorance talking. I thought you were like any other asshole, that you were just killing innocent people because you got a thrill out of it, or it fed your ego, or something. I've seen so many people like that in my work over the years, and it's left me jaded. You're not garbage, Elliott. You're so much more than that. You have such value."

"I don't blame you, Niko. For anything you said. Or did. For trying to stop me. For not believing what I said at first. For trying to find another way. I don't hold it against you at all. In your position, I'd probably have done the same. I think anyone would. I was so alone and so lost, and you kept catching up to me again and again, so I tried to reach out."

"I'm grateful that you did."

"And I'm grateful that you actually listened to me," Elliott said. He studied Niko quietly. "I love you too, Niko."

Niko wrapped around the other man, simply holding him, and rested his head on top of his chest, ear pressed against him. Then he closed his eyes. A warm sound filled his ears, better than any song—the faithful and steady beat of Elliott's human heart. The quiet draw of air in and out of his lungs, a life measured one breath at a time.

*You're still alive.*

Elliott had experienced so much pain.

Far more than Niko could ever have imagined. He'd been so blind to it all, had neglected to see what was right in front of him. What Elliott carefully hid away in self-loathing and trauma.

*What could drive someone to this sort of depravity?* the reporters had asked again and again, circling through theories on never-ending newsfeeds that Niko had gladly eaten up from the couch of his old apartment.

The question should have been, *What could drive someone to this sort of desperation?*

Niko stayed like that for a while in silence before speaking, his voice gentle but sober with the seriousness of what he wanted to say. "Elliott."

"Yes?"

"I love you so fucking much. More than I even have words for. I— It's like we just talked about before, right? I want you to know you don't ever have to hide anything from me. Anything. Even the darkest, most difficult things. If you ever want to talk about what happened to you there, or about anything on your mind at all, I'm more than happy to listen. I'm not going to think any less of you. There's nothing shameful about what you went through, other than that *they* should be ashamed. I'm not going anywhere. I'm not going to turn you down, or treat you differently. I'll still keep waking up next to you. But if you don't ever want to tell me, you don't have to. Either way, it's alright."

"I..." Elliott exhaled, a long-held tension slowly leaving his body. He was silent for a long while, before finally speaking. "Okay... Okay."

"Okay," Niko said gently.

It was as though he'd been waiting to hear those words, to be given permission to share his pain. To know that this time, doing so wouldn't leave him betrayed and abandoned. Niko wouldn't fail him the way Liam Soren had. He couldn't even fathom it.

Elliott tentatively began telling him, his voice steady and quiet, about all the details of what had happened to him after Cleo's death, of the things Uru Taal had enacted on him. On how he'd felt himself leaving his own body, so delirious he'd wondered if he was dying or already dead. That later in his research, he'd found recordings of himself too, but they'd all since been long erased from the dark web in Honeybliss's house cleaning efforts. He hadn't saved them, like he had all the others. Niko was glad they were gone.

They talked for hours, Niko mostly listening, never once stopping in holding him as tightly as Elliott's injuries allowed for. Any other urgency in the galaxy could wait. Elliott laid himself bare before him, sharing the most painful, raw memories of his life, his darkest hours, his greatest agony. It was devastating to hear. It was all the suffering and misery of the Honeybliss files but multiplied by ten thousand, to know it had happened to the man in his arms whom Niko loved so deeply now. The surprisingly sweet, tender, sensitive assassin who shared his bed.

Elliott didn't cry. His tone had no anger, nor even bitterness, instead remaining quiet and drained as he spoke the memories. It was clear they took everything out of him to share. But once he finished, something in him changed subtly. There was a shy light peeking through the tumultuous, torrid dark. A relief, a peace at finally having been heard. At having someone to trust in and share his own story to, who had promised not to turn away.

Niko knew he would be the only one Elliott would probably ever share these things with again. He was fiercely glad to bear this man's pain, to help him carry the heavy burden of it in any way he could. He would keep it deep inside himself, all his memories and words, hidden away and protected in layers and layers of plated armor, until Elliott's voice was inseparable from his own heart.

Afterwards, when Elliott drifted off into the peace of sleep, exhausted and worn down to the soul, Niko finally let himself cry.

He wept for two people named Cleo Marie and Elliott James Kestrel. Siblings who had been each other's only sunlight. Who had loved sushi, and cafes. Parties, and sometimes movies. They had been driven in their careers. Cleo had loved fashion. Elliott had loved engineering, loved fixing broken things. They'd had passions, they'd had dreams. They'd still been trying to find out who they even were.

They had been so young when Honeybliss took them away.

All Niko could do now was give a patient home to Elliott's heart, and hope that one day, when all of this was over, the beautiful, beloved man could finally learn to live again, somewhere outside of revenge.

Niko would be waiting for him on the other side of it with open arms.

# CHAPTER TWENTY-ONE

# READY FOR DESTRUCTION

THREE DAYS HAD PASSED since Niko watched Cleo's—and Elliott's—video. Elliott had kept mostly to their room in the daytime, seeming exhausted and needing time to recover. Niko had stuck by his side all the while, planting gentle kisses on his temple and rubbing at his back. When his fingertips had glanced the subtle ridge of Elliott's scar where it lay hidden away beneath his shirt, his heart ached.

In the evenings, Elliott expressed that he wanted to go work on T1-N4 some more. When he was gone, Niko quietly combed through the Honeybliss files, reading everything he could about the Heenva who'd filmed those videos. He was a trust fund heir from old generational money, who'd gotten in thick with Uru Taal and had stayed friends with him for over a decade. His name was Yerudu Hesaakan. Niko could barely read about him without his blood pressure spiking, his pulse pounding in his temples and throat.

Oliver and Loolae cooked for them in Niko's absence, bringing trays of food with extra helpings of the more indulgent parts for Elliott, which made Niko smile. They quietly asked after him when Niko accepted the food. All he could tell them was that he'd just needed time. Their genuine care and concern for him made Niko feel such gratitude he didn't even know how to process it.

They'd spent the days together in a timeless sort of cocoon, hidden away from everything that was outside. Niko could grant him that, at least. For those few days, they were just people, boyfriends simply existing and lounging lazily around their shared bedroom. They lay in bed and talked. They watched Niko's favorite romance movie, *When the Stellar Wind Comes Calling*. And they watched the newsfeed, laughing over some of the press speculation of why Niko had abandoned his former job to work with Elliott and the nature of their relationship. To one particular major news outlet, they were the most infamous professional roommates around. Ones who'd enigmatically called each other 'babe' on live broadcast.

To Niko's shock—though as usual, the response was complicated and varied across a wide spectrum—they truly were gaining sympathy. Elliott had seized the attention of an entire galactic civilization with his actions, and now that he had it, he'd asked them to listen.

They were.

Planets, space stations, moons, scattered all across the stars. Every known and sentient alien species. They were listening. And many of them, just as Niko had, were beginning to see why Elliott had done what he had.

Endless videos, photographs, and newscasts showed the shockwaves Elliott's speech and the distribution of his painfully curated files had made across the galaxy. Headlines filled Niko's vision in hologram blue, hour after hour.

PROTESTS ERUPTING ACROSS GALAXY
'STARHAWK INITIATIVE' FORMING IN SUPPORT OF KESTREL
QUEEN DALATH UNDER ARREST
GALAPOL UNDER FIRE FOR POTENTIAL COVERUP
CHANCELLOR IINCHA'CUL TO BE INVESTIGATED
KESTREL AND ESTRELLA CALLED 'HEROES' BY SOME

On the morning of the third day, a new headline filled Niko's vision that made his eyes prick with the sting of warm tears.

BOUNTIES ON KESTREL AND ESTRELLA CANCELED

He lay side by side with Elliott, and reached out to pull the other man into a tight embrace. Elliott returned the gesture, holding him so tightly the pressure of it made Niko ache. It was a good sort of hurt, though.

"*Niko...*" he murmured, face buried in Niko's shoulder. "Niko... Niko... Niko..."

Elliott spoke his name again and again. Niko had never heard another person frame it in their voice with such reverence, such love. It made him ache all over.

"Hey," Niko said, pulling away and taking his face in his hands. "It's only going to get better from here. We're almost done, Elliott. We're going to win this."

"They've gone into hiding—"

"I know. I know. But we'll figure something out. Don't we always? With your intellect, and my good looks..."

Elliott laughed, a sound that had become so precious to Niko.

"Hell, who am I kidding?" Niko continued. "With your intellect, and good looks, and charm... You have the whole package. It's not even fair."

"Niko," Elliott complained. "You have all of that too. You're my favorite roommate."

This time, Niko laughed. "But seriously, we'll figure out a way."

Elliott smiled, a warm joy painting his features brightly. "You're right. We will. I believe it now. I believe it, when it comes from you. We'll find a way through, won't we?"

Niko leaned forward and kissed him on the forehead. "We will. We—"

The ringing of his phone interrupted their moment. He sighed and brought up the holographic caller ID—Lady Death.

"Give me a few, okay babe?"

"Take however much time you need, Niko."

Niko slipped out of bed, transferring back to the chair, then wheeled out of the bedroom and into the nearest empty room. "Hey, Deleera. Is everything good?"

"Everything's great, Niko. Have you looked at the news?"

He felt the smile make its way across his lips. "Yeah. We did. They canceled it."

"Even governments can still have some common sense, it seems."

"Yeah, sometimes," Niko said.

"I tried texting you about it, but your phone is rejecting new messages. I think your cache has gotten too full from spam. It takes a hell of a lot of messages to get to that point. You'll probably want to clear it out soon. I thought I'd let you know."

"Oh," Niko mumbled, shocked. He hadn't even known that was possible. "Oh, shit. Okay. Thanks, Deleera."

An icy discomfort snaked its way up through him at the memory of the last time he'd dared comb through some of the thousands of messages left by strangers on his phone. So many people had wished death and suffering on him—and on his family. Strangers had gone out of their way to tell him they were glad his mother and brother had died. Niko felt sick at the thought.

And there were undoubtedly a hundred times more now, likely pouring in by the day, unasked for, unwanted. So many filled his phone now that he couldn't accept new messages at all anymore.

"No problem. Hey. And let me know when you guys need help again. We're ready to go, over here."

Niko blinked. "I— Deleera, I've asked so much of you already."

"And? What, do you think we're soft? That it's too much? Do you think we're getting tired?"

He winced. *Should have known better than to put her pride on the line.* "No. No, of course not. I just—"

"I told you, Niko. This is bigger than any of us now. There's no favor for this one. It's not personal. This is just trying to hit back at people who do nothing but punch down. And that is *exactly* what I live for."

He knew that. "I... Alright. Yeah, we will. We'll let you know. It's getting harder to find them now, and it's going to stay that way, I think. We tried to hit Enva'ruu, but he wasn't there. It turned into an ugly ambush by another hunter who was being funded by Honeybliss."

"Mh," Deleera grunted. "Yep. Getting those files out is going to change up the whole game in a big way. Everyone knows what these insects did now. But it also means you just turned on the light, so the roaches are going to scatter and hide."

"Yeah."

"I'll look into it. See what I can find. See if any of my connections can dredge anything up."

"Great. Just... be careful, D. I've been bitten before."

"I will. You too, Niko."

He hung up with her, then drew in a long, grounding breath. Niko opened his text messages, trying not to look at nor read any of their previews. He moved his thumb over the holographic

DELETE ALL button, figuring it was best to just purge and not look back. But something stopped him.

He was too curious. He had to know. Even if it was to his own detriment.

It seemed he still didn't know when to hold back.

Niko let himself glance through a few. To his surprise, they weren't anything like the same messages he'd been getting shortly after joining Elliott.


They were something entirely different now.

*Those guys had it coming. Monsters. Don't s*

*Thank you for doing it.*

*hi is this niko? my daughter was killed whe*

*You guys are just doing what should have be*

*FUCK THE GOVERNMENTS WE LOOK OUT FOR OURSEL*

*u know what u guys kinda have a point*

*Niko Estrella? I'm Nhanri Dunn with AV News*

*TELL ELLIOT KESTRAL I LOVE HIM HES MY HUSBA*

*Thank you*

*THEY TOOK MY BROTHER NOBODY BELIEVED ME THA*

*Im an actress. Horu Duu'mari had a reputati*

*You guys want help? CALL ME!!! I'M READY*

*REMEMBER THE LOST — STARHAWK*

*you guys are so freaking hot lol just sayin*

*thank u thank u thank u...*

*I believe in Starhawk!!!!*
*I miss my dad everyday someone took him too*
*DEATH TO RAPISTS KEEP IT UP*
*I didnt understand why you did it but now i*
*We salute you STARHAWK*
*CVN News. Would you and Elliott like to spe*

Somehow, Niko had become the receptacle of the galaxy's whims. First, their condemnation and fears. And now, the pleas and quiet gratitude of those who'd suffered similarly to Elliott. People who had lost loved ones of their own to Honeybliss or other situations like them. People who couldn't abide by that wounding injustice that turning a blind eye to it all had caused.

He scrolled through hundreds upon hundreds of similar messages. *So much for glancing.* Occasionally there were still the same hateful messages and death threats as from previous weeks, but they were swallowed up in a sea of what, shockingly, was support. Approval. Gratitude.

Niko was about to delete them all and wipe the slate clean, when a message from several days ago caught his eye.

*My name is Angela Kelsa. I have something*

He didn't know why, but the name stood out to him. It was on the tip of his tongue, buried somewhere deep in the corridors of memory. Then it came back to him: he'd read that name before. And it had been delivered on Elliott's handsome voice once, desperate and pleading as he'd listed Honeybliss's victims before the ears and eyes of trillions.

*"Daranu. Jayson Cohl. Angela Kelsa. Marco Fulari."*

Niko blinked. He hesitated, goosebumps prickling up along his skin, before archiving this particular message thread, then finally wiping the rest.

Was someone fucking with him? Was someone pretending to be a dead woman? The absolute and utter cruelty of that idea made his stomach churn.

He opened it.

*My name is Angela Kelsa. I have something that belongs to Elliott, though I don't know if he'll want it. You're familiar with those files, so you'll probably know my name. I don't have any other way to reach you but this. I was one of Uru Taal's victims too, a year and a half after Elliott and Cleo Kestrel had been.*

Attached was a photograph that left Niko breathless. A delicate, golden ring sat in a human woman's open palm. It had a tiny opal and asymmetric floral engravings on it. Niko knew that ring. It had been used to ruin Elliott's life. Several more surprisingly long messages followed.

*He gave it to me. Put it on my finger. It was a sick joke. He said it belonged to a dead woman. Someone who he'd done the same things to that he'd done to me. I wanted to throw it away, but something in me made me keep it all this time. I guess I wanted that woman to never be forgotten. I'm glad I know her name now. She had a name. Cleo. She felt like a sister to me too in some ways, though I never knew her. We'd both had to endure... him.*

*They think I'm dead. Everyone thinks I'm dead. It's better that way. I never went back to my life. I was terrified they'd figure it out.*

*That they'd come for me. But like Elliott, I've been watching them too. And when I saw your broadcast, I rejoiced. His files showed me whose ring this was all along.*

*Let me know if you want help with those scumbags. I have a few unique and useful skills. You and I aren't so different in that.*

*If anyone could hate another person more than the seething disdain I have for every one of these Honeybliss bastards, I would be surprised, believe me. To say they've ruined my life would be a gross understatement.*

*Every time the galaxy has one less of these assholes in it, it's a better place for everyone.*

Niko glanced up and around the empty room, its four metal, sterile walls giving no answers. Above him, a single fluorescent light buzzed softly. He hesitated. Should he talk to Elliott about this? But showing him the ring right now made Niko a little wary. Bringing anything up like this right now might not be the best idea. The last thing he wanted to do was set off his trauma all over again when he was still recovering from having gone there.

Instead, he went to Zann.

"Niko," Zann greeted him. He'd been sitting on his bed in his own room, one long leg stretched out, a cluster of research and news holograms scattered in the air around him. They cast the entire room in a spectral glow. Beside him on the bedside table was an ashtray full of spent cigarette butts. The room smelled of a combination of stale smoke and Zann's typical aftershave. "Come in. You hear about your bounty?"

"Yeah."

Zann sat up fully now, swinging his legs so they draped over the side of the bed, and waved the holograms away. "How's it going? I tried texting you a couple times, but I think your phone is full and didn't wanna bug you guys. Is, uh—" he hesitated, genuine worry filling his eyes. It made his face softer than it usually looked. When he looked like that, Niko couldn't help but see the resemblance between him and their father. "Is Kestrel, uh, doing okay? Seemed like that was kind of some big shit."

Niko appreciated that he cared. Zann hadn't always been the greatest at showing warmth, but underneath it all, he was someone who cared a lot about the people close to him. And it seemed Elliott now fell under that umbrella, even if it was at its very edge. Gone now were the quips, jabs, and little nicknames. All that remained in this serious moment was concern. "Yeah, he's, um. He's alright. He's just taking some time."

"Yeah?" Zann eyed him. "How the fuck did you get this far without knowing about that, Niko?"

Niko glanced away, shame crushing him tighter than the gravity of a gas giant. He hated the question. But it was a fair one, nonetheless. "I—I actually don't know, Zann. I watched every one of those videos, but I just couldn't see hers. I figured I had a pretty good idea how they were going to go, you know? And then after that, he'd just never really talked about it much, or in detail. He just said he was saving Uru Taal for last, and that Taal had been there when Cleo died. Things like that."

It *had* gone like that... hadn't it? Niko tried to wrack his brain, tried to remember, tried to see if there was any detail he'd missed along the way. Maybe Elliott had told him. Maybe someone else had, and he just hadn't truly heard it. It was lost to him now, if so. He'd thought he'd known, so any hints given otherwise simply hadn't soaked in. And he'd been so focused on surviving the complexities and challenges that always lay ahead of them.

"Shit," Zann said, shaking his head. "Hers were actually the first I watched. I wanted to know what made that guy tick, you know?"

"Yeah," Niko mumbled. He didn't want to talk about this right now, and it wasn't why he'd come here, anyway. "Hey, uh, so I was trying to clear out my messages, when I came across a pretty interesting one. I wanted to see what you thought."

He wheeled over to the bed and showed Zann the message history from Angela, including the photograph. Zann read the details quickly, his dark eyes darting back and forth, a glint of blue reflected in them from the light.

"Huh. I'll be damned."

"Right? So, like, do you think it's legit?"

"Hard to say. The tone of her messages seems pretty personal and legitimate. And that's definitely the ring from that old video. Could be a knockoff. Are there any specific details about it Kestrel might know that we could ask her about? Hidden engraving, that sort of thing?"

It wasn't a bad idea. Though, it would involve bringing Elliott into this after all. Niko sighed. "Yeah. I can talk to him."

Zann thumbed through his own phone for a moment, before bringing up his copy of Uru Taal's files from Elliott's research. Sure enough, there was a folder in it titled ANGELA KELSA. He opened it, bringing up several photographs of a human woman with pale skin, fluffy, deep brown curls, and dark eyes. Her visage was familiar to Niko. He'd just struggled to match visuals to a name before.

Zann let out a whistle, looking impressed. "Damn. Worked as a skip tracer. That must be what she means by 'useful skills.' If this *is* legit, then she might be our new best friend."

"Huh," Niko marveled softly. A skip tracer. They weren't so different from bounty hunters, though focused more on information gathering and locating fugitives in the first place. In Angela's case, it seemed she'd worked for the Internal Revenue Regulation of Kaalan-10. Her specialty had been in tracking down fugitives of tax evasion and other financial crimes so that Kaalan-10's government—or hunters like himself—could sweep in and bring them in once they'd been found.

Galapol had employed a few skip tracers of their own, though at this point, Niko wouldn't trust them as far as he could throw them. They were probably earning their current paychecks by diligently trying to track Elliott and himself down.

"Probably what got her taken, actually," Zann hypothesized. "She might have been investigating one of Taal's friends, so he decided to make her not a problem anymore."

Zann had an excellent intuition for those sorts of things. Niko figured he probably wasn't wrong. Or if he was, that he wasn't far off from the truth.

Either way—if she really was Angela Kelsa, and was willing to help, this could be a massive boon in finishing off Honeybliss once and for all.

Zann started playing her victim footage from Honeybliss. Niko flinched away, casting his gaze to the corner of the room. He'd seen this multiple times already, had it imprinted into his brain. He'd had nightmares about it. Her screams were familiar. She had been defiant, more angry than afraid, spitting curse words in several languages at Taal, even actually spitting on him once.

That last offense was what had proven—or so Niko had assumed, until now—a fatal mistake. Uru had shortly after thrown some concoction that was likely acid or watered-down bog-theun corrosive on her. It was gruesome.

After that, Angela Kelsa had never resurfaced again. It only made sense to assume she'd, like almost every other one of Honeybliss's victims, died from their treatment and had been discarded afterward.

"Sorry, Niko," Zann said, closing the video out again. "Go get him. He needs to know about this. This could change everything for you guys."

Niko returned shortly after, with Elliott in tow. The other man looked sleepy and a little disheveled, still in pajama bottoms and a plain white t-shirt. His feet were in socks. Cowlicked waves hung in his face as he folded his arms across his chest.

"This room smells awful," he said.

"Yeah, hi to you too. Good to see you're still your usual sunshiny self," Zann quipped.

"I just can't help but be *inspired* by you."

Niko sighed, realizing their weird rivalry had been resurrected. Maybe it was a good sign, though, if Elliott was now up for trading jabs.

"Anyway," Zann continued, "come here. Look at this. This is the same one, right?"

Elliott grudgingly leaned in and eyed the image of the ring that Zann had now zoomed in on and expanded. Niko was intensely aware of him, his gaze fixed on the blond man's expression. Elliott's brow drew into a subtle frown at the sight of the ring, though it was something that felt more wounded than angry.

"Yes, that's it."

"Right. Can you tell me anything else about it? Was this some mass-produced thing? Are there any unique features? An old nick in it you might remember?"

"I believe it was unique. One of a kind. It was our maternal grandmother's. Cleo and I had been really close to her when she was alive, but especially Cleo. We'd even discussed moving in with her. She died when we were pretty young, though. But that had been her wedding ring."

"Huh." Zann looked at him.

"It also has an inscription inside. '*My heart resides within you.*'"

Something about those words made Niko ache in a deep, inconsolable sort of way. Maybe because he felt every one of them now—profoundly, personally.

Zann gestured at Niko impatiently. "Alright, so ask her what it says inside. Just in case some jackoff made a copy from the video for this."

Niko sighed and steeled himself, then started typing. *Hi, Angela. I hate to ask, but the ring says something inside of it. Can you tell me what it says?*

The three waited in tense silence, when Niko's phone pinged.

*Sure. I understand. There are a lot of messed up people out there. It says: my heart resides within you.*

"Ask her for a picture of herself," Zann pushed.

"Fucking god, Zann," Niko said. He understood the reason for the request, but actually asking it made his skin crawl. "You saw the video. She—"

"I know. But we need to know, Niko. It's the last thing. She's sounding pretty fucking legit. Either that, or someone managed to get that ring. But we need to know."

Niko glanced at Elliott. He'd half expected him to push alongside Zann, to let his paranoia take over and insist it needed to be done. But, instead, he gave Niko a pitiful look, barely shaking his head. Niko ran a hand over his face before starting to text anyway. "Fuck."

*Okay. I'm sorry, Angela. I have to ask one last thing. Do you have a photo of yourself?*

This time, there was a long delay before her response finally came. *I don't really want to do that. I'm sorry. I'm not the same anymore. They ruined me. If it helps, I'm willing to speak with you on the phone.*

Niko felt like a monster. He wished he hadn't asked.

"Do it," Zann said. "Call her. We need *something.*"

Niko hesitated again, casting another glance at Elliott.

"Do it," Elliott agreed, nodding subtly.

He put a call through. Angela answered on the third ring. For a moment, Niko wasn't sure what to say. She spoke first.

"Hello? Is this Niko?" It was the same raspy, deep but feminine voice from the videos. The same one that had dug into Niko's mind and would never leave. He cast a flickering glance up toward the others and nodded. Zann returned the nod, silently agreeing with his assessment. It was her. "Hello?"

"Uh, hi. Angela. Yeah, this is Niko."

"Thank you for reaching out. I didn't know if you even read any of these messages. I figured it was a long shot, but... Anyway, I'm glad it worked."

"Yeah. Um. Thanks for reaching out to me, too. You—" He glanced up at Zann, who impatiently gestured for him to get on with it. Niko looked away from him. "Listen, sorry if this is too personal, but are you alright? I mean in the sense of— Are you safe right now? Do you need any kind of help or shelter?"

Niko had no idea what he could possibly offer her, but if another of Uru Taal's surviving victims needed help, he would do anything to see it done. Maybe Lady Death could house her.

Angela paused for a beat. When she spoke, she sounded a little touched—and, maybe, a little sad, too. "That's... kind of you to ask. But I'm alright. Since it happened, I've learned how to evade them pretty damn well. I can take care of myself. I'm used to it now."

"Okay," he said. He prayed that their stirring things up with Elliott's speech and file distribution hadn't put her in even greater danger somehow. A thought occurred to him, then. Niko wondered how many people there might actually be out there, who'd slipped through the cracks and were forgotten or managed to survive the atrocities of Honeybliss, only to quietly disappear, like Angela had. Like Elliott had—until he'd embarked on his mission.

"Do you know if there's anyone else out there like you? Anyone who survived—"

"No," she said, and they both fell quiet for a moment. "Sorry. I really, really am. Most people don't survive this. I've searched relentlessly, just in case. I'd only ever caught on that there may have been someone else recently, and it turned out to be Elliott Kestrel. They have years of experience burying this shit."

"Yeah. That's— Yeah, that's fair. Um," he continued, stumbling again over his words. "Speaking of searching. You said you might be able to help us. I think... we could use a little of that right now, honestly."

"It would be my pleasure, believe me. You've probably seen it in the files already, but I used to work as a financial skip tracer."

"Yeah. That's—that's actually exactly what we need right now. Since we distributed the files and had the broadcast, we think they're all going to go into hiding. I mean, it wouldn't really make sense to just hang around and wait to get killed."

"Makes sense," she agreed. "You're right. I'm confident I can find any of them. I've been keeping tabs on them over the past year anyway. *Fuckers.*"

Niko let out a soft snort at that last word. It said so much, with so little. "Are you sure? I mean, they're probably going to have a lot of help covering up their locations, too."

"Yeah, actually. You might not think so, but hiding someone who wants to stay alive is a lot harder than hiding the corpses they created can be. These assholes will need food, they'll need shelter. Maybe even entertainment, depending. They'll need to exchange income for those things. They can hide it well, but there will be receipts and transaction histories *somewhere.* Tell me who you want to pick off next, and I'll get you their location," Angela said. Niko glanced at Zann and Elliott; both nodded back at him.

"Yeah. Okay." He caught Elliott's gaze from the corner of his eye. The other man mouthed *Enva'ruu* to him, but Niko continued on, all force and will. "We're going for Yerudu Hesaakan next."

Elliott gaped at him, but said nothing. He paled slightly.

It had to be Yerudu, though. It couldn't be anyone else. Niko could honor Elliott's wish to save Uru Taal for last—though only barely—but he couldn't tolerate Yerudu Hesaakan living to see another day. That Heenva shitstain was fair game.

"Alright. Sure. I can do that."

"Is there anything we can do for you, Angela? Anything at all?"

"No. You just stay put and let me do what I do best. Trust me. By taking care of them, you're doing me *plenty* of favors." She hesitated, before adding, "Actually. Is—is Elliott around?"

Niko looked at him. Elliott was quiet for a moment, before speaking. "I'm here."

There was a strangely charged silence, something full of such deep emotion Niko could barely begin to touch it. These were two people who'd both endured and shared a very particular nightmare.

Finally, Angela spoke again. "I... I wanted to say thank you. For everything that you've done. It must have been so hard for you, alone and without anyone listening."

"It was." Elliott paused. "For you too, I imagine."

"Yeah. I've been following them, this whole time. But I was too afraid to ever actually act. It felt too big. Hopeless, I guess."

"Yes," he said. "I didn't... go into this with hope."

"I'll find Hesaakan for you. It's the least I can do, after everything that you've done for all the people they hurt."

Elliott didn't reply, so Niko answered her instead. "Thanks, Angela."

"Sure." She seemed to still be addressing Elliott with her next words, though. "There are probably a lot of people out there right now just living their lives, going about their days. Not knowing they would have been next. Not knowing that they owe their futures to you. And if there *is* anyone else out there who survived, too, they've probably been waiting for a long, long time for someone like you. I have."

Elliott said nothing.

Five and a half hours later, Niko received a set of text messages with an address to a remote bunker on the opposite side of forestial Vorna-12 as Baouban's destroyed safehouse was. Crowded into the Murder Room now, he poured over their information with Zann and Elliott.

"Could still be a trap," Zann mused. Niko hated the thought, but he was right. Everything about Angela seemed genuine, but then again, so had Baouban once, and the fact that her coordinates led to the same planet they'd been so deeply betrayed on set a sick sort of irony to it all. "She got this pretty fast, given everything.

Might be Galapol agents camping out there again, just like with Khaathra."

"Yeah," Niko mumbled.

"Wish we had a way to check it out. Drone footage, or something. Should have tried to nab one of those from Galapol too."

"Actually," Elliott said, "in a way, you did." He went and retrieved T1-N4 from a shelf. Niko did a double take, looking at her now. The little bot was polished clean and fixed up, with a ridiculous new paint job that had crudely illustrated flames along the bottom of her and a skull and crossbones above the beautifully preserved Lord Fukkaho sticker.

One arm now terminated in what appeared to be a miniature flamethrower instead of her usual prehensile pincers, with a tiny fuel canister attached. A partially-concealed camera was installed on her front, just above her interface. Niko barked a laugh as he took it all in.

"What the hell? You did that, Elliott?"

Elliott shrugged. "I... needed to get my mind off things lately and working on this helped."

"Is that a fucking flamethrower?" Zann marveled.

"It is," Elliott said. Niko couldn't help but notice the carefully concealed pride in his tone that still managed to subtly slip through. "Fully functional, too."

"You got her to work again?" Niko asked.

"Yes, but I had to rewrite some of her neural network and jailbreak the programming. I'm not talented with machine AI the way some of the other people at LaraTech were, but to put it simply, she won't send feedback to Galapol if you do anything illegal."

"So, what's this about a drone?" Zann pushed.

"Right. See this camera? I'd had it from before I even started killing. I gathered a lot of supplies and tech components, just in case I'd need them eventually if a situation arose. I've made her into a fully functional drone. She can be used for surveillance. And see this?" He opened her side compartment, then pointed to delicate wiring and a chip of some kind. "She has ophthalmic refraction tech installed, too—"

"What." Zann stared at him.

"Uh, the stealth tech stuff," Niko offered.

"I've programmed her to switch stealth on and off, adjust the camera, transmit signal, internal emergency kill switch, things like that, all from remote control," Elliott continued.

"And the flamethrower?" Niko asked.

"And the flamethrower."

"Well, shit," Zann marveled. "Everything's kinda falling into place for once, huh?"

"Please don't jinx it," Niko said. The last time things had started falling into place for them, he'd received news that his father had been kidnapped by literally the worst people in the galaxy.

"Don't expect anything extraordinary," Elliott warned, though Niko thought any of the wonders he'd managed to create could easily be categorized as 'extraordinary.' "The camera doesn't have the range most modern drones do, and it's still, in the end, a very basic T1-N4 model. It's just a project I've been putting together in my free time. But we could deploy her and scout the area while she's under stealth. Check if Angela's information is good, or if we're about to walk into another trap. Then go from there."

"Sounds good," Zann said. "When do we start?"

"Why not now?"

"Good afternoon, Niko!" T1-N4 exclaimed cheerily as her interface activated, a familiar, pixelated emoji smile lighting up her screen. The shine of its glass reflected the thick, cerulean treetops of Vorna-12 above. All around them, the scent of soil and petrichor filled the air. Niko only now realized how stale the air in places like the facility seemed. Even Kaapra-19 and Dainna, while full of their own vibrant tapestry of city scents, never held the sort of quiet, soothing splendor that nature inherently did. "It's very good to see you again!"

Niko blinked. "Wow, she remembers me? I thought she had to be, like, rebooted."

"She did. I had to wipe everything. But I wanted her to recall you, so I programmed it in," Elliott said. That detail struck Niko hard and he ached, looking over at Elliott. It was such a simple, small thing, but meant so much.

Elliott tossed her into the air, and her little whirring engines took over. "Are you ready to *murder some assholes?*" she chimed in her singsong voice. Niko barked out a laugh.

Elliott smirked at him. "I may have added a few personality additions."

"So, you made her into a mini you." Zann snorted.

"Beats being nagged at about keeping hydrated, I guess," Niko said.

"She'll still do that," Elliott muttered. "Time to test the controls." He played around with a small but simple holographic interface. T1-N4 moved in a gentle circle, then floated up and down. He opened a second hologram which revealed himself, Niko, and Zann from the viewpoint of T1-N4's camera, all slightly distorted in fisheye view.

"I am ready for *destruction!*" she exclaimed, then emitted a small jet of flames aimed toward the sky.

"Okay, you might have to tone that thing the hell down, before it sets us all on fire in our sleep," Zann mumbled.

Elliott ignored him. A moment later, she vanished from view. "Everything seems to be functional."

Niko caught a glimmer of distorted air from the corner of his eye as she ascended. He and Zann crowded around Elliott to watch the holoview from her camera as it swept up now through the treetops, heading toward the coordinates Angela had provided them.

"There's a branch—" Zann warned. T1-N4 swiftly pivoted around it. "You should stay clear from any settlements too, even with the stealth on. You might want to go a little higher, and—"

"I know what I'm doing," Elliott snapped.

"Zann, stop backseat driving the drone," Niko mumbled.

The camera view soared up above the treetops, giving a breathtaking view of the azure forest at large. In the distance, a flock of diamond-shaped creatures that reminded Niko of manta rays soared along, before diving one after the other into the foliage. Eventually, T1-N4 reached Angela's coordinates, pausing to hover above dense overgrowth and tall, crowded trees. The area looked completely inconspicuous—nothing at all appeared to be around for miles.

"Bring her down under the canopy," Zann said impatiently.

"*I know!*" Elliott barked. T1-N4's view began to descend, slow and careful as Elliott had to navigate her through the branches. Once the leaves cleared from view, the undergrowth of the forest spread before them, shady and azure with dim shafts of sunlight peeking through occasionally.

Elliott rotated T1-N4 slowly.

"There. There!" Zann said, pointing. Elliott paused, zooming in with her camera on the spot Zann had indicated. Peeking out from among several tangled bushes was a heavy set of concrete doors that led straight into the ground. Elliott swiveled the camera more, and two ships—one smaller and built for luxury travel, the other more sizable and for utility—sat parked two dozen yards away in a subtle clearing. A particularly rough and scarred looking

Toliai stood leaning against the side of the plainer ship, smoking a cigar.

"Get a close up of their serial numbers," Zann said. Elliott zoomed in on the small, sixteen-digit numbers printed on the sides of each, and Zann immediately began running them through some of the data he'd swiped from Galapol. "One on the left belongs to Hesaakan. The other... is harder to track, but seems to be registered in Dolloss, Thoro."

The capital city of Thoro, which seated the Toliai royal throne.

"So, these guys are a favor from Taal to his best buddy," Niko mumbled.

"Or Taal's here too," Zann said. Goosebumps crept along Niko's skin at the thought.

"Taal's recovering in the Dolloss royal hospital," Elliott said.

Zann shrugged. "Could be a front to throw your murder-happy ass off." He pulled out the pack of cigarettes from his coat pocket and lit up, seeming to savor in the relief only satisfying a gnawing addiction could bring. "Anyhow, I guarantee this guy's big scaly ass isn't the only one here. And they're probably elite, seasoned agents in service to Taal. Or trusted mercs. Either way, your job here just got a whole lot harder. You sure you wanna go through with this?"

Something hardened inside Niko. He wasn't willing to back off on this, wasn't willing to let it go and allow Yerudu Hesaakan to enjoy another day of sentience just because Uru Taal might be there too. And he'd dealt with Toliai before. They were hard as hell to bring down, but they weren't invincible. Especially not with Lady Death and her team backing them up. They could take on a few well-trained mercs.

He glanced at Elliott. "I want it to be him next. Are we still doing this?"

They locked gazes for a long minute, Elliott searching Niko's eyes, his own hard and shadowed in a churning storm of thoughts. He worked his jaw.

After a moment, he gave Niko a single, decisive nod. "But only Hesaakan."

"Fine," Niko agreed reluctantly. He had a feeling Taal wasn't behind those thick concrete doors, underneath the soil—an old gut instinct that whispered to him. But if the Toliai prince—and Elliott's tormentor—was there, Niko would have a hell of a time trying to talk Lady Death into letting him go.

Let alone, himself.

But that was a problem for *Future Niko*, and one he might not ever even have to worry about at all.

Elliott looked back to the camera, guiding T1-N4 across the area to get a full look around. "Underground bunker. Likely fortified. There's probably a back entrance around here, too... Bingo." The camera focused now on another door, similar to the first, hidden in an even thicker set of bushes. "We can flush them out, then pick them off at both exits."

"Yep." Zann crushed the butt of his cigarette under his boot, then kicked a small covering of dirt over it. "Well. Place looks surprisingly clear, too. No Galapol agents waiting around on this one. Nothing fishy. Just an asshole hanging out with his hired protection. Looks like Kelsa's intel checks out. We just earned ourselves a very, *very* useful new best friend."

Elliott began T1-N4's retreat, guiding her up silently through the canopy again, careful not to rustle any leaves and catch the guard's attention. Then he spoke what lay heavy and wrapped with dread deep inside of Niko.

"If Honeybliss doesn't find her first."

# CHAPTER TWENTY-TWO

# WHAT'S UNDERNEATH

THE NEXT DAY, NIKO and Elliott were both up early to prepare for the mission ahead. As usual, Elliott wanted to make haste in taking down their next target. This time, knowing the full context of what Hesaakan had contributed to, Niko was fully on board with moving things along as rapidly as possible.

After breakfast with the others, he suited up and spent the morning in the hangar, tightening and changing out some of the *Soñadora's* parts with spare tools he kept in the ship's cabin. Maintaining the ship had once been one of the greatest joys of his life. Bounty hunting had paid quite well, especially with the caliber of targets he regularly brought in. But he'd chosen to stay in a tiny apartment with cheap furniture—something Zann had relentlessly complained about—pouring most of his income back into modding and keeping his beloved ship in pristine condition, instead.

It was fun and nostalgic to do it all again now. And it helped keep his thoughts both off the mission they were about to embark on in just a matter of hours, and fantasizing how much he wanted to choke the life out of Yerudu Hesaakan.

Satisfied the ship was in good shape after all the abuse they'd put her through lately, he stood and decided to check in on Elliott. If Niko was this enraged whenever he thought about Hesaakan, he could only imagine how the other man was feeling.

The shooting range and lounges were all empty, as was the Murder Room. Zann only shrugged when Niko questioned if he'd seen him. Finally, he checked their bedroom and found him perched on the edge of their bed.

Elliott's slender back greeted him. His hair was a rich, deep honey gold, damp from a recent shower and hanging in heavy waves. A navy-blue t-shirt of Niko's hung off his frame, too big for him. The sight of it made Niko's breath catch in his throat.

Elliott had his earbuds in. Niko could barely hear his music from the doorway, and his heart ached. Time and again, Elliott had said—and shown—that he turned to the comforts of music when his anxiety was eating him alive.

He crossed the room and sank down slowly on the edge of the bed, next to Elliott. The other man looked over at him, lovely green eyes hiding their depths away. Elliott gave him the ghost of a smile, and Niko gladly returned it. Niko reached out and brushed back a few golden curls, and gently plucked an earbud from his ear. Then he put it in his own, a rich and vibrant ocean of sound washing over him now, glistening vocals buoyed by layers of reverb and a dream-haze of pop guitar.

*"Baby, I'll be your shelter.*

*When the meteors come,*

*You can hide in me.*

*We'll watch the stars fall together,*

*Until you'll see*

*Everything that scared you can be*

*Beautiful, beautiful,*

*You're so beautiful.*

*Just open up your heart to me."*

They sat side by side for a while, Kuliedi Taan—or was it Hayura? Niko honestly couldn't discern the difference between their music—singing a lullaby of comfort to them both. He wondered if either of the singers had any idea the effect they had on Elliott Kestrel, the very assassin who'd crashed their duet concert debut. That they brought him a unique sort of comfort in the dark, in the quiet. Elliott leaned over and rested his head against Niko's thick, armored shoulder pad. Something about the gesture hurt—he found himself wishing he could feel and bear the weight of his touch fully, could feel the connection of skin against skin without boundaries.

He wished, above all, that he could give Elliott that comfort, too.

Eventually, the song ended and the music melted away into silence, whatever playlist or album Elliott had chosen concluded. After a moment, Niko finally spoke. "What's on your mind?"

"It's different this time."

"Yeah? Talk to me, babe. You can tell me."

Elliott hesitated. He pulled out his remaining earbud, and Niko did too, setting them on the bedside table. Whatever lay within the other man was swallowed deep, struggling to get out. "I'm..." His voice quieted to barely above a whisper. "Niko, I'm terrified."

"I'm here."

"I hate that I'm scared. It enrages me to fear this—" He bit off his words, clearly not wanting to say 'person'. *"Creature."*

Niko opened his mouth to speak, but Elliott continued on, right over him. He'd obviously summoned something inside himself that lay tangled, caustic, and indigestible, one of those things that if you didn't expel it, it would burn you alive from the inside out. Niko had seen him in this mood before.

"How insulting. How humiliating. How absolutely wretched. To fear something is to give it power. Of which he deserves none. He deserves *nothing*. Why does he get to luxuriate in money and power, while he hurts everyone else? While he films their ruination, and misery, and pain, and death for his fucking entertainment? Why does he get to laugh at it all, just because he was born to a rich family and has wealthy ties? Why do any of them? It's disgusting."

Niko nodded. "I hear you, Elliott. It *is* disgusting. No one should ever be allowed to do those sorts of things to another person, no matter how powerful they are. And no one should try to defend or hide that shit for them because they can be paid off, either." He hesitated. "I'm sorry that any of this is a reminder of what happened. I should have talked to you about it, first. I wasn't thinking. I should have made sure you were okay with it. But I can't... I can't tolerate him living another day. I can't, Elliott. Now that I know, I think it's time this sick animal is put down."

"No. You were right. It's time. It's long *past* time, actually. He'll get what's coming to him. Though he doesn't deserve the mercy of a fast death."

"I see red even thinking about that fucked up asshole. It's taken everything I have not to just go out there and fuck him up myself."

A small smile graced Elliott's lips. "Thank you, Niko. For caring about me. For being angry for me. It's... nice."

"It's okay to be scared. It is. It's not insulting to be. These people *hurt* you. They did more than that. They changed your entire life, and you're still recovering. They took something from you. And they took your sister. It's okay to feel any way you need to. There's no one right way to... to grieve, or to heal, or to process."

"Most people might argue a galaxy-wide murder-spree isn't the best coping method," Elliott deadpanned.

Niko couldn't help but smile, despite the gravity of the situation. "Okay, yeah, maybe not. But you can't argue they didn't have it coming, either."

"I won't argue that, no."

"Elliott, we're almost done now. We're going to make it through this. You got people to finally listen to you and see the truth of the abuse that's really going on. Honeybliss can't hide anymore. And you have friends. You have allies. More than that, you have a family now. We're not going to abandon you, like everyone else did. We're going to take care of you. *I'm* going to take care of you.

"I care about you, Elliott. I care so fucking much. Whatever happens from here on out, it's the two of us, and I have your back. I'll never let anyone hurt you again. They'll have to go through me, first."

Elliott's smile returned. "Yes, I suppose they will, won't they? Somehow, after everything, you're still here."

"And I'll always be. The only place I want to be is at your side."

They stayed like that, simply existing together as the minutes trickled away from them. Niko knew him, knew he was likely spiraling into overthinking. "Let me distract you. Do you want to train for a while?"

Elliott remained silent, his eyes searching Niko's a moment. Niko could sense the change, the thought behind his gaze. His pupils grew into dark, wide pools, vanquishing away some of the sea-green. The cadence of his breathing grew a little more rapid.

"No, I don't want to train."

Before Niko could speak, Elliott leaned in and took up his mouth in a kiss, needy and demanding, molten sugar and spice. Niko emitted a soft, muffled sound, involuntary, greedy.

Elliott pulled back long enough to murmur, breathless, "I want *you*."

Niko searched the other man with his gaze, before leaning in and meeting him in another kiss, and then another. He was delighted to oblige, eager to help distract his boyfriend from everything they were about to face down together, the creeping dark of memories that undoubtedly cut him like shards of broken glass. Niko couldn't get enough of him. Elliott cupped his cheek in his hand and stroked his thumb along it.

He climbed into Niko's lap, straddling him now, and kissed him with a hot passion along his jaw, his neck, sending goosebumps trailing along Niko's skin beneath the suit. Niko cupped the other man's ass, but Elliott reached behind himself and removed his gloved hands. He held them in his own.

*"Niko,"* he breathed, touching their foreheads together. *"I want what's underneath."*

"It's yours," Niko said. "It's all yours. It always has been."

Elliott began to unlatch the gloves, but Niko stopped him. He removed them himself instead, carefully, slowly, freeing the calloused hands beneath, with their countless stories told through old tattoos.

Niko touched Elliott everywhere, greedy for the connection he could feel with his own bare hands now. Then he reached up for his shoulder pads, unfastening one, then the other, letting them fall to the floor beside the bed, the weight of them no longer bearing down on him. Elliott pressed a warm, liquid kiss to his lips, moaning softly into Niko's mouth. Niko wanted to melt into him.

He then moved to his chestplate, eyes on Elliott the entire time. Elliott reached out to join him, elegant, long, pale fingers dancing along the scratched and dented metal of the chestplate, until they found Niko's hand and covered it with his own. Together, they gently pried open the release latch.

With a snap, the piece came loose, and a rush of cool, refreshing air flooded around Niko, its tight pressure released from him now. Elliott pulled it away from him, and with a single warning beep, the neurotech of his suit was disabled. The other man discarded it with the rest of Niko's armor.

Elliott half-climbed off of him as Niko removed the final armor pieces from his legs. He let them fall to the floor, too, until only he—vulnerable, tender, and wanting with a passion that set his heart beating—remained.

"Lover," Elliott said, "there you are."

He straddled Niko again, pinning him under the weight of his lithe body. The heavy sensation of him drove Niko wild. It was something he could put his trust in, something reliable, sturdy, and real. This time, when Niko snaked his arms around him and cupped the other man's ass in his hands, it was allowed.

Elliott buried his nose in the crook of Niko's neck and inhaled deeply. Then he let out a low moan of pleasure, which sent a bolt of white-hot electricity coursing through Niko all the way down to his cock. He could feel himself growing hard, growing hungrier by the second, his heart rapidly taking off and nearly leaving him behind. Elliott raked his fingers through Niko's hair, before gripping it possessively.

Then his lips brushed Niko's fragile throat. He teased something that glanced barely upon the boundaries of a lingering bite, teeth pressing lightly upon skin.

Like the knife from their roleplay, it was a show of power, of dominance. Of something dangerous.

Elliott *was* dangerous, and he was powerful. In just over a year, he had ascended to sit on a throne of a hundred billion stars, a formidable monarch. He'd become the assassin an entire galaxy had come to both fear and respect. The man who even the hard-eyed, shifty denizens of black market back alleys glanced at with wariness and awe. He bent interstellar politics to his will. He'd re-shaped the futures of empires. He'd changed the course of history with a morbid plan and piercing determination, the face of unrelenting justice itself.

And now he sat, pressed against Niko, teeth hovering above his throat, breath hot on his skin. A single snapping of his jaws closed could crush the air—and life—right out of Niko's body.

It was a wordless plea for his trust. The arguably most powerful man in existence had held Niko's life, time and again, in his hands. And he'd only ever taken gentle, reverent care of it. Niko slowly tipped his head to the side, baring more of his neck to him, a quiet acquiescence, and Elliott relented, releasing his pseudo-hold on his throat.

*"Baby..."* Niko whispered, a sunburst of exhilaration quickening his breaths into panting now.

Another quiet moan slipped from the other man as he pressed against him even harder, grinding his own erection against Niko's, an urgent, heated sensation building between them. His fin-gertips dug bruises into Niko's skin, needy and demanding. He bent and nipped at Niko's ear, then murmured into it, all breath, ephemeral. Niko could hear something well-con-trolled slipping from Elliott's voice. It hitched a little, low and scratchy at the edges with wild hunger. "I want to fuck you, lover. I want you pleading on my cock. I want to make you cry for me."

Then Elliott froze. He turned his face away, seeming al-most ashamed.

Niko's breath caught in his chest at the sudden switch from syrupy heat to frigid chill. He could sense Elliott's grow-ing hesitation, and something wounded panged through him at the realization.

He drew in a long, shaky inhale, forcing himself to sober from the euphoria of Elliott's touch and come back down to reality to address this. "Elliott? Babe?"

Elliott pulled away slowly. Damp locks of golden hair hung in his face as their gazes searched each other's now. His green eyes winced with subtle pain and uncertainty. He was retreating back inside himself.

When he spoke, his voice was quieter now. "Am I being too much?"

"No. God no, baby."

In denying himself before, Niko had wounded Elliott too.

He had to let the other man know how much it all meant to him. How much he loved surrendering to Elliott. How much he wanted him in any way Elliott wanted to give himself to Niko. He wanted to be Elliott's submissive lover.

He felt his face heat at the thought.

"Elliott, I... I want it, too." He ran his hand along the length of the other man's arm, a gesture both pleading and meant to comfort. "I want it. I want it like that. I want *you* like that."

Elliott moved in so close that they shared one another's breath. "If you want it, then tell me, Niko. Tell me what you want."

Niko's breath caught in his throat. Elliott wanted him to say it, wanted to draw it out of him. Wanted his commitment, his full-hearted enthusiasm.

Niko would give it to him.

"I..." he began. "I want you to make love to me. I want you to... to dominate me." He could feel the heat stinging his cheeks, but continued on regardless. "I want to s-submit to you, Elliott."

Something in Elliott shifted again. His gaze searched Niko, green eyes locking onto his own and boring in now, assertive.

"Why?"

The heat that pooled in Niko's cheeks now flooded through his entire face and down into his neck. He swallowed back a heavy lump in his throat—something both thrilling and terrifying. But this time, he pushed the fear aside, leaving it to rest among the pile of discarded armor he had left on their bedroom floor.

He didn't need to carry it anymore.

"Because I love it when you do. It—It feels freeing to let go for you. It feels good to give myself to you. I like it when you take over. I like being whatever you want me to be. I like when you use me. It feels... It feels unlike anything I've ever experienced. I didn't know it could feel like that."

"Good boy," Elliott purred, his tone bright and sensuous. Niko bit his lip. It was quite clear that Elliott loved making him squirm. "You did so well, telling me how much you like it when I fuck you."

But Niko was getting bold now. He wasn't done yet, a reckless courage bolstered by Elliott's praise spurring him on. "I fantasized about it. After you'd sent that picture. I couldn't get it out of my head. I used it. I imagined you inside me. I imagined you—" He turned his face away, unable to look at Elliott when he said what lay on the tip of his tongue. It was almost too much to bear. "I imagined you calling me a good boy. Like... Like you had in your first text message. But I don't want to make it weird, or anything— I don't want you to feel obligated to, you know, keep saying that. Or whatever."

"Oh, Niko," Elliott breathed into his ear. "I promise you, it's never an obligation." He leaned forward and nuzzled his cheek against Niko's, his hand snaking downward to glance his fingertips along the swell of Niko's erection through his jeans. Niko let out an involuntary grunt of pleasure, beginning to sweat now. But the other man wasn't finished. "You touched yourself to my picture? While you imagined me giving you a good fucking? Did you like it? Did you wish I was really there to give it to you?"

"I— God, I *loved it,* Elliott. I craved it."

"Did you come for me?" This time, Elliott gave his cock a squeeze that nearly turned Niko's vision white at the edges from the frantic anticipation it aroused. Niko wished he could grind his hips up into that touch. He emitted a strangled, needy sound.

*"Use your words, lover,"* Elliott whispered.

"Y-yeah."

"You imagined me splitting you in half? All while you were hunting me?"

"I... Yeah. I did."

"That's naughty, Niko." Elliott smiled, foxlike.

Niko couldn't help but laugh, a little self-consciously at first. "Maybe it was a little hypocritical, yeah." Then he let go, and felt his mouth twist into a grin, Elliott's smile widening as well.

It was good to laugh, to smile. It was relieving to be able to poke fun at himself and share in this joy with Elliott. All the flimsy walls he'd constructed from years of experience and expectation, of having to carry himself a certain way weren't needed anymore. Not here. Not with Elliott.

It meant everything to have someone he could trust like this—fully, without question.

Elliott pulled him into a tight embrace, arms wrapped around Niko protectively. "Tell me what you want, lover."

Niko returned the hug, melting into the other man. He let out a long, slow breath, setting whatever residual inklings of tension that still stubbornly remained free. "I want you to use me. I like it. I want to serve you."

Elliott hummed as he began to stroke Niko's cheek tenderly. Niko leaned into the touch thoughtlessly, all instinct and delight.

"Then why don't you start by taking my pants off for me, like a good boy. Hmm?"

Niko gladly obliged, his hands—trembling, now, with anticipation and desire—fumbling to unbuckle Elliott's belt, then unzip his fly. He pulled the belt free of its loops and made to toss it aside, when Elliott snapped out a hand and gripped his wrist tightly.

"No. We'll be using that."

Niko's breath caught in his throat at the thought. He laid it on the bed beside them, then pulled Elliott's jeans down. The other man finished kicking them off the rest of the way before straddling Niko again, clad now only in Niko's oversized shirt and a pair of tight, deep gray boxer-briefs which accentuated the ravenous bulge beneath. A wet spot of pre-come stained them that made Niko's breath hitch with need. His hands twitched to pull down that underwear and free the glory that lay beneath as well, but Niko knew better now.

"Can I?"

"Say it all the way."

Niko buried his face in Elliott's neck, lapping at and kissing the other man as though starving. The taste of his skin and scent of his hair—still damp from his shower and smelling of Elliott's unique shampoo—made him all the more lightheaded. "Can I remove your underwear? I want to see you. Please, Elliott."

"You can do that."

He hooked his fingers under the elastic waistline and pulled down slowly, gently, unwrapping a gift for himself. Elliott sprung free once they were down to his thighs, the tip of his blushing cock glistening with his need. Niko salivated at the sight of it, barely able to hold himself back from immediately trying to take it in hand.

Elliott removed his underwear from there before straddling Niko's lap again, staring down at him. Only Niko's oversized t-shirt remained on him now, the hem of it lifted by Elliott's erection. Niko wondered if it was going to get wet, like the underwear had been. The idea of Elliott soiling his shirt sent a heady thrill through him, white hot as lightning.

Elliott picked up the discarded belt—simple, black leather—and examined it for a moment in thought. Then he eyed Niko, his gaze meeting his own in question.

Niko considered for a moment. Another jolt of mixed thrill and fear rushed through him, like it had his first time. He'd loved being restrained and taken by Elliott before—even if his response afterward had been to dissolve into embarrassment and shame. But he wouldn't do that again. Not this time. All the same, he longed, always, to wrap his arms around his boyfriend and pull him close in their lovemaking.

He nodded. "Yeah. I want to." Then he paused, remembering what Elliott had pushed for before. *Say it all the way.* "I want you to restrain me."

"As you wish, lover," Elliott murmured. He took Niko's hands and held them between the two of them in his own, trailing his thumb along their tendons, before turning them palm up. He leaned down and kissed both his wrists, then slowly, gently, wound the belt around them together and pulled it into a knot—tight enough that Niko couldn't free himself, but not so tight as to hurt.

A pang of alarm raced through him at the thought of being so trapped, but he felt his skin starting to burn with an even greater need now, too, goosebumps of anticipatory pleasure racing along his arms.

Something else was beginning to fill him as well, all felt in every part of himself: a sweetly burgeoning joy.

Sex with Elliott and the dynamic they were building through it was something entirely new to Niko. Speaking these thoughts aloud was something he'd never done, nor had ever let himself try. Neither was being spoken to the way Elliott did when they got hot and heavy—dominating, commanding. But it wasn't unwelcome. It wasn't unwanted. It was everything Niko had held deep inside himself, hidden away, yearning to be set free.

He would indulge Elliott in servitude, in softness, just as Elliott would indulge and ignite Niko by commanding him.

"Lay down for me," Elliott instructed.

Niko closed his eyes, a fierce tidal wave of euphoria and joy crashing through him, and let himself slip under its warm waters. Starlight danced beneath his skin, bright behind his eyelids. He melted heavy into the bed below them, a blissful smile pulling at his lips.

He was no longer just a man here with Elliott Kestrel. Under his control and in his care, he became something elemental, a part of everything.

Like this, trusting himself in the hands of the most powerful, dangerous man in the galaxy, Niko could finally be free.

He surrendered to the love of his life, and let him take over.

# CHAPTER TWENTY-THREE
# TOMORROW

BEING WITH NIKO LIKE this was a celebration. He helped Elliott turn off his constant thoughts, kept him from spiraling. Pushed the rage, hatred, and pain away to somewhere quieter. With Niko, he could forget about everything outside for a while. In joining with the other man, Elliott was able to reach out and touch a joy that he had long since thought dead, forever removed from him. Niko Estrella had breathed life into him. With his care, his trust, his intimacy. His love.

Since he'd told Elliott he'd fallen in love with him back on the beaches of Eanan, Elliott hadn't been able to stop running that moment through his head on repeat.

*"I've got you,"* he whispered in a promise.

"I know," Niko said, a smile on his lips. He opened his eyes, looking back at Elliott now, and his smile grew.

With his belt tightened around Niko's wrists, Elliott helped himself to his lover. He would take excellent care of him. That Niko trusted him so completely meant everything to him. That he'd been willing to say aloud what he wanted, what he'd desired, and push past the hangups of fear and self-consciousness that had held him back before made Elliott's heart feel full.

And he was relieved. They could both simply be their honest selves together. Elliott wasn't being too much by expressing his own needs.

He'd been pushing it, he knew. Niko was like a feral stray, nervously edging at the boundaries of sustenance gifted—pacing to and fro and back again, debating if it was safe enough to allow himself to indulge in what would feed him. He could just as easily have been sent running by Elliott's questions.

But Elliott wanted to reach out, to coax it out of him. To let him voice and explore those desires and needs between the two of them. To encourage Niko to become familiar with the joy of submission, to become comfortable with it. To know submission wasn't something to be ashamed of, nor embarrassed about. Neither was letting another top you.

He shifted forward until his cock brushed against Niko's bound hands as the other man rested them atop his waist, then began slowly rutting against them. He could hear his lover's breathing pick up pace, could see the flush of color all over his skin, the way his brown eyes pleaded.

Elliott rocked his hips slowly, pushing himself against the other man's hands again and again. He loved doing this to him, loved making him come undone like such a delicious thing.

He trailed his fingers down the muscles of Niko's strong arms, gently tracing the tattoos there which he loved so much. When his fingertips glanced Niko's washboard stomach through the fabric of his tank top, the other man drew in a sharp breath, his chest rising and falling rapidly now. Two dark, soulful eyes full of myriad depths watched Elliott with desire, with trust, with affection. Elliott dipped his head and left a trail of long, sensual kisses along his neck. When loose strands of his hair brushed Niko's skin, the other man's muscles tightened. He was ticklish.

Niko's throat shifted as he swallowed. "Elliott, you... you can be rough with me. I like it."

He was being surprisingly open—even more than Elliott could have initially hoped for. "You're doing such a good job," he cooed. "Telling me everything that you like."

*Don't treat me like glass*, he'd once told Elliott. *I want everything you can give.*

Elliott met his lips with his own in a deepening, passionate kiss, then another. He nipped at Niko's bottom lip. His lover gave a soft grunt of pain as he did, his breathing quickening in excitement. His erection pushed urgently back against Elliott's own, meeting him.

*You like it best when it's rough, don't you? But you're sweet, too.*

"I'm going to use you," Elliott breathed, sitting back up and shifting forward again, "for my own pleasure. Because you asked me to." He took Niko's wrists by their belt-turned-restraint and pulled his arms up over his head, pinning them back against the headboard and holding them there. Then he leaned down over Niko, eyeing the other man.

Elliott liked it best this way, liked getting to gaze down at him. To have his lover beneath him. To make him serve and service him. It was never something done out of disrespect—in fact, he respected Niko above anyone else alive. Niko was one of the strongest people he'd ever met—in so many ways. That the man beneath him, flushed with desire and eager to submit to him in their bed was so strong, so capable, so profoundly resilient made it all the more thrilling for Elliott to dominate him. He salivated at the thought.

Elliott reached down and stroked gently at Niko's thick, dark hair, his lover's eyes nowhere but on him, looking for instruction, for guidance. "The safeword from before still applies. It always will. But for right now, I want you to give my hand three taps if it becomes too much, or you want me to stop. Because you won't have many opportunities to speak, from here on out."

"What do—"

Before Niko could even finish talking, Elliott shifted forward again and lowered himself onto the other man's face, the wiry stubble of Niko's five-o-clock shadow scratching his ass and spread thighs. Elliott reached down with his free hand and gripped his hair in a tight fistful, then wrenched Niko's head back so his chin and mouth were forced straight up into his opening.

"Eat," he commanded.

Niko gave a moan of what Elliott surmised sounded like a mixture of shock and pleasure both, tensing beneath him. That his lover enjoyed servicing so much made Elliott giddy, but he tamped down on the urge to show it outwardly, his heart leaping into a sprint of excitement now.

Niko wasted no time, working his tongue along and inside him, eager to please, to obey. He squirmed and shifted below him, his bound hands flexing into fists. Elliott ground down on him, his thighs straddling Niko's head. He knew the other man must undoubtedly be struggling to breathe and granted him mercy, pulling up briefly before resuming his throne on Niko's face, hand roughly gripping and pulling at his hair.

Niko drew in sharp, greedy breaths in the seconds granted to him, then gave a muffled groan of pleasure as Elliott shoved the full spread cuisine back into his face again. His lover's slick, wet tongue along and within him was exquisite torture that made it hard to keep still. The exhilaration of it forced a few quiet moans to escape him.

"You're doing—" He gasped. *Steady yourself. Don't come undone yet.* "So well. I hope you're fucking hungry."

The last words emerged as a rough growl, as pleasure wracked Elliott's entire body. His balls gracelessly pressed against Niko's face, adding to the humiliation of it all. His wanting cock dripped pre-come into the other man's hair.

Elliott wanted to be ornery. "Do you like it, Niko? Are you enjoying yourself?"

Another low, muffled groan emerged from his lover. Elliott lifted himself again, giving him another moment to catch his breath. "Is this what you wanted?"

"I—"

Elliott was back on him before he could get out another syllable. Niko let out another pleading sound, already back to penetrating him with his hot tongue, like he was starving and Elliott was a holiday feast.

"Use your words," he taunted, knowing Niko could do anything but. A cocky, self-satisfied smirk crept across Elliott's lips as another long, sensual, wordless moan vibrated through Niko. "Tell me how much you like it. Or maybe, this time, you'll have to show me instead."

The thick muscles of Niko's arms strained and flexed, sweat glistening on them now. His hands drew into tight fists before unclenching, the belt that bound them still held tightly in Elliott's grip. Yet, not once did the other man tap him in their silent safeword.

Elliott knew he was loving it, loving being used like this. It nearly left him breathless to think about. Mixed with the vibrant pleasure of Niko's tongue relentlessly lapping at him, face buried deep between his spread cheeks, Elliott was rapidly hurtling towards release far too early. He finally pulled up and climbed off of Niko, releasing his hold on both his pre-come messed hair and wrists. His lover panted and gasped for air as they both took a moment.

"Elliott... Baby, please."

"Mmm, what's that?" Elliott responded, trying to steady his own voice and not sound out of breath, nor give away how close he'd been to losing himself. Niko always did that to him. It was always this way when they were together.

"I need you. I need you, baby. I want to feel you."

Elliott raked his gaze across Niko. His face was so full of earnest pleading. He wondered if Niko even knew how clearly he wore all his emotions and wants on his sleeve, plain as day.

Niko had once thought he was anywhere near convincing, awkwardly trying to say he hadn't wanted something like this. It was only out of respect for Niko and the dire, painful seriousness of the situation that Elliott hadn't outright laughed at the flimsy lie.

Now Niko lay in their shared bed, face flushed from desire and exertion both, hands tied with Elliott's belt, eyes so openly imploring. He was fully clothed still, his jeans tented from his own untouched erection, the fabric of them dampened now. Elliott reached down and gave his cock another few strokes through the fabric, and Niko made a soft sound.

"I'm surprised you didn't cream yourself," he taunted.

"I, uh, came close a couple of times, actually."

"Would you like me to take you apart, Niko? Would you like me to fuck you, like you fantasized?"

"Please, baby. Just... Just fucking unmake me. Please."

"When you beg me like that, I don't have much of a choice, do I?"

He unfastened Niko's jeans with a slow, tantalizing deliberation, then pulled them off, followed by his boxers—deep blue and covered in a pattern of tiny, illustrated spaceships similar to the *Soñadora Despierta,* charmingly tacky.

He shrugged Niko's t-shirt off himself, finally rewarding his *good boy* with a full and unimpeded view of his own nude body.

Then he looked down at Niko's gray tank top, the only clothes remaining between them, and paused in thought. It would be difficult to pull off him with the other man's wrists bound together. Elliott could leave it on.

Or he could have fun with it.

"How certain are you that we can get steady supply restock from Lady Death?" he asked.

"Huh?" Niko puzzled out, a perplexed frown creasing his brow. "I'm pretty damn sure. But what does that have to do with—"

*Ah, I get to do it the fun way.*

Elliott helped himself to gripping the fabric of Niko's top. He ripped it open with his bare hands.

"Holy *shit*, Elliott."

"A bit dramatic," Elliott muttered, painfully self-aware now.

"But hot as fuck."

Elliott then retrieved the bottle of lubrication from the drawer of their bedside table, pouring a generous amount into his palms and Niko's own opening, massaging at him with his fingers, taking his time in loosening and opening him up. It was taking less effort with each time he'd let Elliott top him. What had started as an awkward tangle of trying to fit their bodies together the first time Niko had been willing to trust him in going there was now relented and relaxed with ease.

"So eager," Elliott teased. "Do you want it, Niko?"

"Yeah. I fucking do. Please. I can't wait any longer."

Elliott bent forward and laced a trail of slow kisses between his lover's thighs. He knew Niko had issues of self-image and self-worth. The other man's gaze always seemed to dull or flicker in another direction whenever he saw Elliott touching his legs. "Look at me, Niko."

Niko did, turning his gaze back on Elliott again. Elliott knelt and kissed further down his legs and stroked them tenderly. It didn't matter to him that Niko couldn't physically feel it; this was meant as a loving touch felt more in the mind, in the soul. "I want you to know how perfect you are. You're perfect for me. You're perfect in my eyes. I love every part of you. You're so beautiful to me."

"Elliott, I—" There it was, the subtle hitch in his lover's voice that always came when Elliott gave him attention there. "Thank you."

"You don't have to thank me for anything. I'm not saying it as a favor. I'm only telling you my truth."

"Yeah."

*And I'll keep telling you, again and again, until you believe it too.*

He stood and stroked his hands down Niko's side and let his fingertips glide low across the other man's belly, just above his groin and over the soft hair there. "Are you ready for me? Do you think you can take all of me? You've done such a good job at letting me fill you in the past."

"Please, Elliott. I need it. I need you. Please let me take you."

He loved making Niko beg for it. Something bright and shimmering danced behind his eyes upon hearing those words. He lined himself up with Niko and pushed in—with hardly any resistance this time. The sensation elicited a sensuous moan from his lover. Elliott sunk himself in his tight heat up to the hilt. He could feel his pulse in his entire body now, vibrant with excitement, arousal, and need.

Then he gave Niko everything he'd begged for, thrusting hard into him again and again, leaning forward over the other man and prying his legs as far apart as they could go. He stroked Niko's cock in time with his own movements, until his lover began gasping softly from the motions.

"Harder. Please, baby," Niko said, his voice hoarse and breathy as he began to lose himself. "I want it harder, deeper. I want... I want it to hurt. I like it when it's with you."

Elliott railed him now, pushing his entire weight onto his lover with each thrust. If Niko wanted to be destroyed, he would gladly oblige.

"Elliott—Baby—Please—I—I need to come. Please, can I?"

"No."

Niko emitted a low whimper that nearly made Elliott's legs buckle beneath him. All his adult life, there had been something about taking a man and reducing him to pleading, whimpering, and begging for him. And it meant especially much coming from Niko, the fiercest opponent and strongest man he'd ever encountered.

*Fuck yes.*

Elliott loved being his Dom.

"I can't take it anymore. God, baby," Niko pleaded. "I can feel you everywhere. I can't— Please. I can't last. Not when you fuck me like that."

"Hmmmm." Elliott pretended to consider, still giving it to his lover nearly as hard and rough as he physically could. It took a heroic, willful effort to not lose himself and spill hot and runny inside of Niko. He'd done it before, the first time the other man had let him top. The thrill, the sensation had been too good. The way Niko had begged him—then and now—was too good. Knowing he was taking such a strong, capable man to pieces, making him plead for release, sent a rush of goosebumps and electric thrill all the way down to his toes. An indulgent moan escaped on his exhale. "Since you begged for it so sweetly, I'll let you come... On one condition."

"Wh-what's that?" Niko's voice broke on the words, barely more than an exhaled breath now. He was so close that it had become hard for him to speak.

Elliott stayed silent another moment, wanting to tease him.

But his lover was an impatient man. "Baby...?"

"I want you to look at me, when you do."

He thrust into Niko even harder and faster, knowing it would trigger the other man's release. As if on cue, Niko's neck arched back on the pillow and for a brief moment, he wrenched his eyes shut, lips parting. He was beautiful in his rapture, like a painting.

"Niko."

Then those dark eyes opened again, fixed only on Elliott as he railed him into ecstasy now, his own moans escaping as he pressed deep into his lover, wanting to escape into him, become a part of him. The expression painted on Niko's face was one that Elliott wanted to commit to memory forever—cheeks flushed, eyes wild and pleading, mouth opening as a low, throaty set of cries emerged with each of Elliott's thrusts. Seconds later, a stream of come spattered across Niko's bound wrists and heaving chest.

"Oh f— Oh *fuck,*" he whimpered.

Elliott reluctantly pulled out of him, already missing the tight warmth of his lover. He was too close now to keep going. Not after that performance.

*Exquisite.*

He continued stroking himself, crawling over Niko. The other man reached up to try and aid him, even with his wrists bound.

"*No,*" Elliott murmured, his own voice low and liquid with mounting, frantic need. "No. Open your mouth for me, darling."

Niko did, obedient as always.

*How lovely you are.*

"You ate it earlier like you were starving," Elliott said, "so I'll nourish you." He jerked himself until it came, the grand rush of pleasure that rocked through him like a crashing storm. It was all Elliott could do to keep kneeling over Niko; his knees threatened to give out again from the intensity of it. He spurted into Niko's mouth, his come coating the man's tongue.

"Swallow it all."

Niko did, eyes meeting his own the entire time. It gave Elliott another trembling thrill of pleasure, his giddy heart nearly bursting in his chest. Then he collapsed down onto the bed beside Niko. He gave him a long, sensual kiss along the jaw.

*"Good boy."*

Elliott then untied the makeshift restraint, tossing the belt lazily off the side of the bed, exhausted. He felt around on the blankets behind him until he found the shredded tank top, and used it to clean Niko off.

Some distant part of his brain nagged at him that they shouldn't have worn themselves out, shouldn't have expended the energy before what lay ahead of them today, but he willfully pushed the thought away, not wanting to entertain it. Thinking of Hesaakan in any capacity—even ending the creature's life—made him sick. It was like a black hole that began to eat all the light out of him.

He could think about it later. This was their moment.

Being with Niko was the only time he was able to *stop* thinking.

"Niko, are you alright?"

"Yeah, babe. I'm... Yeah. I'm alright. I'm really good, actually. Thank you. For everything. For being patient with me through my bullshit."

"Turn over," Elliott said softly. Niko turned so his back was facing Elliott now. Elliott traced his fingertips along all the strong muscles there, before silently signing his own name between Niko's shoulder blades. It briefly appeared as a pale imprint against his lovely, dark bronze skin before vanishing into him. Then Elliott wrapped around him possessively, pressing his body against the bigger man's. "Will you tell me if you're not? Will you tap my hand? Will you say our safeword?"

"Yeah, Elliott. I will. I won't pull what I did again. I never should have. I wasn't used to this, and so I pushed you away. I wish I could take it all back. I don't ever want to push you away. I don't ever want to hurt you. Not you."

"You were phenomenal today, Niko."

"Eh, you did most of the work—"

"No. Stop. It's not like that. You were wonderful. But I meant more than that, too. More than the physical. I'm proud of you. It takes courage to say what you want. And it takes a lot to admit what you're afraid of."

That was something Elliott knew all too painfully well.

"Yeah. It does." Niko fell quiet for a moment before glancing back over his shoulder, dark hair falling across it. "Are *you* okay, baby? It's... a lot. All of it. Today, everything. This. Me."

"Niko, this is the best I've been in a very long time."

"Really? I'm glad."

Elliott held him tighter. For a moment, they simply lay there, before he found himself breaking the spell of their shared silence, which had begun edging on falling into a sleep they couldn't afford right now.

"I never moaned."

"What?" Niko said, the word nearly slurred from his bliss-laden exhaustion. He looked at Elliott from over his shoulder again.

"Before. With anyone else. With Liam. With anyone. I never moaned during sex. I stayed quiet."

"Wait, what?" Niko was awake now, eyes widening with shock. "But every time we..."

"I know." This time, he was the one to blush, it seemed. "I suppose you just do that to me."

"Do I?" Niko's voice rose in pitch, the excitement and elation in those words clear. The man was ridiculously pleased with himself. It made Elliott's lips curl into a smile.

There was something he wanted Niko to know.

"Haven't you realized?" he began quietly, resting his cheek against Niko's back. "You're the only one who's ever held power between us. I belong to you, Niko, wholly. You have me in the palm of your hand. You always have."

"I love you, Elliott."

It was Elliott's turn to be a little needy now. "Say it again. Please."

"I'll say it as many times as you want me to. I'll say it every night before you sleep. I'll say it every morning when you wake. It'll be the last and first thing you'll hear every day, for the rest of your life. I love you, Elliott. I love you, I love you."

Niko was too good for him. Elliott hardly deserved this. Those words were meant for someone far better than the wretch that he was. But he clung to them anyway, with greedy desperation. Niko's love was what had even kept him alive at this point, longer than the rage and resentment ever could have.

"I love you too, Niko. I'll take care of you."

Such a meager, simple offering.

But it was all that Elliott had to give. He had never meant any words so intensely, so truly, with such ferocity in all his life as those.

He wished he could show the urgency of them, how they were words that were more than words, that when he'd said them, he'd spilled out a part of what little was left of his soul and gifted it to Niko.

But his lover only grinned, his eyes squinting with that kindling warmth that came to him so easily as breathing.

Niko understood.

"I know, babe. I'll take care of you, too." He was always so brilliantly intuitive, acutely tuned-in to Elliott. It was one of the greatest comforts he had ever known, to simply be understood. Even when he tried not to be, hiding away in the very shadows he'd created.

Perhaps especially then.

With this man by his side, Elliott felt capable of anything. Maybe, even, that he was deserving of love, after all.

Niko had given him something unspeakably precious, unfurling and blooming within him like a wounded flower battered by the rain, turning its bruised petals to the light of his sun.

He gave him a tomorrow.

# ACKNOWLEDGEMENTS

I'm grateful to so many people who have been a part of this wonderful, turbulent journey, but some I'd like to give my thanks to by name include:

**TJ Rose.** I would probably still be lost and floundering, if not for you. When I was brand new to this all, you took the time to reach out to me. You asked how I was doing, and taught me where to find resources. You introduced me to the writing community. Your acts of kindness genuinely changed my trajectory, my path, and my life. I'll never forget that kindness, and I try to spread it as much as I can to new authors I find along the way. I wish you every success in this world, and I know you'll achieve it. Your books are so beautiful, and it brings me joy whenever I see how much love they've been getting.

**Logan Sage Adams.** You were one of my first friends in this community, and every time we talk, it is a pleasure. I've gotten to see you release so many incredible books, and I've loved them all. Thank you for commiserating with me when times were hard. Thanks for checking in on me, and for sharing your work with me. Thank you for reading mine too. Your enthusiasm and excitement for getting the next chapter honestly pushed me to keep going when the light had started leaving my world. I can't wait to see what you do next. Your stories are full of so much heart and love, and I hope the whole world loves them as much as I do.

**Mars Quinn.** When you'd read *Kestrel,* then generously taken the time to review it, I was star-struck. I'm so happy we met. It honestly feels like we've been friends for years and years. It's been such a delight to find another sci-fi romance author! And your beautiful, romantic stories have left me feeling so excited and invigorated. I adore your *Cosmic Romance* series, especially *Cosmic Captain.* I love how you're able to effortlessly weave romance, sci-fi fun, and deep, poignant themes together all at once. You're doing great, and your future is only going to get brighter and brighter. I'm rooting for you.

**Sam Northman.** Our (for me) early morning and late-night chats have been some of the greatest joys of my writing career. Thanks for commiserating with me and kicking my butt. You're doing so much better than you think you are. Every single day that you show up, you're winning. Reading your *Viking Bloodlines Saga* series has been one of the most exhilarating and fun times of this year. It was, genuinely, one of the only sources of joy I had during some hard times this winter. Keep doing your wonderful thing. I can't wait to see where your career goes in the future... And I'll be cheering you on every step of the way.

**Thea Verdone.** I owe so, so very much to you. You've been such a lovely friend to me, and you've built a community that has helped not only me, but so many other indie authors thrive. Your support and generosity have helped keep me going. Thank you for helping me with *Killjoy*. And thank you for trusting me with the beautiful, fragile, delightful gift that is your own words. Can I selfishly call myself the number one fan of *What Death Forgets?* I genuinely think about that book every day. I'm so excited for the day when I get to celebrate your publication of it. You work so hard, always, and it shows in everything that you do.

**Zoë Partyka.** I'm so happy that we met. We get each other! I've loved getting to chat about books and the weird adventures of life with you. You have a way of turning the mundane magical, and have made me look at everything through a new lens. Getting to read *The Midnight Dolls* was a truly life-changing experience for me, one I'll never, ever forget. Thank you for loving my space books too, and for the critical but kind feedback to help me grow as a writer. You bring such art into this world, and it's a better place because of you.

**Jon Paul Hart.** Thank you so much for being you. You've picked me up and kept me going when things were getting dark. Your humor, friendship, and kindness mean more to me than I could ever even begin to express. Thanks for helping critique *Kestrel* and *Killjoy* for me. The truth is, your writing absolutely blows mine out of the water, and I can't wait to see you publish something too. You're going to wow the world when you do. And I'll be here for every minute of it, grinning and cheering you on.

**JT Adria.** Thank you for being such a great friend to me. You were my critique partner, my alpha reader, and my confidant of story secrets. It's been such a pleasure getting to know you and see you grow in your own beautiful writing! Your stories have given me immeasurable joy, and I'm so honored you shared them with me. I can't wait until I can give you all the love and support online that you've given me in my published author journey. And I know it's going to happen soon. I'll be here when it does. (Also, meow.)

**Kasey Landergren.** Thank you for being my friend. You've stuck with me and chosen me again and again for most of our lives now. And your determination and staunch encouragement pushed me to keep going, even when my belief in myself was faltering. Thanks for letting me both brag all my little triumphs to you and complain all my hurts alike. I couldn't ask for a better friend than you. I hope we'll be friends for the rest of our years. I can't wait to see what the future brings.

And thank *you,* dear reader, for your support. Everyone who has made a post, or shared a story. Everyone who has rated or reviewed these books. The people who have signed up to ARC read. The people who beta read for me. The people who took the time to draw fan art of Niko and Elliott. The readers who made such lovely and artistic visual edits on Instagram. The people who have reached out to and messaged me to say how much these books have affected them. You keep me going. You really, really do. I keep every one of those kind comments and interactions in my heart, like little treasures. And I call upon them on dark days.

I can't wait to bring you the final book of the *Starhawk* trilogy and conclusion to Niko and Elliott's story. It would mean a lot to me if you left an honest review on Amazon or Goodreads of this book. Reviews help boost visibility of indie authors' books, and help us continue to bring you more content in the future.

And as always, remember: be gay, do space crime.

Until next time.

**ADRIENNE LOTHY** lives in Illinois with two cats and approximately one million houseplants. When she's not writing interstellar love stories, dreaming up new plotlines, or trying to negotiate peace in the Felines vs Foliage war, she can be found journaling, photographing the sky, haunting coffeehouses, and (of course) reading.

You can read more about her, stay up to date on new content, and access exclusive free bonus stories through her newsletter.
Sign up at **www.adriennelothy.com.**

She is also active on Instagram, at **@adriennelothy.**

www.ingramcontent.com/pod-product-compliance
Lightning Source LLC
Chambersburg PA
CBHW030329010826
48973CB00004B/933

9 798990 497733